Secrets on Cedar Key

TERRI DuLong

KENSINGTON BOOKS
www.kensingtonbooks.com

KENSINGTON BOOKS are published by

Kensington Publishing Corp.
119 West 40th Street
New York, NY 10018

All Kensington titles, imprints, and distributed lines are available at special quantity discounts for bulk purchases for sales promotion, premiums, fund-raising, educational, or institutional use.

Special book excerpts or customized printings can also be created to fit specific needs. For details, write or phone the office of the Kensington Special Sales Manager: Kensington Publishing Corp., 119 West 40th Street, New York, NY 10018. Attn. Special Sales Department. Phone: 1-800-221-2647.

Kensington and the K logo Reg. U.S. Pat. & TM Off.

ISBN-13: 978-0-7582-8813-4
ISBN-10: 0-7582-8813-1
First Kensington Trade Paperback Printing: December 2013

eISBN-13: 978-0-7582-8814-1
eISBN-10: 0-7582-8814-X
First Kensington Electronic Edition: December 2013

10 9 8 7 6 5 4 3 2 1

Printed in the United States of America

Secrets on Cedar Key

Also by Terri DuLong

Spinning Forward

"A Cedar Key Christmas" in *Holiday Magic*

Casting About

Sunrise on Cedar Key

Postcards from Cedar Key

Published by Kensington Publishing Corporation

*In memory of my Cedar Key friend Ingeborg M. Worth,
who had the same zest for life as my character Maybelle*

Acknowledgments

For this novel, I take my readers on a short trip to Paris, France, with my main character, Marin. The real-life apartment in the Latin Quarter that my husband and I rented earlier this year is what inspired the creation of the apartment where Marin stayed. So thank you to the owners, Amy and Oscar Schatcher, for the inspiration and especially for your kindness and understanding during my husband's unexpected health issues during our Paris visit.

A huge thank-you to Ellen Johnson, owner of the real Serendipity Needleworks, in Tuscaloosa, Alabama, for the support and warm welcome I always receive at your shop for my book signings. Also to her patrons Dolores DelRio Tabor, Lois Kramer, and Mary Rhodes, who always show encouragement and love for my books.

My cup runs over with gratitude for other yarn shop owners who have supported the Cedar Key series since *Spinning Forward*. Thank you to mother-and-daughter team Pauline and Sandi, at the Ball of Yarn, in Ormond Beach, Florida; Rhonda Jones, at the Yarn Cottage, in Fairhope, Alabama; Elyse Anderson, at Only Ewe & Cotton Too, in Alpharetta, Georgia; Teri Gabric, at Northwoods Fiber Farm, in Inman, South Carolina; and Barbara Zory, at Yarnworks (my "home" yarn shop), in Gainesville, Florida.

And a huge thank-you to the more recent yarn shop owners who now support the Cedar Key series and host my book signings: Susan Post, at A Good Yarn, in Sarasota, Florida; Roz Moore, at Fiber Art, in Odessa, Florida; April Cordell, at Fleece, in Cumming, Georgia; and Diane Hardin, at the Yarn Lady, in Summerfield, Florida. I hope you know how much your support means to me.

Another huge thank-you goes to Sue Hootman, Jan Holman, and Linda White. You attended my knitting retreat and then you were instrumental in setting me up to sign books at your local yarn shops. I deeply appreciate your support!

I also owe a huge debt of gratitude to mother and daughter

Barbara and Marjorie Competiello for your unfailing support of my work, for your loyalty, for your friendship, and most of all for proving that mother-daughter relationships do not have to be complex and difficult.

For Robbie Lee, my fan in Tasmania who made sure that her local bookshop carries the Cedar Key series, I can't thank you enough for your support! And a huge thank-you for coming from the other side of the world, literally, to actually visit Cedar Key. You're the best!

Over the past four years I've been very fortunate to build up a wonderful fan base on Facebook. Not only have you supported my work, but you've made me laugh when I really needed a smile, you've encouraged me during some difficult times, and you've shared the fun moments with me. For all this and so much more . . . thank you to: Mary Jane Hoffman, Janice Freedman, Denise Woods, Christine Murphy, Darlene Gibson, Bonnie Thomas, Fran Currier, Gayle Cooper, Angelique Carlson, Mary (Mar) Little, Linda Wilson, Karla Bradbury, Carolyn Biddle, Terry and Gloria Irvin, Leslie Ann Beaster, Becky Whitt, Agatha P. Townsend, Dirk Bauman, Joyce King Collins, Jackie Imhoff, Linda Thurmond DeCristofaro, Mary N. Connolly, and so many others that space prevents me from listing. A million thanks to all of you!

For my wonderful French friend, Nicole Coutand. Thank you for showing me many years ago, in your Le Bourget kitchen, how a blowtorch is used with crème brûlée. And I still say . . . your crème brûlée is the best I've ever tasted! *Merci beaucoup* for sharing the creation with me and for your friendship, which makes our visits to Paris even more special because of you and Jean-Jacques.

A multitude of thanks to the entire Kensington team for allowing me to share my work with readers, and especially to my editor, Audrey LaFehr; her assistant, Martin Biro; my publicist, Vida Engstrand; and the team in the Art Department, who always seem to outdo themselves with each new cover!

Special thanks to my first two readers, Alice Jordan and Bill Bonner. You've both been with me from the beginning, and I hope you know how much I appreciate your input, suggestions, and support!

As always, love and thanks to my daughter, Susan Hanlon, and my husband, Ray. After all these years . . . you know why.

And to my readers . . . I hope you know how much I appreciate that you allow me to take up some of your time with my stories. It truly means the world to me!

1

I stood there, arms folded across my chest, staring at the gaping hole that separated Yarning Together from our new business venture. After the events of the previous day, I now wondered if perhaps my mother's plan to expand the yarn shop to include needlepoint might be foolhardy.

"Oh, Marin. I'm so sorry about what happened. Are you okay?"

I turned around as Chloe walked into the shop and scooped me into her arms for a hug.

"Wouldn't you know I'd be in Gainesville yesterday when all the commotion was going on here?"

I patted her back, trying to pass on what little reassurance I had.

"I'm okay, and Ned's wife called me this morning. It was a heart attack but he's going to be fine. They'll keep him for a few days at Shands and then he'll be discharged home."

Chloe blew out a breath. "Oh, that *is* good news. Thank goodness. But . . . and I almost feel guilty asking . . . how long before he can resume work?"

My guilty thoughts matched hers. "According to Eileen, the doctors have said six to eight weeks."

"Oh."

"Exactly. Here I was hoping that I'd be able to open the needle-point shop by Christmas, and we're not even sure Ned will be back to work in two months."

Chloe headed to the coffeemaker and began spooning Maxwell House into the paper filter. "Hmm, true," she said before going to the back room and returning with the carafe, filled with water.

"How's Dora dealing with the news?"

"Fine," I said, settling myself on the sofa. "You know my mother. She always seems to do well in a crisis. Unlike me." The phone call from the university in Gainesville seven months before, telling me that my husband had collapsed in his classroom and had been taken by ambulance to Shands Hospital, had proved this to me.

We both turned as the wind chimes on the door tinkled and my mother walked in. "Good morning, girls," she chirped in her usual cheery voice.

Not for the first time I hoped that her health and longevity genes ran strong in me. At seventy-eight, she showed no signs of osteoporosis, her striking white hair had recently been cut into an attractive bob, and most days her energy level surpassed mine. But it was her optimism that enhanced her youthful vitality and appearance.

"You think?" I mumbled. Having our contractor out of work with a heart attack didn't amount to a good morning for me.

"Oh, Marin," she said, placing a kiss on the top of my head. "Cheer up. We just might have a replacement to finish the work."

"Really?" I sat up straighter on the sofa.

"Possibly," she replied, settling down beside me. "Well, I had a call from Worth Slater this morning, and it seems he's willing to take over for Ned."

"*The* Worth Slater?" Chloe's excitement caused me to sit up even straighter.

"Who's that?" I had relocated from Gainesville after my husband died to move in with my mother on Cedar Key, but I still didn't know everyone in town.

"Worthington Slater," Chloe explained. "Rumored to be one of the richest guys in Marion County. His family owned horse farms in Ocala. Not to mention he's pretty darn good-looking and quite the eligible bachelor."

I laughed and looked at my mother. "You're joking, right? Why on earth would somebody like him even want to get his hands dirty?"

My mother shook a finger in my direction. "Marin, how many times have I told you not to be such a quick judge of character. It just so happens that Worth owned his own architecture business, and that included refurbishing a lot of older homes and apartments. He knows we're in a bind and has offered his services."

"Oh. Well, good. So when can Mr. Rich Guy start?"

"I'm not sure. He's coming by later today to look at the work we need done. He said he'll honor the estimate that Ned has given me, which is very nice of him."

"That's encouraging," I said, getting up to walk toward what was supposed to be the new archway separating the shops. Instead, what greeted me was an uneven hole in the wall that led into a dark and dusty room.

"God! It's such a mess. We'll never have that turned into anything decent."

I wasn't sure if the tears I felt stinging my eyes were more from the residual grief about the loss of Andrew or from the fact that something positive in my life was on hold.

"Of course we will," my mother said as her arm went around my shoulder.

"Right. It's just a little setback," Chloe said. "What we all need is a cup of this freshly brewed coffee." She held the pot in the air and then proceeded to fill three mugs.

I fished a tissue from my pocket, blew my nose, and settled back on the sofa. "I feel so selfish. Poor Ned could have died in this very shop yesterday, and I'm worried about opening the needlepoint section."

My mother patted my hand. "He's going to be just fine. Might be a while before he'll be back to work, but it was a mild heart attack, so he was lucky."

"Unlike Andrew," I said and heard the tinge of envy in my voice.

Chloe passed us the coffee before sitting down. "Gosh, he was lucky he wasn't alone when it happened. You must have been frightened, though, Marin. There wasn't anybody else in the shop, was there?"

I took a sip of the strong brew and shook my head. "No, I'd just come back from lunch. Mom had taken Oliver home for the afternoon, and I'm glad she did, what with the paramedics arriving and everything. Ned had already returned from his lunch when I got back, and he was working away. A few minutes later he came over here to sit on the sofa, and I knew something was wrong. He was white as a ghost, sweaty, and looked terrible. Said he was just having some mild pain in his upper left arm. Thought it was from the work he'd done earlier breaking through the wall. But I didn't want to take a chance. It could have been a muscle pull and exertion, but he was also having classic signs of a heart attack, so I called 911 just to be on the safe side."

"Thank goodness you did," Chloe said.

I nodded. "I'm just glad he's going to be okay."

"Eileen said he'll be home in a few days, and if all goes well, he can return to work in a couple months."

I got up to go look at the wall again and shook my head. "Geez, we didn't even really get started, and there's so much to do in there. Putting in the bay window in the front wall, redoing all the walls and floor, wallpaper, painting . . . I sure hope this Worth Slater will be willing to take it over."

"Yeah, I know what you're saying." Chloe joined me at the wall and peered into the dark room.

"So does the yarn shop have to live with that ugly hole in the wall until Worth or somebody can begin to work on it?" I heard the whiny tone to my voice, which made me sound more like a teenager than a fifty-six-year-old woman.

"I think we should be able to find a sheet or big piece of plastic to cover it. It'll be fine," my mother said in an attempt to reassure me.

"Are you still thinking of adding on a patio out back and taking over the old carriage house?" I knew my mother liked how Chloe was able to push a conversation toward a different subject rather than focusing on the negative. That was one of the reasons they worked so well as partners at the yarn shop. When my mother had purchased the shop from my cousin Monica a few years before, one of her best decisions had been asking Chloe to be her partner. She was a joy to work with. Not only had she gotten a degree in textile design many years before, acquiring an exceptional knowledge of fibers and colors, she was also a great asset for the shop, always ready to pitch in and do that little extra for customers, staying late if it was required, doing everything she could so that the shop would be a success. And now, due to my mother's desire to expand the shop to include needlepoint, I would have the opportunity to work there as well.

"Yes," she told Chloe. "I've been giving that a lot more thought, and I think we should do it. Having a screened patio built between the shop and the carriage house will give our knitters a wonderful place to sit outside during the nice weather. And I think we'll be almost forced to remodel the carriage house. Once that archway is finished, we're going to lose that entire corner over there," she said, pointing to where the credenza held our coffee supplies and the old-fashioned desk that served as our checkout area. "Everything can be rearranged in here, and a lot of the stock can be put in the carriage house. We could get really creative with displaying the various yarns, rather than just in cubbyholes and cubicles."

"Oh, I agree," Chloe said. "Besides, I think knitters love to wander around, browsing, touching all the different yarns. If a shop is too small and cramped, I think that takes away from the experience. It'll be a lot of fun getting it all put together."

"And your needlepoint shop will become a reality, Marin." She patted my hand again. "We just have to be patient."

"I know. You're right, Mom," I told her. "Like you've always said, it'll happen in its own time. I'm sorry for being so childish about all of this. I guess I was really counting on being a needlepoint shop manager by Christmas." I blew out a breath and turned toward the boxes of yarn that UPS had delivered the day before. "Well, I need to get to work and get those unpacked. And you have the morning off, so go. Chloe and I can handle things here."

"Lucas told me the book I ordered would be at the shop today, so I'm going to stop by and get it. Oh, and it's my turn to do dinner, so you don't need to rush home. Lasagna and salad. Is that okay?"

"It's wonderful," I told her before giving her a hug good-bye. Living with my mother these past seven months had been good for both of us. Although I was ashamed to admit it and it was probably unknown to others, Andrew and I had evolved over twenty-six years of marriage to a bland and stagnant relationship. I had been looking forward to his retirement this past summer, hoping to re-capture some of the spark that had been missing. But his death had prevented that from happening. Despite the lack of passion, I missed him. I missed the day-to-day conversations and routine we had shared. So I welcomed the company and companionship of my mother. We also seemed to be in sync as far as housemates. She re-spected my quiet time, we shared chores around the house, and overall, I was happy that she had invited me to move in with her after Andrew died.

"I'll see you at home about five," she said before leaving.

Chloe gathered up the mugs to take into the back room to wash. "Moving in with your mother seems to be working well for you. I know Dora is thrilled to have you there."

"Yeah," I said as I cut open one of the boxes of yarn. "She's al-ways been easy to get along with. I'm fortunate."

Chloe laughed. "You've got that right. Many adult daughters would cringe at the thought of moving back with their mothers. I'm sure I couldn't have done it."

I fingered the new sock yarn that had been made in Germany before I arranged each skein in a wooden cubbyhole. With the vi-brant pinks, greens, blues, and lavenders, I knew we wouldn't be keeping this yarn in the shop for long.

As I continued unpacking yarn, rearranging various skeins, and making a sign to place on the front table for yarn that would be dis-counted, I allowed my mind to wander and couldn't help but wonder what the rest of my life had in store for me. Was this all there was? Married at age thirty, the mother of two grown sons, a retired professor of English . . . and now a widow at fifty-six, living with her mother and soon to run a needlepoint shop. I let out a sigh. It could be worse. Certainly, it could be much worse.

2

Chloe was still at lunch when he walked into the yarn shop. When I first looked toward the door and saw the good-looking older man enter, I assumed he was here on a knitting errand for his wife or to purchase a gift certificate.

"May I help you?" I asked, walking toward the front of the shop.

"Yes, I'm looking for Eudora Foster."

It was then that it hit me that he was Worthington Slater, and in a heartbeat I realized Chloe hadn't been exaggerating when she said he was *pretty darn good-looking*. At least six feet tall, he wore a casual short-sleeved shirt tucked into khaki trousers. A deep bronze tan and silver hair complemented his good looks. He appeared more likely to be sitting behind the desk of a successful company than swinging a hammer as a workman.

"Yes," I said, clearing my throat and extending my hand. "I'm Dora's daughter. Marin Kane. Nice to meet you. She's at home this afternoon but told me you'd be stopping by to take a look at the project."

I felt his hand grip mine as a friendly smile crossed his face.

"Nice to meet you." His gaze moved to the hole in the wall. "I take it that's the area to be remodeled?"

I nodded. "Yeah, it looks more like a bomb zone at the moment," I said, walking toward the wall. "It's hard for me to visualize what my mother keeps saying will be so nice."

Worth laughed. "Oh, you don't trust my abilities?"

"Oh, it's not that," I stammered. "I mean . . . it's just a dark, dingy area right now. And so much needs to be done to transform it into a needlepoint shop."

He produced a flashlight from his pocket before stepping into the adjoining room.

"Hmm," he said, shining the light toward the ceiling, walls, and floor. "Well, yes, it does need extensive work, but like Ned told me, it's certainly doable."

"Really?" I could feel my excitement building. "You're willing to do it for us?"

Worth nodded, and I followed him back into the yarn shop.

"I am," he said. "I'll get with your mother to confirm, but when do you think she'd like me to start?"

"Yesterday?"

He laughed again. "In a bit of a rush, are you?"

"Well, a little. I was hoping to be able to have it open by Christmas."

"It's early October. That gives me about ten weeks. I don't think that'll be a problem."

In addition to his good looks, I liked this man's enthusiasm.

"Oh, that would be great."

"Okay, then," he said, heading toward the door. "Tell your mother I'll give her a call at home this evening, but I should be ready to begin on Friday."

"Thanks so much."

The moment Chloe returned from lunch, I shared the good news with her.

"Terrific. Then everything is back on track. Oh, and by the way . . . what was your opinion of Worth?"

I was surprised when I felt warmth creeping up my neck. Damn hot flashes. "Oh . . . he was nice. Very nice. And friendly. Very businesslike too."

Chloe laughed. "In other words...I wasn't lying, huh? Pretty hot?"

"Yeah...I guess so. I mean, I really didn't notice. He wasn't here very long."

"Right," she said, and I saw the grin that crossed her face. "You know, Marin, just because your husband passed away, it doesn't mean your life is over. You can still appreciate a good-looking and pleasant guy."

All of a sudden I felt flustered. "Yes, of course. I know that," I said and was grateful when Berkley walked in the door, putting an end to further discussion.

I spied the basket of hand-dyed yarn she was carrying. "Oh, good," I said. "You spun more yarn for us."

"Yup, another ten skeins."

Chloe reached over to touch the soft greens, yellows, blues, and lavenders. "Gorgeous. Jill did another great job with the dyeing."

Berkley had relocated to Cedar Key the previous year from Salem, Massachusetts, opened up the chocolate shop on Second Street, and provided us with yarn from her alpacas, which were kept at her friend's farm in North Yarmouth, Maine. She had also fallen in love with Saxton Tate III, a British mystery author who lived on the island.

"Thanks," she said, and I saw her gaze take in the hole that dominated our wall. "Geez, I heard about all the excitement here yesterday with Ned. Is he okay?"

I brought her up to date on Ned's condition while she walked over to take a peek into the room on the other side.

"I'm glad he'll be all right. But what a shame about the delay in the work."

"Not exactly," I told her and explained about Worthington Slater taking over.

"Oh, that's great. So maybe you'll have the needlepoint shop up and running by Christmas after all."

"Here's hoping. Do you have time for coffee?"

"Yeah, a quick cup would be nice. Oh, I have some news. Saxton's daughter, Resa, and her husband arrive here next week."

"That's great," Chloe said. "Do you think they'll really end up purchasing the bed-and-breakfast?"

"I think there's a pretty good chance. Resa's husband, Jake, has been doing a lot of research about opening a pediatric practice in Gainesville, and it seems he's found another physician who's interested in being his partner. So that will enable them to relocate here. They have an appointment with Alison next week to look at the B and B, so if they like it . . . who knows? They could end up making an offer on it."

"I'm sure Saxton is thrilled that his daughter might be living in the same town."

Berkley accepted a mug of coffee from Chloe. "Thanks. Oh, he is. I think he still feels guilty for not seeing her for thirty years, so it's like he's getting a second chance. I'm hoping it will all work out for the two of them."

I nodded. "Resa was pretty understanding, wasn't she? I mean, not all daughters would be so quick to forgive a father who made no attempt to see her since she was a child."

"Yeah, I think Resa's pretty special. She feels that her parents' divorce was the cause of the estrangement with her dad, so she doesn't blame him."

"What time are you closing today?" I asked. "I wanted to stop by and get some chocolate."

"I'll be at the shop till five. I'm out of truffles, though. My shipment from Angell and Phelps is due in tomorrow."

"That's fine. I'll get some dark chocolate pieces."

"Well, there you are." All of us turned toward the door to see Grace Trudeau walk in holding her six-month-old daughter, Solange.

Chloe ran over to scoop the baby out of her sister's arms. "And how's my favorite niece?" she cooed, holding the baby up in the air, which produced giggles and a trail of drool on Solange's chin.

"Oh, sorry," Berkley said. "I closed the shop to run down here and drop off some yarn."

Grace waved a hand in the air. "Not a problem. Just thought I'd pop in to replenish my chocolate supply."

"That baby gets prettier every day," I told her, and it was the truth. Grace, who was extremely attractive, and Lucas, with his French good looks, had produced a gorgeous daughter with olive skin and dark curly hair who was a combination of both her parents.

Grace laughed. "Thanks. We happen to think so. She tends to be a bit fussy lately, though. She's teething."

"Well, you just let Aunt Chloe take her when she's fussy." She placed a kiss on the baby's cheek. "That's right. Aunt Chloe doesn't mind and will have her laughing in no time."

As if to prove her aunt correct, Solange broke out in another round of giggles, causing all of us to laugh. Chloe was besotted with her niece, but I also felt that part of it was that she was grateful to be reunited with her sister. After ten years of a rocky relationship, their aunt Maude had paved the way for the sisters to put their differences aside, and I knew Chloe treasured the love they now shared.

"Time for me to reopen the shop," Berkley said. "And thanks for the coffee."

"I just want to pick up some yarn to make a sweater for Solange and I'll be down to get my chocolate."

"*Another* sweater?" I kidded her. "That child is going to have more sweaters than anybody in Levy County."

Grace laughed. "Actually, I'm going to make this one in a size two. She has plenty to get her through this winter, so I may as well start working ahead."

"Oh, look at this great mint green linen that came in the other day," Chloe said. "Perfect for Florida, even in the winter."

I returned to unpacking the new shipments while Chloe tended to Grace.

Shortly after four-thirty, I rang up another sale while Chloe worked away on a gorgeous teal cable sweater done with baby alpaca yarn that would be displayed in the shop.

"Well, if you don't mind, I think I'll scoot along. I want to make the chocolate shop before Berkley closes."

"No, not at all. I'm going to finish up this row and then I'll be closing. I don't think we'll get any last-minute customers today."

"Okay, then I'll see you tomorrow. You have a good evening," I said, gathering up my sweater and handbag.

I walked into the living room to be greeted by my mother's dog, Oliver. A black standard poodle, Oliver had been rescued by my mother a few years before and was one of the great joys in her life.

"Oh, no, sorry," I told him as he sniffed my bag of chocolate. "No chocolate for you, I'm afraid." A pat on his head and a stroke beneath his chin made him happy as he followed me to the back of the house.

My mother was in the kitchen putting the finishing touches on a bowl of salad.

"Ah, you're home. Lasagna's in the oven. We'll be eating in about an hour," she said as my cell phone rang.

I answered to hear a male voice inquire, "Could I speak with Andrew Kane, please?"

Surprised by the request, I mumbled, "Who's calling?"

"This is Rick at Mail Boxes in Gainesville."

"Oh... well... Andrew was my husband. But he passed away in March."

I heard the surprise in the caller's voice. "I'm terribly sorry, Mrs. Kane. Please accept my condolences."

"Thank you. What's this in relation to?"

"Well... Mr. Kane had a mailbox here with us, and... um... the payment for the box is overdue. So I needed to call and see if he... or somebody... wanted to bring the account up to date. Otherwise, I'm afraid we'll have to cancel the rental of the box. I tried to call the number he gave us, but that phone was disconnected. This is the number that he listed as an emergency backup."

What on earth was he talking about? Andrew didn't have a private box for mail. Our mail had always been delivered to our home. Or did he?

"Well, no. If my husband did have this mailbox, there's no longer a need to keep it. If there's a balance due, I'd be happy to pay it."

"Oh, no. That's fine. I'll just discontinue the rental. However, there was one piece of correspondence in the box. Would you like me to forward that to you?"

"That would be nice. Thank you," I told him and gave him my mailing address at the Cedar Key Post Office.

Disconnecting the call, I shook my head. "Well, that was odd."

"You look bewildered," my mother said. "Everything okay?"

I explained the call to her while still trying to sort out why Andrew would have this rental mailbox.

"Perhaps it had to do with the university," my mother said. "Maybe he needed a post office number rather than a physical address for some particular reason."

"Hmm, maybe." Then why did I suddenly feel so uneasy?

⤜ 3 ⤛

I spent the next day wondering what the correspondence for Andrew could possibly be. In all honesty, I think I felt more left out than curious that Andrew had set up a means to receive mail privately and hadn't bothered to inform me.

By that afternoon I had to discuss it with somebody other than my mother, so I shared the phone call with Chloe.

"It's probably not all that unusual. Like your mother said, maybe it has to do with receiving school-related material."

"Yeah, well, why couldn't that be sent to our home address?"

Chloe looked up from her row of knitting. "Maybe he subscribed to porn?"

The thought of it made me laugh. Andrew was far from romantic or passionate. But I suppose that didn't rule out a fondness for something kinky.

"Could be, but I doubt it. Besides, the fellow said it's an envelope, not a magazine or anything. Plus, my cell number was listed by Andrew as an emergency backup."

"Who was it from? What was the return address?"

Stupid me. "I didn't think to ask," I said with disappointment.

Chloe smiled. "Well, don't let your imagination run away with you. You should have it by tomorrow."

"Chloe's right," my mother said. "Come on, girls. Time to close so we can get back here at seven for the knitting group."

I always enjoyed the Thursday evening gathering of women at the yarn shop, and tonight provided me with a diversion from thinking any further about the piece of mail being sent to me.

I settled myself on the sofa and was joined by Corabeth Williams. Corabeth had been a bit of a celebrity in town the year before when it was discovered that she was the number one best-selling author of erotica, writing under the pen name Lacey Weston. Just shy of her seventieth birthday, Corabeth resembled a cookie-baking grandmother more than somebody who penned sexual escapades. But once the surprise died down, Corabeth resumed her ordinary life on Cedar Key while continuing to write her novels.

"How're you doing, Marin?" she said, reaching into her bag to remove a beautiful lavender sweater.

"I'm doing good. Oh, that's gorgeous. Is that a Malabrigo yarn?"

"It is, and the shade is called periwinkle. I just love this hand-dyed merino wool. I'm hoping to have it finished to wear for Thanksgiving."

I looked up to see my cousin, Sydney, and her daughter, Monica, enter the shop. Sydney Webster had relocated to the island four years ago, surprising the entire town when it was discovered that my mother's sister, Sybile, had given birth years before to a daughter we knew nothing about.

They took a seat on the sofa opposite me and I smiled in greeting. I certainly loved my two sons, but seeing Sydney and Monica together always made me wish that I'd also had a daughter.

"How are those adorable triplets?" I asked Monica.

She laughed as she pulled an almost completed pink knitted hat from her bag. "Going through the terrible twos, I think. I'm hoping when February comes and they turn three, things will calm down."

Sydney smiled. "Don't count on it."

"How's the day care going?" I asked. Cedar Key was fortunate to now have a nice day-care center on the island for the young mothers who needed to work or just needed a break like Monica.

"Oh, it's great. Leigh is so good with the kids. It's only two mornings a week, but I think it's as good for them as it is for me. They're learning to play with other children rather than just each other, and they seem to love it."

"I'm here," we heard and looked up to see that a flustered Grace had joined us.

Normally looking well-groomed and stylish, Grace had arrived with her curly hair looking like it hadn't seen a brush for a couple days, her face bare of makeup, and the tee shirt she wore had a large yellow stain down the front.

"I know," she said, plunking into one of the chairs. "I'm a mess. Solange has kept me up for two nights. I'll be so happy when that tooth comes in. I didn't want to leave Lucas alone with her, but he insisted that I come."

Monica laughed as she reached over to pat her friend's leg. "Welcome to motherhood. I'm glad you came. You need the break. And, yeah, that tooth should be breaking through soon."

Sydney looked across at me and smiled. "Makes ya kinda glad those days are behind us, huh?"

"Yeah, but the thing is when you're going through them it's like there's no end in sight, and then all of a sudden those kids that gave you the sleepless nights are grown and gone."

Sydney nodded. "True. How are the boys doing?"

"Good. John loves living and working in Boston. With the economy still not great, he feels fortunate to have landed a position there with a good company. And Jason likes his job in Atlanta. He's thinking he might return to school for grad work, though."

"That's really great," Grace said, beginning to work on the new sweater she had started for Solange. "But don't you miss them? I mean, I know my daughter's only six months old, but just the thought of her moving away makes me want to cry."

I let out a sigh. "Yeah, I do miss them. A lot. But . . . that's a parent's role, isn't it? Bring them up the best we can, and then we have to let them go to make their own lives. Unless, of course, you're like me and return to the nest in your fifties."

"I love having you with me, and you know that, Marin," my mother said.

"And besides, under the circumstances it was the practical thing to do. It was silly for you to stay in such a large house in Gainesville by yourself," Sydney added.

"I agree," Corabeth said. "I think selling that house was right, and nobody says that you can't eventually buy your own place here on Cedar Key."

"Hey, watch that, Corabeth. You'll have my housemate moving out on me."

I laughed, but after seven months I had recently been giving this idea some thought myself.

By seven-thirty the room was full of chattering women knitting away. I always loved seeing the yarn the women had purchased at the shop magically being turned into various items. I looked over to see Chloe and Grace's aunt Maude working on what appeared to be a dress.

"Oh, Maude. That's gorgeous. Is it for Solange?"

She looked up from reading her pattern with a smile. "Yes, it's from *The Sugar and Spice Collection,* by Elsebeth Lavold. The dress is called Saffron and I thought it would be pretty using the aquamarine Hempathy yarn."

"I just love it, Aunt Maude. Solange will look adorable wearing that."

"Well, it'll be a little while. I'm making it in a size two."

I saw my mother look around the shop. "Anybody know where Berkley is tonight?"

"No," Chloe said. "I saw her earlier today and she was supposed to be here."

Five minutes later Berkley walked in.

"Gosh, I'm sorry I'm late," she said. "I'm afraid I have some bad news. Miss Maybelle has passed away."

My mother's hand flew to her face as gasps filled the room. "What?" she said, jumping up from her chair.

Berkley nodded. "I know. It was quite a shock. Saxton had tried calling her all day like he usually does to check on her. By five o'clock, he became really worried and went over to her house. He let himself in with the key she'd given him...and he found her slumped in her chair with her knitting in her lap. He called 911, but he knew she was already gone. It must have been a heart attack."

"Oh, my," Maude said. "How terrible. Maybelle did have a heart condition...but still."

I got up to put an arm around my mother. She had been good friends with Maybelle for more than fifty years. I knew the loss wasn't going to be easy for her.

"Did anybody contact her goddaughter, Victoria?" Sydney asked.

"Yes, Saxton had her number in New York and he made the call. Of course, she was pretty shocked. It happened so fast."

Corabeth shook her head. "Such a shame. But thank goodness that Victoria reconnected with Maybelle and was able to spend two months here with her this past summer."

Chloe nodded. "Yes, Maybelle really did enjoy that visit, and she adored Victoria's little boy, Sam. Is it too soon to know about any funeral arrangements? Is Victoria in charge of it?"

"Yes," Berkley said. "Maybelle had just recently changed her will. Victoria is the executrix. She told Saxton that Maybelle's wishes were to be cremated. She said she'll call him tomorrow with details about a memorial service."

"Gee," Chloe said. "I wonder what Victoria will do with the house. Maybelle's had that since the early sixties."

"Yes, she has," my mother said. "She loved that house and called it her safe harbor. Maybe Victoria will use it to visit here with her son. This certainly is very sad news. Why don't we have our coffee and pastry now and break up early this evening."

"Good idea," I said, patting my mother's back.

✲ 4 ✲

Chloe and I had both insisted my mother take the next day off from the yarn shop. The two of us were able to handle the customers and any deliveries.

"How's your mom doing this morning?" Chloe asked when I walked in at ten.

"Pretty good, I guess. It's hard for her losing another person in her life. First Sybile, then Saren passed away, then my husband, and now a good friend. She was quiet this morning, but you know my mother. She's resilient. I think she'll be okay."

Chloe nodded. "I didn't know Miss Maybelle very well, but she was quite the character. She certainly seemed to have a zest for life. How old was she? Do you know?"

"She turned eighty-one in July. She was happy her goddaughter could be here to celebrate it with her. Yeah, Maybelle was one of those people who weren't the life of the party—she *was* the party."

Chloe laughed. "Berkley told me she was a Copa Girl back in the fifties. She said she got invited with Saxton to go to Maybelle's home for tea last year. I guess Maybelle showed her a lot of the costumes she used to wear as a dancer at the Copa."

"Oh, yeah. I saw those years ago when I was in my teens. I was so captivated that she offered to let me borrow one of the gowns for my prom. My mother said absolutely not." I laughed recalling the memory.

We both looked up as the door opened and Worth Slater walked into the shop. God, I had forgotten he was coming this morning. Dressed in jeans, tee shirt, and work boots, he did look like a contractor ready to report for work, but his style of dress certainly didn't detract from his good looks.

"Good morning, ladies," he said, a cheery smile covering his face. "Is Miss Dora here?"

"No, I'm afraid not. My mother won't be coming in today. A very good friend of hers passed away yesterday."

"Oh, Maybelle Brewster? I had heard about that. I'm very sorry. Well, I spoke to your mother the other evening, and I'm ready to begin if it's okay with you."

"Sure," I said. "Work away. Is there anything you need?"

He shook his head as he walked toward the open space. "No, I'm all set." He held up a large toolbox. "I'm going to begin with that bay window. I think once we get some natural light in there for you, you'll be able to see the possibilities. Oh, and I have a fellow dropping by to help me in about an hour. His name is Kyle, so just send him in."

"Will do," I said and caught the grin on Chloe's face.

I rolled my eyes at her as I began straightening out yarn in the cubicles.

Fridays were generally fairly busy with tourists on the island, so I wasn't surprised to look at my watch and see it was already twelve-thirty.

"Hey, time for lunch," I said. "Did you bring yours or are you going out?"

"I told Grace I'd meet her and the baby at Pickled Pelican. I'll be back in an hour."

"That's fine. Take your time. I brought my lunch, and when you get back I'll go to the post office."

Post office. I'd almost forgotten about the letter that should be there waiting for me.

I was setting up my sandwich and coffee on the desk when Kyle hollered, "Bye," on his way out and I realized that Worth might be eating his lunch alone in the next room. I peeked in to see him leaning over a makeshift table—a cardboard box—about to take a bite of his sandwich.

"Gosh," I said. "There's barely any light in here. You're certainly welcome to join me at my desk. I'm just about to eat too."

He looked up and smiled. "Oh, thanks. That would be nice," he said and followed me into the shop.

I cleared a space on the desk for him as he pulled up a chair. Sitting across from him, I suddenly felt awkward. "Oh," I said, jumping up. "Would you like some coffee? I just brewed it."

He raised a hand in the air. "No, thanks. I have bottled water, but I might take a rain check on that coffee later this afternoon."

"Sure." I sat back down and proceeded to take a bite of my chicken salad sandwich.

"I'm sorry for your loss," he said, surprising me. "Your mother told me your husband recently passed away."

I nodded. "Yes, this past March. A massive coronary."

Worth shook his head. "Sudden death is a good thing for the victim but difficult for those left behind," he said, like he had experience.

"Are you married?" I asked and then wondered if I was being too nosy.

"No. My wife passed away ten years ago. Breast cancer."

Now it was my turn to say I was sorry.

"Children?" he inquired, which assured me I hadn't been too inquisitive.

"Two sons. Grown and gone." I explained that John and Jason lived out of state. "How about you?"

"Yes, a daughter. Married and living in Paris."

"Paris?" I said with surprise. "How nice."

Worth took a long swig of water and nodded. "Caroline went there for college, met a Frenchman, married, and the rest is history. I have two grandchildren. Yvette is twelve and Christophe is ten."

"Oh, how nice, but you probably don't get to see them that often."

"No, I do. I go over to Paris fairly often, and they try to get to Florida during the summer."

"Grace's husband, Lucas, is from France. He owns the bookstore in town."

He nodded. "Yes, I know Lucas quite well. Nice guy. So have you ever been to Paris?"

"Actually, I have. The summer after I graduated college I went with two friends for a couple weeks. I have to say, it was an instant love affair."

"Ah, but you never went back?"

"Regrettably, no. After I got married, we just never seemed to find the time." I didn't want to mention the fact that despite my repeated begging, especially after the boys were older, Andrew had no interest or desire to visit France. So, therefore, I didn't go either.

"Are you living on Cedar Key?"

"Yeah, I decided to sell my home in Gainesville and move in with my mother after my husband died. With the boys no longer living at home, the house was way too big for me. Chloe said you're from Ocala. Will you be traveling back and forth every day to do the work here?"

"No, it's an hour's drive each way, so that wouldn't be very convenient. I took a cottage at the Faraway Inn. I have a dog and they're pet friendly. I love Cedar Key. I've thought about selling my place in Ocala and just moving here, but somehow that hasn't happened yet. Guess I never really had a reason to."

Was it my imagination or did his gaze seem to intensify when he said this? I took the last bite of my sandwich and nodded.

"My mother said you owned your own architecture business. So are you retired now?"

Worth laughed, and I noticed that the laughter seemed to touch his eyes as the sound of it created a happy feeling.

"Well, now, that depends. Officially, yes, I'm retired. I had an office in Ocala and I've given that up. But I'm still open to doing side jobs like this one. I turned sixty-five this year, so I thought it was time I slow down from work a little and enjoy other things in life. But the problem is I also enjoy working. That's why taking a job like this is perfect for me. Nothing too involved or long-term."

"That makes sense," I said and thought of Andrew, who had been months away from retiring but never got the chance. "Good for you. I think we all reach a certain age where we should be able to do what we want."

"My thoughts exactly," he said as he balled up the wax paper from his sandwich. "Well, thank you for sharing lunch with me, but time for me to get back to work."

"Me too," I said, standing up, but I was surprised to find that I really could have kept sitting much longer just talking to him.

Chloe returned from lunch and I headed to the post office. In my box was a manila envelope from Mail Boxes in Gainesville. I decided to wait till I got back to the yarn shop to open it, mostly because I was beginning to feel nervous about what I'd find inside. Then again, if Andrew had given my cell number as an emergency backup, whatever it was couldn't be too damaging, could it?

I walked in to find Chloe surrounded by customers all trying to get her attention. She shot me a look that said *help*. I threw the mail on the desk and went over to assist a group of women. More women filtered in over the next couple of hours and more sales were done.

"Wow," I said, glancing at my watch, surprised to see it was going on four. "That was a busy afternoon."

Chloe nodded as she went to wash out the coffeepot. "Certainly was. Is there a group or something in town?"

"Not that I'm aware of, but could be." We often had various boating groups or organizations coming to the island for the weekend. "Hey, you came in early this morning. Go home. I'll stay till four-thirty and close up."

"Are you sure?"

"Yup. Go." I could still hear saws and various tools from the next room and wondered how long Worth intended to stay and work. I wouldn't be able to lock the shop till he was ready to leave.

Chloe replaced the coffeepot, got her knitting bag and purse, and said, "Okay, thanks. See you tomorrow."

That was when I was finally able to sit at the desk and open the manila envelope. I removed a business-size envelope and the first thing that caught my eye was the return address. Coburn, Draper & Marshall. Commonwealth Avenue in Boston. It appeared to be an attorney's office.

I reached for the letter opener on the desk and carefully slit open the envelope. Unfolding the white paper, I began to read.

> *Dear Mr. Kane:*
>
> *We are sorry to inform you that it has been brought to our attention by the Boston Bank and Trust Company that Ms. Bianca Caldwell was involved in a fatal car accident on April 23.*
>
> *As per your previous instructions, the bank will now issue a check to Ms. Fiona Caldwell for the amount balance in the account.*
>
> *They will need your signature on the enclosed documents. Could you please sign them at your earliest convenience and return them to our office? I am also enclosing a copy of the most current bank statement.*
>
> *If you have any questions, please do not hesitate to call me.*
>
> *Sincerely,*
>
> *James Coburn, Attorney*

Not able to comprehend what I'd just read, I reread the letter and felt even more confused. My gaze flew to the top, where it was dated May 15—five months ago. What the hell! What the hell *was* this? *Who* were Bianca and Fiona Caldwell? I'd never heard those names in my life. Surely this was some sort of mistake. Surely it was meant for another Mr. Kane.

With shaking hands I dialed the Boston number and asked for Mr. Coburn.

"I'm terribly sorry," a thickly Boston-accented voice said. "Mr. Coburn will not be back in the office until next Wednesday. May somebody else help you?"

"No," I mumbled. "Thank you." I hung up the phone as I sat there numbly staring at the papers in my hand.

"Everything okay?"

I heard Worth's voice and jumped.

"I'm sorry. I didn't mean to startle you."

"No . . . no, it's okay. I'm okay. It's okay. Really." I knew I was talking ragtime and couldn't help it. All of a sudden I felt like I had no control over anything. Not even my voice.

I felt Worth's hand on my shoulder, and that was all it took. One small gesture of kindness and I began sobbing. I utterly and completely broke down as he stood there helplessly trying to soothe me with words.

After a few minutes I began to get control of myself, hiccupped, and reached for a tissue to blow my nose. I shook my head back and forth, swallowed, and said, "I'm sorry. I've just received some rather shocking and upsetting news. I feel like a fool."

"No, no. Don't be silly," he said and placed his hand on my shoulder again, but this time it didn't bring forth a torrent of tears. It felt comforting.

"Thank you."

"Tell you what. I'm finished for the day and I'd say you are too. How about you join me over at the Black Dog for a drink. I think you could use one."

"Oh, no. I couldn't. My mother is expecting me," I said and realized I sounded like some silly teenager with a curfew.

"Under the circumstances, I'm sure she won't mind. Give her a call to let her know you'll be late."

And I did.

5

We were seated at an outside table on the deck of the Black Dog, a glass of wine in front of each of us, and I let out a deep sigh.

"Feel like talking about it?" Worth asked.

I took a sip of my cabernet. "I'm not even sure where to begin."

He nodded and remained silent as I gazed out over the water. I had grown up on this area of the Gulf, fishing, boating, being a kid, then a teenager. Yet all of a sudden it looked foreign to me. After reading the letter from the law firm in Boston, I felt like everything I thought I had known about my married life was a fraud. As much as I wanted to deny it, I was pretty certain there was no mistake that the letter had indeed been intended for Andrew, but I had no idea what the contents were about.

I took another sip of wine, reached into my handbag, removed the letter, and passed it to Worth. "Read it," I said.

He put on reading glasses, read the paper, raised his eyebrows, and put the letter down. "Do you know who these women are or what this is about? How did you get a letter like this that was sent to your husband?"

I proceeded to tell him about being contacted by Mail Boxes and how the letter had been forwarded to me.

"And, no, I have no idea who these people are. I've never heard these names in my life."

Now it was his turn to let out a deep sigh. "And how much money are we talking? What did the bank statement say?"

It was then that I realized I hadn't even bothered to look at that. I reached in my bag and removed the statement. I felt my eyes widen. Fifty thousand dollars. Wordlessly, I passed it to Worth and heard him whistle.

"Yeah, that's a significant amount. I thought maybe it would be a small sum. Have you contacted this attorney?"

"Fifty thousand dollars that I knew *nothing* about, and yes, I called him as soon as I read the letter this afternoon. He's out of the office till next Wednesday." A wave of nausea shot through me. Whatever this was about, I knew it wasn't going to be good.

"Well," Worth said, and I looked up to see concern on his face. "I think at this point we can assume a few things. It's apparent that your husband made specific instructions, and one of those was the fact that if something happened to this Bianca Caldwell, the balance of the account was to go to Fiona Caldwell. Are they relatives? Nieces or maybe cousins?"

I shook my head and took another sip of wine. How is it that when the bad things in life happen, when we look back in retrospect, many times we realize our gut feelings were usually correct? And I had a gut feeling now.

"No," I said. "No nieces. No cousins." I could feel moisture burning my eyes and reached into my bag for a tissue. "But maybe a lover and a daughter."

"You knew your husband," Worth said softly. "Do you think that's possible?"

I let out an angry chuckle. "I'm beginning to think I didn't know him at all . . . and anything in life is possible."

"I'm sorry," he said and reached out to pat my hand. "I'm sorry you have to go through this."

The words were kind, but what I noticed most was that they sounded very sincere.

"Thanks. Somehow I just have to get through the next five days, which won't be easy. I want answers now."

"That's natural. Another glass of wine?"

"I think I will. I told my mother not to wait dinner for me."

After the waitress brought the wine, I found myself telling Worth about how Andrew and I met and surprised myself because I normally didn't open up to somebody I'd known for only a few days. But it felt right.

"So you met at UF in Gainesville," he said. "Majoring in the same program?"

"No. I was English lit and Andrew was a science major, but we didn't meet as students. We were both on the faculty teaching there. I was already twenty-seven, dating different guys but nothing serious. Actually, the first few months after we met, it was a platonic relationship. We were just friends, and then he asked me out. After that we began to get serious. We got engaged a year later and married two years after that."

"So you weren't a kid."

"No, I was thirty when we got married. We both had our positions at the university, so we bought the house in Gainesville. We were married two years when I had Jason, and then John two years later. So I gave up my teaching position." I didn't mention the fact that Andrew wouldn't even consider me working part-time. He wanted me home, raising the boys and being a professor's wife.

"Oh, I thought you said the other day you were a retired English professor."

"Right. When the boys were in high school, I did return to teaching," I said, recalling the problems it created with Andrew. "I'd probably still be there, but the university began downsizing a few years ago. I figured I could keep busy for a year, because Andrew was supposed to retire this past summer and we had plans to travel."

"That's a shame that didn't work out," Worth said.

I nodded. "I guess so. We were still disagreeing on the travel when Andrew died. He wanted to get a motor home and drive cross-country. I wanted to return to Paris and then take time to travel throughout France. But none of it was meant to be."

I took the last sip of wine and looked at my watch. "Oh, my

God. I can't believe it's seven-thirty. I really have to get going."
How had the time flown so fast just sitting there talking to him?

"Could I interest you in joining me someplace for dinner?"

I had to catch myself before saying yes. "Gosh, I'd love to, but I really should get home. Oh, by the way, I'd appreciate it if you didn't say anything about this letter to anybody. I'm still not even sure what it's all about, and, well, you know . . . in a small town news travels fast."

Worth stood up and placed some bills on the table. "You don't need to worry. Your information is safe with me."

"Thanks," I said, heading toward the stairs. When we got on the sidewalk, I said, "Thanks for listening."

I walked toward my car and realized that while I was feeling far from great, maybe there was a possibility that I'd be able to get through whatever was ahead for me.

I walked into the house and found my mother in the family room knitting and watching TV.

"Did you and Chloe go out for dinner?" she asked.

"Actually, no," I said, then paused. I wasn't sure how she'd react to where I'd been. "Worth invited me to the Black Dog for a glass of wine."

She looked up at me with surprise on her face. "Oh, that's really nice. Did you have a good time? He seems like such a nice fellow."

I smiled. Leave it to my mother. Never one to judge anybody.

"You don't think it's too soon?"

Now her expression looked confused. "You mean since Andrew passed away? You only went for a glass of wine in public, Marin. Nothing wrong with that."

She was right. I realized I was hungry. "Any leftovers?"

"Yes, just heat the tuna casserole in the microwave, and there's salad in the fridge."

"Thanks," I said and headed to the kitchen.

I poured myself a glass of sweet tea while I waited for the casserole to heat. I had made the decision on the drive home to not tell my mother about the letter. I still wasn't sure what it was all about, and quite honestly, I didn't feel like discussing it with anybody yet. Except for Worth.

I set up a TV table in front of the sofa and sat down to eat.

"Oh, Saxton called me earlier," my mother said. "Victoria called him today. She's planning a memorial for Maybelle sometime next month, before Thanksgiving. He'll keep us posted with the information."

"That's good. How're you doing?"

"I'm okay. When you get to be my age, I think you become more accepting of the fact that each year you're going to lose more friends."

After I finished eating, I put my dishes in the dishwasher, got into my nightgown, and settled on the sofa with a cup of herbal tea and my knitting.

My mother retired to bed at ten, but I sat up knitting and thinking.

6

I had always found needlepoint, like my knitting, to be a soothing way to pass time. But by Sunday afternoon neither of my current projects held my interest. I was consumed with a million questions in relation to the letter from the attorney's office.

Who was this Bianca Caldwell? Somebody Andrew knew from years ago? A woman he was having an affair with before he died? And Fiona Caldwell? Why would Andrew have arranged for her to receive money upon his death? As much as I hated to admit it, over the past few days it had been becoming more clear to me that she had to be his daughter. But how was that possible? And how old was she? A small child now left motherless? The attorney's office was located in Boston, as was the bank. Did that mean Bianca Caldwell had also lived in Boston? Had Andrew ever been there? Although he had traveled a lot over the years for teaching seminars, I honestly couldn't recall his itinerary. So many questions and three more days to wait for the answers.

I looked up from the needlepoint canvas I held in my hand and let out a deep sigh. I normally loved the peacefulness of sitting on my mother's patio overlooking the water, watching ibis and heron sweep across the saw grass. But today nothing seemed to settle me or diminish the unease I felt.

"Doing okay?"

My mother settled herself in the lounge beside me and removed the sweater she was working on from her knitting bag. Although she had to have known that I picked up the correspondence from Mail Boxes on Friday, she hadn't questioned me about the contents. But that was my mother. Never one to pry. Always allowing me to open up to her in my own time.

"Not really," I said, getting up to go in the house to get the letter.

Walking back out to the patio, I passed the envelope to her. "Here. I'd like you to read it. This is what was in Andrew's mailbox." My mother removed the paper, adjusted her eyeglasses, and began to read.

When she finished, she swung her legs to the side of the lounge to face me. "Do you know what this is all about?"

"No. I have no idea."

"Did you contact the attorney's office?"

I nodded. "Yes, and James Coburn won't be back in the office until this Wednesday. I've been going nuts trying to figure it out."

"From what I can gather, this Bianca Caldwell was killed in a car crash this past April. It would appear that this law firm has no idea that Andrew has also passed away. They're requesting his signature in order to transfer funds from an account to Fiona Caldwell."

"Right," I said, and could feel anger slowly beginning to build inside of me. "And who the hell is this Fiona? Did you see the bank statement? Fifty thousand dollars. It has to be a mistake . . . either a mistake or a joke, but I'm not finding it humorous at all." I jumped up and began pacing the patio. "How could this happen? Did Andrew have a secret life I didn't know about? I don't understand. I just *don't* understand." But even as I said it, I had a sick feeling in the pit of my stomach that I did understand.

My mother remained silent for a few moments and then let out a deep sigh. "You knew Andrew better than anybody, Marin. Is there any chance that this Fiona could be his daughter?"

I felt moisture stinging my eyes. "Do we ever *really* know anybody?" I shook my head back and forth. "Anything's possible, isn't it? Secrets are buried all the time. Look at what your own sister did—gave birth to Sydney, gave her up for adoption, and never told a soul."

"Very true, but secrets usually have a way of surfacing just like Sybile's eventually did."

"I don't even know how old this Fiona is. The attorney's office and the bank are in Boston, but that doesn't mean she definitely lives in that area. I don't know a thing."

My mother reached over to pat my hand. "And you won't until Wednesday, I'm afraid. But there's one thing that you must remember, Marin."

My head shot up. "What's that?"

"The reason you found out about any of this now is because it was Andrew who gave your cell number to Mail Boxes as an emergency number. That tells me that if something happened to him, he wanted you to get any correspondence related to this situation."

My mother was right. "But why? Why the hell would he want me to find out after he was gone about money he had provided for somebody? Why couldn't he just tell me when he was alive?"

"Shame. Fear. There could be a number of reasons, but until you get the entire story, I don't think you'll know for sure."

"You're right," I replied as the doorbell sounded inside the house.

"That's Sydney," my mother said as she stood up. "I hope you don't mind, but with Noah away for a few days, I invited her to have supper with us. And it's up to you if you want to share any of your news with her."

"Aunt Dora, that was delicious," Sydney said. "Nobody cooks up mullet like you do."

My mother laughed. "Good thing your mother isn't here to hear you say that. She always thought she cooked mullet better than anybody on the island."

I smiled as I reached for the wine decanter on the table and refilled our glasses. "That's one thing you and I never experienced," I told my cousin. "We were both only children, so no sibling rivalry."

"Yeah, that's true. I told Monica if that begins with her four, I'm afraid I'll have no advice to give on that subject. How about your boys, Marin? Any rivalry there?"

I took a sip of wine and shook my head. "Not really. Oh, the usual squabbles when they were little, but for the most part they got along and I never noticed any jealousy. I think girls might be more prone to that anyway, don't you?"

Sydney nodded. "Could be. Look at what Chloe and Grace went through. Chloe's jealousy caused a ten-year estrangement between them. I've always felt, though, that if somebody is happy and adjusted with their own life, it doesn't leave any room to want what others have. But I don't think it's just between sisters. I see it with the younger girls, like Clarissa. They all have to have the same clothes, the same style hair. It drives Monica crazy, and she's trying to teach Clarissa to be her own person. To be an individual and different. I do think raising daughters can be more complex than raising sons, though."

"Hmm, probably. But I wouldn't know. My mother had one daughter, your mother had one daughter, and you had one daughter. Yet I was the one to have two sons. It was Andrew who got the daughter," I said, and as soon as the words were out I felt the anger returning and saw the confused expression on Sydney's face.

The three of us sat there in silence for a moment, and then I let out a sarcastic chuckle. "Yeah, well, at least I'm pretty sure he has a daughter that I only recently found out about," I said and went on to explain the story to my cousin.

When I finished, she took a sip of her wine and patted my hand. "I have to be honest and say that I'm not that surprised." When she saw the look on my face, she went on, "No, no. I have no reason at all to even think that Andrew cheated on you. It's just that at this stage of the game, Marin, not too much surprises me. You have to remember what I went through when Stephen died and then coming here and discovering my biological mother. All of my own experiences have only forced me to believe that truth truly is stranger than fiction."

She was right. If anybody could understand, it would be Sydney. Finding out two weeks after she buried her husband that he had been a compulsive gambler was bad enough, but being evicted from her posh home, which she'd thought was long paid for, had rocked her world as she knew it.

"Sydney's right," my mother said. "Of course this is shocking to you, Marin, but it's life. Shocking and bad things happen. But it's how you choose to get through it that will be important. Just know that you have people who love you, and we'll be there for you, no matter what."

I heard the words, and while I appreciated them, they didn't take away the anger that surged through me. "But damn him. Damn him for doing something like this. I thought we had a good marriage. I thought he loved me. We always got along so well, had so much in common, and enjoyed each other's company. How many times other people even commented on what a great couple we were and how perfect we were for each other. It was all a lie, a sham. Here I am grieving for a husband who was nothing but a fraud." I felt the tears sliding down my face and didn't bother to wipe them away. "This is what Andrew left me with. Not his love . . . but his secrets, and I hate him for that."

I felt my mother's arms around me as Sydney passed me a tissue. "That's not entirely true," she said. "I felt the same way when Stephen died. I knew nothing about those loans he took on our house, which ultimately caused me to be evicted. You have a right to be angry, Marin. Damn angry. But that doesn't cancel out the love that you did share with each other. It doesn't wipe away the fact that you raised two sons together or the good times and happy moments. Those *did* happen. You might not want to admit that right now, and that's only natural. But I agree with Aunt Dora— what's important now is how you go forward from here."

I wiped my eyes again with the tissue. They were right. I knew that. But I also knew that the happy couple Andrew and I projected to family and friends was probably as much of a fraud as I now felt he was to me in death.

7

I woke at five-thirty after a fitful night of tossing and turning. Too much to think about. It was still dark as I brushed my teeth, threw on a pair of jeans and a tee shirt, and then headed to the kitchen.

I waited for the coffee to brew as I stared out the window to the sky over the water getting lighter. After filling my insulated Starbucks cup, I made my way through the family room to the front door. No sign of my mother or Oliver. Slipping into the golf cart, I turned the key and headed downtown to the City Beach.

The sun was just peeping over the horizon as I sat on one of the benches watching a new day begin. The only sound was water splashing onto the shore. I thought back to shortly after I met Andrew. I was teaching at the university and sharing a small house in Gainesville with Bella, my friend and colleague—now known to the reading public by her full name, which graced her book covers, Orabella Vitale. I had invited Andrew to Cedar Key for the weekend to meet my parents, along with Bella and a fellow she had been seeing at the time. Bella stayed with me at my parents' home, and the fellows got a room at the Island Hotel.

The weekend was pleasant enough. My parents seemed to like Andrew, but I recalled a bit of awkwardness during the Saturday evening dinner my mother prepared for all of us. Sitting around the table with coffee and dessert, Andrew began questioning my father about some best-selling novels on the *New York Times* list, asking if he had read them and what his opinion was. My father was a fisherman. He worked from dawn to dusk providing a decent living for us. Many days he barely had time to scan the newspaper before falling into bed shortly after supper.

I saw the embarrassed expression that crossed my father's face at the same time that Bella did.

"Yes, well," she said. "We can't all be bookworms, can we? Tell me, Mr. Foster, which do you find to be more popular, crab or oysters?"

My father visibly relaxed as he launched into an explanation of both, depending on the season, and I wanted to lean over and kiss my friend's cheek. It was the first time that I suspected Andrew was an academic snob, but it wasn't the last.

Another incident on Sunday afternoon was mentioned by Bella later that evening. The four of us had taken my father's pontoon boat out for a ride. It was August, hot and steamy, so Bella and I had worn our swimsuits under shorts and tops. I had grown up on the water, knew how to drive and operate a boat from the time I was ten. But for some reason Andrew seemed hesitant about me being at the helm. Bella's friend cajoled him, saying he had the utmost faith in me.

We headed out from the City Marina, through the channel, and I steered the boat north. I could see the tide was going out, and after a ride to North Key I turned the boat around and headed back. As luck would have it, I hit a sandbar and we got stuck. For those of us who had grown up on the island, it wasn't a big deal. The water is pretty shallow, and with a bit of pushing and prodding, a boat was easy to dislodge.

Bella and I began laughing when we realized what had happened. I whipped off my shirt and shorts and said, "Not to worry," as I jumped over the side of the boat into the water, where I was quickly joined by Bella. The two of us were now giggling as I sputtered out instructions to Andrew and Bella's friend to back the boat up as we pushed. It was then that I saw the look on Andrew's face: a mixture of anger and, if I wasn't mistaken, fear.

Within a few minutes we had the boat off the sandbar, Bella and I jumped back in, and we were on our way.

"What the hell were you thinking?" I heard Andrew yell; I honestly didn't know what he was talking about.

I turned around and stared at him. "What do you mean?"

"Getting us stuck like that and then jumping in the water. You could have been injured," was what he said, but I had a gut feeling it was more his safety that he was concerned about, rather than mine.

"I'm fine," was all I managed to say. I remained cool toward him the rest of the afternoon and during the drive back to Gainesville that evening.

After we got home, I now recalled Bella saying, "Are you sure he's for you, Marin? I'm afraid a fellow like that could suck the spirit right out of you."

I blew out a breath before draining the last of my coffee and standing up. Had my spirit disappeared over the years with Andrew? I wasn't sure. I got in the golf cart to head down Second Street to the coffee café and wondered if Andrew had not only diminished my spirit but also betrayed me in a way that I wasn't sure I'd be able to forgive.

Monday mornings at the coffee café were always busy—tourists leaving the island after their weekend wanting to get that cup of coffee for the drive home and locals gathered to catch up on news. But when I walked inside, the chatter from the locals sitting in small groups at the tables was louder than usual.

I spied Chloe and Grace and joined them. Solange sat in her stroller gumming a teething biscuit and looking around at everybody talking at once. I bent down to kiss her forehead.

"Hey, sweetie," I said and was rewarded with a huge smile before I sat down.

"What's going on? Did somebody win the lottery?"

Chloe laughed. "Not quite. Seems Mr. Carl was in the Welcome Center yesterday and overheard something. According to him, the phone rang and the volunteer answered. Of course he eaves-dropped, and bear in mind that his hearing isn't the best. But he insists that he heard a conversation about a film company wanting to come to Cedar Key to make a movie."

This *was* big news. "Are you serious?"

"That's just it," Grace said. "Who knows? The volunteer was Martha and she's not talking. Said it was a private conversation and Mr. Carl shouldn't have been listening, never mind spreading gossip."

I shook my head and laughed. "Yeah, but we all know that gossip is what this island thrives on. Any small town does. Imagine if it's true, though, the income it could generate for the merchants."

Chloe smiled. "Hmm, I wonder how many of the crew or cast are knitters? This could put Yarning Together on the map."

"I think I'd hold off ordering extra yarn for a while," Grace said.

"Ah, well, it's fun to dream, isn't it?"

Suellen came over to the table laughing and shaking her head. "Can you believe this? Mr. Carl has really started something. Your usual, Marin?"

"Yeah, thanks," I said and heard somebody standing in back of me say, "Well, they just might be looking for extras, and I was chosen as Clara in *The Nutcracker* in fifth grade."

I turned around to see the one speaking was Mr. Carl's wife, Raylene, and couldn't control my laughter.

"Oh, my God! Is she for real?"

Suellen nodded. " 'Fraid so," she said before heading to get my coffee.

"Well, you do have to admit Cedar Key would be a beautiful place to film a movie. With the water and nature everywhere. We're a funky little fishing village, but I think we have a lot to offer."

Chloe took a sip of her coffee. "If it's true, I'm wondering what type of movie it would be. Small Southern town? Maybe based on a novel?"

"Only time will tell," I said as Suellen returned with my coffee.

Chloe leaned toward me and dropped her voice to a whisper. "I haven't seen you since you picked that letter up on Friday. Is everything okay?"

I stared into my coffee mug, shook my head, and took a sip. "Not really."

"Oh, I'm sorry. Anything you want to talk about?"

Why not? I thought. If it was true that Andrew had a daughter, and I was pretty sure that it was, the word would make its way around the island eventually.

I proceeded to explain the call from Mail Boxes to Grace and then brought them both up to speed on what the letter contained.

"Oh, gosh. I'm so sorry, Marin." I felt Grace squeeze my hand.

"Do you think this could really be Andrew's daughter?" Chloe questioned.

"Well, I don't have any proof yet, but why else would he have money in an account for this Fiona Caldwell?"

"And you say her mother died in a car crash this past April?"

I nodded and took another sip of coffee.

Chloe blew out a whoosh of air from between her lips. "Wow. It was bad enough when Parker left me to marry his trophy wife a couple years ago and their baby arrived just after they exchanged their I dos . . . but I did know Wifey Number Two was pregnant. I can only imagine what a shock this has been for you. How old is the child, do you know?"

"Nope, I don't know a thing. And I won't for two more days. The attorney who sent the letter won't be in the office until Wednesday."

Chloe got up and scooped me into a tight embrace. "Well, no matter what you find out and no matter what happens, I want you to know that we're all here for you, Marin. Right, Gracie?"

"Absolutely," she agreed, right before I felt moisture stinging my eyes once again.

8

I woke Wednesday morning after another sleepless night. The digital clock on the bedside table read five-fifteen. I wasn't due into the yarn shop until two in the afternoon. It was going to be a very long day. I decided to get up, get dressed, and grab some coffee, and instead of taking the golf cart, I'd walk downtown with Oliver. Good exercise for both of us. After leaving a note for my mother to let her know that I had the dog, we stepped outside just as dawn was breaking.

We walked along Gulf Boulevard and turned onto Whiddon. Only one vehicle passed us, a truck pulling a boat, most likely headed to Anchor Cove to launch the craft for a day of fishing. Not pleasure fishing but working for their livelihood, like my daddy had done for so many years.

Walking along G Street, I glanced out at the tide coming in and once again thought of Andrew and my father. My dad had never held that initial snobbery against my future husband. He was always friendly toward Andrew, but I often wondered what he really thought of my choice, whereas I had always felt, although she never said a word, that my mother wasn't all that pleased with Andrew for her son-in-law. What was it that she might have seen and I hadn't? Or more honestly, what was it that maybe I had preferred not to see?

As I approached the City Park, there was a figure farther down the beach with a dog on a leash, and when I got closer I realized it was Worth. He turned around, saw me, and waved.

"Good morning," he said, walking toward me.

I smiled and returned his greeting. "And who is this?" I asked, putting my hand out for the Labradoodle to sniff.

"Ah, my best girl. Meet Suzette."

"She's beautiful, and this is my mom's dog, Oliver. I'm not sure if you met him yet in the yarn shop."

Worth also extended his hand for Oliver to sniff and shook his head. "No, I've never had the pleasure. What a handsome fellow."

"Do you let Suzette loose? I was going to let Oliver run a bit."

Both dogs were already doing the requisite sniffing of each other.

"Yes, I like to give her a bit of exercise before I leave her to go in to work," he said as he unclipped her leash.

I did the same and we watched the two dogs run off together through the park. Worth and I took a seat on one of the benches to watch them.

"How've you been?" he asked. "I was a little concerned about you over the weekend, and your shop has been closed for two days."

I nodded. "Right. We're closed on Mondays and Tuesdays. I'm doing okay. I think. I'll know better later this morning after I speak with that attorney."

"This is a rough thing for you to go through. I hope whatever he tells you won't be too disturbing."

"The thing is, I have a million questions. I just hope he'll be able to answer them."

"I have some good news for you. That bay window will be installed this afternoon. Will you be in the shop today?"

I nodded. "That *is* good news. Yeah, I'll be there around two."

"Good. I think that will make a big difference. After I get the window installed, I'll begin working on the ceiling and walls."

"That'll be great. That windowsill will allow me to display some finished pieces, which might entice people passing by."

"I don't know much about this type of thing, but is your needle-point similar to tapestries? I've seen a lot of those in France."

"They're actually pretty similar. It's the technique and methods that might differ. Needlepoint is done on open-weave canvas using wool, silk, or cotton threads. Many designs use only a simple tent stitch, which relies on color changes to construct the pattern."

"So you do needlepoint in addition to knitting?"

I laughed and nodded. "Yeah, most women have a variety of handwork that they enjoy doing and usually a favorite. I go back and forth on both knitting and needlepoint, depending on my mood."

We both turned around as barking caught our attention. Suzette was bowing low, and as Oliver ran toward her, she spun in circles, forcing him to chase her.

"They seem to be having a great time," I said.

A smile crossed Worth's face. "Yeah, I'm afraid she's flirting with him."

My smile matched his. "Nothing wrong with that." I glanced at my watch and saw it was going on seven. "Oh, gee, I have to get going. Come on, Oliver," I hollered.

"I wish you luck with that phone call, and, well . . . I was won-dering if maybe you'd like to have dinner with me this evening."

I clipped Oliver's leash to his collar. "That's really nice of you. I think I would. Thanks."

The smile on his face broadened. "Great. How about I pick you up at seven? And is the Island Room okay?"

"Sounds good."

"Okay. Then I'll see you later today at the shop."

As I headed home I had the comforting thought that no matter how the phone conversation went with the attorney, I had a nice dinner to look forward to. With quite a handsome man.

I waited until my mother had left for the yarn shop and then placed the call to James Coburn in Boston, Massachusetts.

I explained to the secretary who I was and requested to speak with the attorney. My hand grew clammy as I gripped the phone tighter and listened to a piece of classical music on the line.

A few moments later, I heard, "James Coburn. How may I help you?"

Clearing my throat, I said, "I'm Marin Kane. Wife of Andrew Kane, one of your clients."

"Mrs. Kane," he said, and I heard the surprise in his voice. "I've been attempting to reach your husband since April."

"Yes, well . . . My husband passed away in March, and I'm calling to find out about the letter you sent him in reference to Bianca and Fiona Caldwell."

"Oh, I'm so terribly sorry for your loss. My deepest condolences. I had no idea. Was it sudden?"

"Thank you," I replied, detecting sincere sympathy in his tone. "Yes, it was. A heart attack."

"Again, I'm so sorry. Well, this does complicate the situation a bit."

"Perhaps you could start at the beginning and explain to me who these women are. Why was there a bank account for this Fiona Caldwell?"

A deep sigh came across the line. "I take this to mean that Andrew never did explain the situation to you?"

"Never. The first I heard of it was when I was contacted about a piece of correspondence at his Mail Boxes account that I also knew nothing about. Andrew had given them my cell number as an emergency contact. That was how I came to receive your letter sent to him in May."

"I see." Another sigh. "This is a bit awkward, and I hate to have to be the one to tell you. I really thought that over time Mr. Kane would explain the situation himself."

"Which he did not," I said as my anger began to build.

"Right. Well . . . Fiona Caldwell is the daughter of Mr. Kane and Bianca Caldwell."

There. The words had been spoken. What I was pretty sure I knew had just been confirmed. There was no turning back now. And yet, I could feel hurt and betrayal spreading through me. Hearing it said out loud made it all heartbreakingly real.

"Mrs. Kane? Are you still there?"

"Yes," I whispered. "I'm here."

"Not that hearing something like this in person would make any of it easier, but I hate having to do this by telephone."

He was right. Finding out something like this would not have been one bit easier in person, but without seeing his face, I focused more strongly on his voice. And I couldn't deny the compassion I heard.

I swiped away the tears that had started to fall. "It's not your fault," I said. "It's certainly not *your* fault. I need some answers, though. I need to know about this . . . girl. This Fiona Caldwell. How old is she? Does she live in Boston? Does she know Andrew is her father? Was he still in touch with her mother?" I felt the questions tumbling out of me as my tears subsided and the natural desire for answers took over.

"I don't know the entire story," he said. "Andrew and I were classmates in college, but we had lost touch until he contacted me about this situation, so I'll tell you what I know. Fiona is not a child. She turned nineteen this past April, born . . ."

I heard him rustling through papers.

"Ah, I have the file here. Born April 22, 1994."

My mind did a quick calculation. April of 1994. That would mean she was conceived in July of 1993. Andrew and I were married. Jason would have been five years old and John three. I couldn't think beyond that.

"What else?" I questioned. "How did Andrew know the mother? Where did she live?"

"From what I recall Andrew telling me, Bianca Caldwell was a colleague of his. They had both been teaching a course at the same college. She did live in Amherst, Massachusetts, when he first came to me. About five years later she relocated north of Boston to Marblehead."

Amherst. The summer of 1993. A teaching position that Andrew had been offered. Could it be possible? While I stayed behind in Gainesville to care for our two sons, he was having an affair with another woman?

"And did Andrew continue seeing her? Did he visit...his daughter?"

"I can't answer that for sure, but I think not. That was why he came to me. He wanted to set up an account to provide for the child until age eighteen. So I can assume he had no further contact with either the mother or the daughter. All of the financial arrangements were done through my office and the Boston Bank and Trust Company."

"But I don't understand," I said. "If he was providing money for that girl's support, why is there still fifty thousand dollars in the account?"

I heard the attorney clear his throat. "Well, over the eighteen years Bianca Caldwell only withdrew a portion of what the balance was, and I have no idea why she never took the full amount, which continued to grow monthly, and it accumulated interest as well. But as my letter stated, sadly, Bianca Caldwell was killed in a car crash in April. That was one of the stipulations that Mr. Kane had put in place. If anything were to happen to Bianca Caldwell, he was to be notified, we would send him the required documents to be signed, and the balance of the account would be put in Fiona Caldwell's name."

"It seems my dearly departed husband thought of everything," I said and heard my sarcasm. "Except factoring in his own death. So now what?"

"This is where it becomes a little complicated. Because you are his legal spouse and next of kin, it now becomes necessary for us to obtain your signature on the documents."

I couldn't suppress the chuckle that bubbled forth. "So you mean to tell me that my signature is what stands between my husband's love child, this Fiona Caldwell, receiving the handsome sum of fifty thousand dollars and getting nothing?"

There was a pause on the other end of the line. "That's precisely what I'm telling you."

I shook my head. *How ironic,* I thought. *Andrew was the one who cheated, but I now hold the final card.*

"I don't even know this girl. I know nothing about her. Why would I pass over fifty thousand dollars to a total stranger?"

"You're very right," James Coburn agreed. "You're certainly justified in your thinking. However, I do want you to know something else. I have an updated contact number for Fiona Caldwell that was given to me by the bank. They are handling her mother's estate and had been in touch with Fiona. The bank manager told her about the account set up by her father, and she contacted me. We spoke for quite a while, and like you, she had many questions that I wasn't able to answer."

When I remained silent, he went on.

"This has all been quite shocking for you, and I certainly understand the anger and betrayal you must be feeling. I don't know you at all, but just from speaking with you on the phone, I have no doubt that you're a good person. I would just like you to bear in mind . . . no matter what happened, no matter the terrible wrong that your husband and Bianca Caldwell committed, Fiona Caldwell is the innocent victim of two adults behaving badly. She had asked me for your name and phone number, but I didn't feel at liberty to share that with her. She then asked if I would give you her number and requested that you call her."

After a few moments, I said, "Give me her number."

9

After hanging up the phone with James Coburn, I walked out to the patio, plunked onto a lounge, and stared out at the water. What the hell had my life come to?

So I now had confirmation that not only had Andrew been unfaithful but that union had resulted in the birth of a daughter. A daughter he had chosen to tell me nothing about. It was then that the irony hit me. After the birth of our two sons, I would have liked to try once more for a girl. I recalled how Andrew had not welcomed this idea. He felt two children were enough. We should be thankful that we had two healthy sons, he had said. Although I truly would have welcomed a daughter, I didn't push the subject.

No wonder, I thought. *He already had that third child that he was paying for, and it just happened to be a daughter. His daughter. Not mine.*

I forced myself to think back to that summer of 1993. For whatever reason, our marriage seemed to be on shaky ground. We argued a lot over seemingly trivial matters; we no longer pursued activities that we both used to enjoy; our sex life had come to a virtual standstill. Plain and simple, we were drifting apart. So when Andrew had told me about the offer to teach a summer class at

Hampshire College in Amherst, Massachusetts, I'd thought the time apart might do us both some good.

I walked into the house, filled the kettle with water, and placed a teabag in a mug. Leaning against the counter, waiting for the kettle to boil, I remembered that when he had returned home almost three months later, things had seemed to improve.

I had spent a lot of that summer with the boys at my parents' home on Cedar Key. By the time Andrew returned in late August, both of us were refreshed and definitely happy to see each other, and there appeared to be a subtle shift in our relationship. Thinking about it now, I wondered if perhaps acceptance was what had been acquired. Acceptance of each other, acceptance of our life together, and acceptance of a marriage and love that had always lacked a certain romance and passion.

The whistling of the kettle cut into my thoughts. After pouring water into the mug, I took my tea, along with the papers on the counter, and went back out to the patio.

I let out a deep sigh and allowed myself to breathe in the warm October air. Butterflies flitted on one of the flowering bushes at the side of the patio. I looked above me to see a bright blue sky dotted here and there with white puffy clouds. I realized that the grief I had been feeling since the loss of Andrew had lightened. Did this mean that I no longer mourned his passing? Or even worse—did it mean I no longer loved him? Was the anger and betrayal that I felt able to supersede any love that we may have shared over twenty-six years of marriage? I had no answer for that.

I took a sip of tea and then glanced at the papers in my lap, scribbled notes from the information that James Coburn had given me.

I wondered if Bianca Caldwell had continued her teaching career after her daughter was born. Since she had not touched much of the money that Andrew had contributed, I assumed that she must have continued to work. I also wondered if any other family was involved in Fiona's life. Perhaps an aunt or a grandmother. Although I realized that it was probably natural for her to want to speak with me, the thought of it left me uneasy. What, exactly, would she be hoping to hear about the father she had never known? With the anger and betrayal that I was dealing with, I wasn't at all sure I was the person to give her a clear and unbiased picture of this man.

I glanced at my watch and was surprised to see it was already noon. And here I sat, still in my shorts and tee shirt, no shower taken and no desire whatsoever to go into the yarn shop in two hours. It was then that I remembered the dinner date I had agreed to with Worth. This held no appeal for me either.

I got up, went inside, and called my mother.

"Are you very busy at the shop today?" I asked.

"Not especially, no. Why?"

I fibbed about not feeling so well, which really wasn't very far from the truth. Except that my symptoms were more emotional than physical.

"Oh, don't worry about coming in, Marin. Chloe and I are just fine here, and I can close around four."

I breathed a sigh of relief. I just wasn't up to going there and pretending everything was fine, and I still wasn't ready to discuss what I'd learned this morning.

"Thanks, Mom. Oh, and could you do me a favor? Could you tell Worth that I'm not feeling well? I was supposed to join him for dinner this evening . . . but . . . maybe you could ask him if he's free on Friday evening . . . I'll take a rain check."

"I'll take care of it. Now, lie down and get some rest."

I wasn't sure if it was because I felt guilty about not going into the yarn shop or because I just needed to keep busy, but I spent the afternoon preparing dinner for my mother and me.

Comfort food. That was what I needed, and I proceeded to put together a batch of homemade macaroni and cheese. Putting that aside to slip into the oven later, I then prepared a salad and placed it in the fridge.

I began removing all the ingredients necessary from the cabinets to make a chocolate cake. But not just any chocolate cake. Decadent. Sinful. So delicious it would send my taste buds into orgasm.

By the time I poured the rich, dark batter into the cake pans, the entire kitchen was filled with the wonderful scent of chocolate. I had even melted a pound of truffles from Berkley's shop to include in the batter. I carefully put the pans into the preheated oven, closed the door, stood back, and let out a deep sigh.

I hadn't even tasted it yet, and already I was sure my endorphin levels had notched up a degree. No doubt about it—chocolate had a way of easing a woman's sadness. Who knew—maybe it could even promote world peace.

I was just about to make myself another cup of tea when the phone rang and I answered to hear my eldest son's voice.

Oh. My. God. It suddenly hit me that eventually both of my sons would have to be told and learn the truth about their father.

I pushed aside my concern as my motherly voice took over. "Jason. How nice to hear from you. Everything okay in Atlanta?"

"Yeah, fine. Just calling to see how you're doing. I called the yarn shop but Grandma said you were home today, not feeling well."

"Oh, no, nothing serious," I fibbed. "Just a bit of a sinus headache. Probably all the fall trees and flowers in bloom. How's your job going?"

"Very well, but I'm still thinking about returning to grad school. Maybe next year." He paused for a moment. "One of the reasons I was calling . . . I know you were counting on me being there for Thanksgiving. Especially since it's the first year without Dad. But, well, I've met this girl . . . September Callahan . . . and . . ."

I interrupted my son as I broke out in a chuckle. "Her name is September? Like in the month?"

I heard Jason's chuckle match mine. "Yeah. A bit unusual, huh? I'm not sure, but I think her parents might have been hippies. They now live in Manhattan and her father is an attorney, but . . . that's her name."

I felt the smile cross my face. "Well, yes, it's certainly different, but I like it. So are you saying you won't be coming for Thanksgiving?"

"Yeah, September's parents have a country home in Connecticut and they've invited me there for the Thanksgiving weekend, but . . . I don't want you to feel bad."

I had been counting on both of my boys being with my mother and me for Thanksgiving, so I felt a jolt of disappointment. But I summoned up a happy tone and said, "No, don't be silly. Of course you should go, Jason. Is it serious with this girl?" It was the first I was hearing about her.

"Well, if you're sure, Mom. We've been seeing each other for about six months now, so I think it could be leading to something serious. I met her at a dinner party through mutual friends."

Six months they had been dating? I had to admit, I felt a little left out and couldn't help but recall that old saying, *A daughter's a daughter all of her life, but a son's a son till he takes a wife.*

I forced happiness into my voice. "That's just wonderful, Jason. I'm really happy for you, and I'm sure you'll have a wonderful time. Hopefully, you'll be able to make it here for Christmas."

"Oh, thanks, Mom. Thanks for being so understanding. I have to get back to work, but I'll call you again soon. Love you."

I hung up and then realized Jason had not given me an answer concerning Christmas.

10

"That was just delicious, Marin." My mother wiped her lips with the cotton napkin. "And I can only imagine what that chocolate cake will taste like a bit later with a cup of coffee."

During supper I'd brought my mother up to date on Jason's phone call.

"Oh, that *is* a shame he won't be joining us, but at his age it's to be expected."

As I began to clear the table, she said, "Do you think it's serious with this girl, September?" A smile crossed her lips. "That's an unusual name, isn't it?"

I nodded as I began filling the dishwasher. "I know. Can't say that I know of anybody else by that name. Jason didn't really confide in me about the seriousness of it. I think that's where daughters and sons differ, don't you?"

"Oh, I'm not sure about that. But then, I've never had a son."

I thought again of Andrew's daughter. I hadn't yet told my mother about the phone call with the attorney, and even though she knew I had called him that morning, she hadn't asked.

"Oh, before I forget. First of all, Worth seemed disappointed that you couldn't join him this evening for dinner, but he said Friday evening was fine. And the window looks wonderful. He did a very professional job, Marin. I think you're going to like it a lot. It really opens up that room, and now, of course, you have some natural light in there. He began working on the sill and said that should be finished tomorrow."

"Oh, good. I'm looking forward to seeing it. But even better, everything seems to be on track. Hopefully, I'll be able to open in time for the Christmas shoppers."

"Yes, I would think so. And the catalogs arrived today from the various distributors, so you can begin looking through those to get an idea about the stock you want to order."

"Great," I said as I pushed the button on the dishwasher. "Coffee's ready. Do you want a slice of cake now or later?"

My mother reached over to give Oliver a pat. "I think I'll just have the coffee for now, and it's such a nice evening, let's have it on the patio."

Oliver walked over to sniff some bushes as my mother and I sat down.

"Oh, I met Worth's dog this morning at the park. A very pretty Labradoodle named Suzette. Oliver seemed to take quite a liking to her, and she returned the interest."

My mother laughed. "Yes, Oliver can be quite the ladies' man."

I took a sip of coffee and then said, "It's true. My suspicions were correct about Andrew. Fiona Caldwell is his daughter."

My mother reached over to pat my arm but remained silent.

"She's younger than Jason and John. Just turned nineteen in April."

"Oh." I saw my mother press her lips together. "I guess I was hoping that perhaps if it was true, it had occurred before he even met you . . . but I guess not."

I shook my head. "No, it happened the summer he went to teach in Amherst, Massachusetts. Do you remember that? The boys and I spent a lot of time here with you and Daddy."

"I do remember. It's none of my business, but were you and Andrew having a difficult time? Is that why he left to teach a summer semester there?"

"I was giving that some thought earlier today. Yeah, probably. Although I wouldn't admit it at the time. Not even to myself. But we weren't getting along great. And now . . . I have to question my entire marriage."

My mother shifted on the lounge to face me better. "What do you mean by that?"

I shrugged. "I don't think we ever had a marriage made in heaven. I think I see that now more than ever."

My mother shocked me by saying, "Does anybody?"

"What?" I gasped. "You and Daddy certainly did."

"Oh, Marin. Your daddy was a good man. A hardworking man and a good father. But he was human like any other man, and that means he had his flaws."

I had never heard my mother say this before. "But you always got along so well. I can't ever recall you fighting or name calling."

"No," she said, leaning back in the lounge to look out toward the water. "I don't think we ever did. At least not in front of you. But housewives in my time did what they were told. We didn't speak up very much. Certainly not like today." She let out a chuckle. "Well, my goodness, today the word *obey* has been taken out of almost all marriage vows. But when I was married . . . that word *obey* was taken very seriously."

I wasn't sure what surprised me most—the fact that my parents' marriage wasn't what I had grown up to think it was or the fact that my mother was now sharing this with me.

"So what are you saying?" I asked, not even sure I should be asking this question. "Are you saying you never loved Daddy?"

"No, no," my mother said quickly. "I did love him; of course I did. But, Marin, you're a grown woman. You have to know the definition of love isn't always neatly tied up in one little package. There are different kinds of love. The young, romantic, passionate love, which may or may not go on to become something deeper, something more enduring. And there's the kind of love that grows between a man and a woman based on a mutual admiration and respect for one another. But yes, I did love your father."

I had a feeling that what my mother felt for Henry Foster was her latter definition of love. She had known him all her life, growing up on the island.

I followed her gaze out to the water and softly asked, "Did you ever experience that romantic and passionate love?"

To my surprise, she replied, "Yes. Yes, I did. Before your father and I married. I was a young girl of eighteen."

I refrained from saying anything, but I suddenly felt a stab of envy. I wasn't sure that I could honestly say that I had ever felt that particular kind of love.

"What happened?" I asked, uncertain if my mother would continue.

But she did. "His name was Julian Cole. It was 1953 and your father was in the army. We had no commitment to each other, no engagement or anything like that. Just friends who had grown up together. Julian was a writer. A journalist, actually. He was from California and came here to write some articles about fishing communities in Florida. That spring of 1953 we fell hopelessly, desperately in love."

"So he loved you back?"

"Oh, yes. There was never any doubt about that. From the first moment we met at the Island Hotel."

I was almost afraid to ask. "Why didn't you end up together?"

My mother let out a deep sigh. "I'm afraid it wasn't a good time in our country. McCarthyism was going on. People were suspicious of one another. In Hollywood, it was a very dark time, with many actors losing their careers for being accused of communism. Most of it was false, and this was later proved. But it didn't matter. Lives were ruined and the damage had been done."

"But I don't understand. You said Julian was a writer. A journalist writing articles about fishing communities."

"That's right, but although he wasn't a communist, he was a liberal. He believed in equal rights for everybody, and the year before he had written for a progressive magazine. Articles supporting what unions wanted to do for the workers and other left-leaning topics. Actors weren't the only ones singled out. Professors and writers were among the accused, and Julian was one of them."

I was soaking in this story as if it had happened to somebody else, but here was my seventy-eight-year-old mother telling me about a man who appeared to have meant the world to her.

"The magazine he was working for contacted him that October and told him he had to come back to California, that charges were pending against him and he had to try to clear his name. But at the time, I knew none of this. All I knew was one evening he told me something had occurred and he had to leave the next day. He promised to be in touch as soon as he could. And then . . . he was gone."

"But you know why he left, so he did get in touch with you again?" I knew this story did not have a happy ending, and I felt sadness for my mother's loss.

She nodded. "Not until almost a year later. A letter arrived with a Paris, France, postmark. Julian explained he had never been formally charged, but many of the accused were leaving the country. Better to be safe than sorry, they felt. And so . . . he left. He began a new life in Paris, writing for an American magazine that welcomed the news that the expats could provide. He begged me to join him there. Julian asked me to marry him and assured me we would have a good life."

"Why didn't you go?" I whispered.

"Quite simply, because of my sense of duty. Sybile had already left home the year before to go to New York and pursue her modeling career. Daddy was ill by then, and I couldn't leave Mama alone to care for him."

"So instead you gave up your own life?"

"I didn't look at it that way. Until I received the letter from Julian explaining why he had to leave . . . I hated him for leaving me. Had things been different, we might have married right here in Cedar Key and eventually moved away for his career. But once I received his letter, I couldn't help but feel that everything happened exactly as it was supposed to. Your father asked me to marry him the following year, and I accepted. And over time, I came to forgive Julian, and by forgiving him, it enabled me to learn the true meaning of forgiveness, because forgiveness and love go hand in hand."

"And you never saw him or heard from him again?"

"When you were about ten, I saw an article written by him in one of the top American magazines. At the end was a small bio, which said he was married to a French woman, had one son, and lived in Paris. And last year . . . I saw on the Internet that he had passed away at the age of eighty-five in Paris."

I got up to squeeze my mother's shoulders. "I'm so sorry," I told her.

"No, no. Don't be sorry, Marin. We should only be sorry for what we *don't* experience in life. Not for what we do—both the good and the bad." She held out her hand so I could assist her to stand. "Okay, now I do believe it's time for a piece of that wonderful chocolate cake, and perhaps you'll share the rest of your conversation with the attorney."

With the cake plates empty, I took a sip of tea and said, "So there you have it. That's what I learned this morning."

"So you also don't know if Fiona grew up knowing about Andrew or if she ever met him?"

I shook my head. "No, I have no idea. The attorney seemed to feel that there hadn't been any contact between Andrew and Bianca over the years, but he wasn't certain."

"And the money that Andrew has paid over eighteen years. Fiona wasn't aware of that until after her mother died?"

I shrugged and nodded. "Right. I believe the bank informed her, gave her the attorney's information, and that was the first she learned about the money."

"Apparently her mother shared very little with her about her father. I guess it stands to reason that Fiona is now looking to you for some answers. You do plan to call her, don't you?"

"I'm not sure."

My mother got up to place her cake plate in the sink. "I see," was all she said.

❧ 11 ❧

As I drove down Second Street, the bay window caught my eye immediately. I pulled the golf cart in front of the shop and gazed at the new addition. It looked wonderful, and I was excited as I unlocked the door and stepped inside. I could hear Worth working in the other room.

"Hey," he said, turning around as I walked in. "What do you think?" His arm gestured toward the window.

"I think it looks great. I love it. It already makes the room look larger." I walked closer to get a better look. The window jutted out from the building with a large pane of glass in the center and side sections that each held six smaller panes.

"I'm glad you like it, and I think it was a good choice to go with this type of window. It will increase the flow of natural light into the room."

"I love the oak wood and the wide sill attached to it." I trailed my hand across the smooth finish. "This will be perfect for displaying finished pieces of needlepoint."

"I still have to get it stained, but other than that, this project is about finished."

"Terrific," I said, feeling my spirits lift. "What's next on the agenda?"

"We'll be working on the ceiling and walls today, getting them sanded down, and I'm hoping the ceiling light will be delivered by the middle of next week. There was a back order on the fluorescent ones with the oak frame."

"Hmm. I hope you're right and that won't cause a delay. And the ceiling fans? You'll be installing one at each end of the room, right?"

"Yes, I picked those up yesterday in Gainesville."

"Great," I said, heading back to the yarn shop. "We're right on schedule. I'm going to brew some coffee. Would you like some?"

"Sure. Kyle should be here shortly, but I think I have time for a quick break."

I brought Worth's coffee to him when it was ready.

"Thanks," he said, shooting me a smile. "We're still on for dinner tomorrow evening, right?"

I nodded before taking a sip. "We are, and thanks for understanding about last night."

"Not a problem. I'm glad you asked for a rain check. How're you doing?"

"Okay," I said, but before I could say any more, Kyle walked into the room. "Well, I'm going to let you guys get to work. If you need anything, just give a holler."

My mother had the day off, but Chloe would be in at noon. I turned on the computer and was going to check e-mail for any recent orders, but instead I found myself doing a Google search for Fiona Caldwell in Marblehead, Massachusetts.

I clicked to bring up a Boston University website on the screen where her name was listed. She was a student at BU? According to the article, she was. I read that Fiona Caldwell had participated with a group of freshman nursing students passing out toys the previous Christmas at Boston Children's Hospital. She was studying to become a nurse? Had she inherited an aptitude for science from Andrew? And had Bianca Caldwell also had a career in science or nursing? The link below this one told me that Fiona also had a Facebook page, but when I clicked I discovered it was private and a friend request had to be sent, which of course, I wasn't about to do. Not even a photograph was available to the public, which left me feeling oddly disappointed. I realized that the main reason I had even done the search was in the hope that I might be able to see what she looked like. Silly me. Those were the only two mentions listing Fiona Caldwell, so unless I made the decision to call her, the limited information I had would be all I knew about Andrew's daughter.

Closing the screen, I went to the e-mail account to check for new yarn orders.

Shortly after Chloe arrived, Raylene came into the shop accompanied by Mr. Carl.

"So," she said, her tone indicating she was here for a chat and not yarn. "Now we know why you're adding on the needlepoint shop."

I looked at Chloe, who shrugged her shoulders and raised her eyebrows.

"You do?" I asked.

"Yup, we do," Mr. Carl confirmed. "You've known about this film company coming to town and you wanted to spruce up the shop and make it look better."

I shook my head and pursed my lips. "Hmm. You found us out, didn't you?" I couldn't resist. There was no sense in trying to set them straight, so I might as well play along.

I heard Chloe cough and turned around to see she was actually stifling a giggle.

"See," Raylene said, jabbing her husband in the arm. "See, I told you some people know for sure what's going on. I knew you were right about this."

"Well, I'll be!" A huge smile covered his face, making me feel a tad guilty. "So when will the rest of us be told? Do you know what the movie's about? When is the film crew coming?"

"Geez, I'm really not sure, Mr. Carl. Maybe you should go back over to the Welcome Center and see if you can get some information there."

"Good idea," Raylene said, pulling her husband's arm as they headed out the door.

Chloe broke down laughing. "Oh, you are *so* bad. But that was priceless the way they both lapped it up."

"Hey, there was no sense trying to tell them that the needlepoint shop has nothing to do with a movie that any of us know a thing about."

Laughter broke out later that evening as we sat knitting at the yarn shop.

My mother was wiping at her eyes and still laughing. "You naughty girl, Marin. Shame on you leading Raylene and Mr. Carl on like that."

Corabeth had gotten her laughter under control. "I'd say they both deserve it. They thrive on rumors, the both of them. I think that was rather clever of Marin."

All the other knitters agreed.

"Well, sometimes no matter what you say to people, they still only believe what they want to, so I figured I'd let them do just that."

"Yeah, and it might keep them from nosing around in other business for a while," Flora said.

We all looked up as Berkley walked in. "Hey, is it really true about the film company coming here?" she asked, and that brought forth another round of laughter. "What?"

I quickly explained what I had done, and Berkley shook her head, grinning. "Aw, geez. I was all set to spruce up on my acting skills."

"Well, don't toss that idea aside," I told her. "Apparently Mr. Carl did overhear something at the Welcome Center. We just don't know yet what's going on."

Berkley pulled up a chair and began working on a pair of multi-color cotton socks. "So I guess we'll just have to wait and hope it might be true."

"Did Saxton's daughter and her husband arrive today?" Corabeth asked.

Berkley nodded. "Yes, Resa and Jake are here, and they're meeting with Ali tomorrow to look at the bed-and-breakfast. Saxton and I have our fingers crossed that they'll purchase it."

"Oh, Polly," Monica said, looking up from the blue knitted hat she was making for her son. "I need to call you tomorrow and make an appointment for Clarissa. She wants her hair cut."

"Sure. Probably a little trim? I have a couple openings on Saturday."

Monica shook her head. "Ah, no . . . not a little trim. She wants all of it cut."

Sydney shifted to face her daughter. "What?" she gasped. "That gorgeous long hair of hers? Why?"

Sydney was right. Clarissa had just turned thirteen. Her beautiful hair fell to the middle of her back, thick and wavy and envied by her classmates.

"Well, Adam and I wanted her to be her own person, rather than a follower copying everybody else, but I guess we didn't have to worry. You remember her friend Zoe, who moved away when her mother died?"

"Right," Flora said. "Sandy Collins's daughter. Zoe went to live with her dad and stepmom, didn't she?"

Monica nodded. "Yes, and one of the girls in Zoe's class was recently diagnosed with cancer. She's going to be going through chemo and of course will probably lose her hair. So Zoe and a few of her friends decided to get their hair pretty much shaved off, and they donated the hair to that program Locks of Love."

"I've heard of that," Dora said. "The organization then makes wigs for the children who have lost their hair from chemo."

"That's right. Zoe e-mailed a photo of herself to Clarissa last week and told her all about it, so now Clarissa has decided she'd also like to do this."

"Wow," Berkley said. "What an admirable thing to do."

"I agree," I told Monica. "That's really quite brave of her."

"I know. Adam and I have discussed it with Clarissa; we told her while it's a very nice thing to do, once her hair is gone, it will take a while for it to grow back. But she's determined to do it."

"I'm really proud of her," Polly said. "And I'd be very happy to participate. Isn't there a minimum on the length?"

"Yes. It has to be ten inches or longer, and the hair must be sent as a ponytail or braid. Clarissa pulled up all the guidelines on their website, so she'll bring them with her when you cut it."

"Very good, and tell her there'll be no charge for the cut. Just call me tomorrow and we'll figure out the time for Saturday."

Shortly before nine my mother prepared the coffee for the group.

"It was my turn to bring the snack," Chloe said. "And I brought fudge from the Cedar Key Fudge Company." She opened a box to display the various flavors.

"Oh, my." Flora sighed and leaned forward for a better look. "So much for that diet of mine tonight."

I laughed as I stood up and stretched. "Look at all the great flavors."

"I'm not familiar with this shop. Where's it located?" Berkley asked.

"The fudge is made at Ada Blue's restaurant out on 24," Chloe told her. "My favorite is the key lime."

Conversation continued while we enjoyed the fudge and coffee, but my mind wandered back to Clarissa and the bold step she was taking with her hair. I admired the fact that a thirteen-year-old girl could be that brave and make a decision that might wind up causing her ridicule from her friends for being different. But she didn't seem to care; nor did she seem concerned about the outcome.

Unlike me. I wasn't even brave enough to make a telephone call to gather more information about Fiona Caldwell.

❧ 12 ❧

I had left the yarn shop at three after being prodded by my mother and Chloe to go home, relax, and then get ready for Worth to pick me up at seven.

I had poured myself a glass of sweet tea and decided a luxurious bubble bath might be fun when the phone rang.

"Bella," I said after hearing my friend's voice. "How are you?"

Her laugh came across the line. "Better now that I made my deadline. My manuscript is finished and I feel like I can breathe again. But how are *you* doing?"

I realized that we hadn't spoken for a few months. She had been busy working on her next novel and I had been busy trying to adjust to being a widow.

I let out a deep sigh. "God, where do I begin? A lot has happened since we last spoke. But I'm doing okay . . . or as well as can be expected, I guess."

"I know. I'm sure it's hard being without Andrew, but it sounds like more is going on than just losing him."

You have no idea, I thought and proceeded to bring Bella up to date.

"Wow," she said when I finished. "I almost don't know what to say. And you haven't made any contact with the daughter yet? Do your boys know? How did they take the news that they have a half sister?"

"No, I've made no contact. I just can't bring myself to make that call. And, no, I'm ashamed to say that I haven't said a word to John or Jason about this yet."

"Hmm, well, there's no hurry on telling them. They'll find out from you eventually, but you might want to consider calling this girl to gain more information. Especially since it's up to you to sign those documents if that's what you decide to do."

I let out another sigh. "I know."

"So all of this happened the summer he went to teach in Amherst, huh? I came back to Gainesville to spend a week with you while he was gone, remember?"

I did remember. I also remembered the long, comforting conversations we had in the evening over wine after the boys had gone to bed. I remembered being grateful that I had a close girlfriend I could confide in, one who never judged me. And even though I had opened up to her about my less-than-perfect marriage, she had never once said *I told you so*. Like I knew she wouldn't now.

"Yup," I told her. "That was the summer it happened. You and I both know that Andrew and I were having problems, but I sure as hell didn't think he was off screwing another woman." Just like that I felt my anger flaring again. "Much less getting her pregnant. I mean, God! They weren't even responsible enough to use protection."

"You know I'm on your side, Marin, but that's not necessarily true. Contraception can fail, but at any rate, a child was the outcome. And now . . . Andrew is gone, the mother is gone . . . and it looks like, my friend, *you* are the one that's left to deal with this. And deal with it you will."

"Don't be too sure of that," I retorted.

Bella's soft laughter came across the phone, and I could almost see a smile crossing her face. "Oh, but I am sure of it, Marin. You seem to forget. I knew you when. I knew you before you even met

Andrew. When you took chances, when you knew where you were going, and when your strength was one of your best qualities."

I shook my head. "That woman is gone."

"No, she's not. You just have to find her again. And you will. I'm sure of it."

"Tell me your news," I said, tired of my own drama. "What's going on in your life?"

"Well, as I said, my manuscript is finished. So I have a few months to catch up on other things. Oh, and after the first of the year I'll be traveling to Tuscany, the setting for my next novel, so I'll be over there for a few weeks doing research."

"Tuscany? Really? Gosh, that's great, Bella. Are you going by yourself?"

I heard her laughter again. "Oh, yes. Just me. That's one of many things I like about being single. I don't have to check with anybody. I can go where I want, when I want."

Bella was extremely attractive and she had male companions, but she had always preferred companions to a spouse. And knowing her as I did, I could verify that at age fifty-seven, she never once regretted having no husband or children. She had a lovely town house in Savannah and three dogs that meant the world to her, and Bella had always been one of those women who created her own happiness and felt fulfilled doing so.

"Oh, by the way," she said. "Any chance I could get an invitation to Cedar Key for Christmas? Do you think your mother would let me have that guest room?"

I jumped up from the stool in the kitchen. "Are you serious?" It had been a while since anything had caused me to be this happy. "Oh, Bella, of course you can come. I'd love to see you. I haven't seen you since Andrew's funeral . . . and that certainly wasn't a visit. When will you be here?"

"Well, you know I have to bring my babies, but they'll get along just fine with Oliver, so we were going to drive down on that Sunday, the twenty-second. I'll stay five or six nights if that's okay."

"Of course it's okay. Gosh, you've made my entire month with this news."

"Okay, well, great. Oh, I meant to ask you. Why are you home so early on a Friday afternoon? I meant to call the shop first but dialed this number instead. Isn't the shop still open till five?"

I smiled. "Yeah, it is, but my mom and Chloe are there. Besides . . . I'm going out for dinner this evening. Getting picked up at seven."

"Getting picked up? Well, now, that sounds interesting. I'd say you have a lot more to tell me. We're not anywhere near ready to hang up."

Now I was laughing. "Ah, but we are. I have a bubble bath planned, and then I need to get ready. But I *will* tell you . . . his name is Worthington Slater, it's *just* a dinner, and I'll call you next week with details. Love you," I said, hanging up before she could ask any more questions.

I was still smiling as I placed my empty glass in the dishwasher. I adored Bella, and I had always considered myself fortunate to have such a good friend. I saw that it was going on four o'clock, so decided to pour myself a glass of wine and then take it with me to relax in that bubble bath.

Turning in front of the full-length mirror in my room, I caught the doubtful expression on my face. I didn't exactly look bad, but I didn't look great either. Walking closer, I could see shadows under my eyes caused by lack of sleep. And when had those extra lines appeared near my jaw? Even my hair seemed to lack any luster. A medium brown, it fell in a nondescript style to my chin. I had chosen to wear tan slacks with a pale yellow blouse. My weight was in proportion to my five-four height, and I wore the outfit well, so that wasn't what was causing my doubts. I let out a deep sigh. It was the fact that at fifty-six I looked weary. I looked like a woman who had gone through a wringer and had emerged looking used, wrinkled, and dull.

The doorbell interrupted my thoughts. Grabbing a sweater and my bag, I headed to the living room to open the door.

Despite what I had been thinking a few minutes before, when I saw Worth standing on the porch wearing jeans, an open-collar shirt, and a navy blazer, I felt good. I'm not sure if it was the way his eyes quickly scanned my body or the sexy smile on his face, but not only did I feel good, I knew for certain that Chloe had been right about him being hot.

"All set?" he asked.

"I am." I hollered to Oliver to be a good boy and take care of the house. "My mother's gone to a friend's for dinner," I explained.

It was then that I noticed the vehicle parked in the driveway. A silver Porsche Carrera convertible. I looked at the car, looked up at Worth, and blurted, "Is that *your* car?"

"Yeah, but I can put the top up if you'd prefer."

Here was a car worth more than four hundred thousand dollars and he thought I was worried about the wind? I recovered my composure and said, "Oh, no. That's fine. It's just . . . I thought you drove a truck. I saw the truck parked in front of the yarn shop."

He threw his head back and laughed as he opened the door for me to slide in. "Oh, I use the truck for work. I went to Ocala this afternoon and brought the car back with me. Would you have preferred I kept the truck?"

I glanced at him as he walked around the car and got in. He was serious, not joking.

"Oh, I didn't mean that. No. This is fine."

Fine? I thought as he backed out of the driveway and headed toward Gulf Boulevard. Oh. My. God. I had never been in a car this luxurious. Or expensive. I settled back in the leather seat and allowed myself to soak it up. The speed limit was only twenty, but the wind still managed to blow through my hair and make me feel incredibly carefree.

"Were you busy this afternoon at the shop?" he asked, making me realize that this magnificent piece of machinery was simply a means of transportation to him. Here I was just about drooling and he was asking about my afternoon.

"Yes," I said, now focusing on him. "Yes, we were. Fridays usually bring the tourists. Was everything okay at your home? You hadn't been there for a while, had you?"

"Right. A little over a week, but everything is fine. I have a woman who comes in to check on things and clean."

I shifted in my seat to get a better look at him, and that was when I became aware of the close proximity we were physically sharing. And I liked it.

"Will you be going back to Ocala tonight?" I asked as he pulled into the parking lot at the Island Room.

"No. I'll be working on the shop again tomorrow and I'll head back to Ocala on Sunday to drop this off and get my truck."

Before I had my seat belt unclipped, Worth had walked around and opened my door. *He doesn't just drive a killer car; he's also a gentleman,* I thought as I stepped out to join him.

Walking into the restaurant, I felt his hand at the small of my back guiding me through the door, and I stupidly almost tripped as we approached the podium to be seated.

His hand shot out to grab my arm. "Are you okay?"

"Just feeling dumb," I said and laughed. "My heel caught on the carpet."

We were directed to a table outside and I was grateful for the cool air on my flushed cheeks.

After we gave our order for wine, Worth leaned back in his chair, smiled across the table at me, and said, "This is nice."

He was right. Sitting across from him, just the two of us, it *was* nice. I returned his smile. "It is, and thank you for inviting me to dinner."

He leaned forward with his elbows resting on the table edge. "My pleasure. Now . . . tell me about yourself."

I laughed. "I have a feeling you probably know way more than you ever wanted to."

"That's not true, but I mean tell me about you. What you like. What you don't like. Your favorite books or movies. Those sorts of things."

I was reminded of Andrew and how I always felt like I was boring him when I wanted to share any of those subjects with him.

"Oh... well." I paused as our wine was brought to the table and Worth told the server to give us some time before we looked at the menus. "Let's see. Favorite books? I have a variety of favorite authors, so my reading tastes are a bit eclectic. But my favorite book is probably *To Kill a Mockingbird*."

Worth nodded. "Good choice." He lifted his glass to touch mine and said, "Here's to a long and lasting friendship."

I smiled and took a sip. "And favorite movie? That would have to be *Casablanca*."

"Another good choice. Favorite type of food?"

"Hmm, definitely French, with Italian as a close second."

"I agree. And how about flowers? What would be your favorite?"

Without hesitating, I said, "Oh, yellow roses. I adore them. But I also love lilacs and lily of the valley. My turn—favorite book and movie?"

"I'm afraid I'm not quite as decisive as you are. I read a lot of nonfiction, history, politics, and I have read all of Saxton's mysteries. I enjoy his novels a lot. And believe it or not, my favorite movie is also *Casablanca*."

I smiled. It would have been easy for him to fib, but I knew that he hadn't. I was beginning to realize there were a few things I definitely liked about Worth, and his genuine sincerity was one of them.

By the time we'd ordered dinner, both of us choosing escargot and duck confit, I marveled at how comfortable I felt in his company. There had been no groping for a topic to discuss, no nodding of the head to be polite, no awkward silences. We discussed a variety of topics, and I discovered I loved listening to him, but even more surprising was that he never took his eyes from mine and he made me feel special.

Dinner was followed with coffee as we finished off the last of the wine. I realized he hadn't questioned me at all about speaking with the attorney on Wednesday, but I knew it wasn't because he wasn't interested. It was because he knew it was up to me if I wanted to share the information.

"The dinner was wonderful, Worth. Thank you again."

He nodded and glanced out to the water and the lights now twinkling on Dock Street. "I'm glad you enjoyed it, because I did too."

"I spoke with the attorney," I said as I twisted the napkin in my lap.

"Hmm, and how did that go?"

"Well, I was right. Fiona Caldwell is Andrew's daughter."

He nodded but said nothing.

"But because Andrew is now dead, it's all become a bit more complicated as far as the money in that account," I said and started at the beginning to tell him what I had learned.

When I finished, he reached across the table to grasp my hand. "And how are you dealing with all of this?"

It was difficult to focus on his question when I could feel the warmth of his hand on mine.

"Probably not well," I said after a few moments. "Not well at all. I still haven't even called Fiona."

"There's no rush. I think you need some time to absorb all of this. Give yourself that time."

He was right. But the longer I delayed speaking to Andrew's daughter, the longer all of this would be hanging over my head, and I verbalized this to Worth.

He nodded as he let go of my hand and sat back in his chair. "Do you honestly think that once you sign those documents that will be the end of it?"

Chalk up another trait I liked about Worth. He had a way of saying something that enabled me to face the truth; this very thought had been running through my mind for two days.

I blew out a breath of air. "I had hoped it would."

"Have you given any thought to the fact that Fiona might want to meet you? Might want to meet her half brothers?"

I had, and that was when I would push the situation from my mind.

"Yes, but I've tried not to think about it. Because I honestly don't know how I feel about this or what I would tell her."

"Exactly. This is why I'm saying you need time. Time to set everything right in your mind." He paused for a moment, putting his hand on top of mine. "And don't take this the wrong way—but the attorney is right. No matter what, Fiona isn't to be blamed for any of this."

❧ 13 ❧

I woke on Sunday morning with the sun streaming through my windows. I stretched and glanced at the bedside clock. Seven-thirty. Later than I normally slept, but I knew that stress easily caused fatigue. I recalled Worth's invitation from Friday evening when he brought me home and felt a smile cross my face. He had asked if I'd like to take a drive with him later this morning to return his car to his home, and intelligent woman that I am, of course I accepted.

Walking into the kitchen, I was greeted by Oliver.

"Good morning, fella," I said as I stroked his ears and headed to the coffeepot. I saw my mother sitting on the patio, poured myself a mug, and joined her.

"Good morning," she said, folding up the newspaper she had been reading. "How are you this morning?"

"Good." I inhaled the wonderful scent of salt air on the breeze. "What are your plans for today?"

"Since you'll be gone, I accepted Maude's invitation to lunch."

"Oh, good. Be sure to tell her I said hello." I heard the phone inside the house ring. "I'll get it."

I answered to hear my younger son's voice. "John, how are you? How's everything in Beantown?"

His laughter came across the line. "I'm good, and so is Boston. How're you doing?"

"Fairly well," I said, trying not to feel guilty for not sharing the news I now had. "So what's up? Your job is going well?"

"It is. The leaves are beginning to turn up here now. I think I'm going to like New England in autumn."

Having been raised in the South, I could understand that. "Well, I hope you'll like it just as much once that snow starts falling."

John laughed again. "Oh, I don't think I'll mind. Listen, Mom, the main reason I'm calling . . ."

I could hear the hesitation in his voice. "Are you okay?" Why is it when an adult child sounds nervous, a mom always thinks a terrible tragedy is about to befall him?

"Oh, yeah, yeah. I'm fine," he quickly reassured me. "It's just that . . . I hope you won't mind, but I won't be coming home for Thanksgiving this year."

"Oh," was all I could manage to say.

"Yeah, well, we only get the Friday off with the weekend, so a bunch of my friends thought we'd just all pitch in and cook Thanksgiving dinner together. One of the guys has a place in Cambridge, so we're going to go there rather than try to book flights for a quick trip home."

"Oh, I see," I said and hated that I sounded bitchy.

"Are you okay with this, Mom? I mean, I figured that Jason would be there, and I promise I'll be home for Christmas."

Get a grip, Marin. No kid likes a control-freak mom.

"Yes, of course I'm okay with it, but, no, Jason won't be home this year either. Apparently, he has a girlfriend and they're going to her parents' home in Connecticut for the weekend."

"Oh, really? He's going to September's family?"

My disappointment quickly morphed to jealousy. "You knew about your brother's girlfriend?" I questioned, feeling terribly left out.

"Yeah, they flew up to Boston for a weekend a couple months ago, so we got together for dinner."

It was times like this that I knew how hurtful parenting could be. And yet, wasn't that the point of raising a child? To raise them so well that they are fully prepared to go out and face *their* world—even without you.

I cleared my throat and blinked back the moisture I felt in my eyes. "Oh, that was nice that they came to Boston. So . . . what did you think of her?"

"I liked her. She's very pretty, but even better . . . she's intelligent."

I smiled and realized that one statement said volumes about how Andrew and I had raised our sons.

"So is it okay, Mom? That I won't be there for Thanksgiving?"

I smiled again. Here was my twenty-two-year-old son basically asking my permission to skip a family Thanksgiving, when no permission was even required.

"Well, you know Grandma and I will miss you and Jason both, but . . . of course it's okay. What's your contribution for the dinner?"

"Oh, another thing I meant to ask you—could you e-mail me Grandma's recipe for squash casserole?"

I shook my head and laughed. "Ah, you won't be down here in the South with us, so you want some of the South up there with you, huh? Yes, I'll send it off to you this week."

"Thanks, Mom. Love you, and I'll talk to you soon."

I stood for a few moments holding the phone in my hand and let out a sigh. I couldn't lie. I was very disappointed that this would be my first Thanksgiving without my sons. But I attempted to brush off my mood and headed back outside to tell my mother, who, of course, took it better than I had.

"Oh, that *is* too bad that neither boy will be with us, but I guess that was bound to happen eventually. But we'll be surrounded by family, Marin. This year it's Sydney's turn to do Thanksgiving, and I'm doing Christmas here. So Monica and Adam will also be there with the children."

This did manage to brighten my mood a bit.

My face was uplifted, capturing the sun as the wind blew through my hair and Worth turned the Porsche onto SR 27 in Bronson. Unlike Friday evening on the island, with a speed limit of twenty, once we left Cedar Key and he was able to increase the speed on 24, I could really appreciate the car he owned. I felt like I was floating, and with Springsteen's voice coming from the Bose speakers, it was difficult to remember the last time I had had such a sense of freedom.

"Not much longer down 27," I heard Worth say, and I nodded. I wasn't sure I ever wanted this ride to end. But about fifteen minutes later he was pulling into a long, paved driveway. A tunnel of live oaks partially obscured the enormous house at the end.

I sat up straighter in my seat. *Wow* was the only word that immediately came to mind as an image of Southfork from the TV series *Dallas* flashed before my eyes. The house was redbrick, two stories, and, just guessing, I'd say it was at least five thousand square feet.

Not wanting to gush and trying to contain my amazement, I thought, *I'm impressed,* but only said, "It's beautiful, Worth. Absolutely beautiful."

"Thank you," he said simply as he pulled the car into the circular drive.

We walked to the entrance, where he unlocked the door. When we stepped into the huge foyer, he punched a code into the pad on the wall, deactivating the alarm system.

"Welcome," he said in a tone of voice that was absent of ego, gesturing with his arm. He could have been inviting me into a small, moderate home and not this elaborate domain that oozed money and success. "Come on in the kitchen. How about a mimosa? And then I'll give you a tour, if you like."

"Sure," I said, following him to the back of the house along a wide hallway framed on each side with photos. I wanted to stop and take time to stare at each face on the wall, but I kept walking.

I entered a designer kitchen that I was sure would be the envy of even Paula Deen. It was large, bright, and cheerful, with a multitude of oak cabinets surrounding the circular room and a huge rectangular oak island in the center.

"Have a seat," Worth said, indicating the tall captain's chairs at one side of the island. He proceeded to open the oversize stainless steel fridge and remove a plate of various cut cheeses along with a bowl of green and black olives soaking in olive oil and herbs. "Help yourself," he said, adding breadsticks and crackers to another plate.

"Do you need any help?" I asked, suddenly feeling like I should be serving *him*.

"No. Not at all. Just have to get this open." He had removed a bottle of champagne from the fridge and expertly popped the cork without spilling a drop. Filling two crystal flutes halfway, he then topped them off with what I was sure was fresh-squeezed orange juice.

I had a feeling that a phone call to his cleaning lady had arranged all of this.

He leaned across the island, that sexy smile covering his face, as he lifted his flute toward me. "Here's to friendship and many good times ahead."

I noticed that his words were a bit more personal than his toast of Friday evening. "To friendship and good times," I repeated before taking a sip. I was right. It *was* fresh-squeezed juice. "Delicious."

"Good. I'm glad you like it."

I glanced out the windows that looked to the back of the house. A flagstone patio held chairs, tables, and at the far end an in-ground pool. Beyond that were acres of land.

"So," I said. "This is quite the place. Especially for one person."

Worth nodded. "Yeah. Now you can probably see why I want to sell it."

I wasn't sure that I could. "Won't you miss it, though? Wouldn't it be difficult giving up something like this?"

He took a sip of his mimosa before answering, and I could have been mistaken, but the expression that crossed his face looked like sadness. "It's only a house," was all he said. "Come on, take your drink and I'll show you around."

We walked through the dining room off the kitchen into a huge great room. For as large as the house was, it didn't have a stuffy feeling. Two buttery yellow leather sofas were arranged in front of a fieldstone fireplace. Matching club chairs with ottomans were placed before enormous French doors giving a view out to the patio and pool. I noticed beautiful framed paintings on the walls that I was positive were scenes of Paris and the South of France. And on the large oak coffee table was a crystal vase filled with fresh deep purple asters and orange mums. The entire room gave off a warm and cozy ambiance.

"What a nice room," I said, following Worth to another hallway.

He nodded. "Yes, I spend a fair amount of time in there when I'm home."

I noticed a beautifully decorated half bath off this hallway, and Worth gestured to two guest bedrooms as we walked along. When we reached the end we stepped into a large room that could only be a library.

Standing in the center, I took in the four walls lined floor to ceiling with shelves and books. At one end there was even a brass rod with a mahogany ladder attached.

"Now, this is impressive," I said, taking in the chintz easy chairs, tables, and lamps comprising the middle of the room. Two long, rectangular windows allowed just enough sunlight in, and I noticed that one of them had a window seat with three large cushions. A book lover's fantasy.

"I have to admit, I do love this room," he said as I wandered over to browse some of the titles, which did reflect his preferences. History and politics, and against another wall I scanned Shakespeare and various books of poetry.

"Come on, I'll show you upstairs."

We had made a complete circle, and I now found myself back in the foyer but entering from the east side of the house. To the left of the front door was an intricately carved oak staircase, and I followed Worth to the second floor. Two more guest rooms were off the long, L-shaped hallway, separated by a sitting room. Both were beautifully decorated, and I couldn't help but think perhaps Worth was right—all this room for one person did seem a bit foolish. I followed him back out to the main hallway, and at the far end we stepped into what I knew was the master suite.

I caught my breath before saying, "Oh, wow," as my eyes took in the exceptionally large room dominated by a king-size canopy bed positioned to look through a wall of French doors to a deck and directly out to the woods bordering the property. I walked toward the doors and saw lounges and tables sheltered by a partial roof overhang, allowing both shade and sunshine. I shook my head and marveled at the beauty.

"It's a bit ostentatious," I heard Worth say at my shoulder as he let out a sigh. "But . . . it was what Claire wanted."

So that was his wife's name—Claire. I felt his hand at my back as he directed me toward the attached bathroom, and once again the word *wow* came to mind. A large sunken tub took up one entire corner, surrounded by potted plants, candles, and two steps leading into the tub. A glass-walled walk-in shower took up another corner, complete with two benches and double showerheads. A long vanity sink, toilet, and bidet completed the room, with a large skylight above me and oversize paned windows flanking the tub.

"I wouldn't say it's ostentatious," I said. "All of it is absolutely stunning."

"Thank you," was all he said as I followed him back downstairs to the kitchen.

He reached for my empty glass. "One more?"

"Yes, that would be nice," I said as I positioned myself on the stool. "Did you raise your daughter in this house?"

"Yes, we moved in here when Caroline was three months old, so this is where she grew up."

"Lucky girl. Thanks," I said, taking the champagne flute.

Worth nodded. "I think Caroline did always feel fortunate."

I noticed that he didn't say the same about his wife. "Did you do the plans for the house and have it built?"

"Yes, I did all of the blueprints with Claire's input. She had been hoping to move in before Caroline was born, but the contractors had a few minor setbacks. As large as the house is now for me, being alone, we did entertain quite often with my business. We also had various fund-raisers held here for the university and other organizations. So it was nice that I had the space to be able to do all of that."

I smiled as I got the distinct feeling that Worth was a strong believer in giving back.

"As a matter of fact," he said, and I saw that sexy smile appear again. "That was where I first met you—at one of the fund-raisers at the university."

I was certain he was joking, as I had no recollection of ever having met him until he walked into the yarn shop a couple of weeks before.

He threw his head back and laughed. "I've been waiting to see if you'd say something, but obviously I didn't make much of an impression. One of the professors brought Claire and me over to meet you and Andrew. We did only chat for a few minutes, and it was about fifteen years ago."

All of a sudden I had a flashback of being at one of the many functions that Andrew and I were required to attend. I did recall an extremely handsome man in a tux accompanied by a tall, slim, blond woman wearing an emerald-green gown. Of course I had forgotten their names over the years but the one thing that now stood out in my memory was how friendly the man had been and how his wife had displayed an air of coolness and boredom.

Now it was my turn to laugh. "I *do* remember now, and I apologize that I didn't recognize you right away."

Worth leaned across the island and patted my hand. "No need for an apology . . . but I'd like you to know that I never did forget meeting you that night."

I felt the energy of his hand on mine and I was certain that our friendship had been notched up another level.

⤜ 14 ⤛

By Tuesday afternoon I was finding it difficult to suppress the smile that kept appearing on my face. It had been a while since I'd felt so good. I had been at the yarn shop earlier and saw the archway to the needlepoint shop almost completed, and Worth had done a wonderful job with it. So the work was moving along on schedule, and that gave me cause to be happy. Although I had no idea what might happen, if anything, I was also happy about my friendship with Worth. I liked him and I liked being with him.

I had just filled the washing machine with towels and turned it on when the phone rang. I answered to hear Victoria's voice. "How're you doing?" I asked.

"Okay, but I'm afraid Sam is having difficulty understanding that Maybelle is gone. He really enjoyed spending the summer with her."

"I can understand that. Death is difficult no matter the age, but for kids, even more so."

"I was calling to let you and your mother know that the memorial service will be held on November sixteenth. It's a Saturday, which I thought might be more convenient and not too close to Thanksgiving. Is your mother at home or at the shop?"

I glanced at the calendar hanging on the kitchen wall. "Okay," I said and saw it was three weeks away. "And, yeah, my mother's still at the shop."

"I'll give her a call there with all the details, but the memorial is being held at Maybelle's house in the garden near the water. It's what she specified in her will."

I thought of the ideal location of Maybelle's property and smiled. "She was right to choose that. Safe Harbor is the perfect place to remember her. Have you decided yet what you're going to do with the house?"

There was a pause before she spoke. "I haven't said anything to anybody yet . . . but yes, I'm going to put it up for sale. With a young son and a business to run up here in New York, I just know I wouldn't be able to get down there much to use it, and that's not right. Somebody could be enjoying that house. I think Maybelle would have wanted that. But, Marin, do me a favor—don't say anything to anybody. I'd rather the word didn't get out just yet."

I will never be able to explain why, but before I could even stop myself, I blurted, "I won't say a word if you promise to do me a favor—please don't list the house with a Realtor until you offer the sale to me first."

"Absolutely," she said, and I heard the surprise in her voice.

After hanging up with Victoria, I brewed a pot of coffee, poured myself a mug, and went outside to sit on the patio. I still had no idea why I had made that request to Victoria. I'd known the house might go up for sale but hadn't given much thought at all to actually purchasing it. Until that moment on the phone. Did I really want to buy Maybelle's house? I hadn't even seen it since I was a teenager. God only knew what it looked like inside. I glanced up and noticed a swarm of dragonflies hovering in the air near the fence. It had been ages since I'd seen any. For some reason they seemed to come to the island only sporadically. At the same time I noticed the dragonflies, I heard the radio in the kitchen begin playing an old song from the fifties that I also hadn't heard in ages, "It Wasn't God Who Made Honky Tonk Angels," by Kitty Wells. The wind had increased, coming in from the water, and I shivered as I listened to the words about married men thinking they were still single. I let out a deep sigh and got up to go back into the house.

Leaning against the kitchen counter, I took the last sip of my coffee and knew what I had to do. Finding the phone number on the paper in my handbag, I placed a call to Fiona Caldwell. My hand gripped the phone as I heard the rings and then a female voice saying hello.

I hesitated before inquiring, "Is this Fiona Caldwell?"

"Yes. Who's calling?"

The voice was soft, with an annoyed tone. The one we use for telemarketers.

I cleared my voice. "This is Marin Kane. Your . . . father's wife. James Coburn, the attorney, said you wanted to speak to me."

I heard a surprised gasp from the other end of the line, and the annoyed tone was now replaced with excitement, as she said, "Oh! Thank you for calling me. I wasn't sure that you would. You know . . . under the circumstances and everything."

"What is it that you wanted to speak to me about?" I knew I sounded abrupt but couldn't help it.

"Yes . . . well. How did my father pass away? Was it an accident or had he been ill?"

"A heart attack. He had been teaching a class at the university and collapsed. It was quite sudden."

There was a pause before she said, "I see. I'm truly sorry for your loss, and I can only imagine what a shock it was for you to learn about me. At least I always knew I had a father out there somewhere."

"What exactly had your mother told you? And . . . I'm sorry for the loss of your mother."

"Thank you. I was only told that he was married, that she hadn't seen him since before I was born, and it would serve no purpose for me to know his name or where he lived. So he lived in Florida?"

"Yes, Gainesville," I said and couldn't help but feel Bianca Caldwell had maintained an aloof attitude toward her daughter where it concerned Andrew.

"Do I have any siblings? I'm an only child, so I've always wondered if maybe I had any sisters or brothers. Well . . . half sisters or brothers."

"You do," I said as a wave of guilt came over me for not yet telling Jason and John about their half sister. "You have two brothers. Andrew and I had two sons by the time you were born."

"I do?" Even across a phone line it was easy to detect an increased excitement in her voice. "So they're older than I am?"

"They are. Jason is twenty-four and lives in Atlanta, and John is twenty-two and lives and works in Boston."

"Boston? I'm in Marblehead, just north of Boston. Oh, my God! Who would have thought I had a brother living so close. Are they married, any children?"

"No. They're both still single ... and they don't know a *thing* about you." The sarcasm in my tone slipped out before I realized it.

"Oh," I heard her say. "Yes, of course. I can understand that. So, ah ... they're never going to know about me? Is that what you're saying?"

I heard a bit of defiance in her question. "No, I didn't say that. I just haven't told them anything yet. They'll both be home for Christmas. I was planning to tell them then. Do you have any other family? On your mother's side? Grandparents or aunts and cousins?"

"No. Nobody. My grandparents both died when I was small, and my mother was an only child. So ... it's just me."

So this girl truly was an orphan, but I refused to allow my emotions to rule the conversation. "Do you know how they met? Your mother and Andrew?"

"She told me she met him when she was teaching a summer course in Amherst. My mother had a degree in business and was teaching economics. She was twenty-six when she had me."

So Andrew was about eleven years older than Bianca.

"I see. And you're in college?" I questioned.

There was a pause before she said, "I was. I finished my freshman year at BU, but I didn't return for this semester." Another pause before she said, "I needed some time off."

I wondered if the reason had anything to do with finances or perhaps the fact that she had lost her mother the previous spring. "Do you work?" I asked. I felt like I was being nosy but assumed if Fiona didn't want to answer, she wouldn't.

But without hesitation, she said, "I'm working at a restaurant in

Marblehead. Just waitressing. Maybe I'll return to college next year. What I really wanted to speak to you about"—and another pause came across the line—"was...I was wondering...if it might be possible to come down there and meet you and my brothers—half brothers. I mean, I know you said they don't know about me yet, so we could wait until after the first of the year. You know...until you've told them about me."

I certainly was not prepared for this. Okay, I could understand her wanting to meet Jason and John, but she could travel to Atlanta and Boston to accomplish that. So why me? I wasn't related in any way to this girl.

"Oh...well...I'm not sure the boys will even be back here after Christmas." I felt myself stammering for something appropriate to say. I was at a loss for words and annoyed that she was directing this request at me. "Listen, let me think about this. Let me explain the situation to the boys at Christmas and see what their reaction is. And then...maybe we can arrange for you to visit if they'd like to meet you and can manage a return trip to Cedar Key."

Silence came across the phone.

"Would that be okay?" I questioned.

"Yes," I heard her say softly, knowing I hadn't given her any other option. "Okay. Then that's what we'll do. I'll wait until you call me back after the first of the year."

I said good-bye and hung up the phone, and it was then it hit me that during our entire conversation Fiona had not mentioned money or the account Andrew had set up for her.

∞ 15 ∞

"So what did you tell her?" Chloe asked as she continued stocking the cubbyholes with a new shipment of yarn.

"I told her I wasn't sure that would be possible. I mean, *really*. I don't think I should be expected to meet Andrew's love child. I only called her to get some information so I could make a decision about signing the documents. So I told her I'd need time to think about any possible meeting, and she did seem to understand."

Chloe nodded but remained silent.

"What?" I asked. "Do you think I'm wrong?"

"No," she said, tossing the empty box into the back room. "Not wrong if that's how you feel. How'd Fiona feel about the boys?"

"She seemed excited to learn she had two half siblings."

"Hmm," Chloe mumbled. "And . . . have you made a decision about signing those documents?"

I straightened the knitting needles hanging on the rack as I rearranged the correct sizes. "God, why can't people replace the correct size where they belong? It's such a nuisance going through them every day to keep them in the right place . . . and, no, I haven't made a decision yet."

I had a feeling that Chloe was thinking if I met Fiona in person it might help, but I didn't want to discuss it further. I turned around to see Berkley enter the shop with another woman.

"Hey," she said. "I wanted to bring Resa over so she could meet you guys. I'd like to introduce Resa Campbell . . . the proud new owner of the Cedar Key Bed and Breakfast."

"Wonderful," I said, extending my hand. "I'm Marin Kane and this is Chloe Radcliff. Congratulations."

"And welcome to Cedar Key," Chloe told her, also shaking Resa's hand.

"Thank you. It's not quite official yet. Jake and I made the offer this morning, but Ali accepted right away. So we have to get with the Realtor and do all the paperwork next week."

"I hope you'll enjoy living here and running a business," Chloe said. "I'm sure it'll be a bit different from Seattle."

Resa laughed. "Yes, that was the point of relocating. Jake and I both wanted to live in a smaller town. He's going to be joining a pediatric practice in Gainesville and eventually hopes to open his own. And I'm just thrilled to finally be living in the same town as my dad."

Despite the years apart from her father, she did seem quite excited about their reconciliation. I wondered if Fiona held any animosity toward Andrew. As far as I knew, he had played no role in her life, except financially, and she had only recently found that out.

"Any chance you're a knitter?" Chloe asked.

"I am, and that was another reason Berkley brought me by. I'd like to get some yarn for a sweater."

"Great," I said. "And you'll have to join our knitting group tomorrow evening. We meet every Thursday about seven."

"Yeah, Berkley had mentioned that. Oh, what's that yarn?" she asked, walking toward skeins of cranberry, pink, and black.

"That's the Cascade Ultra Pima Quatro. One hundred percent pima cotton. Nice for a sweater to wear in Florida."

"I love it," Resa said, heading to the book of patterns. "Now I'll choose something to make."

I shook my head and laughed. "I wonder how many women

choose the yarn before they decide on a pattern or if they do it in reverse."

"Hmm, good question," Berkley said.

"It's kind of like, which came first—the chicken or the egg? I'd bet it works both ways. How do you choose?" Chloe asked me.

"Actually, you're right. Depends on my mood, I guess, and which I see first—the yarn or the pattern."

"Marin, have you got a second?"

I spun around to see Worth standing in the archway.

"Sure," I said, following him into the next room. "What's up?"

"Well, I'm afraid we have a bit of a setback. I had really hoped that ceiling light would arrive today. The archway is finished, so I was planning to begin on the light tomorrow."

"But?" I questioned.

"I just got a call from Home Depot. They haven't gotten it in yet, and according to the distributor it looks like it'll be another week."

"Oh." I felt my heart sink. "So will this put us behind quite a bit?"

Worth shook his head. "Not really. It shouldn't. I'll probably have it by next Wednesday, and in the meantime I can do some more sanding of the walls and getting everything ready for painting. Speaking of which, have you decided on a color yet?"

"No. I thought I'd go to Home Depot myself and see what I might like. I also want to look at a border print for the top of the wall. Geez, now that I think about it, I guess I'd better get moving. I also need to choose some furniture and go through the catalogs to order my stock."

"I can't help you with the stock, but I'd be more than happy to go into Gainesville with you to choose paint and paper."

"Oh, that would be great." *Not to mention, it would also be fun,* I thought.

"I have an idea. Do you think you could be free on Saturday, or will you be working?"

"I'm off this Saturday."

"Good. I'll pick you up about eleven. We'll go to Gainesville, do the shopping, and then go to my place for a late lunch. How's that sound?"

Perfectly divine. "Like fun. Okay, it's a plan."

I stopped at the chocolate shop on the way home to replenish the supply for me and my mother.

"Hey, Berkley," I said, and my gaze was caught by three beautiful iridescent dragonflies hanging from a rack on a table filled with crystals and other gems. "Oh, gosh. That's pretty."

"I know. They're done by a local artist and they're for sale."

I walked over to get a closer look. They really were gorgeous. I lifted a finger to touch one, and although there was no wind in the shop, a chill went through me, causing a shiver.

"What is it about dragonflies?" I asked.

A smile crossed Berkley's face. "What do you mean?"

I removed a turquoise one from the rack and held it in the palm of my hand. "Aren't they supposed to mean something?"

Berkley came to stand beside me and nodded. "Yes, dragonflies are very special creatures that have a lot to teach us. They rarely make it to old age, so they understand that time is short and they live life as though today may be their last."

I ran my finger along the delicate wing. "Kind of like *Seize the day*?"

"Exactly. They also symbolize renewal and a sense of self that comes with maturity. So they represent change."

"Interesting." I passed her the one I was holding. "I'll take it. It'll look nice hanging on the patio. And also I'd like a half pound of your signature Cedar Key clam chocolates and a half pound of the truffles."

We chatted as Berkley boxed my order.

"Resa seems very nice," I told her. "I hope she'll join us tomorrow evening."

"Oh, I'm sure she will. She's anxious to meet all the locals."

"So she and Saxton have a good father-daughter relationship now, huh?"

"Very much so, and I'm thrilled because I know how much it meant to him."

"That's great," I said as I wondered again about Fiona and Andrew. "Thanks." I reached for the bag, paid for my purchases and headed home.

My mother and I were enjoying our after-dinner coffee on the patio, each lost in her own thoughts. I watched the sky turning from a light pink to a darker crimson with streaks of blue. Both sunrise and sunset had always seemed like magical times to me. Sunrise held such promise for the day ahead, and sunset allowed one to contemplate how well the day had been lived. I glanced over at the dragonfly that now hung from a hook on the post in the yard. It swayed gently in the breeze off the water. What was it Berkley had said? *Dragonflies represent change and renewal.* In the almost eight months since Andrew had died, I was certainly experiencing change.

"I have something to tell you," I said. "Actually, I'm not supposed to mention it, but I know you won't say anything."

I glanced over as my mother shifted in her chair to better face me. "What is it?"

"Well, when Victoria called me the other day . . . she said she's definitely going to be selling Maybelle's house. But she didn't want the word out just yet."

"I see," was all that my mother said.

"Yeah, she said what with Sam and her business up north, she really wouldn't get the chance to come down here much and use it."

"I suppose that makes sense."

I nodded and remained silent for a few minutes, trying to form the words in my head.

"And so," I said, "I told her to please not put it on the market or list it with a Realtor until . . . she offered it to me first."

"You?" I heard the surprise in my mother's voice.

"Yeah. I don't know. I can't really explain it, because up until I said that to Victoria, I hadn't really been thinking about buying Maybelle's house."

My mother adjusted her position in the chair but remained quiet.

"What do you think?" I asked. "I haven't even been in that house since I was in my teens. You used to go visit Maybelle. Do you think it would be a good house for me?"

"I'm not certain."

She paused for a moment, causing me to think she was definitely not in favor of my purchasing the house, which was odd because my mother was always so open-minded, allowing me to come to my own decisions.

"You think it might be a bad idea?" I asked. "Is it just that particular house or any house in general?"

She reached over to pat my hand and shook her head. "No, no. I didn't mean to indicate that you shouldn't purchase that house if you want to. I'm sorry if I gave you that impression. I guess I was just surprised. You'll need to go look at it when Victoria is here for the memorial."

"I will," I said. "I think I will." But I was certain I still detected uneasiness in my mother.

❧ 16 ❧

Who knew that shopping in Home Depot could be so much fun? At least with Worth it was. He joked with me about being as insistent on the name of the paint as I was about the actual color.

"You're kidding, right?" he said as we stood in front of the display of cards listing all the various paints. "You don't like this shade of blue because it's called Jazz? But you like this one because it's called Beside the Ocean?"

I nodded, and although, yes, he was correct, I had all I could do not to burst out laughing, because hearing Worth say it, I did sound a little nutty.

"But wait," I said. "Yarn is the same way. I think yarn designers are very careful when they name their various yarns. People like a pleasant name. You know—something catchy."

I could now see that Worth was having difficulty holding back his laughter. "And does the name of the yarn affect the outcome of the project?"

"Well . . . yes . . . it certainly could. And that's why I think this shade of blue would be much better for the needlepoint shop."

He put his arm around my shoulder, emitted a deep laugh, took the sample from my hand, and said, "Then Beside the Ocean it is."

After getting the paint mixed, we put the pails in the shopping cart and headed to the next aisle to look at border prints. Unfortunately, just as I was turning the cart I was distracted by a display of lamps. My cart bumped into a table arranged with stacked balls of twine, causing most of them to topple, flying every which way across the floor.

"Oh! God!" I quickly began running to catch the balls and caught a glance at Worth doing the same. Bending down to scoop up more, I wasn't able to hold back my laughter and saw that Worth was shaking his head and also laughing.

"You're a disaster in a home improvement store," he said, making me laugh even harder.

I rushed down the aisle to grab a few more balls of twine and returned to the table to see a sales clerk, hands on hips, fighting to suppress a giggle. "I would say you guys are having way too much fun," she said as the giggle erupted to laughter.

"I am *so* sorry," I told her. Talk about feeling stupid. "My cart just bumped the table, and, well . . ." I gestured with my hand.

She stooped to pick up a ball at her feet. "Don't worry about it. I told the boss that stacking those like a pyramid was looking for trouble. I figured some kid would knock them over."

"Thanks." I looked around. "I think we got all of them, and I'm really sorry."

She waved a hand in the air. "Not a problem."

I retrieved my cart and walked down the aisle with Worth beside me.

"You do provide some good entertainment," he said.

I looked up to see a grin covering his face.

"It wasn't intentional, but I'm glad you enjoyed it. Okay, on to border prints."

After much deliberation, I was convinced I just wasn't going to find anything that appealed to me, when my eye caught a border print on the highest shelf.

Attempting to reach it, I said, "Oh, that one. I need to see that one."

I felt Worth's hand go around my wrist. "Ah, no you don't. We don't need the entire shelf coming down. I'll get it," he said, removing a roll and passing it to me.

"This is it," I said and felt a strange sensation as I looked at it. It had a pale blue background and some tiny yellow flowers, and dominating the paper were blue dragonflies. I couldn't believe it.

"Really?" Worth questioned. "You like this one?"

"I do. Do you like it?"

"Very pretty, and it'll go nicely with the paint."

By the time we checked out and got to Worth's house, it was after two o'clock.

"You must be starved," he said as we walked in and he deactivated the alarm system.

"Well, I am ready for lunch." I followed him to the kitchen. Even though it was my second time in his home, I was still captivated by the beauty and luxury of it.

He opened the fridge and said, "Some sweet tea?"

"Sounds great." I settled myself on the stool as he removed a pitcher and filled two tall glasses.

"Thanks," I said and watched as he placed two plates in the microwave.

"I hope you like quiche, and we have some clam chowder to go with it."

"I do. But tell me, you didn't actually do this cooking, did you?"

A grin covered his face. "I can't lie. No, I didn't, but I do know how to cook, and actually, I'm not too bad. But my housekeeper got it all prepared for me last night."

"That was delicious," I told him after we finished eating. "My compliments to your housekeeper."

"Would you like some coffee?" he asked, and when I nodded he removed a French press from the counter and proceeded to prepare it.

I watched as he filled a saucepan with water and placed it on the stove to heat and then removed a bag of coffee from his freezer. He did seem quite comfortable in his kitchen as he placed coffee beans into a grinder. The whirring sound filled the room along with the strong fragrance of coffee.

"I bet you got those coffee beans in France," I said.

Worth looked up and smiled. "I did. One of my weaknesses. I always bring back a few bags stashed in my luggage. I'm afraid I'm spoiled by the rich, dark French coffee."

"I agree with that. I really missed it after I returned home from my visit there years ago. Right along with the French wine and chocolate."

Worth laughed. "Ah, a woman after my own heart. I admire your taste."

As he filled the press with coffee, added the boiling water, and gently pushed the plunger down so it could brew, I sat there feeling very much at home. I had known Worth for only two weeks and yet it felt so right being with him.

He filled two mugs, passed one to me, and said, "Let's go sit out by the pool. It's nice out there late afternoon."

I followed him to the patio table and sat across from him as my gaze took in the pool, the landscaping of bushes and flowers, and the woods beyond.

"This is such a pretty spot," I said, taking a sip of coffee. "And this is every bit as good as I remember French coffee to be."

"I'm glad you enjoy it," he said, ignoring my comment on his lush surroundings.

We sat there in a comfortable silence, and then I said, "I called her. I called Andrew's daughter."

I could feel Worth's gaze as I continued to stare at the pool.

"And how did that go?" he questioned.

I let out a deep sigh and turned to face him. "Probably not well. Fiona was very pleasant. Friendly. Me? Not so much. She did know that her father was married to somebody else, but that was about all she knew. She wanted to know how he had died and then seemed very interested to find out she had two half brothers."

"That makes sense."

"It does?"

"Well, yes. I can understand how finding out she has a blood connection to somebody else might be important to her. I know my daughter has mentioned over the years that she wishes she had a sibling. Somebody to share a history with."

I was also an only child, and I knew what he was saying. "Hmm, I suppose you're right."

"So did you find out anything about her that might prevent you from signing the documents?"

"I haven't even given the documents another thought, and what surprised me was the fact that Fiona didn't mention them or money at all during our conversation."

"Maybe it's not about the money to her."

"What do you mean?"

"Maybe getting information is more important to her. Learning about her father and brothers, being able to make a connection to somebody other than her mother."

I remained silent for a few moments before saying, "Yeah . . . she asked if she could come down here to meet me and the boys."

"She did? Well, that certainly sounds like somebody trying to reach out. So what did you tell her?"

I felt a wave of guilt and hated to have to admit my reluctance at having Fiona visit. "Well, I told her I needed time to think about it and I explained that the boys didn't even know about her yet, that I'd be telling them at Christmas and would get back to her after the first of the year."

Worth nodded. "And she was okay with that?"

"I really didn't give her much choice."

"This is a difficult situation for everybody involved," he said, and I knew he was trying to make me feel better.

"Yeah, right. For everybody except Andrew. He conveniently died and left his mess in my hands." As soon as I said it, I knew I sounded bitchy, but I had no control over the anger that seemed to bubble up intermittently.

Worth didn't appear to judge me, though, as he reached across the table and grasped my hand. "You have every reason to be angry, but I think you handled the call with Fiona just fine. You answered her questions, you explained about the boys, and you told her you'd think about her coming to visit and get back to her. At this point, I don't think she can expect more than that. I have no doubt you'll make the right decision."

I wished I had his confidence. I nodded and, wanting to change the subject, blurted out, "By the way, I might be moving."

I saw the startled expression on his face. "You're leaving Cedar Key?"

I realized my hand was still in his and gave it a squeeze before letting go and shaking my head. "No, no. But I'm thinking of purchasing a small house there. It was Maybelle Brewster's house," I said and went on to explain that Victoria might be selling it.

"I know that house. It's quite . . . different," he said, and I saw the grin covering his face. "It was Ned who did the original refurbishing of the cottage when Maybelle bought it. Gosh, that was back in the sixties and the summer before I began college. Ned let me go out there with him a few times to help him with the kitchen." Worth shook his head as he began laughing. "I'll never forget those red appliances and the white cabinets with strawberries painted on them."

I joined his laughter. "I know. I'll probably have to do a complete renovation of that kitchen. Even when the stove and fridge broke years later, somehow Maybelle was able to replace them with the same vintage red ones."

"Aw, no. Don't replace them. They add to the quirkiness and charm of that place."

I laughed again. "Hmm, that depends on your definition of *charm*. I'm not sure I could wake each morning to stare at what resemble giant tomatoes in my kitchen before I've even had my coffee."

"Seriously, it's a nice little house and a very pretty setting right on the water. Have you made an offer yet?"

"No. Victoria said she'll discuss it with me when she comes down for the memorial service in a few weeks, but I made her promise not to list it with a Realtor until I did have a chance to see it and make an offer if I'm interested."

"I hope it'll work out for you. As Maybelle proved, it's an ideal house for a woman alone."

"Yeah, I just wish my mother were a bit more enthusiastic. I was kind of surprised at her reaction when I told her."

"Maybe she just doesn't want to lose you. She's had you living with her almost eight months now."

"I don't think that's it. She's normally very open-minded, and she knew that living with her wasn't going to be permanent, that I'd be getting my own place eventually. No, it seems there's more to it. I just wish I knew what it was."

The rest of the afternoon flew by, and before I knew it, Worth was turning onto Andrews Circle, bringing me home. I noticed that when we were together, time seemed to move faster.

Maybe because I was trying to prolong that time, or trying to be hospitable, I said, "Would you like to come in for a while?"

He looked genuinely disappointed. "Gosh, I really can't. I left Suzette with Doyle Summers for the day. He's great for offering to pet sit dogs on the island, but I didn't bring her food, so I need to collect her and bring her to the Faraway to get her fed."

"Oh, okay," I said, surprising myself with the disappointment I felt. "Thank you so much for a great day. The shopping was fun and the lunch was delicious."

"It was my pleasure. I'll keep the paint and border print and just bring them to the shop on Monday," he said, before leaning over to allow his lips to brush mine.

Feeling flustered, I reached for the door handle and stammered, "Yes, that'll be fine. Thanks," before getting out, heading toward my mother's front door, and feeling like an awkward teenager returning home from a first date.

∽ 17 ∾

The following Wednesday ended up being one of those days that reminded me of a bad hair day, Murphy's Law, and the universe being out of alignment all rolled into one.

It began with me stopping by the coffee café to get an iced latte before opening the yarn shop. In the process of juggling my handbag, a tote bag containing my current knitting project, a copy of the *Cedar Key News*, and my coffee cup while attempting to unlock the door, the lid popped off the latte, dousing my white blouse with a large, wet, tan stain.

"Oh, great," I moaned, making my way inside to drop everything on the counter while managing to hold the coffee cup aloft.

I glanced down at my blouse and realized that I'd mistakenly put on a black bra rather than a white one at the same time Worth stepped into the shop from next door. I also realized that I was probably a good candidate to win a wet-blouse contest.

"Everything okay?" he inquired, and I was positive his gaze had settled where my B cups were visible through the transparent wet blouse.

Grabbing one of the display shawls hanging from a hook, I wrapped it around my upper body as I nodded and mumbled, "Yup. Fine. Everything's fine. Just spilled some coffee."

I heard him say, "Okay. Just checking," but not before I saw the grin on his face as he turned to go back into the needlepoint shop.

My mother was coming in to work at noon, so I put in a distress call requesting that she bring me a clean, dry blouse.

About an hour later, as I was trying to stock yarn and maintain a grip on my shawl, I looked up to see Mr. Carl walk in. *Lovely,* I thought.

"Mornin', Miss Marin. Oh . . . are you not feeling well?" he asked with concern in his voice.

"I'm fine. Why?"

He pointed to my shawl. "It's almost eighty degrees out there. Are you cold?"

"No, I'm not cold. Spilled some coffee on my blouse earlier. What can I do for you?"

The confused expression on his face told me he had no idea what I was talking about.

"Right. My Raylene sent me over. She needs two more balls of that there yarn."

"Which yarn?"

"Um . . . well . . . you know. For the thing she was working on."

Yup. It was going to be one of those days.

"Mr. Carl, Miss Raylene probably has about three projects going. Do you know which one, exactly, she needs the yarn for?"

The look on his face told me he did not.

"Okay," I said. "Let's start over. Do you happen to know what color the yarn is?"

He shook his head slowly as he shifted from one foot to the other.

"Look, just give her a call. You can use the phone right there," I said, pointing to the one on the counter.

"Oh, Lord, I couldn't do that."

Was that fear now covering his face?

"And why not?" I questioned.

"Raylene would kill me. She's always telling me that I forget everything."

Yup. That was definitely the look of fear.

"Well, I'm sorry, Mr. Carl. But I just don't see how . . ."

I was interrupted as he removed his hand from his pocket and began waving a paper in the air. "I have it! I have it! She wrote down what it was she needed."

I reached for the paper and shook my head. I wasn't sure if I was happier for Mr. Carl or for myself.

"Right," I said, walking toward the wall. "Two skeins of baby alpaca with this dye lot number."

I rang up the sale and passed him the bag.

"Thanks so much, Miss Marin. Oh, hey, do you think your new shop will be finished by the time the film company gets here to do the movie?"

Oh, God, not that again, I thought. But all I said was, "I certainly hope so."

He nodded, hollered good-bye, and left.

About an hour later I looked up from the needlepoint catalogs I'd been browsing to see a woman enter the shop. Nobody I knew and most likely a tourist. And one that looked out of place wearing a designer dress and stiletto heels and carrying a Coach handbag.

"Hello," I said. "May I help you?"

Ignoring both my greeting and my question, she walked to the cubbyholes filled with yarn, examining each one, and then waved a manicured hand in the air.

"Is this all the yarn you carry?"

We were normally told by tourists that we had an excellent selection.

"What exactly are you looking for?" I asked.

"Cashmere," she said in a tone that made me feel like I should have known that. "Don't you carry cashmere?"

I got up and walked to the bottom shelf. "We do have a few skeins down here," I said, removing one in a shade of pale pink. "But because it's so pricey, there aren't many requests for cashmere."

"Really?" she said, surprise covering her face. "Well, that color will never do. My dog is a male and wouldn't be caught dead wearing pink."

"Your dog?" She was joking, right?

"Yes, I want the cashmere to make a sweater for Lucifer. We live in a cold climate and he needs to be kept warm."

Nope, she wasn't joking, and I could feel the beginning of a headache across my forehead.

"Hmm, well, I'm sorry," I told her. "I guess the best we could do would be an alpaca or wool."

She walked toward the door, shaking her head. "No. That won't work. He's allergic to those."

And with that, she was gone. What on earth was she even doing on Cedar Key? Did she not realize that we're just a small fishing village without all the upscale amenities found in large cities? And did she not know that this was precisely how we liked it?

By the time my mother arrived with my clean blouse, I was more than ready to escape to lunch for an hour. I had brought a smoothie that I'd prepared that morning and decided to sip it as I drove around the island on the golf cart getting some fresh air. I found myself taking a left at Whiddon and heading out toward the airport. Pulling off the road, I sat and stared at the Gulf in front of me. A perfect late October day. Sun shining, no humidity, and the kind of weather many people in the North move to Florida for. I let out a deep sigh as my mind wandered to the recent conversation with my mother about my call to Fiona.

After I told her everything we'd discussed, she was quiet for a few moments and then said, "So this girl is going to be alone for the holidays?" making me feel like the child she would reprimand when I didn't want to share toys with a friend. I told her I really had no idea what Fiona had planned for the holidays and left it at that. But I wondered when it had become my responsibility to find out what she was doing for Thanksgiving and Christmas.

I released the brake on the golf cart, got back on the street, and took a right farther down, following the dead-end road to the end and Maybelle's cottage. Getting out, I opened the black wrought-iron gate attached to the fence enclosing the small side yard. Walking to the back, I stared out at Safe Harbor as ibis and blue heron circled farther out above the water. I felt enveloped by peacefulness, a tranquility that I hadn't felt in a long time. Taking in deep breaths and releasing them, I then noticed the dragonflies—a swarm of them hovering above bushes close to the shore. After a few minutes, I turned toward the house, hoping to peek in some windows, but all of the blinds were drawn tight. Getting back on the golf cart, I turned it around to head back to the yarn shop, gave a last look to the house, and knew without a doubt that *I* was meant to live there.

By the time late afternoon arrived, my headache had subsided and I was feeling better than I had that morning.

My mother had run down to the post office to collect the mail and I'd just finished waiting on a customer when Worth walked into the room.

"Busy?" he asked. "Have you got a second?"

"Sure. What's up?"

"Well . . . I really hate to have to tell you this, but . . . I'm afraid we've run into a problem."

"The ceiling light?"

"No. Actually the light arrived this morning. I'm afraid it's a bit of a larger problem than a light."

I could feel a knot forming in the pit of my stomach but remained silent.

"It's . . . ah . . . the ceiling. I cut into it a little while ago, prepping it so we could get the light installed . . . and . . ."

"And?"

"There's been some major water damage in that ceiling, which leads me to think there's probably a leak in the roof. So that will have to be repaired and then . . . a whole new ceiling put in. All the wiring will have to be checked, too, and then, of course, everything will have to be inspected."

I stood there, biting my lip, shaking my head, and desperately trying not to cry. Closing my eyes, I took a deep breath and whispered, "How long? How long will all of this take?"

I heard Worth clear his throat, and my eyes flew open.

"Well, I'm not certain." He ran his hand through his hair, a gesture I'd never seen him do before and which led me to believe he was nervous. "But, in all honesty, it won't be done in time for you to open before Christmas. November first is Friday. I don't even have anybody lined up to do the roof. I can do the ceiling, but I'll need some help with it and Kyle doesn't have enough experience. I'm so sorry, Marin. I know how much you were counting on all of this to be finished by early December."

We both turned toward the door as my mother walked in, saw the expressions on our faces, and said, "What's wrong?"

I grabbed my handbag, my knitting tote, and the keys to the golf cart. Walking to the door, I said, "Worth will tell you. I need to go home a little early," and as I stepped outside onto the pavement, I knew exactly what I needed to do.

18

I got home a little after four-thirty, poured myself a glass of wine, let Oliver out in the yard, and sat on the lounge thinking. By the time I finished my wine, my decision had been made and I headed inside to the computer.

Thirty minutes later I grabbed the papers that the printer spit out at me and took a deep breath. What the hell had I just done? I couldn't recall having ever made such a spontaneous decision, and yet the papers in my hand proved that I had done just that.

I glanced down to see copies of electronic tickets for a flight to Paris, France, on November 25, three days before Thanksgiving, with a return flight two weeks later. I felt a smile crossing my face as I experienced a mixture of excitement and uncertainty. It was then that I heard my mother coming in the back door. *She'll probably think I'm nuts,* was my first thought.

"Marin. I'm home," she called from the kitchen.

Damn. I felt every bit the sixteen-year-old about to face punishment for some incredibly stupid deed.

"Hi," I mumbled, walking into the room.

My mother turned around as she removed a casserole from the fridge. "Are you okay? I'm so sorry about the delay at the shop, but Worth has a few calls out to find somebody to do the roof."

I watched as my mother tapped the pad on the stove to preheat the oven.

"Yeah, I'm okay. I guess I overreacted on the setback."

"I know you're disappointed, Marin, but what with Thanksgiving and Christmas just around the corner, you'll be busy, and before you know it all the work will be done and you can open. Worth is pretty sure everything will be completed by early January."

"Right. Well . . . I won't be here for Thanksgiving. The boys aren't coming and this is the first year without Andrew and I don't think I can bear to pretend I'm even interested in celebrating this holiday. You'll be going to Sydney's, so I don't feel like I'm deserting you, and, well . . . I just booked myself a flight to Paris. I leave out of Gainesville to Atlanta, where I'll catch an Air France flight direct to Charles de Gaulle. I'll be gone for two weeks, and . . ." I knew I was babbling and couldn't help myself, and I also couldn't control the tears that were now streaming down my face.

"Oh, Marin," I heard my mother say as she scooped me into her arms. "Good for you."

"Good for me?" I hadn't quite expected to hear her say those words.

She gave me a tight squeeze before stepping back to reach up and wipe the tears on my face. "Yes. You're a fifty-six-year-old woman. You've had a very difficult year. You've been under a lot of stress. You need to get away and clear your head. I think going to Paris is a wonderful idea. You've wanted to return there since your college days. Believe me, life is too short not to do what makes you happy. So let's celebrate with a glass of wine."

I sat at the table and watched as my mother poured two glasses of pinot grigio, passed one to me, and lifted hers in the air. "Here's to Paris and a whole new adventure."

I touched the rim of her glass and smiled before taking a sip. It was in that moment that it really hit me. I *was* going back to Paris! It wasn't a daydream. It wasn't a wish. It was reality—and *I* had made it happen.

"My God," I said. "I'm really going to do it. Are you sure you don't mind me leaving you over Thanksgiving?"

My mother waved a hand in the air. "Don't be silly, Marin. As you said, I'm not going to be alone. I'll be with Sydney and the family. So not another thought about that. I think you really need this trip. It'll be good for you. Now, where did you book yourself to stay?"

I let out a laugh. "Oh, I didn't get that far. I only booked the flight."

"Hmm, well, don't let it go too long. Even though Thanksgiving is an American holiday, the hotels might be pretty full."

I nodded. "I'll get back on the computer after supper and see what I can find."

"What was the date again? Will you be here for Maybelle's memorial service?"

"Definitely. I don't leave till the twenty-fifth, and besides, I really want to talk to Victoria about the sale of the house."

My mother remained silent. What was it about that house? Why was she supportive about my trip to Paris but not about purchasing Maybelle's former residence?

"You really don't want me buying that house, do you?"

I watched as she got up to place the casserole in the oven and waited for her answer.

After a few moments she joined me at the table, took a sip of her wine, and said, "It's just that there are so many other houses on the island for sale. That house will probably need some refurbishing, and it's out at the tip of the island. Wouldn't you prefer something closer to the downtown area, maybe in the historic district?"

"But it's such a pretty location. Right on the water. And besides, I plan to purchase my own golf cart, so I can be downtown in a matter of minutes."

My mother nodded and let out a sigh. "You're probably right, and it's your decision after all. By the way, I haven't had much of a chance to talk to you. Did you get the paint and border print purchased over the weekend?"

I had a feeling my mother wanted to change the subject. "Yes.

Worth has it. I did get it on Saturday when we went to Home Depot. We went to his house for lunch after. What a gorgeous home he has, but so large for one person."

"That's right. I had heard his wife passed away quite a few years ago. Such a nice man. He was quite concerned about you this afternoon."

"About me?"

"Yes. He felt just terrible about the ceiling and the delay."

The disappointment that I'd felt earlier had lightened with my decision to go to Paris.

"Gosh, it wasn't his fault. Not at all."

"That's true, but I think it bothered him that it was just one more thing to give you frustration. He's a nice man, Marin."

She had just said that. I moved my fingers around the stem of the wineglass.

"What? Are you playing matchmaker?" I let out a forced chuckle and glanced up to see a smile cross my mother's face.

"And would that be so bad?" she asked, with a hint of humor in her tone.

"Well . . . I don't know. I mean . . . Andrew has only been gone for eight months, and . . ."

"Marin, there's no time frame on grieving, and it isn't up to anybody but you to determine what that time frame is. You're never going to forget Andrew. He was your husband, the father of your two sons. You spent twenty-six years together. You have a history and nothing can erase that. But it also doesn't mean that you can't enjoy the company . . . or even love . . . of another man during your lifetime. I just want you to know this. Don't live by other people's standards. Live with what you know is right for *you*. Like making the decision to fly to Paris."

She was right. It had been so long since I was on my own, capable and free to make my own decisions, that I'd forgotten what an exhilarating feeling it could be. I thought about the dragonflies I'd seen in Maybelle's yard. How they seemed to follow their instincts, how they seemed to seize the day, enjoying life to its fullest.

"My biggest wish for you," she continued, "would be that when you're my age, you have no regrets."

I couldn't recall hearing my mother ever say that, and before I could stop myself, I blurted, "Do you have any?"

It was a few moments before she answered, and I caught the expression of sadness that briefly came across her face before she let out a deep sigh. "I have a few, but I've come to realize that with age we learn forgiveness. Not just of others, but of ourselves. Youth can be notorious for causing us to be judgmental, but most of the time the years have a way of softening that judgment."

I wasn't quite sure what my mother was referring to. My judgment of Andrew? My difficulty in forgiving his indiscretion? My reluctance to accept Fiona as a part of my family?

I knew the conversation was at an end when she got up to remove the casserole from the oven, and I also knew that, as usual, my mother had given me a lot to think about.

Later that evening I got back on the computer and began to Google hotels in Paris. I narrowed down my search by arrondissement. From my last visit there, I knew I preferred the Left Bank with its Bohemian atmosphere at the sidewalk cafés and restaurants. I knew I loved the Latin Quarter, the boulevard Saint-Germain area, and Montparnasse. So I began checking various hotels for availability with my dates.

Three hours later I realized that trying to find accommodations in Paris over Thanksgiving was proving to be a daunting task. Either there was no availability, I'd have to sell my firstborn child to afford the rates, or the write-up on the hotel from previous guests wasn't enticing.

I rolled my chair back from the computer and massaged my temples. Hours of staring at a screen had brought back my headache of earlier that day.

Damn. Now what? I had already purchased my airline ticket. Had even made my seat selection. Way at the back of the 777, where the configuration was two seats across. I chose the window seat, and with a bit of luck, the aisle seat would remain empty, giving me some stretch-out room.

But I had no place to stay. There *had* to be a decent hotel, with availability at a reasonable price. Didn't there? My day had definitely been one that I wasn't sorry to see come to an end. Despite my lack of accommodations, I drifted off to sleep thinking about French wines, patisseries, and sidewalk cafés.

❧ 19 ❧

By the time I arrived at the knitting group Thursday evening, I was no closer to finding a place to stay in Paris. Maybe my plan would fall apart before it even began. I turned around to see Monica and Clarissa walk into the shop.

"I know it's almost time for your knitting group to begin, but I was wondering if Clarissa could purchase some yarn."

"Of course," I said, taking in Clarissa's extremely short hairstyle. Gone was the long, wavy hair cascading down her back, and in its place was about a half inch of hair covering her scalp. "I really like your cut," I told her. And I did. With a pretty face like she had, the length of her hair didn't detract from her looks at all.

A huge smile covered her face. "Thanks. But I think my head might be a little cold this winter, so I want to knit myself a hat."

"Smart girl, and I applaud you for donating your hair to the Locks of Love. It's a very worthy organization, and a lot of girls wouldn't part with their hair like you did."

"Thanks," she said and walked over to inspect a new shipment of baby alpaca.

"Is she really okay with it?" I whispered to Monica.

She nodded. "Yeah, she is. Adam and I are so proud of her, but I think Clarissa would prefer to stay low-key about it."

I nodded back and looked up as some of the women walked in the door.

Flora looked around before settling herself on the sofa. "Is your mother coming tonight?"

"She is and should be here shortly."

Clarissa returned to the counter holding up a skein of beautiful pale pink baby alpaca. "Do you think this would be okay?"

"Perfect," Monica and I said at the same time.

"Do you have a pattern at home or do you need to get one?"

"Monica found one at home for me. It's a French beret and really cute. Is this enough yarn, do you think?"

Monica read the label and said, "No, for the beret you'll need one more skein."

"Can you stay for the knitting group?" I asked as I rang up the order.

"Not tonight. We left Adam at home with the triplets and he has papers to grade for tomorrow, so we promised we'd just come down to get the yarn."

"Maybe next week, then," I said, as my mother walked in, followed by Raylene, Sydney, and Corabeth.

I was just sitting down when the door chimes tinkled again and we looked up to see Shelby Sullivan walk in.

"Gosh," I said. "I haven't seen you in ages."

"It *has* been a while," my mother agreed as she waved a hand toward a chair. "Welcome, Shelby. Come and join us."

Shelby Sullivan was Cedar Key's first best-selling author. Now in her early sixties, she lived out by the airport with her husband and continued to sell romance novels that women across the country loved.

"Thanks," she said, sitting down beside me. "I just finished my novel a few days ago and it's on its way to my editor. Now I'm on holiday till early January."

"You have a good schedule worked out, don't you?" Sydney said.

Shelby nodded as she reached into her knitting bag and removed a gold and tan cable sweater she'd obviously just recently started. "I always plan to finish my last novel for the year by early

November, and then it's my time to get ready for the holidays, do my Christmas shopping, baking, and cooking. Not to mention allowing me time to get more knitting done."

"Well, good for you," Corabeth said. "And congratulations on another manuscript finished."

"Thanks, and how's your latest one coming along?"

"As spicy as ever, and I should have it completed in a few months."

"So what's the latest news on the island?" Shelby asked. "When I'm writing, I feel so isolated. Bring me up to date."

"Well," Raylene said, leaning forward in her chair. "We hear that a movie company is coming to Cedar Key to do a film. Any chance it could have something to do with one of your books?"

Shelby laughed. "If so, I don't know a thing about it. From your mouth to Spielberg's ears," she said, causing all of us to laugh.

"So you're denying it has to do with your books?" Raylene persisted.

"I'm afraid so," Shelby told her.

"How's Josie doing?" my mother asked. "We don't see much of her lately either."

"She's doing very well. Hard to believe she's already graduated from her RN program."

"That's right," I said. "This past June. I heard she took a position at the Urgent Care Center in Gainesville. Does she like it?"

Shelby nodded. "Yes, she seems to. It's very good hours and only one weekend a month. So she certainly accomplished what she hoped to do—having a career with a decent salary and being able to spend more time with Orli."

"I saw Orli in the post office last week." My mother shook her head. "Goodness, she's a young lady now. No more little girl."

"True. She turns sixteen the end of December. So far the teen years haven't been too bad." I saw her glance stray to the archway in the wall. "I heard you're going to be opening a needlepoint shop. Gosh, I haven't done that in years, but I'm looking forward to browsing in there. When are you planning to open?"

I refrained from lifting my head from my knitting or from answering and heard my mother say, "Well . . . we've had a bit of a setback. We were hoping to open before Christmas, but I'm afraid that won't happen now. Apparently there's a small leak in the roof that caused ceiling damage, but Worth is attempting to find some workers to get it all fixed. So . . . we won't be opening now until after the first of the year."

"Oh, that *is* a shame," Sydney said. "I know how anxious you were to open, Marin."

I nodded and heard my mother say, "She was. However, I think Marin has found something to occupy some of the time between now and then."

I looked up from my knitting to find a group of expectant faces looking at me, waiting for an answer, and I smiled. These women allowed no possible information to escape them.

"Well . . . I'm planning to take a trip to Paris. But . . . now I'm not sure that will even happen. I was foolish enough to book my flight first and now I'm finding it almost impossible to find a place to stay."

"Oh, how exciting," Sydney said. "When are you planning to leave?"

"November twenty-fifth, a few days before Thanksgiving, and I guess that's the problem. I didn't think about so many hotels being booked solid during that time. The ones I've found so far that are available are so pricey I can't justify paying that."

"Yeah, the holidays can be a busy time in Paris," Sydney said. "Let me talk to Noah and see if he might have some suggestions for hotels, and you should also talk to Lucas and Grace. They're very familiar with Paris also."

"Good idea. I'll do that tomorrow."

"Did you say you plan to be there for Thanksgiving?" I heard Raylene question.

"Yes. I'll be there two weeks, so I'll be back early December, in time for Christmas."

"Well, that doesn't seem very proper. Leaving your mother alone and all."

Before I had a chance to reply, I heard my mother say, "Proper has nothing to do with it, Raylene. Marin is a grown woman and should be able to make her own choices. She's had a very difficult year, and besides, I won't *be* alone. I'll be spending the day with Sydney and Noah."

Raylene shrugged her shoulders before giving off a sniff. "Well, I know it's none of my business, but I'm just saying . . . in my day, a daughter was always present for any holiday gathering."

"Right," Corabeth said. "This is none of your business, and Marin, I think it's a wonderful idea."

"I agree," Flora said. "Weren't you there after you graduated college?"

"I was, and I've always wanted to go back. I spent some time there with a couple girlfriends, and then time got away from me and I never had the chance to return until now."

"And you're traveling there alone? All by yourself?" Raylene asked.

"Yes," I told her. "Contrary to what many might believe, Paris is a very safe city. Of course I'll take precautions and not do anything or go anywhere foolish, so I think I'll be just fine."

Raylene sniffed again. "I just can't imagine being there alone. What if something happened? What if you got sick?"

"God, Raylene, stop being such a downer," Flora said. "They do have doctors in Paris, and believe it or not, many French people speak English, although I have no doubt that Marin will be brushing up on her French before she leaves."

In all honesty, I hadn't thought about that but made a mental note to dig out my old French translation book or purchase a new one.

"Whatever," Raylene mumbled before she resumed her knitting, and I couldn't help but wonder what had happened to the woman who had seemed to mellow earlier in the year. Normally cranky, judgmental, and a gossip, for a time Raylene had become almost sweet. Her husband, Mr. Carl, had insisted that the transformation had all come about because of Berkley's signature clam chocolates. He made a point of telling everybody that the rich, dark delight had magical qualities that Berkley had added to the recipe. So much for magic, I guess.

✥ 20 ✥

I was the first to arrive at the yarn shop on Friday morning. My mother would be in after lunch and Chloe was due to arrive in an hour. I peeked through the archway and then remembered that Worth had said he'd be in a little after ten, as he wanted to make more phone calls about finding somebody to do the roof.

I went to prepare the coffeepot and recalled his apology of the day before. Poor guy. It wasn't his fault about the roof leak and setback for my opening, but I got the feeling he somehow felt responsible.

And I was right. Because when he arrived he gave me another apology before saying, "But I do have good news. I've found some fellows from Williston that have experience with roofs. They'll be here this afternoon to take a look at it."

"Oh, that *is* good news, Worth. And, please, no more apologies. It's not your fault this happened. Really."

A smile covered his face. "Okay, but how about joining me this evening for a drink at the Black Dog?"

My smile now matched his. "Sounds great. I'll meet you there around seven?"

"Perfect," he said, before turning to go into the other room.

A little while later I looked up to see Josie Sullivan enter the shop. "Hey, Josie. Nice to see you. Your mother was at the knitting group last night. How've you been?"

"Busy. That's why I haven't been in here for a while. Between graduating in June, taking my state boards, and then starting my new job, I haven't had much time for knitting. But things are slowing down a little and I'm missing those needles and yarn in my hands. I know I don't have much time between now and Christmas, but I thought about making a vest for Orli."

"I have just the thing," I told her, walking to the book of patterns. Flipping through, I found the one I had in mind. "How about this? It's really easy, just knit and purl, and it works up very fast. Plus, it can be done in a cotton yarn, which is perfect for a Florida winter."

"Oh, that *is* cute. I think Orli would like that. Maybe a pima cotton?"

"Yes, that would work well." I pointed to the wall and then shook my head. "Darn. We really need more room in here. We got in a new shipment of pima the other day, but I haven't unpacked it yet because I'm not sure where to put it. Browse through those in the cubbyholes, and if you don't see a color you like, I'll open the new boxes and let you look through those."

"Thanks."

Chloe arrived a few minutes later and walked in waving an index finger in my direction, a frown on her face.

"What?" I questioned.

"I missed the knitting group last night and only found out this morning that you've planned a trip to Paris the end of November. Shame on you for not telling me."

I saw a smile emerge and knew she was joking with me. "I'm sorry about that. I only made the plans two days ago, and believe me, they were very spontaneous."

"Well, good for you, I say. You should go, Marin. Your boys both have plans for Thanksgiving, Dora is all set for dinner, and *you* need to get away and clear your head."

I laughed. What was it about another female backing you up

and encouraging you that made you feel even more empowered? "Thanks, but I'm not sure it'll even happen. I'm having a real problem trying to find a place to stay."

"Well, I just came from the coffee café, and Grace said to pop over later. Lucas has some names of hotels to give you. You can't let a little thing like accommodations keep you from going."

"Right," I said, letting out a chuckle. "I could always sleep on the pavement along the Seine."

Chloe laughed as Josie approached the counter, her arms full of yarn.

"Josie, hi. I didn't even see you over there in the corner. How are you? It's been a while."

"I know. But it's time to get back to my knitting. I think I'm having withdrawal."

"That *does* happen. Are you making a sweater?"

"A vest for Orli for Christmas. I hope. Marin assures me this pattern will work up fast."

Chloe glanced at it and nodded. "She's right. It will, and I love that color of yarn."

"Yeah, Orli loves turquoise, so this is perfect. Okay, ring me up, ladies."

Chloe totaled the amount while I placed the pattern and yarn in a shopping bag.

"How's Ben doing?" Chloe asked her.

I recalled how my mother had related to me a few years before that Josie had reconnected with Ben Sudbury. Mr. Al's nephew, Ben, had spent childhood summers on the island with his mother, Al's sister, Annie. But when Annie passed away, Ben had not returned since the funeral—until a few years before, just before Christmas, in an attempt to place his uncle in a nursing home and sell off the house. Poor Mr. Al was being accused of not being of sound mind because of the mess his property had become. But through the efforts of Josie's eleven-year-old daughter, Orli, and other children, the community had banded together to clean up the property, preventing Mr. Al's placement in a nursing home and the sale of the house. In the process, Ben and Al reconciled, and although they'd had a rocky start, Josie and Ben had begun a long-distance relationship.

"Oh, he's fine," Josie said, but she didn't sound very enthusiastic.

"Does he have any plans to get back down here soon?"

"Oh, yeah. He'll be here for Christmas. He knows that Mr. Al is getting up there in age, so he feels it's important to spend the holidays with him."

"Good," Chloe said as I passed the bag to Josie.

"Thanks," she said. "And maybe I can make the knitting group next week."

"That would be great," I told her. "We look forward to seeing you."

After she left, I looked at Chloe. "Wasn't Ben supposed to relocate down here a few years ago?"

She nodded. "Yeah, that was the plan. He was going to resign his position as editor at that publishing house and sublet his apartment in New York City. His plan was to come here in order to spend more time with his uncle and also to work on a novel. I think it was also in his plans to try and develop a relationship with Josie."

"What happened?"

"Well, the economy got even worse, Josie got accepted to nursing school, and I think the timing was all wrong. From what I heard, he thought perhaps he should keep his job for the time being and just fly down here as often as he could, which is what he's been doing. And with Josie in school, she was extra busy studying, so it really didn't leave her much time for romance."

"Hmm, that's too bad. Well, she said he's coming at Christmas. Maybe the timing will be better."

"Could be."

When I finished lunch, I headed down Second Street to the coffee café to speak to Lucas about possible hotels. I was pleased to see Grace sitting at a table with Solange on her lap when I walked in.

"There's my cutie pie," I said, leaning over to place a kiss on the baby's head. "I swear she's growing by the day, Grace."

She nodded and smiled. "I know. She'll be seven months old already in a couple weeks. Not only did the one tooth come in, but she now has two."

"So she had plenty of reason for all that fussing." As I glanced at Solange, I felt my heart turn over. Those baby years went way too fast for most mothers to appreciate and enjoy them. Maybe it was because we were so caught up with the actual care we didn't take the time to slow down and enjoy the moments. It was difficult to remember when John and Jason were that age, and I realized that perhaps this was the reason women in my age-group were so enthralled about becoming grandmothers. They now had the time, and less responsibility was involved, allowing them to truly enjoy all the precious moments. I couldn't help but wonder how long I'd have to wait before John or Jason made me a grandmother.

"The usual?" I heard Suellen say.

I looked up and smiled. "Yes, thanks. That would be great."

"So," Grace said. "I hear you're going to be on your way to Paris. I'm so excited for you. I think you know that France is my favorite place to be. Of course, being married to a Frenchman could account for part of that."

I laughed and nodded. "Hmm, you could be right. Yes, I'm hoping to get there, but you probably heard I'm having a problem trying to find a place to stay last minute."

"Yeah, but Lucas has jotted down the names of some hotels for you to contact. Oh," she said, looking up, "here he is now."

"Hey, Lucas," I said as he approached the table, placing a kiss on Grace's lips first and then on Solange's cheek. I noticed how the baby's face lit up at the sight of her father, and for some strange reason I had a flashback to my boys' faces doing the same thing. I was the one who spent all day with my sons, feeding them, cleaning up after them, playing with them, but when Andrew walked in the door each evening, they only had eyes for him. The flashback momentarily made me think of Fiona, and I pushed the thought aside.

"Grace said you're having trouble trying to locate a hotel over Thanksgiving. That can be a busy time in Paris, I'm afraid. My cousin owns an apartment there, so I gave him a call, but unfortunately it was rented months ago to a family from the States. So the best I can do is this list of names," he said, passing me the paper.

"Oh, Lucas, that was so nice of you to even call your cousin. I really appreciate that. And thanks for this list. I'll get on the Internet over the weekend and see if they have availability."

"These hotels are on the Left Bank. I'm familiar with most of them, but they're not anything fancy. Actually, some of the rooms might be quite small by American standards."

"Hey, that's what I get for waiting till the last minute. And besides, I'm not planning to spend much time in my room. Too much to see and do."

Both Lucas and Grace laughed.

"Very true," she said. "Anything in particular you have in mind to see?"

"Well, I saw all the touristy things the first time I went there after college. So maybe I'll revisit a few, but mainly I just want to sit at the sidewalk cafés, watch the world go by, and soak up Paris."

"That's the best way to really experience that city," Lucas said. "Well, I have to get back to the bookshop. Let me know if I can help with anything else."

"Thanks," I said as I stood up. "I'm going to get my latte and get back to the yarn shop," I told Grace. "Take care and thanks again."

I walked into the shop to see Worth and my mother hunched over a large piece of paper on the counter, with Chloe looking on from the side.

"What's up?" I asked.

"Well, Marin, I think we have some good news for you," my mother said.

I was ready for good news and saw my mother nod at Worth.

"The fellows came about the roof, and they'll be able to begin work in three weeks. They have a few other jobs to finish up first, but they said it should only take a couple weeks to complete both the roof and the ceiling. After that I can get the rest of the work done. So . . . it'll be tight, but you just *might* be able to open before Christmas."

"Really?" All of a sudden my compulsion to open before December 25 didn't feel as strong. "Well, maybe I shouldn't rush it. If it happens before Christmas, great. But I still have to order the stock, and it really won't be the worst thing in the world if I can't open till after the first of the year."

I saw Worth and my mother exchange a glance.

"We have more news," she said, pointing to the paper on the counter. "Since Worth will have a few weeks free from working on the needlepoint room, he said he can begin work on the outdoor area and the carriage house. Come on, we'll show you."

I followed them through the small back room and outside.

"Okay," Worth said as he gestured with his hands. "This area here with the grass will be covered with cement, and the screening on the side will connect the carriage house and the yarn shop."

"This will be so perfect." I heard the excitement in Chloe's voice. "It's a good size and will be ideal for the ladies to sit out here and knit."

Worth nodded. "Right. This area is approximately three hundred square feet, so you'll be able to fit in tables and chairs and not feel cramped."

"Exactly," my mother said, leading the way into the carriage house. "This is going to need new walls and new flooring, and I'm praying the roof on this structure is okay and you won't find leaks when you do the ceiling in here."

"We'll have the guys take a look at it when they come to do the other one." He shined a flashlight upward. "But from what I can see, I think we're going to be okay."

"Won't it be great to have more room for our yarn?" Chloe said. "I can't wait to get in here and start arranging everything."

I smiled. "I know the feeling," I told her. "It all sounds great, and you think you'll be able to get started on this part of the project soon?"

"Absolutely," he assured me. "Next week, in fact. I've gone as far as I can with the other room, so Monday morning Kyle and I will begin working out here."

I was able to see that things were slowly beginning to fall into place. Now if only I could decide what to do about Fiona and find a hotel room in Paris. I wasn't naïve enough to think that those two things would make everything right in my little world—but they might go a long way toward helping.

❧ 21 ❧

I arrived at the Black Dog later that evening to find Worth standing on the sidewalk with Suzette's leash in his hand.

"I hope you don't mind," he said. "But I've been gone so much lately, I hated leaving her alone again this evening."

I knew Worthington Slater was a good man, but I kept discovering more proof of this.

"Of course I don't mind," I said, bending down to ruffle the dog's curly chest. "She's adorable and quite well behaved, I might add. Suzette is very welcome to join us."

The huge smile on Worth's face was my reward.

I led the way up the stairs and to the outside deck, where we chose a table in the back. The sky was darkening quickly and I realized that this first weekend in November was when we'd be changing our clocks back one hour, which would mean it would be dark even earlier.

We gave our order for wine and I caught the smile that Worth gave me across the table.

"I was pleased to find the fellows to do the roof," he said. "I don't want you to get your hopes too high, but as I'd said earlier, you just might be able to open the shop before Christmas."

I nodded and realized that not only had I not told Chloe about my Paris plans, but I hadn't shared them with Worth either.

"That would be good, but . . . I began making some plans the other day that will keep me occupied until that happens." I thanked the waitress when she placed a glass of Ecco Domani in front of me, and I saw the curiosity in Worth's expression. "I'm taking a trip to Paris at the end of the month."

"Really? Well, good for you. From what you've said, it's about time that you return there. Here's to a great trip," he said, lifting his glass to touch the rim of mine.

"Thanks." I took a sip and then shook my head. "Well, I'm not all that certain that it will even materialize. I booked my flight before I even thought about booking a hotel room, and now it seems . . . well, either there's no availability or the prices are way out of my league."

"And you've tried some of the smaller, out-of-the-way hotels? If they're not in the touristy areas, you might have better luck."

"I've tried quite a few of them, and Lucas gave me a list today that I plan to check out. Now that I've actually taken the first step with booking the flight, I've allowed myself to get excited about going. I think it might be good to get away for a couple of weeks. You know, clear my head, figure out what I'm going to do about Fiona, just . . . chill out. Alone."

"I think it's a great idea, and I think you need to do it." He took a sip of wine and seemed to be deep in thought. After a few moments, he said, "Listen, I don't want to be presumptuous or anything . . . but I might have a solution to your problem."

"You do? What? Do you own a hotel in Paris?" I kidded him.

"Ah, no. Not a hotel, but I do own an apartment. Three of them, actually."

I stared across the table at his face, trying to decipher if he was joking with me, but his expression was perfectly serious.

"You do?" I replied as I wondered what other secrets this man might have. "How come you've never mentioned this?"

He shrugged, which led me to think that owning three apartments in Paris wasn't all that important to him, and he confirmed this when he said, "I guess I didn't think it was a big deal. I bought them quite a few years ago, mainly as investments when the prices were good. Over the years I've been able to upgrade and refurbish two of them, and I have them listed with a management company as rentals. But the third one I use when I go over there on business and to visit my daughter, so it's never rented out."

"Oh," was all I could manage to say.

"It isn't anything fancy, but it's a great location in the Latin Quarter on rue des Lyonnais. A two-bedroom on the ground floor, and I have a small garden outside the living room, which is nice for sitting outside in good weather."

And so? Was he offering to rent me his apartment? Not quite—as I found out a moment later.

"You said you're flying over the end of the month?"

I nodded. "Yes. I leave on November twenty-fifth and I'll be there for two weeks, flying back on December ninth."

He took another sip of wine and then said, "Well, the solution to your problem would be that you take my apartment to stay in."

"Really?" I could feel my excitement building as Paris was becoming more of a reality. "You'd be willing to rent me your apartment? God, I'd be so grateful! Would it be about the same price as one of the smaller hotels?"

Worth laughed. "No, no. I'm not going to *rent* you my apartment. I'd like you to just stay there."

Okay, so maybe he was the wealthiest guy in Marion County and didn't need the money, but it didn't seem right for me to take his place rent-free.

When he saw my hesitation, he said, "Well . . . there is *one* minor problem."

My head jerked up and I saw a smile cross his face as I waited for his explanation.

"I had already made plans a few months ago to fly over in early December. I do this every year to spend time with my daughter and grandchildren. We exchange our Christmas gifts then and have our holiday together. I'd prefer to be here in the States on the actual day, and Caroline and her husband usually take the kids skiing over the Christmas holidays, so this works out well for us."

I nodded and said, "That's a nice arrangement," still not understanding his meaning.

His smile broadened. "Well, my plans have been made to fly over on December third for five nights."

Oh. Now I understood, and the first thing that came to my mind was, *And that would be a problem, why?* Spending quality, private, alone time with this handsome man was becoming more enticing each time I was with him. But what I said was, "Oh, then I couldn't possibly come and be there at the same time you need your apartment."

Worth reached across the table and grasped my hand, creating a surge of heat in my body. Something I hadn't felt in a very long time. Maybe too long.

"On the contrary," he said, staring into my eyes. "It *is* a two-bedroom, so you'd have your own space, and you certainly wouldn't be intruding on mine. In fact, I'd welcome your company. Besides, it's the least I can do after the setback with opening the needlepoint shop."

Needlepoint shop? At that moment that was the last thing on my mind. I wasn't sure if it was the glass of wine that I'd just consumed or my vivid imagination, but I had visions of lovers strolling hand in hand along the Seine, couples clinking champagne glasses at sidewalk cafés, bouquets of flowers on the pavement in front of florist shops, everything about Paris enveloped in a romantic cocoon.

I felt Worth squeeze my hand and heard him say, "Well? What do you think? Is it a deal?"

I recalled my mother's words about Andrew and my moving on: *It doesn't mean that you can't enjoy the company of another man— or even love—during your lifetime.*

I squeezed Worth's hand in return and smiled. "It *is* a deal, and thank you for your offer. You're helping to make one of my dreams come true."

"I hope so," he said, and I detected huskiness in his tone that I hadn't noticed before.

* * *

We had another glass of wine as we discussed our schedule and instructions for me about the apartment before we left the Black Dog. When I returned home, I found that my mother had turned in early, so I prepared myself a mug of herbal tea and took it to my bedroom, where I changed into pajamas, removed my makeup, and then curled up in bed.

I felt a smile spreading across my face. For the first time in a long time, I could say I was happy. Or at least beginning to feel happy. Here I was about to embark on a whole new adventure at age fifty-six. And if I was honest—here I was feeling attracted to a very handsome and nice man. And above all, here I was within a few weeks of returning to my beloved Paris. And that was when it hit me, and I let out a deep sigh. The hurt and betrayal that Andrew had inflicted on me returned full force and stabbed me again. I felt tears stinging my eyes. *Damn you, Andrew. Damn you for what you did.*

I had tried to block Fiona and our conversation out of my mind, but I knew that eventually I was going to have to face it and deal with it. Maybe my mother was right. Maybe the best way to deal with it would be by going away for a while, taking a break, and allowing myself *time*.

My inner voice kept telling me that Paris was precisely the place to do this, and—thanks to Worthington Slater—that was going to happen.

∽ 22 ∾

I pulled into the parking lot of the Flying Biscuit and glanced at Chloe.

"So you think I was smart to accept Worth's offer to stay at his apartment?"

"Of course I do. You would have been silly not to, for a few reasons."

We got out of the car and walked toward the restaurant. "Like what?" I asked.

Chloe waited till we got inside and were seated to answer me. "Well," she said, picking up her menu and giving it a quick glance. "For one, at the rate you were going with accommodations, it wasn't looking very promising."

I nodded. "Hmm, true."

"And for another, come on. I doubt that many women would find it a hardship staying with a handsome man like Worth in an apartment in Paris."

"God, you make it sound like a rendezvous. I had no idea he owned apartments in Paris, much less that he'd be there part of the same time."

"Exactly," she said, a grin on her face. "Consider that a bonus."

She looked up at the waitress who had approached our table. "The omelet for me, one of your famous biscuits, and coffee, please."

I glanced down at my menu and realized that even though I'd skipped breakfast before we left the island, I didn't have much of an appetite for brunch, but I mumbled, "I'll have the same."

When the waitress walked away, Chloe looked at me and shook her head. "Don't look so uptight. This trip is supposed to *decrease* your stress, not increase it."

"I know, but God . . . I haven't shared living arrangements with anybody since I married Andrew."

"Worth said the apartment has two bedrooms. You enjoy his company. He's so familiar with Paris, I'm sure he'll point out some of the out-of-the-way places that you might otherwise not see. Go with an open mind, Marin, and enjoy yourself."

I could have sworn I heard her say, "And with an open heart," under her breath, but I let it go.

After we finished eating we headed to the mall, which was the purpose of our drive to Gainesville. I hadn't bought any new clothes in ages and thought perhaps a few new items for my upcoming trip might be in order. I invited Chloe along for company and moral support. I was never sure what looked good on me and what didn't.

Chloe suggested we hit Coldwater Creek first. "I love their clothes. For classy, mature women," she said. "And not girls in their twenties."

I hoped that didn't translate to dowdy. As soon as we walked into the shop, I discovered it didn't.

Two hours later I was certain that I'd tried on just about every item in the store, with Chloe running back and forth acting as my personal fitter. But it had been a very successful shopping spree, as my credit card could attest to.

Driving back to the island, I began to have doubts about some of the items. "You don't think that black dress might be a little too . . ."

"Sexy?" Chloe inserted. "Of course it is. That's the purpose. And those killer heels you got to go with it? Perfect. You know that Worth will take you out to dinner at least one evening, and you have a very stylish outfit to wear. You'll have a coat, but don't forget to take along that gorgeous, black cashmere shawl you knitted in case it's chilly in the restaurant."

Good thinking, I thought. And I never thought I'd be wearing *that* shawl to Paris.

"Do you think the bathrobe is appropriate? Not that I plan to be parading around the apartment in it, but I like having my coffee before I hit the shower and get dressed."

"Very appropriate," Chloe confirmed. "It's a full-length, soft flannel robe. You could greet the UPS driver at the door wearing that and not feel underdressed. Plus, it's a great shade of blue."

I nodded and kept driving. The slacks, blouses, and jacket that I'd bought I didn't have to question.

"By the way," Chloe said. "Do you think you'll meet his daughter and grandchildren while you're over there?"

I hadn't given that any thought. "Oh, I don't think so. I mean, this is family time for them. I'm sure Worth won't want me intruding."

"Don't be so sure," she said, and I glanced over to see a grin on her face. "With all the excitement about Paris, have you given up your idea about Maybelle's house?"

I shook my head. "No, not at all. Victoria knows that I'm very interested. We spoke on the phone the other day and she agreed to show me the inside the day after she gets here."

"Oh, that's good. I'm sure you'll enjoy having your own place again, so I hope it works out for you. Has your mother taken to the idea any better?"

"Not really, and I just can't figure it out. It seems that it's that house in particular and not the fact that I'll be moving out, because she mentioned that there's a lot of other houses for sale on the island. Has she said anything to you?"

"Not a word, and I agree that's odd. Do I dare ask? Any decision about Fiona?"

I approached the blinking red light at US 19, looked both ways to cross over to SR 24 for the final twenty-minute drive to the island, and let out a deep sigh. "None whatsoever. My plan is to tell the boys about her when they come for Christmas. Beyond that—nothing. I'm hoping when I'm in Paris, alone, with time to think, I'll be able to decide what would be the best thing to do."

Chloe nodded. "Yeah, but since she already said she wanted to meet you and the boys, there's no doubt she'd like to learn about her father."

"That's just the problem. I can't forgive Andrew for what he did. So I don't think I'd be a very good candidate to be the one extolling his virtues to his daughter."

"She already knows what he did, Marin. I'd bet anything she just wants to find out what kind of person he was."

"Exactly," I said and heard the edge in my tone. "A cheating husband would cover it pretty well."

I arrived home to find my mother sitting on the patio, a glass of wine on the table beside her and an old photo album in her lap.

"How'd the shopping go? Get yourself a glass of wine and join me. Meatloaf is in the oven and dinner's in about an hour."

"Sounds great," I said, heading back inside to pour myself a glass of cabernet before sitting in the lounge across from my mother. "Shopping was great. Chloe was a huge help and I got some nice things for my trip."

"That's good, but I have no doubt you'll be doing some shopping in Paris too."

"I'm planning to get some Christmas shopping done, but I might pick up one or two things for myself."

"That was so generous of Worth to offer you his apartment, and it'll be nice to have his company there for a few days."

I nodded. "It *was* nice of him, and I'm getting excited about going."

"Oh, before I forget. Jason called you a few hours ago. I told him you were in Gainesville shopping, and he didn't want to bother you on your cell so he said to call him when you get a chance."

"Did you tell him that I'm going to Paris?"

"No. I think you should tell him, but I know he'll be happy for you."

* * *

And he was. I called him later that evening, and after a few minutes of getting his news, I said, "By the way . . . since you and John won't be home for Thanksgiving . . . I've made plans to fly to Paris for a couple weeks."

"Wow! Really, Mom? That's great. You've always wanted to go back there. Who's going with you?"

"Nobody." Well, technically nobody was going *with* me. I just neglected to add that Worth would be arriving a week later. "I'll be going on my own, and I think this might be a good thing."

"Oh, I agree," my son said. "You've never taken off alone. All of our vacations were family vacations with me, John, and Dad. Remember when I went to Germany the year after I graduated college? I went alone and I really enjoyed it. I think this will be good for you."

I smiled. "Thanks. You're still coming home for Christmas, right?"

"Absolutely. And I'll want to hear all about your Paris trip, so take lots of pictures. Which hotel are you staying at?"

"Actually, I'm not staying at a hotel. A . . . ah . . . friend of mine. Well, he's a friend but he's also the one that's doing the work for the needlepoint shop. I was having a terrible time trying to book a hotel, and he owns an apartment in Paris . . . so . . . he's offered to let me stay there."

"Boy, you lucked out, didn't you? Staying in an apartment, rather than a touristy hotel, you'll really be able to soak up the Parisian lifestyle. Didn't you rent an apartment the last time you went?"

"I did, with my two friends, and you're right. We got to experience so much more than if we'd stayed in a hotel."

"Well, I think that's great, Mom. I'm glad you're going."

"And you're still going to be with October and her family for Thanksgiving?"

I heard Jason's chuckle come across the line. "Her name's September, Mom, but yes. We're still going."

"Sorry about that. Okay, if you speak to John, you can tell him about my travel plans, but I'll be giving him a call over the weekend."

When we hung up, I couldn't help but wonder if Jason married September and they had a daughter—was there a chance I could end up with a granddaughter named after a month, or even a day of the week? I felt a grin cross my face. Yes, I suppose there was that chance.

✖ 23 ✖

The following Sunday afternoon I was sitting on the patio at Worth's home watching him toss a ball to Suzette in the yard while steaks sizzled on the grill. He had invited me over to have an early dinner and discuss my Paris trip. I took a sip of my coffee and smiled. Worth seemed to take pleasure in the smallest things—like playing catch with his dog. He turned around, caught me staring at him, and shot me a smile. I had quickly discovered that Worth was one of those men who smiled not only with an expression, but also with his eyes. Somehow that seemed even more meaningful.

"Okay, Suzette," he hollered as he returned to the grill. "That's it for now."

He turned the steaks over and adjusted the flame, which caused me to jump up.

"What can I do?" I said. "I feel bad enough that you're doing the cooking for me again."

He laughed and came to join me at the table. "Don't be silly. I'm sure you've done your share of cooking over the years, but come on. You can help me bring out the dishes and get the table set."

I followed him into the kitchen, where he began placing plates and silverware on a tray. "You can grab some napkins and place mats out of that drawer," he said, indicating an oak hutch.

I opened the drawer to find an array of nicely pressed linen napkins in various colors along with matching place mats. I chose a set of the blue ones and added them to the tray. Worth placed a salad bowl on another tray before putting rice pilaf into the microwave to heat.

"Okay," he said, looking around. "That should do it. If you'll take this out and get the table set, I'll be right out with the rest."

As I arranged the two place settings, I knew that the china, silverware, and napkins were all top quality. No doubt about it. Worth's deceased wife had had very good taste.

"Here we go," he said, depositing the bowls, a bottle of wine, and two glasses on the table before going to remove the steaks from the grill.

Sitting down across from me, he shot me a smile. *"Bon appétit."*

"Merci," I said. "I guess I'd better start practicing my French."

"As long as you know the basics, you'll do just fine."

I accepted the salad bowl he passed me and helped myself to some rice. "Yeah, I remember I did okay my first time there, and actually, by the time I'd left I had learned even more words and phrases."

"Exactly. And besides, more Parisians can speak English than Americans realize. If the American is at least trying, even if they're butchering the French language, they usually discover the French person understands English."

I laughed before taking a bite of my steak. "Right. I think the French just like to know that we've made some effort to speak the language of the country that we're in, which only stands to reason, because Americans tend to get pretty annoyed when people from other countries come here and don't speak English." The steak was juicy and cooked to perfection. "Oh, this is delicious, Worth. I can't remember the last time I've had such a good steak."

"Good. I hope you'll enjoy it."

We were both silent for a few minutes as we focused on the food. I realized that once again I had skipped breakfast, making me extra-hungry later in the day.

"Oh, I wanted to tell you," he said. "When you arrive at the apartment building, you can go to the concierge and she'll give you a key. I could give you one of my spare ones, but I'd like you to meet Madame Leroux when you arrive."

"Oh?" I questioned, thinking that was an odd request.

"Her apartment is on the first floor, just above mine. Very easy to find. I'll let her know to expect you. How are you planning to get from the airport?"

"I thought I'd take the RER. I'll only have one piece of luggage."

Worth smiled. "You already sound like a true Parisian. And your flight arrives at eight-thirty Tuesday morning?"

I nodded.

"Then I'll let Madame Leroux know your arrival time and that you'll be at the apartment before noon. She's pushing ninety, and except for severe arthritis, which limits her mobility, she's in very good health. Both mentally and physically. She's an extremely interesting woman to talk with. She was a young wife and mother living in Paris during World War II. I think you'll enjoy meeting her, and my reason for having you get the keys from her is my way of an introduction."

"I'm intrigued," I said, and I was. "She does sound interesting, and I'm sure I'll love meeting her."

"She also doesn't get much company, and most of her family are gone, except for her niece, who tries to visit often. So maybe if you get a chance in the afternoon, you could pop upstairs for coffee and a chat with her. She speaks perfect English, so that wouldn't be a problem."

For some reason, this seemed important to Worth, and I smiled. "Of course I will. I'd love to."

He returned my smile, reached for my hand, and gave it a squeeze. "Good."

We had just finished clearing the table and filling the dishwasher, and we were about to enjoy our after-dinner coffee when the phone on the patio table rang. Worth glanced at the caller ID screen and said, "Sorry. It's my daughter calling from Paris."

I waved a hand in the air. "Not a problem. Go ahead, take it," I said, thinking he'd get up and go into the house, but he answered and continued to sit with me.

"Caroline," I heard him say. "Nice to hear from you. What's up?"

There was a pause before he said, "Tuesday, the third. I left a message on your recorder last week."

I sipped my coffee and glanced up to see a frown forming on Worth's face.

"No, you didn't inform me of that. Had I known, I would have planned my dates accordingly."

Another brief pause before he said, "Well, I'm sorry . . . and I think Christophe will understand that."

He let out a deep sigh before saying good-bye and flipping his cell phone closed.

"Sorry about that," he said.

"Everything okay?"

"Just typical of my daughter. She's always much too busy to check her phone messages and then insists that she told me something when she didn't. Apparently Christophe has a Christmas play at school on the Sunday before I'm scheduled to arrive. Had she told me before I booked my flight, I would have flown over the week before."

I could tell that he was annoyed. "I'm sorry. Will Christophe be terribly disappointed?"

He waved a hand in the air and smiled. "Oh, no. Knowing my grandson as I do, I'm sure he'll be fine with it. He sent me an e-mail the other day and he knows when I'm due to arrive. This is all about Caroline. It usually is."

"Oh. Can she be difficult?"

Worth nodded. "Very much so. I'm afraid she got more of Claire than I would have liked. Don't get me wrong. She's my daughter and I love her . . . but yes, at times she can be downright difficult. I'm afraid Roland gets the brunt of it, but every now and again it flows over to me."

I wondered if Worth got the *brunt* of it when he was married to Claire.

"Okay, enough about her," he said, reaching for the coffeepot to replenish my cup before standing up. "Something else I wanted to discuss with you about your trip. I'll be right back."

I watched him walk into the house and realized that his minor display of irritation toward his daughter was certainly justified, but it was the first time he had shown an emotion other than upbeat and happy, bringing to mind Andrew's frequent bouts of moodiness. Funny, when one lives with it all the time, maybe one becomes immune to it, but recalling the unpleasantness of Andrew's episodes made me realize that both Claire and Caroline were pretty darn fortunate to have a man like Worth around—and yet, they probably took him for granted.

"Here we go," he said, coming back to the patio and interrupting my thoughts.

I looked down at the table, where he had placed a cell phone, and looked up at him questioningly.

He laughed before saying, "It's an international cell phone. I want you to have it while you're in Paris. You don't need to worry about minutes on it or anything like that. It's all set."

"What? Why would you give me a cell phone?"

"Because," he said, looking at me in a way that made me feel our relationship had definitely notched up from only friendship. "I want to be able to talk to you during the week that you'll be there and I'll be here. I'm going to miss you. A lot."

He reached for both of my hands, bringing me up to stand in front of him, where I was inches away from his handsome face.

"I like you, Marin," he whispered before placing his lips on mine, at first gently, teasingly, and I felt an emotion that I thought I was long past ever experiencing again—that breathless, excited feeling of desire. When his hands cupped my face, his kiss became deeper, more passionate, and I allowed myself to simply *be*.

When we pulled away, we were both breathless, staring into each other's eyes. I blew out a breath of air and nodded. "I like you too, Worth . . . and I'm very glad our paths have crossed."

❦ 24 ❧

During the following week, two things occurred to me—that Worthington Slater was an expert kisser and that perhaps my mother and Chloe knew better than I had what was good for me.

I saw him at the yarn shop while he was there working, and I was relieved that nothing had changed or felt different between us. I recalled from my dating years that sometimes when a relationship moves in a different direction it can feel awkward or uncomfortable. But with Worth—it only felt right.

For the first time since I had moved in with my mother, I wished that I had my own place. It would have been nice to invite him over to *my* kitchen, cook him a nice meal, and spend an evening together. Maybelle's memorial was in three days and Victoria had arrived the day before. We had plans to meet at the house at three.

"You must be getting so excited," I heard Chloe say as I looked up from the computer. "You'll be leaving for Paris a week from Monday."

I stretched my arms above my head and nodded. I had been sitting at the computer for more than an hour tending to all of the online orders and felt stiffness in my shoulders. I stood up and stretched again.

"I am pretty excited, but I'm also excited about going out to see Maybelle's house this afternoon."

Chloe removed the last of the yarn from the shipment box and arranged it on the shelf. "Gee, with a private sale, you could be in there by Christmas, couldn't you?"

"I guess I could be, but with Bella and the boys coming, I think I'll stay put at my mother's, get through the holiday, and probably move in the following week. If I buy it."

Chloe laughed. "Who are you kidding? The way you've been going on about that house—I think it was meant to be."

We both turned around to see Berkley walk in, accompanied by her aunt, Stella Baldwin.

"Hey, Stella," I said. "Welcome back to the island. I didn't know you were here."

"I got here yesterday. I'm planning to stay till after Thanksgiving."

"Great. Did you bring that cute little Yorkie, Addi, with you?"

Stella laughed and nodded. "Oh, yes. I don't go very far without her. She's napping back at the Faraway."

"And how's Doyle?" I asked, knowing that although she came to visit her niece, meeting Doyle Summers the year before had added to Stella's desire for return visits to the island from Atlanta.

"Oh, he's very well. He's taking Berkley and me to dinner this evening at the Blue Desert." She walked toward the archway. "Oh, this looks wonderful, Marin. When will the needlepoint shop be open?"

"Well, it should have been before Christmas, but we had a bit of a glitch, so it'll be after the first of the year."

She peeked into the other room and nodded. "It's going to be perfect. It already looks nice. So what you are naming it?"

Naming it? I hadn't given a thought to that. "Gosh, I guess I thought it would just be an extension of the yarn shop."

"No, no. You have to have your own name for it. You know, something that will be special for you and be meaningful. Like when Sydney named the yarn shop Spinning Forward and then Monica renamed it Yarning Together."

"She's right," Chloe said. "Even though it's on the other side of the wall, it'll be a separate shop."

"Hmm, true," I agreed.

"I go to a nice shop in Tuscaloosa. It's a combination yarn shop and needlepoint. They have a wonderful selection of everything, and the owner and her clientele are so friendly. It's called Serendipity Needleworks."

"Serendipity," I repeated. "I like it a lot."

"Oh, me too," Berkley said. "I've always loved that word because it means coming upon fortunate discoveries when not in search of them."

I knew she was referring to the needlepoint shop, but I couldn't help but think of Worth. I certainly had not been searching for him, and yet—he'd walked into my life.

"Serendipity Needleworks it is," I said and laughed as all three women clapped.

I headed over to Safe Harbor a little before three. When I pulled the golf cart onto the gravel beside the house, I sat for a few moments staring at the sun casting a glow on the water as dragonflies once again dipped and swirled by the shore, which made me wonder if perhaps purchasing this house might also be serendipitous.

Victoria opened the door to my knock and greeted me with a hug. "Come on in," she said, gesturing to the open-plan living room and kitchen.

My eyes immediately went to the red appliances. Worth was right. They were quirky, but they also held a hint of Maybelle and her vintage style.

"You've been in here before, right?" she questioned.

"Yeah, but not since I was a teenager."

Victoria laughed. "Knowing Maybelle, probably not too much has changed. Well, this is the living room."

I took in the good-size room with French doors that gave an unobstructed view of the water. "I have my own furniture," I said. "Were you planning to take Maybelle's?"

"No. I've made arrangements with Flora to hold an estate sale for me and get it sold. But if there's anything that you'd like, just speak up. I'll include it in the sale price."

I followed her to the kitchen. "I like how the counter and cabinets divide the two rooms, but yet if you're cooking in the kitchen, you can see right into the living room."

"Yes, I've liked that myself when I've stayed here. If I'm busy in the kitchen, I can still keep an eye on Sam."

I looked around. "Where is he? Didn't he come down with you?"

"Oh, yes, he's here, but he's over at Clarissa's house. Monica offered to take him for a couple hours. Come on, this way to the bedrooms and bathrooms," she said, and I followed her to the back of the house.

"This was Maybelle's bedroom," I said, stepping over the threshold. "I remember this is where she showed me all of the costumes she wore as a Copa Girl." A beautiful double mahogany bed dominated the center of the room, and a matching bureau and armoire took up space against two walls.

"Right," Victoria said. "And this is the master suite bath."

I followed her to the en suite bathroom and was surprised to see modern upgrades. A Jacuzzi tub was positioned in a corner, and next to it was a walk-in shower, along with a toilet and double vanity.

"This is a great bathroom," I said, noticing the high windows, which allowed for privacy but didn't require any covering, letting in full sunshine.

"It is. Maybelle only had this remodeled a few years ago. I love soaking in that tub."

I had visions of myself doing exactly that—and maybe not solo.

Before my mind could wander any further, I heard her say, "And the other bedroom and bath is this way."

Down the hall was another good-size bedroom with attached bath. Although this one didn't have a Jacuzzi, it did have a wonderful claw-foot soaking tub with combined shower. This guest room would be perfect for Bella and the boys when they came to visit. We walked back into the kitchen, and I knew my decision had been made.

"I want it," I said. "I'll take it."

"Really? But you haven't even seen the outside yet." Victoria gestured toward the French doors. "There's a wonderful patio out there, and a brick path leads right down to the water."

"I came here snooping," I told her. "I've already checked out the outside property. Let's talk price, because I'd say that Safe Harbor has a new owner."

After we went over all the financial details and they were agreeable, Victoria hugged me. "I'm so happy that you're going to be the new owner, and I have no doubt that Maybelle would be happy too. Gosh, I can't believe you're doing a cash sale."

I nodded. "Yes, I think I'm meant to be here in this house, and because I sold my house in Gainesville, it's enabled me to purchase this one." I recalled my mother's reluctance about my choice but hoped that now that it was a done deal maybe she'd feel differently.

"Okay. Then I'll have my lawyer . . . well, Maybelle's lawyer . . . get in touch with yours. I'll sign my part of the papers before I head back to New York next week and I'll get with Flora about doing the estate sale soon, so the house will be empty for you to move in."

"Sounds good. Oh, I'd like to have Maybelle's bedroom set, if you're sure you don't want it. I'd like to put it into the guest room and have something of hers still here. I'll pay extra for it."

"That would be nice, but absolutely not. You were very generous in the sale offer. The bedroom set will be included in the price. And here," she said, handing me a set of keys on a ring. "Here's the keys for both doors. Congratulations, Marin. You're almost the new owner of Safe Harbor."

She pulled me into a hug and I felt my eyes blur with moisture. Yes, it had been a very rough year, but I had a feeling that maybe the tides were now turning, and I felt ready to charge ahead.

⁓ 25 ⁓

When I woke the following morning, the thought uppermost in my mind was the fact that by the end of the year, I was going to be a home owner. Yes, I had owned a home before—but jointly, with Andrew. This time only *my* name would be on the deed. I realized that many single career women had also accomplished this feat, but for me, it was a big deal. Especially when I recalled that there was a time in our country when married women were denied the right to own property.

I smiled and thought of Maybelle. She, too, had purchased Safe Harbor on her own and had gone on to live a full and happy life there for more than fifty years. And this morning many of us would be gathering to remember her and pay her tribute.

My eyes strayed to the bedside clock and I saw that it was already seven. I put on my robe and could smell the aroma of coffee drifting into my room.

My mother was seated at the table, head bent over the newspaper, when I walked into the kitchen.

"Good morning," I said, heading to the coffeemaker.

"Good morning, Marin. Sleep well?"

"I did. How're you today? Ready for Maybelle's memorial?"

"Yes, I'm ready to say good-bye." She got up to refill her coffee mug. "I sure miss having her around."

"Yeah, Maybelle was quite a character. Did you get your words written down for what you want to say?"

My mother nodded. "Yes, I'm all set to read them. I know Victoria will be speaking, but I don't know who else."

I hadn't instructed Victoria not to say anything about me purchasing Safe Harbor, and I didn't want my mother hearing it from somebody else. I took a deep breath and joined her at the table.

"I have something to tell you," I said and saw her look at me with raised eyebrows. "I wanted you to be the first to know—it's official, I'm purchasing Maybelle's house."

She nodded. "I thought you might. Well . . . I hope you'll be happy there, Marin."

I waited a few moments before I said, "But are you happy for me?" And I realized that even at age fifty-six, I wanted my mother's approval.

She reached over and patted my hand. "Of course I am, Marin. You seemed pretty determined to have that house."

"Do you still think it's a bad idea?"

"I don't recall having said such a thing."

"Well, maybe not in those words, but . . ." There was certainly an indication that she felt this way—and a definite lack of enthusiasm.

She took the last sip of her coffee, placed the mug in the sink, and said, "I'm going to take my shower. Will you be ready to leave a little before eleven?"

"Yes," I said as she walked out of the kitchen.

I had just poured my second cup of coffee when my cell phone rang. I looked at the caller ID and smiled. Worth. "Good morning," I said.

"Hope I'm not calling too early, but I wanted to know if you're the new owner of Safe Harbor."

I let out a laugh. My mother might not be too interested, but Worth easily shared my excitement. "Actually, yes, I am. I fell in love with the house and I think it'll be perfect for me."

"That's great. How soon do you think you'll be able to move in? It won't interfere with you leaving on Monday for Paris, will it?"

"No, not at all. I'll sign all the papers when I return, and Victoria had Maybelle's attorney fax them to her last evening, so the lawyers will get it all squared away. I should be able to move in the week after Christmas."

"That's wonderful. I'm happy for you."

I could tell by his voice that he was. "Hey, listen. I just had a thought. If you're not busy tomorrow afternoon, maybe you'd like to go over to the house with me. Victoria has given me the keys and I'd kind of like to check it all out on my own. Plus, I could use a male point of view."

I heard Worth's chuckle across the line, as he said, "Well, I'll take that as a compliment, and yes, I'd love to go with you. I'll see you at the memorial at eleven and we can decide on a time."

I hung up the phone and felt a smile cross my face. No doubt about it, this man just plain made me feel good.

My mother and I arrived at Maybelle's house shortly before eleven. I was glad we took the golf cart rather than the car. Parking spots were limited on the small dirt road, and most of them already seemed to be taken. I squeezed in on a patch of grass and we walked toward the house.

Folding chairs had been set up on the patio, and people were milling about, talking quietly. We spied Victoria standing in back of a wooden podium talking to Saxton. She turned as we approached, pulling us each into a tight embrace.

"Thank you so much for coming. I've never organized a memorial before, and I don't know what I would have done without all of Saxton's help."

Saxton smiled as he nodded toward the covered bowls in our hands. "Thanks for contributing to the lunch. You can bring them over there," he said, waving to a table set up in back of the chairs. "Flora and Maude will know what to do with them."

We passed our meatballs and macaroni salad to the women.

"Thanks so much," Maude said, adding the bowls to the table, which was quickly filling up with sandwiches, casseroles, salads, and desserts.

"Nice turnout for Maybelle," Flora said. "I think she'd be pleased."

I looked around and nodded.

"We should get a seat," my mother said, walking toward the chairs.

I saw Worth walk around the side of the house and waved my hand in greeting. "Worth just arrived. So we'll need three."

"Hi," he said, a smile covering his face. "Mind if I sit with you ladies?"

"That would be nice," my mother said. "There's three seats together in the second row over there."

We followed her and I sat down between them.

"Beautiful morning for a memorial outside," Worth said.

I nodded. "It is." I glanced at my mother and noticed she was staring beyond the patio to the area near the water, a pensive expression on her face. I was sure it couldn't be easy saying good-bye to her friend.

A little after eleven Victoria approached the podium and the seated crowd refrained from any further talking.

"Thank you," she said. "Thank you for coming here today to remember and honor Maybelle Brewster. I've known Maybelle since I was a little girl and she was my godmother. Unfortunately, due to a falling-out between my mother and her when I was only ten, I lost touch with Maybelle—until last year. After my mother passed away, I contacted Maybelle, and she welcomed me back into her life with open arms. But—that's the kind of person Maybelle was. She didn't judge. I'm fortunate that my son, Sam, and I had this past year to spend with Maybelle. She was a delight to spend time with, and my fondest memory of her will always be the year she introduced me to the wonderful character Eloise and took me for afternoon tea at the Palm Court at the Plaza Hotel. I will greatly miss her"—Victoria paused to dab at her eyes with a tissue—"but a part of Maybelle will always be with me. She would be pleased that so many of you came today, because as you know, she always loved a party."

Chuckles filled the crowd and I saw a smile cross my mother's face.

"And now," Victoria went on, "a few of you would also like to share some memories of Maybelle. Dora?"

I watched my mother walk up to the podium, exchange an embrace with Victoria, and clear her throat.

"My friendship with Maybelle goes back fifty years, almost to the day she moved to the island and made Cedar Key her adopted town. When she first arrived, back in the sixties, many of us weren't sure what to make of her. Maybelle arrived here from the glittering lights of New York City, and as all of us eventually found out, at one time those lights literally shined on Maybelle when she performed as a Copa Girl. She once told me that yes, it had been exhilarating to be part of that dance group, with the exotic costumes and attention from patrons, but she admitted that her true self only emerged once she found Cedar Key. Maybelle loved this town and the people. Till the day she died, Maybelle took pride in a style of dress that had disappeared over the years. I don't think any of us will ever forget Maybelle Brewster strolling Second Street looking like she'd just stepped out of a 1950s fashion magazine— complete with hat, gloves, handbag, and pumps. So it was her distinct style and eccentric nature that added to the flavor of our island. Maybelle was that and so much more. She was a good and loyal friend to me. There were times that she helped me to understand life lessons, so I'm very fortunate that our paths crossed. She had a zest for life that was infectious to all of us in her company— and in death, she will be greatly missed."

I watched my mother bring a tissue to her eyes as she left the podium to return to the seat beside me. Reaching for her hand, I gave it a squeeze and whispered, "That was a beautiful tribute to Maybelle."

We sat quietly as others stood and related touching and humorous stories about Maybelle Brewster. When everybody had spoken, Victoria walked to the podium.

"Thank you again for coming this morning. There's plenty of food, so please, help yourself to lunch. Don't forget to sign the guest book and browse through the photo albums that are on the other table. I took Maybelle's favorite photo as a Copa Girl and had memorial cards printed, so be sure to take one as a keepsake."

Worth and I both stood up as the crowd made their way toward the tables.

"That was a very nice memorial," he said. "I wish I'd had the chance to know Maybelle better."

"It was," I said and noticed my mother was still sitting. "Are you okay?" I asked.

She nodded as she slowly got up. "Just a bit of a headache. Would you mind if I went home, Marin?"

I became concerned. This wasn't like my mother. "Are you sure you're all right?"

She patted my arm. "Yes, yes. Fine. I'm just not very hungry and would like to go home. Would it be okay if I took the golf cart? Worth, do you think you could drop Marin off when you leave?"

"Of course I can," he said.

This was definitely out of character for my mother, making me feel uneasy. "I'll go with you. I don't have to stay."

"No, no," she reassured me. "Really. I'm fine. Just a bit tired. You stay." She leaned over to kiss my cheek and headed toward Victoria to say good-bye.

"She'll be okay," Worth said. "I think the final good-bye today was a bit emotional for her."

I nodded. "Maybe. Are you staying for lunch?"

"Definitely, and I'd like to look through those photo albums," he said, placing his hand at my lower back and guiding me toward the tables.

I chatted with others while we ate and looked at the pictures. After about an hour I found Victoria to say good-bye.

"I'll be in touch," she said. "But I think the attorneys will contact us when the paperwork is all finished on the house. I hope you'll be very happy here, Marin. I'm glad it's you that will be the new owner of Safe Harbor. Give your mother my best. I hope she feels better."

"Thanks," I told her and spotted Worth near the water talking to Saxton.

Almost intuitively he caught my glance and nodded before saying a few more words to Saxton and then heading toward me.

"All set?"

"Yes. I'd like to get home and make sure my mother's okay."

On the short drive to Andrews Circle, I said, "Would you still like to go to the house with me tomorrow afternoon?"

"Absolutely." He reached over to lay his hand on my knee. "I'm looking forward to it."

I felt a smile cross my face. "Good. I'll meet you there around two."

～ 26 ～

Oliver greeted me as I walked into the foyer, tail wagging, a ball in his mouth.

I ruffled the top of his head. "Not now, boy," I said and headed to the family room.

My mother was sitting in her chair, legs on an ottoman, her head back, eyes closed. For a brief second fear shot through me.

"Mom?" I questioned, and when she didn't move, my fear turned to panic. "Mom?" I yelled.

Her eyes popped open as her head turned in my direction.

"Oh . . . Marin. I must have dozed off," she said, sitting up straighter.

"Are you okay?" I walked toward her and noticed that the memorial card of Maybelle was in her lap.

"Yes, I'm fine. You don't need to worry. I didn't sleep very well last night."

I nodded. "Thinking about the memorial today?"

"Yes, that was part of it." She let out a deep sigh. "But I think the time has come to share something with you. I have a story that I'd like you to hear. Maybe you could make us a cup of tea first."

"Of course," I said, curiosity tugging at me. "I'll let Oliver out while I get the tea ready."

I headed to the kitchen, opened the French doors for Oliver, and filled the kettle with water. What on earth was this about? I wondered. Was my mother ill and she hadn't told me? No, she'd said it was a *story*. I smiled as I reached for the mugs from the cabinet and placed an herbal teabag in each one. When I was little, she used to tell me stories all the time. My mother was a great storyteller. I still recalled her washing the kitchen floor on her hands and knees and, when she was finished, saying, "Now, no walking on the floor, Marin, until it's dry." And that's when I'd beg for a story. We'd sit side by side on the chairs that had been moved from the kitchen into the family room while she'd go back in time and tell me about various events from her own childhood, growing up on Cedar Key. The one that had always made the greatest impression was about my grandmother, when she was pregnant with my aunt, Sybile. It was a hot and humid day and she was at the beach at City Park. She must have ventured in too far, had never been a good swimmer, and being top-heavy with pregnancy, she fell and began thrashing about. Mr. Russell, a huge, burly man, built like a wrestler, ran in, scooped my grandmother under one arm, and brought her to safety. That was how my aunt came to be named Sybile—that was Mr. Russell's wife's name, spelled with an *e*, and as a thank-you, the name was passed on.

The whistling kettle brought me out of my thoughts. I poured water in the mugs, let Oliver back in the house, and joined my mother in the family room.

"Thank you," she said, as I placed the mug on the table beside her.

I settled on the sofa across from her and waited.

After a few moments, she said, "First, I want you to know that I'm very happy for you about purchasing Maybelle's house. I know I seemed hesitant and not very encouraging, but it was never about you buying a house or moving out of here. I'm afraid it all has to do with something concerning *me*."

Her? Now she really had my attention.

"Nobody knows the story that I'm about to tell you. There didn't seem to be any purpose for me to pass it on, but now . . . I feel the time is right to share it with you, because . . . well, for a number of reasons, I just do." She took a sip of her tea before continuing. "In order for you to understand the entire story, I need to go back to the beginning. Years ago I had a friend who also grew up on this island, Annalou Carter."

"Annalou?" I questioned. I knew about Flora and Polly and Raylene and all the other women my mother had grown up with, but never somebody named Annalou. "Who is she? You've never mentioned her name before. Where is she now?"

My mother shook her head as she lifted a hand in the air. "No, I never have mentioned her to you, until now. Let me tell her story."

Just as I'd done when I was a child, when I asked too many questions during the telling of the story, I clamped my lips shut and sat back on the sofa, letting my mother go on.

"I knew Annalou from the time I can remember. We started first grade together, and although we both had other friends as well, we were *best* friends. We liked the same games, the same books, the same things to do after school. Annalou's father passed away when we were in third grade. He was a fisherman, like my daddy. Mr. Carter was on his way to Jacksonville to sell his fish and was killed in a fatal car accident. It was tough for them when he was alive, financially, but when he died it became almost downright impossible for Mrs. Carter and Annalou to survive."

I took a sip of tea and had no idea where this story was going, but I already knew it was not going to have a happy ending.

"Mrs. Carter tried to pick up work here and there, but things were tough everywhere. It was the war years and money was scarce. People on the island tried to help as much as they could, donating food and clothes to them, but times were tough for them too. About a year later, a man came to the island from Alabama—John Paulson. Mrs. Carter began dating him, and within a few months, they were married. He was a fisherman, so when he worked, there was some extra money, but he was also a drinker. He moved into the house with Annalou and her mother . . . the house that Maybelle Brewster bought in the sixties . . . Safe Harbor."

"Oh, my God," I said, leaning forward on the sofa. "The house that *I'm* buying?"

My mother nodded. "It was never a happy home. He was abusive to Annalou's mother. She was seen around town with black-and-blue marks on her face and arms, the results of his drunken anger. By the time we were thirteen or fourteen, Annalou tried to stay away from the house as much as possible, coming to my house to spend the night and have dinners."

"Didn't anybody do anything? Like report him to the cops?"

"Oh, yes, many times. But the cops would get out there to the house and Annalou's mother would deny he had abused her. She wouldn't press charges. Think about it, Marin—where on earth could she have gone? She was barely making it on her own before she married him, so she knew it was a dead-end road. No education, no job skills. You have no idea how many women endured exactly those kinds of lives back then. They had very few choices."

I shook my head. How pathetically sad. I thought of Berkley's mother, who had also been a victim of domestic abuse, but at least she hadn't married Berkley's father. She'd had the strength to get away and raise Berkley on her own—but she'd also had a year of college and a mother who was able to help her.

"And that's why you hate that house so much? Because it brings back bad memories of Annalou's stepfather?"

"Yes, that's part of the reason, but there's more to the story. Could you make us another cup of tea?" she asked, getting up and walking toward her bedroom. "I need to get something."

When I returned with our tea, I saw that my mother had a small, wooden chest in her lap.

After taking a sip from the mug, she resumed her story. "Annalou and I remained friends through high school. I knew she wasn't happy living at home. When we were younger, I think she hoped that her mother would leave her stepfather, make him move out—do something to protect them and change the way they were living. But she never did. So Annalou began counting the days till we graduated. She was determined to leave that house and make something of her life, even though her mother never did. She learned to type in high school, and her hope was to go to Jacksonville or Tampa to secure a job as a secretary. She used to say that we could go together, share a room, and be roommates."

My mother paused and let out a sigh as her hand stroked the chest in her lap.

"But that didn't happen?" I asked.

She shook her head. "No, it didn't. The summer after we graduated, she came to my house one evening after supper. I could tell she was upset and figured another outburst had occurred with her mother and stepfather. She said she needed to talk to me—outside of my house. So we walked out back to the dock, and as we sat there, our legs dangling over the edge, Annalou told me that she needed my help. She said she hated to ask me, but she had nowhere else to turn."

My mother paused again, and I knew this story was very difficult for her to share, but for some reason, she felt compelled to do so.

"And that was when she told me she was pregnant. About eight weeks along. Annalou dated a few fellows, but she didn't have a serious boyfriend, so her news was quite shocking to me. In addition to that, in 1953 most girls that did get pregnant out of wedlock were considered fast or cheap. They flirted with the boys, wore provocative clothes—and Annalou was just the opposite. Friendly, but quiet, and what we called back then a *good girl*."

"And what happened?" I asked softly.

My mother cleared her throat. "The help that Annalou requested from me? She wanted me to go with her to get an abortion. We were all so innocent back then—I think I was probably more shocked about this than about the actual pregnancy. So I tried to reason with her. I told her she had to tell her mother; the father of the child would be held liable; she wouldn't be forced to marry him. I told her abortion was illegal, that she couldn't take a chance with some back-alley abortionist. But she told me that she knew of a doctor in Tampa, a well-regarded doctor who did this in privacy to help girls like her. She assured me the procedure would be done in his office, with a nurse present, under sterile conditions. But I still tried to change her mind, telling her that it wasn't a good choice, that she could end up bleeding to death, trying to come up with all kinds of reasons why she shouldn't do this, with the limited knowledge that I had. But she was adamant. When she left me that evening"—my mother paused to dab the moisture in her eyes—

"she said to me, 'Are you sure, Dora? Are you sure you won't go with me? I really need you.' And because I judged her, because I thought her decision was wrong, because I thought I understood when I couldn't begin to understand, and because I was too young . . . I said, 'No, Annalou. We'll work this out. Together. But I can't let you do this and I can't go with you.' She leaned over to hug me, kissed my cheek, and left. That was the last time I saw Annalou."

I assumed Annalou went alone, had the abortion, and died from complications, but that wasn't how the story ended.

My mother wiped her tears with a tissue and shook her head. "No, she didn't get the abortion. The next day the entire town was stunned to learn that Annalou Carter's body had been found near the water in back of their house, a gunshot wound to her head, the gun still gripped in her fist."

My hand flew to my face and I heard myself gasp. "Oh, my God! She committed suicide?"

My mother nodded. "That's what the official report said."

"Did the coroner or anybody ever relate that she was pregnant?"

"No. If they knew, that information was never released. It died with Annalou."

I reached over to give my mother's hand a squeeze. "How terribly, terribly sad. To think that being an unwed mother was so humiliating for her that she would take her own life."

I saw a look of profound sadness cross my mother's face. "That wasn't the reason," she said as she opened the wooden chest and removed an envelope yellowed with age. "You need to read this. I received it in the mail the day after Annalou died."

I reached for the envelope and carefully removed the letter. It had been written with a fountain pen, not a ballpoint, and the small, precise script covered the page. I glanced at my mother and then began to read,

> *My dear Dora,*
> *Above all else, please do not blame yourself. I had*
> *no right to ask such a favor from you. I just didn't*
> *know where else to turn. You were my last hope. But I*

*need you to know that my situation wasn't as it may
have seemed. My pregnancy was not conceived in love,
and I didn't have a boyfriend. No, it was quite the opposite—I was raped by my stepfather. I know in my
heart it wasn't my fault. I know that he is an evil and
horrible man, but I also know that I cannot bear the
result of such a violent and horrific act. I have no
choice and at least now I will be at peace, as I want
you to be, my dearest friend. Please know that I forgive you for denying my request. I love you, Dora, and
I'll always be near you.*

I saw the signature *Annalou*, swiped at the tears now falling
down my face, and shook my head. I couldn't begin to comprehend the guilt my mother must have felt. An eighteen-year-old girl
hit full force with the reality of life.

I replaced the letter in the envelope and passed it to my mother
as I got up to kneel beside her, taking both her hands in mine. "I'm
so sorry. So sorry that you had to endure something like this."

"It was a life lesson, Marin. Oh, I'm not saying it was easy. It
took me years to try to let go of the guilt, but what I learned has
steered my course through the rest of my life. I believe I held the
most guilt because I thought *I* knew what was best for Annalou,
but I truly didn't understand at all. It wasn't up to me to judge her,
but I did. It wasn't like it is today, Marin. Women have choices
today, and they're legal choices. Poor Annalou had no such choice
in 1953. I'm not saying that I condone abortion—but I am saying I
very strongly support each woman in making her own choices."

I nodded and began to comprehend what she said. "This isn't
just about that house, is it? You told me all of this so that I'd better
understand forgiveness, didn't you? Forgiveness of Andrew—and
his choice not to tell me about Fiona."

"Some people have a moment in time they would go back to—if
they could—to change things, to make the outcome different. I
did, and I think Andrew did too. It's not an easy thing to live with."
My mother squeezed my hand. "Before you make any decisions

concerning Fiona, I just want you to be sure of your choice. I want you to make that choice, not in judgment or anger, but in full understanding."

I nodded again and let out a deep sigh. "Thank you. Thank you for sharing all of this with me."

∾ 27 ∾

I arrived at Safe Harbor the next afternoon about fifteen minutes before Worth was due. Before fitting the key into the lock, I stood on the patio staring down to the water. Annalou's story was quite tragic, and I felt sadness that she'd had to resort to taking her own life, but even though I knew that violence and her death had occurred on this property, it didn't sway my decision about purchasing the house. If anything, I probably felt even more convinced that I was meant to live here.

I unlocked the door and stepped into the kitchen. The bright red appliances brought a smile to my face. I walked through each room, allowing myself to soak up the energy, and as I had on the afternoon I'd been there with Victoria—I felt good. Like I was exactly where I was supposed to be.

I heard crunching on the gravel and looked through the window to see Worth pull up, then watched as he got out of the car. Rather than walk directly to the door, he stood for a moment gazing out toward the water. This man enjoyed the moments. He didn't rush through his days but took time to truly enjoy the good things in life. I liked him. I liked him a lot. I saw him reach back into the car for something before he headed to the door.

Without waiting for him to knock, I pulled the door open, a huge smile on my face that matched his.

"Hey," I said. "Welcome to Safe Harbor."

He surprised me by pulling me into his arms and letting his lips brush mine, before saying, "And congratulations to the new owner of Safe Harbor." Holding a bag up, he said, "I thought we could celebrate," and I watched him remove a bottle of champagne.

I laughed. "Gee, I'm not sure I deserve this quite yet. The sale isn't completely official."

"Close enough. Any glasses here?"

I opened one of the cabinet doors and spied champagne flutes on the top shelf. Leave it to Maybelle. "Right up there, if you can get them down."

While I rinsed them, Worth expertly popped the cork and then poured the bubbly amber liquid, filling both flutes.

Raising his to touch the rim of mine, he said, "Here's to many years of happiness at Safe Harbor, Marin."

"Thank you," I said before taking a sip. "Oh, this is delicious."

A smile crossed his face. "Glad you like it. Piper-Heidsieck— my favorite."

"Since you haven't been here for quite a few years, let me show you around."

After I had done so, we walked back into the family room and I sat on the sofa, where Worth joined me.

"Will you be keeping Maybelle's furniture?" he asked.

"Only the master bedroom set, which I'll have moved into the guest bedroom. Victoria has arranged to have an estate sale in the next couple weeks. I think everything will be ready for me to move in the week after Christmas, so I'll contact a mover and have them pick up my furniture from the storage unit."

"Sounds good. How's your mother feeling today? Better, I hope."

I took another sip of champagne and nodded. "Yes, she is." I let out a sigh. "I found out why she was reluctant for me to purchase this house," I said, and although I knew I would never share her story about Annalou with anybody else, I felt a need to share it with Worth.

"It really didn't have anything to do with the actual house or even me moving out. I'm afraid there was much more to it. A very sad story, and unfortunately, my mother has carried a lot of guilt for many years." I proceeded to start at the beginning, and when I finished, Worth shook his head.

"Such a tragic story for both of them. Whatever happened to Annalou's mother and stepfather?"

"My mother said that John Paulson disappeared within a week of Annalou's death. Left the island, and there were rumors that he returned to Alabama. Her mother stayed here a few months and then went to South Carolina to live with her sister."

"And this house just sat empty?"

"Right. Until they both died and it was put up for sale. That's when Maybelle bought it."

"Quite a difference having somebody like Maybelle living here. She brought a lot of happiness and laughter to the house, I'm sure. So it doesn't bother you to learn about what happened on the property?"

"No, not at all. Call me silly, but I have the strongest feeling that it's meant to be and I'm the one who is now supposed to live here."

Worth reached for my hand and clasped it inside of his. "Not at all silly. I think certain places have a way of calling to us. I can't begin to understand it, but I feel that's true."

Such a simple gesture, having my hand held, and yet it felt so intimate. As if confirming this, Worth brought my hand to his lips and placed a kiss on top. I looked up and saw a smile cross his face.

"I also think certain people have a way of calling to us," he said. Taking the champagne flute from my hand, he placed it on the table as he moved closer and put his lips on mine. Just like his previous kiss, it began gentle, seeking, and then became deeper and more passionate. When we broke apart, he buried his face in my neck and let out a deep sigh.

"You make me feel good," he whispered.

Before I had a chance to reply, his cell phone rang. He glanced at the caller ID, gave me a sheepish look, and said, "Sorry. Caroline."

I nodded and let out my own sigh as I sat back against the cushion and listened to him talk to his daughter.

"Yes, Caroline. I got it. I had it shipped last week."

There was a pause before he said, "Trust me, it will be there by the end of the week. In plenty of time."

Another pause. "Okay. I'll see you soon. Love you too."

It was obvious Caroline had created another potential problem, but it was the sound of his words—*love you too*—that touched a chord deep inside of me.

He disconnected and took a sip of champagne. "Sorry about that. Caroline has a favorite Southern relish that she loves. Of course it's impossible to get in Paris, so she asked if I'd bring about ten jars over with me when I came. I wasn't about to lug jars of relish on my flight, so I had them shipped."

Yup, Worthington Slater was definitely a good father. "And she's worried she won't have them?"

"Yeah, but I shipped them priority air, so I know they'll be there in time for a dinner party the night after I arrive. So . . . are you all set for your flight tomorrow?"

"I am. Just a few last-minute things to pack. I have to keep pinching myself, though. I still can't believe I'm actually going."

Worth let out a laugh. "Oh, you're definitely going. By the way . . . I was going to ask you, how are you getting to the airport tomorrow? I meant to mention this sooner and it slipped my mind. I'd be more than happy to drive you."

I felt a surge of disappointment. I would have loved for Worth to be the one to drive me to Gainesville. "Oh . . . well . . . uh . . . Chloe had said she'd take me, but . . ." I paused because I didn't want to appear pushy.

Worth reached for my hand again, leaned over, placed a kiss on my lips, and said, "Why don't you give her a call and tell her she doesn't have to make that drive after all. Because I'd like to be the one to see you off."

I felt a smile cross my face. I liked his plan much better. "It's a deal."

"Good," he said, before reaching for the bottle of champagne and replenishing our glasses. "So the reason your mother told you the story about Annalou was because she wanted you to know the real reason why she felt this way about the house?"

"Well, that was part of it," I told him. "The other part actually had to do with Andrew and Fiona—and forgiveness. I guess she doesn't want me holding it against Fiona for what Andrew did, but she also feels that in order for me to go forward I need to learn to forgive Andrew."

Worth remained silent for a few moments before saying, "And can you do that?"

I shrugged my shoulders. "I'm still not sure. And one of the worst things? He's gone. I can't even ask him *why*. Why he got involved with Bianca."

"Marin, even if he were still here, you might never have the answer to that question. Maybe *he* had no answer. It just happened. One of those things that we do, in a moment of weakness, and yet . . . there's no turning back."

He made me wonder if he had firsthand experience with this, but I also recalled what my mother had said about that one moment in time we wish we could go back to and change. Maybe being with Bianca was that moment for Andrew.

I nodded. "Hmm. You could be right."

❧ 28 ❧

When I opened my eyes Monday morning, I knew immediately that I was about to embark on a journey that would possibly change the rest of my life. And although I was beyond excited about finally returning to Paris, I felt it was about so much more than just my trip. I rolled over, glanced at the clock, and saw that it was almost seven.

I was surprised to see my mother already sitting at the kitchen table, a steaming mug of coffee in front of her.

"Up early," I said, heading to the coffeemaker. "Sleep okay?"

"Very well, actually. I think I'm just excited for you and your trip today."

I smiled and joined her. "I know. It's hard to believe I actually did it—made it happen."

"You're going to have a wonderful visit to Paris. Any particular plans?"

"Not really. Returning to a few museums that I enjoyed years ago, doing some Christmas shopping, and just soaking up Paris."

My mother nodded. "I have no doubt you'll enjoy every second, and I hope you'll return home feeling renewed and refreshed."

She didn't say it, but I had a feeling that she also hoped when I returned home a decision would be made concerning Fiona.

"What time is Worth picking you up?"

"Ten. My flight leaves for Atlanta at twelve-thirty and I'll have about a four-hour layover before the Paris flight."

I thought of my call to Chloe the night before, telling her that Worth had offered to drive me to the airport today. She was more than fine with it, joking with me. "Let's see," she said, "me or a very handsome man, who, by the way, is definitely developing an interest in you? Gee, I'd say the handsome man wins." A smile crossed my face at the thought that perhaps Chloe was right about the interest Worth was showing. And it made me feel good.

My mother got up to remove something from the oven. "I have some cranberry muffins I made this morning. As soon as they cool a bit, we can have one with coffee."

The wonderful aroma of baking filled the kitchen, and for a split second I felt a bit nostalgic knowing that Thursday was Thanksgiving and I wouldn't be here. But I pushed it aside and knew that no matter what I was doing on Thursday in Paris—I would be where I was supposed to be.

"I had an idea," my mother said. "But I wanted to ask you first and see what you think."

"What is it?"

"Well, you're going to be in Paris on Thursday . . . and as far as I know, Worth doesn't have any family here . . . so I was wondering if you thought it might be okay to invite him to Sydney's for dinner. I already spoke with her, and she said she and Noah would love to have him."

I hadn't even given that a thought—where Worth would be spending the holiday. "Oh, I think that's a great idea. And very thoughtful of you to consider him. Absolutely. You can invite him when he comes to get me this morning."

"Good. I'd hate to think he'd be spending Thanksgiving alone."

It made me feel good to know that even though I wouldn't be here, Worth would be spending the day with my family.

After more coffee and a muffin, I headed to the shower. A little before ten, I was zipping up my checked piece of luggage. Looking in the mirror, I decided that my outfit would be both comfortable and practical for my flights. Black slacks, gray cashmere pullover sweater, black wool blazer, beige alpaca scarf, and comfortable black leather loafers for all the airport walking. I peeked inside my red Namaste bag one more time to be sure I had everything I needed in my carry-on piece. Passport. I smiled and gave myself silent kudos for always renewing my passport over the years and not letting it lapse. My knitting, e-book reader, iPad, glasses, wallet, makeup, and a few other items. All set. I let out a deep breath, looked around my room, grabbed the handle of my wheeled luggage, and headed to the family room.

A few minutes later, right on time, Worth rang the doorbell.

"Good morning," he said, stepping inside and placing a kiss on my cheek. "Your chauffeur is here."

"You certainly are prompt," I heard my mother say behind me.

"Well, we can't have our girl missing that flight to Paris this evening," he said.

Our girl? I liked the sound of that.

"And you have everything?" my mother questioned. "Your euros, passport, directions to the apartment?"

I let out a chuckle. I felt like a ten-year-old heading off to summer camp. "I do. I have enough euros to get me through the first day. Worth told me about a place near Notre Dame where I'll get a good exchange, and I've double-checked. I'm all set."

"Okay, then," my mother said and pulled me into an embrace. "Oh, Worth. I wanted to invite you to Thanksgiving dinner at Sydney and Noah's house. She wanted me to extend an invitation. If you have no other plans."

A smile lit up his face. "No, I don't. Thank you, and I appreciate it."

"Good. Sydney said around two."

"How about if I pick you up and escort you there? A little before two?"

A smile now lit up my mother's face as she said, "That would be great."

"See you then," Worth said as he reached for my piece of luggage and headed out to the car.

My mother gave me another hug and kissed my cheek. "Bon voyage, Marin. Have a good flight and a wonderful time."

"I will, and I'll call you tomorrow from the apartment after I get settled in."

I slid into the passenger seat and looked at Worth. "Gainesville Airport, please."

He backed out of the driveway and smiled. "The airport it is."

Worth pulled up to the curb, got out, removed my piece of luggage, and said, "I'm just going to park and I'll meet you inside."

Before I had a chance to say anything, he was pulling away, heading for the small parking area. I hadn't realized that he planned to stay with me while I waited for my flight to Atlanta, but I was happy he was choosing to do so.

I walked into the small terminal and smiled. I loved a regional airport. Large enough to be able to get a connecting flight somewhere, but small enough to avoid long lines in security or at the boarding gate. I felt Worth's hand on my shoulder.

"You still have over an hour till your flight leaves. Why don't you get checked in and then we can grab a coffee."

"Sounds good," I said, walking to the ticket counter.

After we got our coffee, we headed to a small table.

"I was able to check my bag all the way through to Charles de Gaulle."

"Oh, that's good. It'll avoid a hassle when you get to Atlanta."

"Right. I'll find a place to have dinner after I go through security there."

"Do me a favor?"

"Sure."

"Call me after you've had dinner and you're at the gate?"

"Okay," I said and felt him reach across the table for my hand.

"I'm going to miss you. It'll seem strange not to see you at the yarn shop while I'm there working."

I realized that he was right. Maybe we had only met not quite two months ago, but we had spent a large amount of time together. And most of it had been quality time—really getting to know each other.

"I'll miss you too," I said softly.

Almost as if he felt bad for possibly putting a blemish on my trip, he gave my hand a squeeze and said, "But just think, one week from tomorrow, I'll be there with you. In the most . . . in the City of Light."

Was he going to say in the most *romantic* city in the world?

I nodded and smiled. "Right, and I look forward to you being there with me."

"I hope so."

Before I knew it, it was time for me to board and begin the first leg of my journey.

Worth led me away from the crowd before I headed to security. He put his arms around me and then he cupped my face in his hands. Staring into my eyes, he said, "Have a wonderful flight, Marin. I'll be there with you before you know it." And then he proceeded to leave me with a kiss that was far from innocent—a kiss that gave a promise of more to come.

I got in line, inched my way forward, and turned around to give Worth a final wave. He smiled and then did something that I found incredibly sexy, something that stirred me, something no other man had ever done to me. He put his fingers to his lips, gestured his hand toward me—and blew me a kiss.

29

When I arrived at Hartsfield Airport, I got on the tram and made my way to the international terminal, where I found a lounge with a quiet booth and ordered a glass of cabernet. After the waitress brought it, I let out a sigh and thought back to Worth and our parting kiss. That kiss definitely indicated more than just friendship, which made me question whether I wanted *more* than just friendship with him. For a brief moment I felt a twinge of guilt concerning Andrew, but then I remembered my mother's story and the guilt she had carried for years. And I knew that if I was honest with myself, then yes—I was pretty sure that moving beyond friendship with Worth was something that I definitely wanted. I felt a smile cross my lips and reached up to touch the spot where his lips had recently been. Letting out another sigh, I took a sip of wine before removing my knitting from my bag to pass the time before going to the gate.

I arrived there about an hour before boarding and found a secluded seat to place the call to Worth. He answered on the second ring.

"Hey," he said. "I guess you'll be boarding shortly?"

"I will, and I think my excitement level is notching up."

I heard his laughter come across the line. "Good. By the way, I just spoke with Madame Leroux, and she'll be waiting for you tomorrow to give you the key to the apartment. She said the weather is overcast and a bit chilly, in the forties, so be sure you're wearing your blazer when you leave the RER. You'll be getting a taxi from there, right? It's only about a thirteen-minute walk, but it could be raining and you'll have luggage."

I smiled at his concern. "Yes. RER, and then a taxi from Port Royal to rue des Lyonnais. And after I get settled into the apartment, I'll go to the Franprix you told me about on rue Broca to stock up on a few food items."

"Great, and try to stay up at least till six or so to get over jet lag. Then when you wake on Wednesday morning, you'll be on Paris time."

I nodded and smiled again. "Right. Will do."

There was a pause, and then he said, "Okay. Have a good flight, and do me a favor?"

"Call you?"

His laughter came across the line again. "Yes. Please call me when you get to the apartment. *Au revoir.*"

I disconnected, shut my cell phone off, and replaced it in my bag.

I did luck out, because nobody had booked the aisle seat next to me, which allowed me to stretch out a bit. We had been airborne about twenty minutes, the seat-belt sign had just gone off, and the flight attendants were beginning the beverage service. I ordered a glass of champagne, reclined my seat a little, and really did want to pinch myself. I was on my way to Paris! Not only that, but I had met an extremely nice, handsome man who would be joining me there in a week. When I thought back to all of the heartache, shock, and disappointment of the past year, it was beginning to feel like a fuzzy memory. Like perhaps it had happened to somebody else. But I knew it had not. It was simply that I was allowing myself to go forward, to get on with *my* life. And although I had no idea where I would ultimately end up or what would happen, especially concerning Fiona, I knew that if I followed my heart and did what I felt was right, things would fall into place—precisely as they should.

The flight attendant placed a glass of champagne on the aisle tray before passing me a pillow and blanket. "Thanks," I said.

"Going to Paris on business or pleasure?" she asked, eyeing the knitting in my lap.

"Oh, pleasure. Pure pleasure."

She laughed. "I'm a knitter also. That's gorgeous. A sweater?"

I held up the front of the sweater and nodded. "It's from a *Queensland Collection* pattern and done with Pima Lino yarn."

"Gorgeous colors," she said, admiring the pink, coral, and turquoise. "You'll have to visit the yarn shops in Paris while you're there."

"Really? I didn't even think about it."

"Oh, yes. They're so nice. That's the best part of my layovers in Paris," she said with a laugh. "I can never resist going there. I'll jot down their names and addresses for you."

"That would be great. Thanks."

I finished off my champagne with dinner and decided to really splurge, having a cognac with coffee after I was done eating. When the dinner tray was removed, I covered myself with the blanket, adjusted my pillow, and removed my e-book reader from my bag. The cabin lights had been dimmed, creating a glow from the seat-back movie monitors and passenger lights. Rather than watch a movie, I decided to resume reading the cozy mystery by Leann Sweeney I'd started a few days before. I'd never owned a cat, but I always enjoyed reading about them in her novels. I wasn't sure how many pages I had gotten through before the page began blurring and I wasn't able to keep my eyes open. I closed up the e-book, flipped my light off, and snuggled into the pillow, allowing myself to drift off.

The next thing I knew the cabin lights were being turned on and I heard the breakfast carts going down the aisle. I glanced at my watch and realized I'd slept for almost three hours. It was midnight, with only about two hours left to the flight. But being six hours later than the States, it was six in the morning in Paris. I flipped up the window shade, and although it was black directly outside my window, ahead in the distance I could see a bright orange and red sky. Dawn was breaking over the city, and I smiled. Not much longer and I'd be there.

I enjoyed my coffee and juice along with a croissant and yogurt. After I finished, I went to the restroom to freshen up a bit before we landed.

The flight attendant returned to my seat and passed me a slip of paper. "Here you go. I think you'll enjoy these yarn shops."

"Thanks," I said and slipped the paper in my bag.

"First trip to Paris?"

"Actually, my second. But it's been over thirty years since I was last here."

She smiled. "Ah, and I bet you'll see very little has changed. That's one of the beauties of Paris. Have a great time."

As the wide-body began its descent, I leaned my chin in my hand on the armrest and stared out the window. It was completely light now, so I was able to see large patches of green below—obviously the French countryside—and as we dipped lower, I was able to make out farmhouses and then small villages. Before I knew it, the announcement was made to fasten seat belts for our final approach into Charles de Gaulle; a few minutes later I felt a bump, and we were on the runway taxiing to the terminal gate.

First in English and then French, I heard, "Good morning, ladies and gentlemen. Welcome to Paris."

I was suddenly overcome with emotion and felt my eyes blurring with tears. Feeling silly, I reached up to dab them and let out a deep breath, and that was when I did actually pinch my arm. Ouch! Yes, I was definitely here. It wasn't a dream.

Once the aircraft was at the gate, noise filled the cabin as people jumped up and began opening overhead bins and removing their carry-ons. Since I had my carry-on bag beside me, I had nothing to remove from the bin. But I stood, stretched, and, remembering Worth's advice, put my blazer on before adjusting my scarf.

In the terminal, I followed the crowds to Immigration, where I eventually made my way to the officer, who looked at my passport, stamped it, and gave me permission to enter the country of France. I now followed more crowds to the baggage area. By this time, I was very grateful that I'd had the good sense to choose comfortable walking shoes. The carousel had not yet begun to move, but I found a good spot where I'd be able to grab my one piece of luggage when it did. Ten minutes later luggage began tumbling out, and I didn't have to wait too long until my gray Samsonite appeared.

I was waved through Customs and emerged to find another huge crowd of people, some waving and smiling, others holding name signs. Almost immediately I saw directions to the RER and walked along, quite happy that I'd invested in the spinner luggage, which was very easy to maneuver beside me.

I found RER B and waited on the platform to board for Port Royal. About fifty minutes later, I got off the train at boulevard Port Royal and got a taxi to the apartment. I was beginning to feel like I was on overload with the sights and sounds of Paris. When we weren't underground on the RER, I craned my neck toward the window, trying to take in the little villages along the route with stone houses, small shops, and streets that meandered away from the tracks. As I waited for a taxi, horns blared, vehicle brakes screeched, and for the first time since leaving, I thought of the quiet of Cedar Key—but I had to admit I wouldn't have traded standing on a Paris street for anything.

The taxi driver made his way down rue des Lyonnais, pulled up in front of a building, jumped out to remove my luggage from the trunk, and gave me a big smile.

"C'est ici," he said, gesturing with his hand toward the building.

I understood that he had told me, *It's here,* and felt proud that I was able to grasp his French phrase.

I paid him in euros before saying, *"Merci. Au revoir,"* which earned me another big smile.

I rolled my luggage to the front door, punched in the digicode, and heard the door click for me to open. Stepping inside, I saw an outside entranceway leading to an open courtyard and another building, where I used my key and walked inside. Worth's apartment was up two steps on the left. I placed my luggage outside the door and climbed to the first floor to meet Madame Leroux and get my key.

❧ 30 ❧

The door opened almost immediately to my knock. Standing before me was a short, stout woman. Her expression was pleasant and conveyed a youthfulness that belied the fact that she was in her late eighties.

She pulled the door wider. "*Bienvenue.* Come in, come in. You must be Marin."

I returned her smile and nodded, but what drew my attention was the huge mass of fur in her arms. Without depositing what I realized was a mega-cat, she sat in one of the overstuffed chairs and gestured for me to take the one opposite.

"You had a good flight, yes?"

"Very good. Thank you. That's a beautiful cat you have," I said and instantly knew it was a Maine coon breed and very similar to the one that Chloe's aunt, Maude Stone, had. Lafitte was big, but this feline probably tipped the scales even a few pounds more.

Madame Leroux stroked the cat's head, which immediately set up the sound of a trill or chirp. I remembered that Lafitte didn't meow either, but made this sweet sound, which was one of the traits that a Maine coon was noted for.

"Ah, this is my Jacques. He's now ten years old and my best friend. You like cats?" she questioned.

As if on cue, Jacques jumped from Madame Leroux's lap and into mine. I let out a laugh as I felt the weight on my legs. I had never owned a cat before, but Jacques was quickly convincing me that yes, I did like cats. He rubbed his large, dome-shaped head under my chin, forcing me to stroke his ears, which brought forth another trill. "I do like cats," I said. "And he's really stunning. A Maine coon breed, right?"

"Yes. My niece is a breeder, like my sister before her. Jacques is my third Maine coon. They're a wonderful breed."

"They are. A woman in the town where I live has one." Jacques was gray and white with a large, fluffy tail just like Lafitte, but I remembered Chloe telling me they come in various colors. "His name is Lafitte and he's the same color."

"Ah, she also has a *bleu?*" she said, using the French pronunciation of the color. "They are quite handsome."

"Blue? I thought he was gray."

Madame Leroux laughed. "Yes, they do look like a steel gray, but they have accents of blue when the light hits their fur."

"Well, Jacques certainly is a handsome boy," I said, and as if understanding, he now placed his huge paws on my shoulders and cuddled against my chest, causing me to laugh.

"So you are a good friend of Worth's? He is such a nice man. He always helps me with little jobs around the apartment when he comes. I will be happy to see him again next week."

So will I, I thought, and said, "Yes, he's doing some remodeling work for my mother's shop, and that's how we met." I neglected to say that I had a feeling we were becoming more than just friends.

Madame Leroux got up and went to the dining room table as I glanced around the two rooms. They had an old-world feel to them, with the cushy pillows, tasseled lampshades, and heavy mahogany furniture.

She returned with a covered plastic bowl and the key to Worth's apartment. "I have your key," she confirmed. "And I'm sure you're tired from your travel, so I have made you some soup to nourish you."

Jacques jumped down, allowing me to stand. "That's so nice of you. Thank you," I said, and before she passed them to me, she leaned forward and placed a kiss on each of my cheeks.

"I'm sure Worth explained where to shop. Just down the street is a Franprix, *boulangerie, charcuterie,* anything you might need, and on rue Mouffetard is the wonderful outdoor market."

"Yes, he told me, and after I get unpacked I'll venture out for a little while."

"I also wanted to tell you, I know that Thursday is . . . what do you call it? Thanksgiving? Your American holiday. I'm going to prepare a roast chicken, and my niece, Annette, will be coming. I'd like you to join us."

I was quite surprised by her invitation and wondered if Worth had anything to do with it. "That would be very nice. I'd like that. Thank you."

"Good. Around one o'clock, and if you need anything, just knock on my door. I'm usually here."

I gave a final pat to Jacques, took the soup bowl and key, and headed downstairs.

I placed the key in the lock, stepped into a small hallway, and saw the kitchen was to my left, adjacent to the living room on the right. Placing the bowl on the counter, I removed my blazer and put it on the back of the stool. Standing in the middle of the living room, I smiled. So this was where Worth spent his Parisian time. French doors lined the wall, looking out to a small, private garden with table and chairs. Worth was right—nothing fancy, but the furnishings looked cozy and comfortable and the two rooms were bright and cheery. I noticed that despite the cloudiness of earlier, the sun was now making an attempt to break through. I walked to the doorway off the living room and saw a good-size bedroom. Retracing my steps back to the entrance hallway, I now saw where the second bedroom was located. It was then that I realized Worth had neglected to tell me which bedroom was to be mine. This one seemed smaller. Since I was the guest, maybe I should claim it.

I heard my cell phone ringing and went back to the living room to remove it from my bag.

"Welcome to Paris," I heard Worth say as I glanced up to the clock on the kitchen wall and saw that it was close to noon.

I smiled. "Thank you. I just got into the apartment a few minutes ago and I was going to call you."

"Flight over okay?"

"It was very good. I slept for about three hours. I don't even feel tired. I had no problem getting the RER or taxi, and I just left Madame Leroux's apartment. I can understand why you're so fond of her, by the way. She's very sweet, and that cat of hers is adorable."

Worth laughed. "Good. I'm glad you arrived safely and yes, I thought you might like Madame Leroux. And Jacques is quite the cat. So what have you got planned for the rest of the day?"

"I'm going to unpack first. Oh, you never told me which bedroom was mine."

Without hesitating, he said, "The one off the living room. The larger one."

"No, no. I have a feeling that's your bedroom. I'll take the smaller one. Really. I don't mind."

"Absolutely not. Please. I want you to have that one. By the way . . . did you check out the kitchen?"

The kitchen? "Not really. Not yet. I'm walking toward it now, though," I said and then gasped. There on the small round table was a vase filled with gorgeous yellow roses, and beside it was an ice bucket, chilling a bottle of white wine. I bent down to inhale the wonderful fragrance of the flowers. "Oh, Worth. You shouldn't have. But thank you so much. The roses are beautiful. I love them, and I know I'll enjoy that wine later."

"That's what I wanted—for you to enjoy it. So you're going to get unpacked and then what?"

"Madame Leroux gave me a bowl of homemade soup, so I'm going to go to the *boulangerie* to get a baguette to go with it. And I think I might wander around rue Mouffetard for a while, find a sidewalk café for coffee, pick up some items at the Franprix. And I plan to be in bed by six or so. How's everything with you?"

"Fine. It's only six in the morning here, but I'll be heading over to the yarn shop later to get some more work done."

"I'm going to call my mother in about an hour. She should be up by then. Oh, Madame Leroux invited me for dinner on Thursday. She said she's preparing a roast chicken, and her niece, Annette, is also coming."

"I'm sure you'll enjoy their company. Okay, well, I'll let you unpack and get settled in. Enjoy yourself, Marin. I'll talk to you tomorrow. And by the way . . . I already miss you."

I disconnected the phone with a smile on my face before going into the bedroom to begin unpacking. After I got my clothes hung up in the closet and put away in a few of the empty bureau drawers, I arranged my toiletries in the bathroom before stepping back into the bedroom. I looked at the queen-size bed and realized I'd be sleeping in the bed where Worth normally slept. I let out a burst of laughter and found myself scooting smack into the middle of the mattress, arms wrapped around myself as a huge smile crossed my face. *Life is good,* I thought. *Life is damn good.*

After calling my mother, letting her know I'd arrived safely and that all was well, I refilled my Namaste bag with essential items to explore my neighborhood—wallet, French phrase book, and street map. Stepping onto the pavement, I let out a deep breath. Already, I felt like a Parisian heading out on my own.

I walked the short distance to rue Mouffetard, found a table at one of the terrace cafés, and ordered a cup of *café noir.* Normally I added a bit of cream, but in Paris I loved the rich, dark flavor of black coffee.

I allowed myself to soak up the atmosphere. Paris had a strong pulse—unlike that of any other city I'd visited—beating away over many centuries. It was easy to visualize eras inhabited by so many famous people down through the ages. Kings and queens, political activists, poets, artists, writers, and so many more, who all contributed to making Paris the extraordinary city that she was. Surrounded by ancient buildings, cobblestone sidewalks, fountains, and squares, I almost expected to see Hemingway or Gertrude Stein claim the table beside me. *This* was what I loved about Paris; *this* was why I had always longed to return here—all I had to do was *be,* and I was instantly transported back to another time in history, almost making me feel as if time itself had stood still.

31

I opened my eyes, saw a bit of light along the edge of the curtains, and for a moment was disoriented. Then I remembered. I was in Paris. In Worth's apartment. In Worth's bed. I yawned, stretched, and glanced at my watch. Five-thirty. No wonder I felt so rested—I had slept almost twelve hours.

After preparing the coffeemaker, I sliced some bread for the toaster oven and then spied the radio on the counter. Turning the knob, I smiled when I heard something I hadn't heard in more than thirty years. The radio station Cherie FM—the station that we'd always had on in the apartment I'd shared with my friends. While I enjoyed my coffee, toast, and some delicious *fromage* I'd picked up at a cheese shop, French music filled the kitchen. I glanced out to the garden and formulated my plans for the day in my head.

First on the list was a visit to Ladurée, the oldest and most legendary of Parisian patisseries, noted for their famous French *macarons*. Rue Bonaparte would be my first stop to purchase the cream-filled sandwich cookies as Christmas gifts for my mother, the boys, and Chloe.

Following a good night's sleep, shower, and breakfast, I was ready to begin my first full day exploring Paris.

After I had a shopping bag filled with boxed *macarons*, I caught the Métro to boulevard Haussmann and Galeries Lafayette department store. Standing across the street, I marveled at the massive structure in all its beauty before going to admire the beautiful window displays, each one showing a different Christmas theme. Walking into the atrium, I paused for a few moments to take in the elegant belle époque architecture. Surrounded by the balconies of each floor, I saw the giant Christmas tree in the center and looked up in awe to view the stunning turquoise glass dome ceiling above. It was absolutely breathtaking, and I let out a deep sigh.

As I began wandering around, I was easily distracted by all of the festive decorations throughout the department store, but after a few hours I had managed to get some more Christmas shopping done. Just as I had decided it was time to leave, I caught sight of a hair salon—a very trendy, upscale salon—and before I realized what I was doing, I had booked myself an appointment for the following Monday, the day before Worth was to arrive.

Back out on the sidewalk, I glanced at my watch and saw it was nearly two o'clock. No wonder I was hungry. I found a small bistro nearby, chose a table on the terrace in the sun, and ordered a glass of Sancerre just as my cell phone rang. I answered to hear Worth's voice and smiled.

"So how is the Parisian doing today?" he asked, and I was surprised at how good it felt to hear his voice.

"I'd say very well, considering I spent a few hours in Galeries Lafayette doing Christmas shopping. Good timing on the call. I just sat down at a sidewalk café for lunch." The waiter placed my wine in front of me. *"Merci,"* I told him.

"Oh, am I interrupting?"

"Not at all. I ordered a glass of wine and haven't ordered my food yet. So how are you doing and how's everything there?"

"Good. I just got to the yarn shop. The work for the screened area is coming along well. I think you'll like it. Did you sleep well last night?"

I laughed. "I certainly did. Almost twelve hours, but I'm over jet lag. And I love the apartment, Worth. It's so cozy and comfortable." I almost said, *The only thing missing is you.*

"I'm glad you like it. And you've been able to find everything okay? Dishes and all that?"

"Yes, fine. It's very well equipped too. I really enjoyed listening to the radio in the kitchen this morning while I had my coffee. So you're keeping busy?"

"For the most part. When I knock off work here, I've been giving some extra attention to Suzette in the evenings."

"Oh, gosh, I didn't even ask you. Will you be boarding her next week when you come over?"

Worth's laughter came across the line. "No, I'm afraid Suzette isn't a kennel dog. Tried it once when she was younger, and she was miserable. So I hire pet sitters. This time I'll have Doyle Summers watching her. He suggested it and I took him up on his offer. They really like each other, and I think she'll enjoy staying at his house while I'm gone."

"Oh, good. Yes, a much better arrangement than a kennel."

"Have you had any time to do some thinking yet?" he asked, and I knew he was referring to Andrew and Fiona.

"Not yet," I told him.

"That's understandable. You need to just settle in first, relax, enjoy Paris. How's the weather?"

"Much milder than I thought it would be. The sun is shining and it's probably fifty today. Perfect weather to be out and about enjoying the city."

"Great. Well, listen, I'll let you go. You need to have lunch and I need to get to work. Enjoy your day, Marin."

He paused and I said, "I will, and . . . I miss you, Worth. It'll be nice when you arrive next week. Bye." I disconnected the call, blew out a breath, and took a sip of my wine. I hadn't planned to say that. It had just come out—but I did miss him. Being *with* him.

When the waiter returned, I ordered a *croque-monsieur*. The grilled ham and cheese sandwich had been one of my favorites years ago.

As I sat there sipping my wine, watching crowds of people either strolling or hurrying past, my thoughts drifted to Andrew. How did I feel now? Removed from the geographic location of our marriage, did I feel any different toward him? The original grief over his death was lighter, and I guess that was natural. Didn't everybody say time would lighten the grief? But how about the hurt, the anger, the betrayal I'd felt this past month since finding out about his infidelity? Allowing myself to focus on my emotions, I realized that those, too, seemed to be lighter.

If I was perfectly honest with myself, I had to admit that during that summer that Andrew had been away I had given some thought to perhaps a separation or even a divorce. I hadn't been happy in my marriage for a while, and I was convinced that Andrew hadn't been either. But then he had returned from Massachusetts, and although, no, our marriage did not suddenly take on a romantic or passionate quality, something changed—and it changed in such a way as to enable us to go forward.

The waiter brought my sandwich, and it looked every bit as good as I remembered. *"Merci. Encore, s'il vous plaît,"* I said, pointing to my wineglass. The wine was delicious and warranted a refill.

I bit into my sandwich and savored the wonderful flavor of what tasted like Gruyère cheese. As I sat there enjoying my lunch, I glanced a few tables away and saw a young father with two little boys probably between three and five years of age. The father had a glass of red wine in front of him, and the boys were each enjoying a cup of rich, dark hot chocolate. They were having what appeared to be an interesting discussion on a topic that held the boys' interest, and I smiled.

Out of the blue, I could see Andrew with Jason and John having similar discussions when they were that age. This thought led me to remember how much time Andrew always spent with the boys. Maybe not so much during the week, when work occupied his hours. But the weekends were devoted to time spent with our sons. We had a fair amount of family outings, but I could recall that if I had preferred to stay home to catch up on ironing or even to just have some quiet time, then it was Andrew who took the boys to the duck pond or the movies or sports events. It was Andrew who helped in the evening with difficult homework assignments, and when the boys were in high school, it was Andrew who would have long discussions with them about career choices, college applications, and potential job opportunities.

I took the last bite of my sandwich and glanced across at the father and sons again. He must have said something humorous, because both boys were laughing. Their faces were lit up with joy, but it was their expression when they looked at their father that caught my attention. The same expression I used to glimpse on Jason's and John's faces sometimes when they looked at Andrew—admiration and respect.

I let out a deep sigh and then took a sip of wine. No matter what, Andrew had been a good father. He'd spent quality time with his sons. He had been a good role model. Andrew had worked hard and been a good provider for his family. He'd encouraged the boys, supported them, and always been there for them during important times.

I took another sip of wine and nodded to myself. Not only had Andrew been a good father—he had been a good man. A good man who had made one mistake—and for that alone, he deserved forgiveness.

∽ 32 ∽

I woke a little later the following morning, just before seven, and decided that rather than have toast with my coffee I'd go to the corner *boulangerie* and bring back something yummy. Something Parisian. Something with a calorie count that I wasn't going to concern myself with. After all the walking I'd done the previous day, I wouldn't have been surprised if I'd lost a pound or two.

I ran a brush through my hair, threw on a pair of sweats along with my Nikes, grabbed my purse, and headed out hoping the Parisians would forgive me for looking like a very untrendy American. The only thing missing was the baseball cap.

Standing in front of the *boulangerie*'s window, I could feel my salivary glands going into action. How on earth *was* it possible to live here, surrounded by such tempting food, and still manage to maintain the slim figures I saw on most French women? Pushing these thoughts aside, I focused on all the delectable choices in front of me. Once I got my drooling under control, I walked inside, chose both an apple tart and a *pain au chocolat,* and happily made my way back to the apartment.

I sat at the kitchen counter enjoying the coffee and savoring the taste of the tart. When I finished my first cup, I got up for a refill and debated whether to also partake of the *pain au chocolat.* Who could resist the flaky puff pastry with slices of chocolate inside? Certainly not me.

It wasn't until I'd showered and dressed that I realized today was Thanksgiving in America. Because of the time difference, I planned to call my mother around eight in the evening my time. She'd be at Sydney's house then, and I could also talk to my cousin.

Since it wasn't a holiday in France, I knew all the shops would be open and left the apartment for a stop at the local florist. The French loved their flowers, and I felt it would be an appropriate thank-you to Madame Leroux for dinner.

One of the things that had struck me thirty years ago about the shops in Paris was their window displays and presentation. No matter if it was a chocolate shop, bakery, wine shop, or cheese shop, the appealing and creative window displays were like none I'd ever seen anywhere else. They were seductive, enticing a customer to stop, admire, and perhaps step inside to make a purchase. The florist shop was no exception.

Artfully arranged on the pavement in front of the shop were tin buckets holding assorted varieties and colors of flowers—purple iris, red, pink, and white cyclamen, roses, and many more that I wasn't familiar with.

I walked inside and explained to the salesgirl that I wanted an arrangement of flowers as a thank-you for a dinner invitation. She smiled and proceeded to collect this flower and that one, nodding to herself as she moved about the shop, and presently she had worked her magic and produced a large, exquisite bouquet of flowers, which she carefully wrapped in green paper for me to carry back to the apartment.

After dropping off the flowers, I spent the rest of the morning wandering streets in the Latin Quarter, pausing to browse in small shops, and to admire Paris. I allowed myself to simply soak up this ancient and beautiful area.

By the time I returned to the apartment, I had about an hour before I was due upstairs at Madame Leroux's, so I made myself a cup of coffee and settled into the cushy club chair to do some knitting. I decided that I'd pay a visit to one of the yarn shops suggested by the flight attendant the next day.

A little before one I picked up the beautiful bouquet resting on the counter and made my way up the stairs. Like the first time I'd knocked a couple days before, Madame Leroux opened the door almost immediately, with Jacques enveloped in her arms.

"*Bonjour.* Come in," she said as her eyes spied the flowers and her face lit up with a smile.

"*Pour vous,*" I told her, passing her the bouquet.

"*Merci beaucoup.* They are beautiful. Come, sit down, and I will put these into a vase."

I had no sooner sat than Jacques was in my lap and I began stroking his soft fur. "How are you, handsome boy?"

I heard a trill in reply and smiled. I could easily become attached to this cat.

I saw that the dining room table was beautifully set for three, with tablecloth, place mats, napkins, china, and crystal. Two candles flickered in the center, adding a cozy ambiance.

"Ah, they will look good here, no?" Madame Leroux asked, placing them on a marble-topped credenza.

"Perfect," I said and then remembered the word in French was *parfait.*

"Annette will be here shortly. A glass of wine before dinner?"

"Yes, that would be nice."

A red wine had already been poured into a decanter, and Madame Leroux filled two glasses.

"Thank you," I said, as she passed one to me.

"And how is my friend Worth? You have heard from him?"

"Not yet today, but he's fine. I'm sure he's anxious to be here and see his daughter and grandchildren."

I noticed that a brief frown crossed the woman's face. "His grandchildren, yes. But his daughter? Caroline can be very difficult."

"Oh, you've met her?" I asked before taking a sip of wine.

She nodded. "Oh, yes. Many times. I have known her since she was a little girl. Unfortunately, she takes too much after her mother and not enough like Worth."

So she had also met Worth's wife. Having met neither of them, I had no reply and was happy the subject ended because there was a brief knock on the door and a woman about my age entered.

"Tante Blanche," she said, scooping Madame Leroux into her arms and placing kisses on both of her aunt's cheeks. "And you must be Marin. I'm Annette. It's so nice to meet you."

She extended her hand, which I shook in return. "Thank you, and nice to meet you as well."

"And you, you spoiled cat," she said, reaching down to pat Jacques, who was still in my lap. "I see that he has managed to bewitch you with his charm."

I let out a laugh. "He's absolutely gorgeous, and I think I'm getting quite attached to him. I told your aunt that a woman in my town also has a Maine coon."

Annette smiled as she accepted a glass of wine from her aunt and sat on the sofa across from me. "They're very special cats, aren't they? Would you like one to take back to America with you?"

I thought she was joking but looked up to see her face was quite serious.

"Oh, that's right. You're a breeder, aren't you?"

"I am, and I have one male kitten left. He's the same color as Jacques. A blue classic tabby with white. He's now three months old and ready to go to a home."

Annette had caught me by surprise, and I only mumbled, "Really?" which caused her to laugh.

"I'm sorry. I didn't mean to put you on the spot like that."

"No, no," I said, as the idea started taking shape in my head. I would *love* to have a Maine coon cat. And why not? Within a month I'd be moving into my own home. Cats were wonderful companions. Studies had shown that they lowered blood pressure and increased a person's well-being. "But what would be required to fly it from France to the States?"

"You would have to have an approved airline pet carrier that will fit under your seat in the cabin. I could tell you where to purchase one in Paris, and you will need a health certificate from the vet to present to the airlines, which I would give to you. Which airline are you flying?"

"Air France," I said, as Jacques looked up at me with his beautiful almond-shaped eyes. The idea had morphed from *taking shape* to *this might be possible*.

"You would just have to call the airline to let them know for your return flight you would have a kitten in a carrier with you in the cabin. I know this requires a phone call and can't be done online. Going through security at Charles de Gaulle, you might have to remove the kitten from the carrier, let the carrier go through the X-ray belt, and you carry the kitten through the scanner. Other than that, that's about all that's required."

"Really?" I said again and now heard Madame Leroux laugh.

"What better remembrance of Paris than to bring home a French cat. But we mustn't force you," she said, getting up. "I will remove the chicken from the oven and we will eat shortly."

Both Annette and I also jumped up, causing Jacques to move from my lap to the carpet.

"I'll help you," I said at the same time that Annette did, and we followed Madame Leroux into the kitchen.

She carved the chicken while Annette mashed the potatoes and I moved the roasted vegetables into serving bowls.

As I sat at the table with them and as we passed around the platter and bowls, even though I was in France, far from home, with people I had only recently met, the *feeling* of Thanksgiving came over me. That emotion of camaraderie and sharing, making me very grateful to be where I was.

As if reading my mind, Madame Leroux raised her wineglass toward me. "Happy Thanksgiving," she said. "Welcome to my table. *Bon appétit.*"

The dinner was delicious, but even nicer was getting to know both Madame Leroux and her niece over the leisurely meal. We exchanged a lot of information about one another. I learned that Madame Leroux had one son, unmarried, and his job had taken him to live in London. Annette and I were actually the same age; she had lost her husband to cancer two years before, and she had one daughter, married with two children, who lived near Lyon. I liked them both, and I had a feeling that we would stay in touch even after I returned home.

* * *

I was shocked to glance at my watch and see it was going on five o'clock as Madame Leroux got up to begin clearing the table. Annette and I helped, and while her aunt washed the dishes, we dried and got them put away.

Madame Leroux wiped her hands on her apron and announced, "Time for dessert and coffee," and set three ramekins of crème brûlée on the table that looked like they belonged in a bakery window, but I knew they weren't store-bought. She had made them herself.

I took one look at the custardy, creamy, sugar masterpieces and was sorry I'd ingested the high-calorie breakfast earlier, but there was no way I was turning down my very favorite dessert. I smiled because I knew my mother would be proud of me.

Madame Leroux picked up a blowtorch and began burning the sugar on top to caramelize it. She expertly aimed the torch at the outer side, working her way to the inside, and produced a golden look on top, identical to that of any top pastry chef.

"*Voilà*," she said and placed them on a tray to carry into the dining room. "Annette, could you bring the coffee, please?"

After we were seated, Madame Leroux pressed the plunger on the French press and filled our cups before we began eating the magnificent dessert.

"This is wonderful," I said after one bite, and it was. It melted in my mouth, and rather than thinking about calories, I only allowed myself to soak up this culinary treasure. "It's my favorite dessert, and yours is one of the best I've ever had."

"*Merci*," Madame Leroux said, but I had a feeling she was used to high praise concerning her crème brûlée.

I sipped my coffee, and that was when I spied Jacques curled up on a stack of afghans that were folded on top of a wooden trunk in the corner of the dining room. I hadn't noticed the knitted pieces earlier.

"Oh, did you knit those afghans?" I asked, getting up to inspect them. The yarn that had been used looked old, not like the hand-painted and spun yarns available today. But the patterns were beautiful, with cables, bobbles, and various other fancy stitches. "They're gorgeous."

Madame Leroux had remained silent, and I turned around to see a sad expression on her face. She nodded slowly. "Yes," she said. "I did knit them . . . but not for warmth. They were knitted during World War II . . . to be used as a secret message."

I returned to the table and suddenly felt awkward, like maybe I'd said something wrong or brought up a subject that she didn't want to talk about. Not understanding, I took a sip of coffee and said nothing.

After a few moments, Annette reached across the table and patted her aunt's hand. "Tell her," she said. "Tell her the story behind the afghans. You should be proud, not sad."

Madame Leroux nodded. "Yes, I know, but it was such a difficult time in our country." She let out a deep sigh. "The afghans . . . they were used to alert the network that we had children hiding in our apartment."

Oh, my gosh. Of course I knew about this, had read many books concerning the subject, and she was right—it was not a good time for France. Neighbors were pitted against neighbors. It was sometimes difficult to know for sure who was against the Nazis and who might be collaborators. It was a time of great distrust.

"You hid children?" I asked softly.

"Yes, I did, along with many of my friends up and down this street. One of them had been approached by a senior member in the network. They knew we weren't Jewish; we were young mothers and housewives, and they felt perhaps we might be able to help them, by hiding the children for a few days, sometimes longer, until they were able to arrange for their papers and get them out of the country."

"They were Jewish children?"

She nodded, and I knew that if not for Madame Leroux and so many others, those children would have been sent to death camps. The thought of it made me shiver.

"And so . . . we had to devise a plan. A way that the network would know if it was safe to bring a child during the night to be hidden, and then we needed to know when, exactly, to have the child or children ready for them to come and take to the next part of their journey out of the country. They put one woman in charge. She lived down the street. All forms of communication were given to her, she passed it along to the next woman, and so on."

"And you used the afghans?"

"Yes. If it was safe for a child to be brought to our apartment to hide, we were to hang a red afghan out the window. Of course, no afghan meant *do not bring a child*. The woman in charge, Madame Gadreault, she devised the code. My color was blue. If I saw a blue afghan hanging out her window, I would know that during the night a child would be brought here. When the blue afghan appeared again, I knew that was the night they would come and retrieve the child to move on."

I shook my head in amazement. "And nobody suspected the afghans, because back then most housewives hung blankets and linens out the windows to freshen them, right?"

"That's right. It was a very clever plan."

"But still dangerous," I said. "Weren't you scared? You had a small child yourself?"

Madame Leroux fingered the linen napkin beside her coffee cup. "Yes, my Jean-Luc wasn't quite two years old, but my husband and I both had made the decision together to do this. And yes . . . many times, I was scared, should I be caught."

I let out a deep breath and then asked, "Then why? Why did you take such a risk to do this?"

"Because it was . . . women . . . women helping women," she said. "Because . . . it was the *right* thing to do, no?"

Tears stung my eyes as I reached over, clasped Madame Leroux's hand, gave it a squeeze, and whispered, "Yes . . . it *was* the right thing to do."

❧ 33 ❧

Saturday afternoon I was sitting at a sidewalk café near my apartment enjoying a cup of coffee. The weather had stayed unusually mild, and this always brought out Parisians looking to soak up any sun that they could on the terraces of the cafés. I had plans to go to Annette's apartment around three. I had spoken with Worth and my mother, and they had both convinced me to at least go and see the kitten.

As I sat there sipping coffee, my mind wandered to my mother and her first-time love, Julian Cole. This was the city he had come to, to escape the wrongful prejudice that had gripped America during the early 1950s. And because of that, my mother had been forced to let go and move forward with her own life, forgiving Julian in the process.

I thought of my mother's best childhood friend, Annalou Carter. How lost and alone that poor girl must have felt to resort to taking her life. And I thought of my mother and the years she had carried her guilt because of a false judgment. The heartache and pain she had endured until, finally, she had learned to forgive herself.

And I thought of Blanche Leroux—to protect the lives of countless children, she had risked her own life and those of her family, because, as she said, it was the *right* thing to do. But in addition to protecting the children, she was also helping the women, the frightened mothers of those children.

Down through the ages women had bonded and connected, sharing interests, social events, but most of all friendship. The friendship itself was a form of helping another woman. Perhaps a phone call or e-mail to brighten her day, a shopping spree or lunch when a woman might most need a diversion, something as simple as a shoulder to cry on or an ear that would listen.

I now thought of Fiona Caldwell, a young woman of nineteen. A woman who was obviously reaching out, trying to learn and make sense of her identity, of her life. A woman who, through no fault of her own, was the result of two adults not doing the right thing.

I let out a deep sigh before taking the last sip of my coffee. I wasn't sure if I had entirely forgiven Andrew for his infidelity. I wasn't sure if the hurt and betrayal would ever fully disappear. But one thing I did know for certain—I felt compelled to do the *right* thing. And the right thing would be to call Fiona, find out if she had plans for Christmas, and if not, invite her to Cedar Key to meet her brothers.

Before I could change my mind, I rummaged through my bag, found the slip of paper with Fiona's number, grabbed my cell, and placed the call.

After three rings, she answered.

"Fiona? This is Marin Kane. How are you?"

I hadn't been very cordial to her on the previous call, so I was surprised by the friendliness in her tone.

"Oh, Marin. How nice to hear from you. I'm fine . . . and you?" she asked, but now I could hear a bit of hesitancy in her voice.

"I'm good. Actually . . . I'm in Paris for a couple weeks, and . . ."

"Like in Paris, France?" she said, interrupting me.

I couldn't suppress a grin. "Yes, like in Paris, France. I needed some time away, and, well . . . here I am. But the reason I'm calling . . . I was wondering if you had any plans for Christmas."

"Plans?" she asked, like she had no idea what the word meant.

"Are you going to a friend's house or someplace to spend Christmas?"

"Oh. No. No, I'm not. My roommate is going up to Vermont over the holidays for a ski trip, but . . . no, I won't be going. I'll just stay here in the apartment."

My mother had been right, and I instantly felt a mixture of both shame and sadness that this girl would be completely alone on Christmas Day.

"Well, I've been giving it a lot of thought, Fiona. And I'd like to invite you to come and stay with us for Christmas. I don't know when you'd have to be back in the Boston area, but you're welcome to stay as long as you'd like."

There was a few moments' silence, and then she said, "Really? You'd really like me to come there? So you've told your sons about me and they want to meet me?"

Oh, Lord. Jason and John had escaped my mind before I'd placed the spur-of-the-moment call.

"Ah, actually . . . no. I haven't had a chance yet to discuss this with the boys. But I will. I'm staying at my mother's home at the moment. I'm in the process of purchasing my own home on the is- land, but I won't be moving in till the week after Christmas. But my mother does know about you, and she suggested perhaps you'd like to come and stay with us."

"Gosh, that's so nice of her. I would. I'd love to come. I'll have to make flight arrangements. What would be the best airport to fly into?"

"You should try to get a Delta flight out of Boston to Atlanta, where you'll switch to another flight into Gainesville."

"Okay. I'm writing this down." There was a pause. "And when I get to the Gainesville airport, will I be able to rent a car there to drive to Cedar Key? How long a drive will it be?"

"It's about an hour's drive, but . . . no, don't rent a car. You can walk everywhere around the island, so you won't need one. And . . . I'll pick you up, Fiona."

"You will?"

I was positive that was excitement I heard in those two words.

"That's really nice of you. Okay. Well, I'll get started working to book a flight. Oh, when do you want me to arrive?"

Good question. I grabbed the datebook out of my bag, scanning the December calendar. Bella was coming in on December 22; the boys were arriving the next day. God, that didn't leave me much time.

"I know this is cutting it close, but is there any chance you could try and book a flight for the twenty-fourth?"

"Oh, Christmas Eve. Gee, I'll feel like Santa flying through the sky," she said, causing me to smile. "Yes, I'll call the airline right now. Do you want me to call you back on this number?"

"I have plans for this afternoon. How about if I call you back later this evening your time?"

"That sounds great. Oh . . . and Marin?"

"Yes?"

"Thank you. So much."

I heard the line disconnect, and it was then it occurred to me that booking a flight three weeks before Christmas might be quite pricey. Well, I'd discuss that with her when I called her back.

With the excellent Métro system that Paris has, I easily found my way to Annette's apartment, which was located in the residential area of the seventeenth arrondissement.

I looked down at the ball of fur that I had cuddled against my chest. "He's adorable," I said. And he was. The moment that Annette had placed the kitten in my hands, I knew it was love at first sight, and I had instantly become the new owner of this particular Maine coon kitten.

"Does that mean you'll be taking him home?"

I nodded and nuzzled my chin against the top of his head. "Absolutely. This little guy is going to have a new home in Cedar Key, Florida."

Annette smiled. "That's wonderful. I know Worth is arriving on Tuesday for almost a week. Would you like to leave the kitten here till the day before you fly back? I'm sure you'll be out and about a lot, and you'll have to purchase a cat carrier for the flight."

"That would be great. I'll come over a week from tomorrow to get him." I sat on the sofa to take a sip of coffee, allowing the kitten to curl up in my lap, and glanced at the gorgeous mother cat. Céline was a beautiful champagne and white color. "Are you going to miss your baby?" I asked her.

Annette laughed. "Probably not. I think three months with four active kittens was enough for her. She's probably looking forward to a break. Do you have a name picked out yet?"

"His name is going to be Toulouse," I told her. "For the town and also for the painter Toulouse-Lautrec. I just like the name."

"Oh, I love it. That's perfect. And how nice that you chose a French name, based on his heritage."

I laughed. "Then Toulouse it is."

As if understanding his new name, the kitten looked up at me, blinked, and gave a soft trill. "I think he likes his name too."

Annette and I went out for dinner to a restaurant in her neighborhood, and by the time I got back to the apartment it was after eight.

I placed a call to my mother first.

"My goodness," she said, after I had shared my news with her. "A lot has happened today. I think you made the right decision about Fiona. That poor girl would have been alone on Christmas, so I'm glad you invited her."

It was then that I realized Bella would have the guest room. "Oh, no. Where on earth will we put Fiona? I hadn't even thought of that when I invited her."

"Not a problem. I have the daybed in my knitting room. I think she'll be quite comfortable in there."

"That's right. Okay, that problem's settled. The boys arrive the day before she does . . . so that's when I plan to break the news to them."

"I don't think you need to worry about that either, Marin. I think the boys will surprise you in their acceptance of this news."

I twirled a piece of yarn from the skein next to me around my finger. "I hope you're right."

"And I'm so glad you decided to purchase the Maine coon kitten. I adore Maude's cat."

"Do you think Oliver will be okay with Toulouse for a few weeks till I move into my house?"

"Yes, of course. Oliver likes cats. That won't be a problem at all. And Worth arrives this Tuesday, right?"

"Yes," I said and felt my heart beat a little faster at the thought of seeing him. "Is the work going okay there?"

"Wonderful. I know you'll be pleased. The screened area is all completed. Worth did a beautiful job. He doesn't have very much more to do inside the carriage house, and the fellows will be starting the roof work on Tuesday. I'd say we're right on track for you to open early January."

"That's great news. Well, I need to call Fiona and see if she was able to book a flight. I'll give you a call during the week. Love you," I said, before disconnecting and then dialing Fiona's number.

I could tell by the way she said, "Hi, Marin," that she had been successful booking a flight. She told me she was confirmed for Christmas Eve and would arrive in Gainesville at twelve-thirty. I could hear the excitement in her voice.

"Oh, that's great you were able to get a seat. But listen, I'm sure it was quite costly booking pretty much last minute. I'd like to help you with the price of the ticket."

"Absolutely not. I had the money. Really. So call me after you get home and settled in and we'll make the final arrangements for you to pick me up."

After I hung up, I continued sitting on the sofa thinking. It crossed my mind that for the first time in a long time, I felt really good. I also realized that everybody had been correct—with Andrew now deceased, it wasn't about him at all. That was the past. What I needed to focus on was the present. And that included his daughter, Fiona.

⚜ 34 ⚜

When Tuesday morning arrived, in addition to being excited about seeing Worth, I found that I was also nervous, and I wasn't sure why. He was easy to be with. I enjoyed his company. Could it be because being alone, without him, I had discovered how much I missed him? And that led me to realize how much my feelings for him had increased?

I pushed these thoughts aside and gazed at the recipe card that Madame Leroux had given me. She had mentioned how much Worth loved cassoulet, and I had decided to shop for all the fresh ingredients the day before and surprise him with a home-cooked dinner the evening of his arrival. After I showered and dressed, I planned to put it all together in the earthenware casserole to place in the oven later that afternoon, so that it could cook for the required three hours.

Finishing up my coffee and toast, I headed to the shower and then took extra time with my hair and makeup. My new cut and highlights from the stylist at Galeries Lafayette were very becoming, and I admired myself once again in the mirror and smiled, wondering if Worth would notice. I had also indulged in an array of new makeup suggested by the woman at the L'Oréal counter. I decided to wear my blue cashmere sweater, accented with a cotton lace scarf the color of cornflowers, and black slacks. I twirled around in front of the cheval mirror and nodded to myself. *Not bad,* I thought. I looked rested. The new hairstyle and makeup had done wonders to diminish the dragged-out look I had been seeing all year. And I could be wrong, but I swore my overall appearance now had a youthful quality, more vibrant, perky.

Just before noon, I stood in the living room surveying my efforts. Two vases of fresh flowers from the local florist—one on the kitchen table and one in the living room. The cassoulet sat ready on the counter to be popped into the oven in a few hours. Edith Piaf was softly drifting from the CD player. Gosh, if I didn't know better, I would think a bit of seduction was in the works.

A few minutes later I heard a key in the lock and saw Worth walk through the door. Okay. I admit it. My heart did a flip-flop and I know that the huge grin I felt on my face matched his.

"Hi," he said, leaving his luggage by the door and walking toward me, making me feel like a giddy teenager.

"Hi," I replied, feeling his arms around me as he pulled me into a tight embrace.

I felt his lips on mine. Gentle, little pecks before the kiss became deeper, more meaningful, and when he pulled away to hold me at arm's length, I was having a hard time catching my breath.

He cocked his head to one side. "You look gorgeous," he said, and with those three little words he made me feel like the most beautiful woman in the world. "I'm not sure what you've done, but I like it."

He pulled me close again, nuzzled his chin in my neck, and whispered, "I missed you. A lot."

I relished the feeling that he created inside me and nodded. "I missed you too. A lot," I whispered back.

After a few moments, he stepped back again and took my hand. "So. I take it you enjoyed staying in my apartment? I like the flowers," he said, nodding toward both vases.

I liked that he was so observant. He had immediately noticed my hair and makeup and now the flowers.

"I did enjoy your apartment very much, and coming here was a good thing for me. I needed that time alone. You were right. I needed to be on my own, away from home, so that I could think straight." Without even hesitating, I reached up to touch his cheek. "But I'm glad you're here. The apartment was empty without you."

The sexy smile he gave me made me know that he was just as happy to be here. With me.

He gave my hand a squeeze. "I'm going to go get unpacked, and then we'll figure out what we're doing for the rest of the day. Sound good?" he asked, heading to get his luggage and walking into the smaller bedroom.

"Sounds great," I said. "But if you're tired, don't let me stop you from taking a nap."

"Never." He swung the luggage onto the bed and began removing items and placing them in the bureau drawer. "But is there a chance you have some fresh coffee?"

"I do. You unpack and I'll go get us a cup."

I had made a stop that morning at the *boulangerie* after the florist, bringing back some flaky croissants, which I now placed on a plate. The sun was shining, and I went to open the French doors in the living room. Standing there breathing in the air, I couldn't help but feel that the universe was in perfect alignment. Yes, it had been a very difficult year, but my intuition told me things were on an upward climb.

I felt Worth's arms go around my waist as he kissed the back of my neck, and I smiled. I wasn't used to such affection, and I realized that although I wasn't used to it, the lack of this simple intimacy was something I had missed my entire married life.

"It's beautiful out," Worth said. "Let's have the coffee in the garden. Did you sit out here much?"

I shook my head as I passed him the plate of croissants, and I picked up the coffee mugs, following him outside. "This is the first time I'm sitting out here. I had the doors open a few times, but I never actually came out to sit." I looked around the small area surrounded by bushes and plants that looked like they were going into their winter hibernation.

"You were saving it for me," he said. "So you've had a good time here, haven't you?"

I nodded. "I have. I visited all the museums that I wanted to, enjoyed the sidewalk cafés, got most of my Christmas shopping done, and very much enjoyed seeing Paris all decorated for the holidays. It's been perfect. And I'm even going home with a Maine coon cat."

Worth took a sip of coffee and laughed. "I'm glad you're taking one of Annette's kittens. Céline is a wonderful cat, and I think you'll be very happy with Toulouse. We'll go shopping tomorrow to get his travel case and whatever else you'll need."

"Great," I said and then noticed after a few moments that he'd become quiet. "Everything okay?"

"Yeah," he replied, but that sure looked like a sheepish expression on his face.

"Something wrong?"

"Well . . . I've done something and I just hope you won't be upset with me."

I could only stare at his handsome face, which now showed concern, and I wondered if all that good feeling from earlier might be about to evaporate before my eyes.

"I hope you won't think I'm presumptuous." He ran a hand through his thick gray hair, and I knew this gesture indicated nervousness or anger on his part. "But . . . ah . . . last week I got to thinking."

Oh. My. God. Does he not want to see me anymore once we return home? I still remained silent, unable to say anything.

"It just seemed kind of silly . . . you know . . . for me to fly back on Sunday. Alone. And for you . . . to fly back on Monday. Alone."

Okay, he definitely had me confused. What on earth was this man talking about? I raised my eyebrows, let out a deep breath, and said, "What?"

This brought forth a grin and a chuckle from Worth. "What I'm trying to say is . . . I called the airline, canceled my flight for Sunday, rebooked my flight for Monday, with you, and I hope you won't be upset."

Upset? This man had gone out of his way to reschedule his flight just to be with me? To spend an extra day with me? Not to mention the cost that must have been involved. It took a second before I realized that my lips were parted but no words were coming out, probably making me look like an idiot.

I let out a burst of laughter as I shook my head. "Gosh, no. Why would I be upset with you? I'm flattered that you'd go to so much trouble to accomplish this. Of course I don't mind. I think it's great." And I did.

"Oh, good. And by the way . . . I also told them that Toulouse will be traveling with us, so that's all cleared and taken care of."

"Thank you so much. I had planned to do that tomorrow."

"Oh. One more thing."

I waited a second and heard him say, "You don't have your seat in economy anymore. I booked both of us for first class."

This man was amazing.

Three hours flew by with us sitting in the garden, sipping coffee and talking. The air was turning much cooler, and I wrapped my arms around myself, which caused Worth to glance at his watch.

"Hey," he said. "How about we go for a walk and find a place for wine and then an early dinner?"

I jumped up, headed into the kitchen, popped the cassoulet into the oven, and turned around to shoot a smile at Worth.

"I have a surprise for you," I explained. "Madame Leroux gave me her recipe for cassoulet, and I've made one for our dinner. It'll be ready about six."

This earned me another tight embrace. "Are you serious? What a great idea. Okay, then we'll go out, have some wine, get a baguette, and then come back here."

After we were seated at the café and the waiter had brought our wine, Worth surprised me by saying, "I wanted to tell you, Marin. I'm proud of you."

"Me? For what?"

"For allowing yourself to be open about Fiona and not holding a grudge against her."

I looked across the street to another sidewalk café filled with people. "It wasn't easy," I mumbled.

"I'm sure it wasn't. And a lot of women would not have been able to make the decision that you did."

I hadn't wanted to tell Worth about my call to Fiona on the phone, so I had just shared the story with him over coffee in the garden. Apparently, he had given it some thought.

"Well," I said. "I've learned a lot these past few months, and I've come to see that it isn't always easy to do the right thing, and sometimes we're not even sure what the right thing might be. But I finally understood, deep inside, that none of this was about Andrew anymore—he was gone. It wasn't even about Bianca. It's only ever been about Fiona—and I think Andrew proved that by what he did for her, financially, to make certain that despite a mistake on his part, his daughter shouldn't be deprived. And it's not up to me to deprive her of her brothers. Jason and John will have to make that decision."

Worth reached for my hand and bent his head to kiss me. Not a gentle, peck-on-the-lips or cheek kiss. No. A deep and very passionate kiss. But this *was* Paris, and this show of affection *was* quite commonplace after all.

35

By the time I woke on Thursday morning, sharing the apartment with Worth had come to feel quite comfortable and familiar. I glanced up at the ceiling and recalled the previous evening when Worth had returned from dinner at his daughter's home. He said the visit had gone well, they'd enjoyed a nice dinner and exchanged Christmas gifts, and it was obvious that spending time with his grandchildren meant a lot to him. He had then surprised me by saying that Caroline had extended an invitation for us to join them on Saturday afternoon for coffee. I had wondered if Worth would even mention me to his daughter. I now knew that he had, but I also wondered whose idea it had been that we should meet.

I glanced at my watch and saw it was going on seven. After slipping on my robe, I headed to the bathroom and then out to the kitchen, where the strong aroma of coffee greeted me.

"Good morning," Worth said, coming to place a kiss on my lips.

"Good morning," I repeated and couldn't help but notice how sexy he looked with his hair a bit tousled, the hint of a five-o'clock shadow on his face, and jeans and a sweatshirt his outfit.

"Coffee?" he asked, going to pour me a mug from the French press.

"Thanks," I said, taking a sip and heading to the sofa, where he joined me.

"I'm glad the dinner last night went well," I told him.

He nodded. "Yeah, Caroline seemed to be in a fairly good mood. I know she's looking forward to their upcoming ski trip."

He let out a deep sigh, causing me to turn my head toward him.

"You know, Marin, there's been something that I wanted to tell you. About Claire. About our relationship and marriage."

When I remained silent, he went on.

"I'd explained that we met in college. Claire still had her senior year to finish up after I graduated. The new semester had only begun when she informed me that she was pregnant."

So Claire had been pregnant with Caroline when they married. Not something that unusual, and I wondered why he felt the need to share this with me.

"I hated to see her drop out of college without getting her degree, but she insisted that we get married immediately. To be honest, although I certainly had feelings for her, those feelings weren't quite as strong as maybe they should have been to get married." He ran a hand through his hair and took a sip of coffee. "What I'm trying to say is, had she not told me she was pregnant, I'm not sure our relationship would have continued much longer. I was beginning to see that Claire and I didn't have all that much in common. She was much more interested in status and an upscale lifestyle than I was. But . . ."

"But you did what you felt was the right thing and married her."

He nodded. "Yeah. We had the very posh wedding that she insisted on. Claire came from money, and she was used to getting her way and reveling in the fact that she was always the envy of her friends. That meant a lot to her. Having the best."

Not an uncommon trait in some women, I thought. "But then Caroline was born and I'm sure your daughter made the marriage more solid."

"That's just it," Worth said. "Claire wasn't pregnant with Caroline when I married her. Caroline was her second pregnancy. She had a miscarriage a few weeks after we returned from our honeymoon. Well, at least she *said* it was a miscarriage."

I shifted on the sofa to better see his face. "Are you saying she could have had an abortion?"

"Oh, no. No, I'm not saying that. But later I began to wonder if Claire had even been pregnant at all. I came home from work one afternoon and she calmly told me that she'd lost the baby. When I tried to take her to the hospital, she refused. She said she'd called the doctor and his instructions were to rest for a few days. That was it. I remember being quite surprised about her lack of grief and later wondered if my own sadness at the loss wasn't even necessary."

I reached for his hand and entwined mine inside. "Hmm," I said. "Well, she wouldn't be the first woman to try and hook a man with a false pregnancy, but then she did get pregnant with Caroline."

He nodded. "Yeah, but she certainly didn't seem pleased when she discovered she was pregnant. Oh, don't get me wrong, she was a good mother, but I just don't think it was something she truly enjoyed, and of course, there were no more children."

"Makes me wonder if we ever truly know somebody," I said and thought of Andrew and how much I didn't know when we met and married.

"That's just it. Sometimes we don't really know somebody when we take those marriage vows, and over the years when we discover that we're not happy, we realize that we have two choices. We either stay and carry on, which many couples do. Or we decide being apart would give us more happiness than being together. Once Caroline was grown and on her own, I made the decision that separating was the best thing for both of us. Claire definitely was not happy, and we were living a charade in that huge house together."

"Oh," I said with surprise. "I didn't realize you were separated. I thought your marriage ended because she died."

"That *is* how it ultimately ended. I had contacted my attorney, had everything arranged financially for a legal separation . . . and that was when Claire sprung it on me that she'd just been diagnosed with breast cancer. I'm ashamed to say that at first I had my doubts and wondered if this was simply another tactic to hold on to me, but no, she hadn't been lying. But she did beg me to stay with her. She said she couldn't get through any of it alone. And she was right; she couldn't. Claire always depended on others. So I stayed."

I may not have known a lot about Andrew when I married him or even during our years together, but I knew for certain in that moment that there are extraordinary people we *do* know. People we instinctively understand. People we are in sync with and are connected to in ways that defy explanation. And I also knew that Worthington Slater was such a person to me, which also caused me to grasp the fact that although it wasn't planned, I had fallen in love with this man.

I shifted on the sofa, snuggling against his chest, and felt his arm go around me. "And so," I said, "you stayed . . . and you did the *right* thing."

We had spent the morning shopping for Toulouse, purchasing his travel case, a few toys, food, and anything else that Worth felt my new kitten might require.

He had suggested dinner at La Rotonde that evening. I loved Montparnasse and decided it was probably my favorite area of Paris. After dinner inside the restaurant we made our way to a table outside to enjoy coffee and cognac. Sitting there with Worth, once again I felt the ghosts of Hemingway and F. Scott surround me and I marveled at the fact that although it was such a cliché, I had managed to acknowledge the reality that here I was in Paris . . . and in love.

We took the Métro back to the apartment and Worth suggested a glass of wine. I kicked off my heels and settled myself on the sofa.

"I have a surprise for you," he said, passing me my glass. "Here's to us . . . and all our tomorrows."

"What beautiful words. I like the sound of that." I took a sip and then smiled. "Another surprise?"

He got up and headed to the television, slipped a DVD into the player, returned beside me, and gave me the DVD box, causing me to laugh.

"Oh, my God! You are *such* a romantic! *Casablanca?*"

Worth smiled. "It's our favorite movie, right? I thought it might be appropriate to watch it here together."

I moved into his arms for his kiss. There was no denying any longer that what I'd been feeling with Worth was pure desire, an emotion I hadn't felt in years and one that I thought might have entirely disappeared. But I now knew that it had simply been smoldering . . . waiting for Worth to reignite it.

I felt his tongue slip inside my mouth as our kiss deepened, and his hands moved down my back before gliding up to circle my breasts. I heard a moan escape me when his fingers trailed along my thigh to the inside of my leg. When he moved my panties aside and continued touching me, it was Worth's groan I heard, and it was a sound that turned me on even more.

Breathless with kissing, I allowed my own hand to touch his hardness and heard him gasp as he guided me down on the sofa to remove my clothes. Bracing himself above me, he looked into my eyes before his gaze slowly descended my body. I let out a deep breath, and when I saw a smile of approval cross his face, I felt every inch a woman, which heightened my desire.

Removing his own clothes, he positioned himself on top of me, snuggled his face in my neck, and whispered, "I love you, Marin. I've loved you from the first time I laid eyes on you at that fundraiser."

I felt his kisses on my neck and whispered back, "I love you too, Worth. I *do* love you."

His mouth found my breast before he said, with huskiness filling his voice, "God, I want you, Marin. I want you so bad."

I nodded and knew my desire was reaching the ultimate as I said, "I want you too. Make love to me."

Worth stood up, reached for my hand, and led me to the bedroom as Rick and Ilsa were falling in love. Rick's classic statement, "We'll always have Paris," would be etched into my soul.

36

I opened my eyes Saturday morning and felt Worth curled up beside me. Since making love for the first time, he had shared my bed the past two nights. Not only did I like him next to me; I liked how spontaneous he was as a lover. I had been surprised that first night to be awakened at about three in the morning to feel his hands once again stirring my desire. I had also been surprised to discover how much pleasuring me meant to him. Although the first time had been frenetic and even a bit wild with the wanting of each other, the next time had been slow, seductive, each of us enjoying the feelings that we created in each other and captivated with the intimacy of our lovemaking.

I moved slightly to better see Worth's face as he slept, and my heart turned over. I deeply loved this man. Yes, I had probably been attracted to him the first time he walked into the yarn shop, and yes, I had thought him quite handsome, but that chemistry that so many couples might initially experience doesn't always go on to become something more meaningful and solid. Sometimes it's simply lust and a physical attraction, but with Worth it was so much more than that. As I came to know him better, I came to love him for the man he was, and I was very grateful that he had come into my life. I reached up a finger to trace his jawline and saw his eyelids flutter, then open, a smile covering his face.

"Good morning, beautiful," he said, placing an arm over me to pull me close.

I snuggled into him and smiled. Was there a better way to start a day? "Good morning to you," I said. "I love you."

"I love you more," I heard him say before his hands once again caused my body to respond so easily to his touch.

"Are you sure?" I asked for the second time as I glanced in the mirror. I had decided to wear my ankle-length black skirt, gray cashmere sweater, and black fashion boots to meet Worth's family.

He laughed and came up behind me, nuzzling his face in the back of my neck. "You look gorgeous. Perfect. Don't be so nervous. We're only going for coffee."

"Right," I said. *And your daughter will be scrutinizing me,* is what I thought but didn't say. "Oh! Shouldn't we bring something? Like flowers or . . ."

Worth laughed again. "Not to worry. I picked up a box of chocolates that Caroline loves when you were at the yarn shop yesterday."

I nodded. "Right. Okay. I'm all set," I said, reaching for my coat and handbag.

Caroline and Roland's apartment was located in the eighth arrondissement, not far from boulevard Haussmann and near Parc Monceau, a very upscale and pricey area. A very Caroline area.

We were buzzed in via the intercom and took the elevator to the seventh floor. As soon as the doors opened, Worth was enveloped in hugs by a boy and girl I knew must be Yvette and Christophe.

"Grandpère, we're so happy to see you," the boy said as the girl hung on to Worth's arm. "And this is your friend?"

"Yes, I'd like you to meet Marin, and this is Christophe and his sister, Yvette."

"It's so nice to meet you," I said.

Christophe threw me a huge smile, which I found resembled Worth's. "We're happy to meet you too," he said.

"I couldn't wait to meet Grandpère's girlfriend. You are his girlfriend, aren't you?" Yvette inquired as we followed her brother down the hall.

Worth and I both laughed as he said, "Indeed she is."

I saw a tall, slim blonde waiting outside a door farther down the hall. When we got to where she was standing, she leaned toward Worth, kissed both his cheeks, and said, "It's good to see you again, Papa."

Stepping into the apartment, he said, "Caroline, I'd like you to meet my friend Marin Kane, and Marin, this is my daughter."

"It's nice to meet you," I said, noticing that not a trace of a smile had crossed her lips.

"Yes, likewise. Come on in. Michelle," she called.

A woman who was probably in her early fifties appeared in the large foyer, wearing a black dress, stockings, and shoes. A maid? Caroline had a maid?

"Take their coats, please," Caroline instructed.

"Bonjour, bonjour."

I looked up to see a man of medium height come toward us. Hugging Worth, he then placed a kiss on each of my cheeks.

"I am Roland, Caroline's husband. Welcome to our home," he said with sincerity, which was certainly more than I could say for his wife.

"Come, come sit down," he said, and we followed him into a huge living room with floor-to-ceiling windows that even on a dreary day brought brightness.

I sat beside Worth on one of the three sofas, and in one glance I could see the furniture, window treatments, and decorating were all top quality. I felt like I was sitting in a French salon of the 1930s filled with antiques and beauty.

The children curled up at Worth's feet and were clearly enthralled with their grandfather.

Caroline perched on the end of a wingback chair and began pouring coffee from a silver pot into china cups.

"So you are enjoying your stay in Paris?" Roland inquired of me.

"Yes, very much so. I hadn't been here since the year after I graduated college, so it's been wonderful to return."

"Yvette," Caroline demanded, and the child jumped up to retrieve the coffee cup and saucer extended in her mother's hand. "For Marin."

"Thank you," I said and smiled at Yvette as I accepted the coffee.

Roland began discussing some French sports teams with Worth as Caroline continued pouring coffee and Michelle entered the room with a large platter of pastries. I accepted the small dish she gave me before she dipped the platter, allowing me to choose a square of apple tart.

I looked up and smiled. *"Merci,"* I told her, and her smile to me was warm and friendly.

The only coolness in the room was emanating from Caroline. I was finding it difficult to believe that this ice princess was actually Worth's daughter.

"Do you have children?" Yvette asked, kneeling in front of me as she bit into a cookie.

"I do. I have two sons, but they're all grown now. One lives in Atlanta and one in Boston."

"Oh, that's too bad," she said, a serious frown covering her face. "I bet you must miss them."

"I do, but they're coming home for Christmas, so we'll spend some time together."

"We're going skiing for Christmas," Christophe informed me.

I nodded. "Yes, Wor...your grandfather told me. I'm sure you'll have a wonderful time."

"I guess," was all the boy said.

Caroline cleared her throat and Roland ceased talking to Worth, to look over at his wife.

She pushed farther back in the chair, daintily took a sip of her coffee, and then said, "So *how* did the two of you meet?"

I swore I felt Worth stiffen beside me and heard him say, "I've already told you, Caroline. I'm doing a favor for a friend and remodeling Marin's mother's yarn shop. We met there the first day I arrived to work."

She waved a manicured hand in the air and nodded. "Oh, that's right. I must have forgotten."

Hmm, I just bet, I thought. I had no doubt that if my female friends from Cedar Key were here with me, they'd have one word to describe this woman, and it began with a *b*.

"So," she said, placing a strong emphasis on the word. "You're a salesclerk at your mother's yarn shop?"

The question made me feel like a teenager, and although I wanted to like Worth's daughter, she was making it difficult.

I shook my head and grinned. "Ah, no. Not a salesclerk. My mother is opening a needlepoint shop on the other side of the yarn shop and I'll be running that portion of the business."

"I see," was all she said.

"I know how to knit," Yvette said, jumping up. "I'll show you the scarf I made."

She ran from the room, causing her father to smile. "Yes, Yvette has taken lessons at a yarn shop and she seems to enjoy it. I am quite proud of her."

I noticed that her mother said nothing, and a moment later Yvette returned with a beautiful scarf done in what I knew was the rosette stitch.

"See," she said, holding it out to me.

I looked at the beautiful lavender scarf and was surprised with the level of her expertise. "This is gorgeous," I said and saw that Yvette was beaming. "My goodness, that's a bit of a tricky stitch, purling two together and then knitting in the same stitch. You've done a beautiful job. How long have you been knitting?"

She glanced toward her mother and then said, "About a year, I think."

"Well, you're certainly on your way to becoming an expert knitter."

"Thank you," she said, and I was rewarded with another huge smile.

"Have you seen Amalie since you arrived?" Caroline asked her father.

Amalie? Worth had never mentioned this name to me. She sounded like a character out of a French movie.

I heard him clear his throat and looked over to see an uncomfortable expression on his face. "No. No, I haven't seen her," was all he said.

I looked back over to Caroline, and I could have been wrong, but that sure looked like a smirk on her face to me.

She let out a sigh. "Oh, that's too bad. I saw her a couple of weeks ago and she asked about you and when you'd be back in Paris. She said to be sure to give you her best . . . if she didn't see you herself."

The room suddenly became uncomfortably silent until a moment later when I heard Worth say, "What, exactly, are you trying to do here, Caroline?"

I saw a crimson blush creep up her neck to her cheeks as she coughed and looked down, avoiding eye contact with her father. "Nothing. What do you mean?"

That prissy tone of voice that she'd had since I arrived now changed, sounding more like that of a recalcitrant teenager.

"You know exactly what I mean." He reached for my hand, giving it a squeeze but not letting go, and looked directly at me. "Amalie used to manage my rental properties. She's a friend of Caroline's. A few years ago my daughter made a terrible attempt at playing matchmaker for me with Amalie. I wasn't the least bit attracted to her, but somehow Caroline managed to let her think that I'd extended a dinner invitation. Not wanting to embarrass my daughter, I did take Amalie to one dinner and explained to her that I was doing so as her employer . . . and not for any other reason. She quit a couple of weeks later, which was probably the best thing for both of us. I had been close to letting her go, due to her incompetence. And just so you know, Caroline, I want to be crystal clear with you, as I have always tried to be. I've fallen in love with Marin, and to my utmost joy, she loves me in return." He stood up and took my hand. "And now, I think we have to leave."

❧ 37 ❧

The following morning I was sitting on the sofa, enjoying my coffee and replaying the events of the day before in my head, while Worth was in the shower.

Following Worth's announcement, we'd both gotten hugs, kisses, and congratulations from Roland, Yvette, and Christophe, while Caroline had stood by mutely watching. Fond good-byes had been exchanged with Worth's son-in-law and grandchildren, but Caroline had neglected to say a word, allowing us to leave without her speaking to her father.

Worth had been quiet until we reached Le Refuge du Passé for our dinner reservation. After wine had been ordered, he'd reached for my hand, brought it to his lips, and placed a kiss on top.

"I'm sorry about that. Very sorry."

I'd shaken my head. "No. There's nothing to be sorry about. It wasn't your fault."

"Sometimes Caroline can be like an obstinate teenager, but it served no purpose whatsoever to bring up Amalie's name in front of you, except to provoke some jealousy or mistrust on your part, and I resent my daughter for doing that."

I had given his hand a squeeze and leaned over to kiss his cheek.

"You are such an honest person, and I hope you know how much I value that. So there could never be any mistrust on my part. I just feel bad that we left without her saying anything to you."

Caroline's silence hadn't seemed to concern Worth, but I hated that we were leaving Paris the next day without their disagreement being resolved.

I looked up as he entered the living room, bent down, and placed a kiss on my lips.

"Hmm, you smell nice," I said, inhaling a woodsy cologne scent from his cheeks. "Are you trying to seduce me?"

Worth threw his head back and laughed. "After last night, I'd say you're the seductress."

Yeah, he could be right. After three glasses of wine, I *had* been a bit frisky.

I took the last sip of my coffee and stood up. "Okay, I'm heading to the shower. We'll do lunch around two and then go get Toulouse?"

"Sounds great," he said, pulling me into his arms for a hug.

When I emerged from the shower, I had a brief thought about surprising Worth by walking into the living room au naturel, but decided instead to get dressed. When I entered, I'm sure a flush was creeping up my face as I saw Caroline sitting in one of the chairs talking to Worth, and I was glad that I hadn't taken that particular time to be playful.

"Hi," I said, looking first at Caroline and then at Worth, not sure what her unexpected visit was about.

Worth patted the sofa next to him. "Come sit down," he said. "Caroline has come over to tell you something."

I sat beside him, felt his hand on my knee, looked at Caroline, and waited.

Gone was the woman with an attitude of the day before. In her place was somebody who looked distinctly uneasy as she shifted in the chair, cleared her throat, and said, "Yes. Right. I wanted to say that I'm sorry, Marin. I wasn't very nice to you yesterday, and that was . . . unkind of me and uncalled for. I'm not sure what got into me, being so unfriendly, and I apologize for that."

I nodded. "Thank you. Apology accepted."

I saw her eyes dart to her father, and I think that was a look of relief I saw cross her face. "And I also wanted to say . . . I have no idea why I mentioned Amalie. I knew my father wasn't interested in her, so I'm sorry for that as well." She paused for a second and then went on to say, "And I think it's quite obvious that my father cares a lot for you. Even Roland and the children saw that. So I want you to know that I'm happy. I'm happy for the both of you, but most of all that my father won't be alone anymore and will have somebody special to spend his time with."

Well, that was quite a mouthful and quite an admission on her part. Did this mean she was giving her blessing as his daughter for us to pursue our relationship?

"Thank you again," I said and shot her a smile. To my surprise, she sent a genuine smile back to me, which softened her attractive features.

She jumped up and pointed to the kitchen table, "Oh, and I brought you both a little peace offering. Some nice wine and cheese to enjoy on your last night in Paris."

"Why don't we have some now?" I found myself saying. "Then you could enjoy it with us."

"No, no. That's for the two of you. Besides, I have to get back home. More packing to finish up before we leave on the ski trip this week."

Worth and I both stood up, and he pulled his daughter into his arms. "Thank you," I heard him whisper in her ear. "Thank you for coming over. I love you, Caroline."

"I love you too, Dad," she said, and when she broke the embrace with her father, I saw moisture in her eyes as she surprised me by pulling me into a hug, kissing both of my cheeks, and saying, "It was very nice to meet you, Marin. Please let me know when you're coming to Paris again. We can go for lunch and shopping."

"That would be great. I'd like that a lot," I said as I gave her an extra squeeze.

She gave her father one more hug, said good-bye to both of us, and was gone.

I stood there looking at Worth and smiled. "I think you were wrong. I think your daughter got a lot more of you than you realize."

Later that afternoon, I sat curled on the sofa next to Worth as we both watched Toulouse scamper around the living room. His playful antics made both of us laugh.

"Isn't he just adorable?" I said.

"He certainly is. I'm very glad you got him."

As if Toulouse knew we were talking about him, he jumped up into my lap and made that wonderful trilling sound.

"And I think he's already getting attached to you," Worth said.

I stroked the top of the kitten's head and let out a deep sigh.

I felt Worth look at me. "Everything okay?"

"Yeah. It's hard to believe that I'm leaving Paris tomorrow. What an incredible two weeks it's been. So much has happened. I almost feel like a different person."

"In many ways, you are. Do you regret leaving Paris?"

"Yes and no. I love it here. I really do. These days here with you have been so special. Something that I've never experienced before. But I'm also looking forward to going back to Cedar Key. I have some work ahead of me—telling the boys about Fiona, getting ready for Christmas, moving into my new home, and then opening the needlepoint shop. So much going on."

"And all of it good things. Well, anytime you feel the need to return to Paris, just let me know. I'd be more than happy to accompany you here. This apartment will always be ready for us."

I smiled. "I like the sound of those words, ready for *us*."

He was silent for a few moments and then said, "I've been giving some thought to a few things. Like what we plan to do about *us* when we return to Cedar Key."

I turned to face him. "What do you mean?"

"Well, we've had the luxury of spending six wonderful nights together. I won't lie; I don't like the idea of being separated once we get home."

I knew what he meant. I had also been thinking about that but had no idea how we might resolve it.

"Any suggestions?" I asked.

"I think we need to discuss our options and then come up with an agreeable solution. You're at your mother's until the week after Christmas when you'll move into your new place, but you'll have Fiona as a houseguest."

"Right. I'd love for you to stay there with me, but that certainly won't allow us much privacy. And as of right now, I don't even know how long she's planning to stay."

"Exactly, and that's fine. You need to take all of that with Fiona one step at a time. However, one thing that I do wish you'd consider is spending the weekends at my house in Ocala."

I laughed, pursed my lips, and gave him what I hoped was a coquettish expression. "Why, Mr. Slater, are you asking me to live in sin with you on a weekend basis?"

His laughter joined mine as he pulled me into his arms. "Yes, Ms. Kane, that's precisely what I'm asking you to do."

I lifted my lips to meet his before saying, "Then I accept."

After I got Toulouse settled down for the night in his crate in the living room, I joined Worth in the bedroom. Climbing into bed beside him, I let out a sigh.

"This has truly been the most glorious two weeks of my life, and it's all because of you."

"I'm flattered," he said. "But that's not entirely true. It was you who took the risk to come to Paris and make it happen."

"Yeah," I said, sitting up straighter and looking at him. "What would have happened had I not done that? Then you wouldn't have been able to let me stay here and join me. Where would we be then? Still just friends?"

"Oh, I seriously doubt that. We had moved up from friends before you even left for Paris. Some things are just meant to be . . . and I think *we* are meant to be."

I liked the sound of that. "Good, because you're so very special to me—both as a friend and as a lover."

Worth reached over to the bedside table, picked up two champagne flutes, and passed one to me. Touching the rim of mine, he said, "I love you, Marin. I love you so very much." Clinking my glass again, he smiled. "And here's lookin' at you, kid."

My smile matched his, as I knew without a doubt that Paris truly *was* the most romantic city in the world.

❧ 38 ❧

I had been home three days and was now over jet lag. The flights from Paris and Atlanta had gone well with Worth and Toulouse. I won't lie—it was a treat flying back first class seated beside Worth. Toulouse was settling in very well at his new, temporary home. My mother adored him, and Oliver had proved to be the perfect gentleman he was by accepting a feline into his domain.

I had spent my first days back in Cedar Key unpacking, doing laundry, and catching up on sleep, but now I was anxious to get downtown, see the updated work in the needlepoint shop, and visit with my friends. I pulled the golf cart to the curb in front of the coffee café and walked in to see the familiar faces of Suellen, Grace, and Chloe.

Chloe was first to jump up, scoop me into her arms, and proceed to kiss both of my cheeks. "That's how the French do it, right?" she said.

I laughed as I returned her hug. "That's exactly how they do it."

"Welcome back," Suellen hollered from the counter. "Your regular?"

"That would be great," I said as I joined Chloe and Grace at a table.

Solange sat in her stroller, and I bent down to kiss the top of her head. "This child grew while I was away," I said.

Grace nodded and smiled. "Sometimes I think I can actually *see* her growing. So . . . how was Paris? We want to hear all about it."

"Right," Chloe agreed. "Details. We want all the details."

Some of the nights spent with Worth flashed through my mind, and I could feel my cheeks getting warm. "Well . . . let's see. I loved the apartment; being in Paris was like stepping back in time, which was a good thing because so much of it was as I had remembered. I had a great time visiting some museums, doing Christmas shopping, and . . . well, just chilling out."

"It sounds wonderful," Chloe said. "So I take it that it gave you time to think and just relax. You certainly look rested. Actually, oh, wait . . . you have a new hairstyle . . . and your makeup. It's new, isn't it?"

I laughed. "I decided to visit a salon while I was there and update my hair, along with the makeup."

"You look great," Grace said. "Rested and . . . glowing."

"Here ya go," Suellen said, placing my latte in front of me.

"Thanks. Can you join us?"

Suellen pulled up a chair. "For a few minutes. So you had a great time in Paris, huh?"

Before I could say anything, Chloe said, "Grace is right. Look at her, she *is* glowing. Okay, we want the details. What's brought about this change?"

I felt my cheeks heating up again. "It's probably the new blush."

"Oh, come on," Chloe said, leaning forward. "You know we're talking about Worth. He flew over there, you were both in the same apartment, I heard he delayed coming back a day in order to fly back with you, and . . ."

"And I heard he upgraded you to first class," Suellen said, a huge smile covering her face. "So I don't think it's the new blush that's causing that glow."

"You guys are so bad," I said, stifling a chuckle. "Yeah, okay, things went well with Worth. Very well, actually. He's an incredibly nice person, and being with him alone we had a chance to really get to know each other and . . . well . . . I know it sounds cliché, but we fell in love in Paris."

Grace smiled and patted my hand. "Marin, you may not have acknowledged it before you left, but it was pretty obvious the way that Worth felt about you weeks before Paris. I think Paris only enhanced what was already there between both of you."

I nodded. "I think you're right. Being alone with no commitments or responsibilities allowed us to just enjoy each other . . . and we did."

Chloe nudged my arm playfully. "Well, good for you, girlfriend. I'm glad you listened to my advice about living your life."

I shook my head and smiled. If Chloe wanted to take credit for Worth and me becoming a couple, that was fine.

"Anything resolved about Fiona?" Grace asked.

"A lot, actually. I did a lot of thinking and came to realize that no matter what, Fiona wasn't to blame for any of what happened. Andrew is in the past, and I feel I should focus on the present— which is Fiona. So I called her from Paris, and, long story short, she's flying down here Christmas Eve day to spend some time and meet her brothers."

"Oh, that's wonderful," Grace said. "I know that was a difficult decision for you, but I think it was the right one to make."

"I agree," Chloe said. "We certainly get nowhere when we stay stuck in the past." I saw her shoot a glance at Grace. "I'm really proud of you, Marin."

"Me too." Suellen gave my arm a squeeze. "Do the boys know about Fiona yet?"

"No, they arrive on the twenty-third, so I have one day to explain everything before she gets here."

"And everything is still on track for you to move into your new home after Christmas?" she asked.

I nodded. "Yes, Victoria signed everything that was needed, I signed the documents before I left, and the attorney forwarded everything to me in the mail while I was gone. I'm now the official owner of Safe Harbor."

Three cheers went up in the café, and I laughed.

"That's great. Congratulations," Grace said.

"I'm sure you'll be very happy there. Can we help you with moving in?" Chloe asked. "We could have a moving-in party."

"That might be fun," I said. "I have to call the storage company about delivering my furniture and belongings, and I think I'll tell them to come on the thirtieth, so I'll keep you posted." I took the last sip of my coffee and stood up. "It's great to be back, and I'm glad I got to see all of you, but I have to get over to the yarn shop now."

"Oh, I think you're going to be very pleased with all the work that's been done," Suellen said. "I popped over there the other day."

"Great," I said, heading to the door, and heard Chloe yell, "Be sure to say hello to Worth for us," causing me to smile.

My mother was behind the counter talking to Raylene Samuels when I walked in.

"Oh, you're back?" Raylene said. "So how was your Thanksgiving in Paris?"

I saw my mother's eyebrows rise as she tightened her lips.

"Actually, I skipped Thanksgiving this year, but I did have a wonderful dinner that day at a friend's apartment."

Raylene sniffed. "Well, I'm sure the French don't know the first thing about Thanksgiving."

I suppressed a chuckle and thought, *And I guess you don't know the first thing about the history of Thanksgiving.*

"Was Toulouse all settled when you left the house?" my mother asked.

"Yeah, he was fine. I'm sure Oliver will take good care of him."

"Toulouse? Who's Toulouse? Did you bring a friend back from Paris? I didn't know a thing about this." Raylene swiveled her head from my mother to me.

I knew it absolutely killed her to be the last to find out anything on the island.

"I did bring a friend back," I said with a serious expression. "A furry one."

"What? What do you mean? What on earth are you talking about?" Raylene sputtered.

My mother burst out laughing. "Marin brought back a beautiful Maine coon kitten."

"A kitten? All the way from Paris? Well, if that isn't just the silliest thing I've ever heard." Raylene picked up her bag, shook her head, and left the shop.

I shrugged. "That'll keep her talking for a while. Is Worth next door?"

"He is. Working away. Come on," my mother said, taking my arm. "Let me show you all the work he's gotten done."

We walked through the archway, and I gasped as Worth turned around and smiled. "Like it?" he asked.

My eyes took in the painted pale blue walls, the beautiful border print with dragonflies, and the tile floor. "Oh, I absolutely love it. God, you've done a super job, Worth. It looks wonderful."

"That's what I told him," my mother said.

He walked toward me and placed a kiss on my lips. "I'm glad you like it."

"I couldn't be any more pleased." I twirled around in the room. "It's actually looking like a shop now. I can't wait for my stock to be delivered, so I can begin arranging everything."

"Everything should arrive by the first week in January," my mother said. "Now come take a look at the patio area."

We followed her through the yarn shop and back room to the outside, where she gestured with her hand. "What do you think?"

It didn't even resemble the overgrown, grassy area that had existed before I left for Paris. Two sides were screened in, and a partial roof overhang that connected to overhead screening jutted out from the carriage house at the back. Cement flooring covered what had once been weeds, and my mother had already arranged cozy white wicker furniture in the area for the women who would be enjoying this spot for knitting and needlepoint.

"Oh, wow! It looks fantastic! I just love it. What an ideal place for women to relax and visit in the good weather." I gave my mother a hug. "You're a true visionary. Our customers are really going to enjoy this."

My mother nodded. "I think they will. I was just waiting for you to return before I officially opened it up to the women."

"Well, I'd say it's officially available now, and how's the carriage house coming along?"

"Pretty well," my mother said as she removed a set of keys from her pocket and unlocked the door.

We stepped inside and she flipped the light switch. The walls had been painted, the ceiling was finished, and the room had definitely shaped up since I'd seen it last.

"This will be wonderful, and I'm sure Chloe will love the extra room for yarn."

"I think she will," my mother said, leading the way back to the yarn shop. "The only things left are to finish off the roof, and then Worth can get the lighting installed in the needlepoint shop, and the fellows have to get the tile down on the floor in the carriage house. So it won't be much longer till our new business is up and running."

I was definitely excited about my new venture. "Thank you both for making this happen." I glanced at my watch. "Are you sure you don't want me to begin back at work till next week?"

"No, I'm fine here alone today, and Chloe will be in tomorrow and Saturday. Weren't you going to Gainesville today to pick up some Christmas decorations?"

"I am, well . . . we are. Worth offered to drive me. I'm going to get some for the shop, too, and I'll come over on Monday when we're closed to get it all decorated. We'll get the tree at home done tomorrow night."

"That sounds good. Oh, Worth, why don't you join Marin and me for dinner tomorrow evening? We could use your help getting those high spots on the tree."

He laughed and said, "I'd enjoy that. Thanks."

I had updated my mother when I got back from Paris about Worth and me. She had been genuinely pleased, and I knew she liked Worth and was happy we were now together as a couple.

"Okay, I'll be back by seven, but don't wait dinner for me," I told her before we headed out.

39

My mother and I had spent the morning baking and preparing dishes for the Christmas party that evening at the yarn shop. It had become tradition to have a gathering the Thursday before Christmas for our knitting group, and each year seemed to add more people.

The counter was filled with fried green tomatoes, mullet dip, and shrimp. Cocktail meatballs were simmering in the Crock-Pot, and a pistachio cake was in the oven.

"Ten more minutes on the cake," my mother said, coming into the kitchen followed by Oliver and Toulouse.

I stroked the top of Oliver's head as I bent down to scoop up my kitten. "I think these guys like the smell of the food," I said, nuzzling Toulouse's head under my chin. "No shrimp for you, I'm afraid. Maybe when you're older."

"Did you have time to wrap our Christmas exchange gifts?"

"All done. They're in a bag on the dining room table."

"How about another cup of coffee while we wait for the cake?"

"Sounds good," I said, placing Toulouse back on the floor. I smiled as he scampered off with Oliver. He'd been with us only a little over a week but had settled in very well. He was a delight to have around and provided my mother and me with many chuckles.

I joined my mother at the table and took a sip of coffee.

"The house will be filling up come Sunday," she said. "What time do you think Bella will arrive?"

"She said midafternoon, and you're right about the full house. Between her three Scotties, Oliver, and Toulouse, it'll be like a mini-zoo here."

My mother laughed. "It'll add to all the fun," she said, and I knew she meant it. "And everything's all arranged for Fiona's flight for Tuesday?"

"Yes, she arrives at twelve-thirty. I spoke to her on Sunday, and she seems very excited about coming."

"I'm sure she is. I'm looking forward to meeting her."

"Actually, I am too. I just hope the boys take the news okay."

"I think they'll be fine. Do they know about you and Worth yet?"

I shook my head. "No. I was planning to spring that on them as well when they arrive. They'll probably be sorry they came."

A smile crossed my mother's face. "I don't think so. By the way, I'm very happy about you and Worth. I think he's a very nice man. I had a chance to get to know him better that first week you were in Paris. There was no doubt in my mind how much he cared for you."

"Really?"

"Yes. He enjoyed bringing your name into our conversations and would tell me if he'd just spoken to you on the phone. Those last few days, it was obvious he was counting down the minutes to get on his flight to be with you."

That made me feel good. I knew he loved me. He expressed it in so many different ways. But it's always nice to have somebody else confirm the fact.

"He's a very special person," I said and let out a sigh. "I never would have thought it possible that I'd meet somebody like him or have a man like him in my life. The way his daughter acted toward me when we first met could have presented a problem, but Worth wasn't about to accept her behavior." I had told my mother the story about our meeting the day after I got home.

She nodded. "I agree. When he told her you were leaving, that certainly sent her a very clear message. The ball was then in her court, but she knew he wasn't going to put up with her foolishness.

And you're right—if he were a different man, that could have been a major problem. I'm glad she backed down, though, and it all worked out."

"Me too," I said as my mother got up to remove the cake from the oven. "That smells heavenly."

"We'll let it cool and then get the green frosting on it." She placed the cake on a wire holder and said, "Maybe you could beat up the pistachio pudding and Dream Whip? I need to go get something."

"Sure," I said as she headed toward her bedroom.

A few minutes later she returned with a medium-size gift bag and passed it to me.

"Christmas gift so early?" I asked, turning off the beaters.

"No. Not a Christmas gift. Something that I made for you while you were gone, and I'd like you to have it now."

Curious, I reached inside, removed an item wrapped in tissue paper, and opened it to see a gorgeous shawl done in a shade of paprika-colored yarn. "Oh, Mom, this is gorgeous!" I said, holding it up in front of me to better see the design, which looked a little familiar. "Is this the design of the Cedar Key scarf?"

"It is, and along the edges are some yarn overs to give it a bit of a lacy, open look. I designed the pattern, and I've called it the Compassion Shawl."

I wrapped it around my shoulders. "I love it. Thank you. But what's the significance of the name?"

"I designed it for you, Marin. I'm very proud of you for the compassion that you've shown in forgiving Andrew and accepting Fiona. The lace work indicates a willingness to be open, and I wanted you to have something symbolic to mark this milestone in your life."

I felt moisture stinging my eyes as I pulled my mother into an embrace. "Thank you so much. This shawl means the world to me, and every time I wear it I'll remember one of the toughest life lessons that I had to learn."

"Good," my mother whispered in my ear. "That's what I was hoping."

* * *

The yarn shop was filled to capacity with women, the noise level was at an all-time high, and even though the Christmas music playing on the CDs was drowned out by laughter, nobody seemed to mind.

I stood in a corner sipping punch and watched the interaction. Sydney, Monica, and Clarissa sat beside one another on the sofa, eating and talking. Chloe, Grace, and Maude were mingling in the crowd. Leigh Salenger, owner of the daycare center in town, was in a discussion with Resa and Berkley, and my mother was making the rounds to be sure that everybody had enough food on their plates and punch or coffee in their cups. I smiled as warmth filled me. There was so much to be said for female friendships. I recalled Blanche Leroux and the vital friendships she had forged during World War II. I thought about my mother and the friendship with Annalou Carter that was cut way too short. I saw Flora and Corabeth laughing with Polly and Raylene. I loved each and every one of these women for a different reason—and I felt very blessed to have them in my life.

The door opened and Josie and Shelby Sullivan walked in, carrying a Crock-Pot and wrapped gifts.

"I hope we're not too late," Shelby said. "Josie was late getting home from work."

"Not at all," my mother told them, taking the Crock-Pot while I went to greet them and placed their gifts under the small Christmas tree in the window.

"So how have you been?" I asked Shelby when Josie moved to the other side of the room to talk to Monica and Grace.

"Oh," she said with an exasperated sigh. "This time of the year seems to get more tiresome. So much to do with the baking, cooking, decorating, and I just wish Josie showed as much interest in the Christmas season as I do."

I noticed that Shelby did look tired, but she had been working hard all year to finish up her current manuscript and then leaped right into all the work of the holidays. I also knew that Josie did not put as much emphasis on material things as her mother did. I was sure she loved the Christmas season, but in a more subdued way.

"Yeah, it is a lot of work," I told her, "but your decorations in front of your house look spectacular again this year." Worth and I had driven past the night before, and once again, Shelby Sullivan had managed to create a winter wonderland on her property, to the delight of Cedar Key residents and people from surrounding areas.

"Thank you," she said, reaching out to touch my shawl. "This is just beautiful. Did you make it?"

"No, my mother did. She designed the pattern and called it the Compassion Shawl."

"I just love it," she said but didn't question the definition of the name. However, Polly overheard us and turned around.

"I've been meaning to tell you, Marin, that shawl is simply gorgeous. You said Dora made it for you?"

My mother walked up to us as I nodded and said yes.

"What's the significance in the name?" Polly asked.

My mother looked at me. "Well, it has special meaning for Marin, so it's up to her if she'd like to share it."

"Oh, please tell us," Polly said. "And I was thinking, if it was okay with both of you, that maybe we should all make the pattern in our yarn group and then sell the shawls at the Arts Festival in April to raise money for a good cause."

I felt that sharing was a major part of friendship, and what could be nicer than women coming together to make something to help others, like we did with the Cedar Key scarf?

My mother looked at me and waited for an answer.

"I think it's a wonderful idea. After we open our gifts, I'll make an announcement and tell all of you at the same time the story behind the shawl."

By nine o'clock everybody was ready to open gifts, and a lot of oohs and aahs ensued as each gift was unwrapped and held up for everybody to see.

When we finished, my mother gently tapped a spoon against a coffee cup for quiet and attention.

"Merry Christmas, and I want to thank all of you for your patronage throughout the year and for coming this evening. With the opening of Marin's Serendipity Needleworks in January, I think we have an exciting year ahead. After the holidays we'll be ready to move a lot of the yarn out to the carriage house, and I think you'll enjoy having more room to browse all the different yarns. I also wanted you to know that beginning next week the patio area out back will be open and ready for all of us to use."

A round of applause and laughter filled the room.

"Many of you have commented on the shawl that Marin is wearing this evening. I did design the pattern, and I made it for Marin. You might see that most of the design is the same one we used in the Cedar Key scarf, with the addition of a bit of lace along the edges. Some of you have inquired as to why I chose to call it the Compassion Shawl . . . but since it is Marin's, I'm going to let her tell you."

I walked to where my mother was standing and felt a bit nervous. Although I knew each of these women quite well, I couldn't be sure how they would accept what I was about to tell them. I let out a deep breath as I looked down and fingered the edge of the shawl and then looked up to a group of expectant faces.

"Well," I began. "As some of you know . . . I recently found out that Andrew has a daughter. A daughter that I knew nothing about until a couple of months ago." I paused, trying to form my thoughts in my head. "Fiona Caldwell is now nineteen years old and lives in the Boston area. Needless to say, I was quite shocked and had a lot of difficulty dealing with this news. I was informed by Andrew's attorney that Fiona wanted me to contact her. She wanted to meet me and my sons, who of course are her half brothers." I cleared my throat before going on. "I spoke to her once before leaving for Paris and had no idea what to do. However, while I was in Paris I was able to think and sort things out . . . and I've made the decision to have Fiona come here to visit. She will arrive on Christmas Eve. My boys arrive the day before, which is when I will be sharing this news with them." I glanced at my mother. "And because of my decision, my mother felt that I had done the right thing, which inspired her to design this shawl and call it the Compassion Shawl." I swallowed before I continued. "She said it represented the compassion I'd shown by forgiving Andrew and accepting Fiona."

Loud cheers filled the room as I felt myself being enveloped in my mother's arms and heard murmurs of love from the women.

"What a beautiful story."

"Dora, what a wonderful idea you had."

"Isn't it just gorgeous? I have to have that pattern."

I wiped at my eyes and held up a hand. "And I also wanted to explain that the reason the color of the yarn is paprika is because the color of forgiveness is orange. Polly said earlier that she'd like our knitting group to make some of these shawls for us to sell at the Arts Festival in the coming year, and I think it's a great idea."

The agreement was unanimous, and my mother said she'd have the pattern printed and ready to pass out at our first knitting group after the holidays.

Before the evening was over, every single woman had approached me to offer support about Fiona's impending visit, saying they looked forward to meeting her and would welcome her to the island.

Yes, I thought, *there is a lot to be said for female friendship, and I am so very glad to be a part of it.*

40

In the almost two weeks that Worth and I had been back from Paris, we'd managed to have a few nights together. A couple of times I spent the night with him in his cottage at the Faraway, and one evening we went to Safe Harbor to relax with wine and ended up spending the night. But we were far from settling into any kind of regular routine of being together.

So when he asked me to come with him to his home in Ocala on Saturday afternoon and spend the night, I jumped at the invitation. Bella was arriving the next day, the boys the day after that, and then Fiona. Who knew when we'd have time to be alone together in the near future?

I allowed my head to rest back on the car seat, eyes closed, soaking up the warm December sun, which touched my face in the open convertible, and listened to Pachelbel's Canon on the CD player. After a few minutes I felt Worth's hand on my knee and glanced over at his handsome face. His eyes were focused on the road, but I caught the smile on his lips.

"Happy?" I asked.

"Very much so, and you?"

"I am." I liked so many things about being with Worth, but one of the best was the easy feeling he created when I was with him. Over the years with Andrew, a lot of our time together had been stressful, brought about by Andrew's moods and always resulting in an undercurrent of tension. But it was so different with Worth— I didn't have to be careful what I said or how I expressed an opinion. I was coming to understand that if I didn't agree with him, that was okay and not cause for anger or harsh words on his part. I liked this easy feeling, this being myself, this sharing of time and love with another person.

"I have a surprise for you when we get to the house," I heard him say and sat up straighter in my seat.

"You like surprises, don't you?" I asked.

"I like giving you surprises, yes."

"And you're not going to give me a hint, are you?"

I saw the devilish grin on his face and knew the answer was no.

Just before we pulled up to his driveway, Worth's cell phone went off. He answered and I heard him laugh before saying, "Yeah, it's fine. She'd probably enjoy that." There was a pause and he said, "Okay, great. Bye."

"That was Doyle," he explained. "He said he had some Christmas cookies that Suzette was drooling over and wanted to be sure it was okay if she had one."

I smiled. "He's a good dog sitter."

"He is, and with Doyle taking her, it gives us a bit more alone time."

I followed him into the house, with him carrying my overnight bag. Strange, how at almost fifty-seven years old this still felt a bit risqué, and I smiled. It might be risqué, but it also felt right.

"Lunch and some wine first," he said, depositing my bag near the staircase and heading to the kitchen.

I looked out to the patio area and noticed that the sun had disappeared and the sky was becoming overcast. "Are we eating in or out?"

Worth opened the fridge and removed a bottle of champagne along with various plates before glancing outside. "I think we'll be okay out there. The table's under the roof in case it rains."

I nodded and went to the cabinet to remove dishes and to the drawer for silverware. I was beginning to feel quite at home in this kitchen and smiled because I thought that was a very good thing.

I had the patio table all set and walked back into the kitchen to hear the pop of the champagne cork. "I love that sound."

"Me too." Worth filled two flutes with the amber liquid. Passing me one and holding his up, he said, "Merry Christmas, Marin. I know it's going to get pretty hectic over the next week, so I want today to be our special Christmas together. I love you . . . and I'll always love you."

I raised my glass and said, "Merry Christmas, Worth. I'm glad our paths have crossed, and I love you too. You mean the world to me."

He took my glass, placed it on the counter, and pulled me into his arms before touching his lips to mine. It still surprised me that the closeness of him caused me to feel a heat radiating through my body that I wasn't used to. I felt the pressure of his hand on my back increase as our kiss deepened. When we pulled apart, I felt lightheaded and tingly, blowing out a deep breath.

"That was nice," I said.

His lips touched mine again and he nodded. "It was very nice, but . . . I guess we should have lunch before we get too carried away."

I laughed as I picked up my champagne flute and followed him to the patio.

Over a delicious lunch of quiche and salad, our conversation never wavered. Something else I loved about Worth—his ability to talk about a variety of topics and make all of them interesting.

Just as we were about to have coffee and cognac, the first raindrops began to hit the pool, creating ripples in the water, and the temperature began to get cooler.

"Why don't we take this inside?" he said. "We can sit in the living room and I can get a fire going."

I laughed. "I know what a romantic you are, but don't you think it's too warm for a fire?"

"Nah, it's only about, what? Sixty degrees?" He placed the tray with our coffee and cognac on the table in front of the sofa and proceeded to get a fire going in the fireplace as I curled up on the huge pillows on the floor.

Once he got the fire roaring, he sat beside me on an adjacent pillow.

I took a sip of coffee and literally felt my body relax. That was another thing I noticed when I was with Worth—whatever stress I might have been feeling magically vanished.

He reached for my hand, encircling it in his, and I smiled. "This is nice," I said.

"It is," he agreed.

I let out a sigh of contentment.

"Have you given any thought to our long-term arrangements?" he asked.

"Not really. I have no idea how long Fiona plans to stay down here, but I wouldn't think it would be longer than a couple of weeks, if that. I mean, I think she really wants to meet Jason and John more than me, and they're only going to be here for five days. She may be gone before I even move into my new house."

I felt his nod against my shoulder. "True. Well, would you have any problem with me staying at your new place once Fiona leaves? I could stay there during the week, and then on the weekends ... we could come here."

I smiled. "Sounds like the best of both worlds to me."

"Good," he said, getting up. "I have something for you."

He left the room and returned with a small box beautifully wrapped in Christmas paper and ribbon.

"My surprise?" I asked.

He sat beside me and shook his head. "Well, maybe one of them. The one I was referring to will come later. This is your Christmas present, and even though it's still a few days away, I wanted to give it to you now. Alone."

I carefully removed the paper to reveal an imprint from a jewelry shop in Paris and looked up at Worth, who shot me a smile.

Opening the box, I saw a gorgeous gold bracelet with a gold charm of the Eiffel Tower dangling from the center. "Oh, Worth! It's just beautiful." I held it up to the light of the fireplace, and that's when I noticed . . . Were those diamonds arranged down the side of the tower? Oh, my God, they were! I knew without a doubt that this was the most expensive piece of jewelry that I'd ever owned.

"Do you like it?" he asked.

"Like it? My God, I love it. But . . . I'd be so afraid to lose it or . . . have something happen to it."

He let out a laugh. "Don't be silly. What's the sense of having something you love, really love, if you can't enjoy it. Here," he said, reaching for my wrist. "Let me fasten the clasp so you can wear it."

I extended my arm and saw the look of pure joy on his face as he attached the bracelet to my wrist. "Perfect. It's perfect for you. Our time together in Paris was so special that I wanted you to have something meaningful to remember those days . . . and nights."

As if I could ever forget. I threw my arms around his neck. "Thank you, Worth. Thank you so much, but I'll always remember our time together in Paris. You don't need to worry about that."

I thought of the cable sweater and matching scarf that I had knitted for his Christmas present and felt embarrassed. I had it tucked away in my overnight bag, but after the extravagant gift he'd just presented me with, mine seemed shabby in comparison.

"What's wrong?" he asked.

Add another thing to the reasons why I loved Worth. He had this uncanny ability to simply look at my face and decipher my emotions.

"I have your gift with me, but . . ."

"But?"

I held up my wrist. "After this extraordinary gift from you . . . I'm afraid mine can't compare."

He pulled me into his arms. "Don't be silly," he said against my ear. "Please. Don't feel like that. I didn't buy you this bracelet because of the cost. I bought it because I wanted it to have special meaning for you. Please accept it with my love."

He was right. I *was* allowing price to come before his sincere reason for choosing this particular bracelet. I nodded and got up, heading to my bag in the foyer.

I returned and passed him the gaily wrapped box. "Merry Christmas, Worth. I hope you'll like it."

I swear the grin and expression on his face reminded me of a five-year-old as he ripped off the paper and opened the box. He removed the pale blue sweater with twisting cables down the front and held it up. "You made this for me?"

I nodded.

He reached back into the box and removed the matching scarf. "And this?"

I nodded again, and that's when I noticed the moisture gleaming in his eyes.

He took a deep swallow and said, "This is the nicest thing anybody has ever done for me." Pulling me into his arms, he whispered, "Thank you, Marin. I love it and I love you. So very much."

He was definitely right. Price had nothing to do with a gift, if it was given in love. I had made many knitted items over the years for Andrew and the boys, and I couldn't recall ever witnessing such deep sentiment from the recipient.

"I'm glad you like it," I said against his ear. "And I love *you,* Worth. You are the love of my life."

He pulled away and fingered the sweater. "When I wear this, I will feel like your arms are wrapped around me. Thank you again." He replaced the sweater and scarf in the box and stood up.

"Okay," he said. "That other surprise I had for you? You have to give me a little bit of time to arrange it."

I looked up with what I was sure was a bewildered expression on my face.

He laughed, and I saw a mischievous gleam in his eye. "Enjoy the rest of your cognac. I'm going upstairs and I'll be back to get you shortly."

I shook my head and smiled. What on earth was this man up to?

About fifteen minutes later Worth walked into the room, reached down for my hand, and led me upstairs to the master suite.

"Close your eyes," he said, not letting go of my hand.

I did and felt him guiding me forward.

"Okay. You can open your eyes now."

When I did, I saw we were standing on the threshold of the room that contained the Jacuzzi, and I gasped. The entire room shimmered with candles, which had been placed all around the tub, on the vanity, everywhere—all different sizes, creating a seductive glow. On one end of the tub was a large vase of yellow roses. On the opposite end was a silver ice bucket cooling a bottle of what I had no doubt was Piper-Heidsieck. Coming from speakers in the ceiling was the haunting voice of Edith Piaf. The fragrance filling the air was a mixture of patchouli, sandalwood, and musk, and the tub jets bubbled enticingly.

"You did all of this?" I couldn't quite believe my eyes. The romance of it was overwhelming, but to know it was Worth's idea made it all that much more incredible.

"I did," he whispered against my ear as I felt him unzip my jeans while placing short bursts of kisses on my lips. "I thought we could enjoy this special time . . ." He paused to lift my sweater over my head. "Together."

I felt him slide my jeans to the floor as his lips found mine again. His kisses intensified as he unhooked my bra, and it too found its way beside the jeans. Heat radiated through my body as he now slid my panties to the floor before placing his mouth on my breast. Just when I was sure I couldn't control my desire for him another moment, he stepped back, gave me that sexy smile of his, reached for my hand, and led me to the steps of the Jacuzzi.

"Now . . . I will show you what true relaxation is," he said, as that devilish grin returned to his face.

❧ 41 ❧

On the drive back to Cedar Key the following morning, I allowed my mind to recapture snippets of the night before. I knew without a doubt that I had never experienced such a seductive and fulfilling time with any man. Worth was definitely unique. In the ways he gave pleasure and the way he enjoyed pleasure. I smiled to myself as he drove along SR 24 and soft music filled the car. Teenagers and young people think they have the edge on sex, but I would disagree. Perhaps they do with just *sex,* since hormones are raging and lust is uppermost in their minds. But I had come to know that there is a distinct difference between sex and making love. And what Worth and I shared as an adult couple was a genuine connection of two people, not only in love but in sync.

"Thinking good thoughts?" I heard him say as he reached over to rub my leg.

I smiled. "Always. I was thinking about last night. Thank you for that. It was wonderful. All of it."

"It was my pleasure," he said, and I knew he meant that.

We maintained a comfortable silence for the rest of the drive. As we approached the Number Four bridge, I looked to my right and saw that it was high tide. The rain of the day before was gone and sunlight glittered on the water.

Worth reached for my hand. "I'm going to miss you," he said.

Although we would be in each other's company over the next week, I knew what he meant. "And I'll miss you too." I let out a sigh. "We might have to devise creative ways to be together," I told him, and this brought forth Worth's laughter.

"Well, this sports car doesn't have a backseat, so, yeah, we might have to get mighty creative."

I laughed at the thought.

Worth dropped me at my mother's before going to pick up Suzette with a promise he'd be back in time for dinner. He wanted to give me some girl time with Bella, which I thought was considerate.

Toulouse was curled up beside me on the sofa as I sat knitting. Shortly before two, I heard a car pull up out front and looked through the window to see that Bella had arrived. "She's here," I called to my mother before going outside to greet her.

Bella had just gotten out of the car and was stretching.

"Long drive?" I called as I went toward her, pulling her into a hug.

"Nah, it was a good trip, but I'm happy to be here," she said, before standing back and taking a good look at me. "You look terrific. Paris must have agreed with you—in addition to maybe something else?"

I let out a laugh and said, "Ah, yeah, you could say that. A certain Worthington Slater might be responsible."

That caused Bella to pull me into another embrace. "Good for you. And when do I get to meet this special man?"

"He's coming for dinner this evening." I bent toward the backseat window to see Bella's three Scotties sitting patiently. "Aww, Silas, Sammy, and Sylvia are adorable. Come on, let me help you unload the car."

"They have their leashes on, so you can take them and I'll get my luggage."

My mother and Oliver greeted us at the front door. The four dogs circled one another and did the requisite sniffing, and then Oliver ran to get his ball, dropping it right in front of Sylvia.

Bella came in behind me and laughed. "I think that was Oliver's welcome. Where's your little Toulouse?" she asked, going to give my mother a hug.

"Welcome, Bella. I'm so glad you could come to stay with us. I think Toulouse scampered off to the bedroom. You know where the guest room is. You can go put your luggage in there."

I unclipped the leashes just as Bella walked back into the living room carrying Toulouse.

"I found him," she said. "And he's gorgeous." Sitting on the sofa, she called her three Scotties to her. "Now, this is Toulouse and he's only a kitten, so I expect you all to be on your best behavior."

Toulouse sat quietly in Bella's lap, allowing the dogs to sniff him, before all three trotted off to join Oliver.

"So much for that," I said with a smile. "I think the animal kingdom will be just fine during the coming week."

"I have a pork roast in the oven," my mother said. "And dinner will be at five-thirty. Why don't you girls get yourself some wine and go relax on the patio. I'm just going to get the vegetables peeled."

"Oh, can't we help?" Bella asked.

"No, no. You two need to catch up and have a nice visit. I'm fine."

I headed to the kitchen, uncorked a bottle of Beaujolais, filled two glasses, and joined Bella outside.

"Here you go," I said, sitting in the lounge beside her.

She leaned over and touched the rim of my glass with hers. "Thanks. Here's to friendship."

I nodded. "A very long friendship it's been." I took a sip and smiled as I saw Oliver romping in the yard with the Scotties.

"So," Bella said, drawing out the word. "Tell me about Paris. More importantly, tell me about Worth."

"Paris was wonderful. As wonderful as I always remembered it. And Worth." I let out a deep sigh. "He's pretty wonderful too."

Bella swiveled on the lounge to face me. "I'm so happy for you, Marin." She reached out to touch my bracelet. "From Worth? It's gorgeous."

I nodded. "My Christmas present. He wanted me to have a special memory of our time in Paris . . . but I don't think I needed a bracelet for that."

"He sounds pretty amazing."

"I think he is. He's a good person, fun to be with, very considerate, not to mention extremely romantic . . . and I think he knows me better than any man has."

Bella took a sip of her wine. "He sounds like the polar opposite of Andrew."

"I guess he is."

She reached over and patted my hand. "It wasn't that I didn't like Andrew, Marin. I just never thought he was the man for you. God knows, you certainly had a decent life together, you raised two wonderful sons, but . . . I always worried you had relinquished your passion when you met Andrew. That you didn't allow yourself to be the person you were meant to be, but rather conformed to what Andrew wanted."

I took another sip of wine and nodded. "I think you're right. Being with Worth, I feel different. Everything feels comfortable and easy."

"And it shows," she said, giving my arm a squeeze.

Shortly before five, Worth rang the bell, and when I opened the door to see him wearing the blue cable sweater that I had knitted for him, I felt a huge smile cross my face.

"Hi," I said as he pulled me into his arms and let his lips brush mine. "You wear that sweater well."

"I'm glad you like it. A very special woman made it for me."

I kissed his cheek. "And I'm glad I'm that special woman."

He held out a beautiful bouquet of flowers. "For your mother."

"She's in the kitchen with Bella. Come on."

I made the introductions between my best friend and the man I loved and smiled as he gave Bella a hug, saying, "It's nice to finally meet you."

"Same here," she said, sending me a wink of approval.

"Thank you for the gorgeous flowers, Worth. I'll just get these in a vase," my mother told him. "Why don't we all have a glass of that nice Beaujolais on the patio. Dinner will be ready shortly."

Over dinner I noticed that Bella and Worth kept up a steady stream of conversation. There were no awkward lapses like had sometimes happened with Bella and Andrew. I smiled and wondered how it would go when my sons met Worth the next day.

"So you're all prepared to get Fiona at the airport on Tuesday?" I heard Bella ask, and I nodded.

"As ready as I'll ever be. Right now I'm more concerned about telling Jason and John tomorrow. After I get through that, then I'll worry about Fiona."

Worth reached over to take my hand. "It'll all go fine. You'll see."

"I think Worth's right," my mother said. "The boys are adults now. This would be an uncomfortable situation if they were still young, but I think they'll understand that we all make mistakes."

"And you don't know how long Fiona plans to stay?" Bella asked.

I shook my head. "I didn't want her to think she could only stay a certain amount of time. So I figured I'd leave it up to her."

Later that evening after Worth had left and my mother had retired for the night, Bella and I sat curled up on each end of the sofa, sipping herbal tea, reminding me of when we shared our house in Gainesville.

"This is fun," I said. "Having you here. I have some good friends on the island, but nothing compares with a best friend. Somebody who knows your history. Who knows you better than any other girlfriend."

Bella nodded. "I agree. We do have a lot of history together over the years. But I never knew you to hold back on me."

"What? What do you mean?"

"About Worth. You were spot-on in your description of him. It's easy to see what a great guy he is. It's also pretty obvious that he's crazy about you from the way he looks at you. But you neglected to tell me how handsome he is."

I laughed. "Hmm, I guess maybe I did. I think he's a keeper."

Bella arched an eyebrow and smiled. "You think?"

42

Jason and John had flown into Gainesville, hooked up at the airport, rented a car, and driven to the island, arriving at the Faraway in the early afternoon on Monday.

I got a call from John saying they'd just checked in and would be over within a half hour.

"The boys are here?" my mother asked, walking into the kitchen.

"Yeah," I said, letting out a deep breath.

She nodded as she prepared to make a pot of coffee. "Are you sure you wouldn't rather I go in my room or outside while you talk to them?"

"Absolutely not. Bella didn't even have to leave, but she insisted on taking the dogs downtown for a walk."

Forty-five minutes later I saw my two boys emerge from the car and smiled. They weren't *boys* anymore. They were grown men. Within seconds of their walking in the door, I was scooped up in their arms, hearing their laughter and excited chatter, and I knew that they'd always be my *boys*.

"You look great, Mom," Jason said. "Paris must have really agreed with you."

"Yeah," John said. "Gosh, you look younger."

I laughed and took that as a compliment. "Come on, Gran's in the kitchen."

After more hugs, kisses, and laughter, the boys each took a stool and sat down.

My mother poured mugs of coffee while I placed a platter of Christmas cookies on the counter in front of them.

"Oh, I was hoping you both made these," Jason said, reaching for one and taking a bite. "As good as I remember."

"The tree looks great," John said, looking into the family room.

It *did* look great, and it had been fun getting it all decorated with Worth helping us.

"So bring me up to date on your news," I said, joining them at the counter.

"No. First we want to hear all about your trip to Paris," Jason said, and John nodded.

I looked over at my mother and cleared my throat. "I had a wonderful time. It was exactly as I remembered it. The apartment was great." I neglected to make any mention of Worth being more than just somebody who allowed me to stay at his place. "I visited museums, sat at the sidewalk cafés, did Christmas shopping . . . and, well, it was everything I hoped it would be . . . and more. But . . . there's something I need to tell you. To talk to you about."

I stopped to formulate my thoughts and saw the boys exchange a glance.

"Anything wrong?" Jason asked.

"No, no," I said, attempting to reassure them, then let out a deep sigh. "Gosh, I'm not sure where to begin. Ah, well . . . a couple of months ago I got a call from Mail Boxes in Gainesville telling me that your father had a box there—a box that I knew nothing about—and I was told there was a letter that had never been picked up. They had no idea your father had passed away, but he had given them my cell number as an emergency contact. So that's why they called me." I stopped for a moment to take a breath.

"Did you get the letter?" John asked, his expression full of curiosity.

"I did, and it was from an attorney in Boston. Actually, it had been sent last May."

"Two months after Dad died?" Jason said.

I nodded. "Yes. And this is the part I'm finding difficult to explain . . . It seems . . . that in nineteen-ninety-three, when your father was teaching that summer at Amherst College . . . he met somebody."

"Met somebody? Like a woman?" John said, clearly surprised.

"Yes. A woman. Her name was Bianca Caldwell. She passed away in April of this year. A fatal car crash. And . . . they had a daughter together."

"What?" John's surprise had now notched up to shock. "You mean Dad was screwing around on you?"

"Did you know about this?" Jason asked, always my more sensitive son.

"I did *not* know. Not until I got that letter, called the attorney in Boston, and had him explain everything to me. Their daughter, Fiona, was born in April of nineteen-ninety-four, and . . ."

John leaned across the counter. "So I was three when she was born?"

I nodded again. "Yes, you were."

"Did Dad have contact with her or her mother? Did he see them after she was born?"

"I don't think so, but I don't know for certain."

"So why was that letter being sent to Dad?" Jason questioned.

"Because your father had paid monthly support for Fiona, year after year, till she was eighteen. However, most of the money had never been withdrawn by the mother, so the balance remains in this account. Your father's stipulations were that if anything happened to the mother, any money in the account was to revert to the daughter at age eighteen. He was to be notified of this and sign the appropriate documents."

Jason shook his head. "Oh, wow! And since Dad is now gone . . . you are next of kin and that's how you were drawn into all of this."

I nodded as he got up and came around the counter to pull me into his arms. I looked over his shoulder at my mother, who had been sitting quietly, and saw a gleam of moisture in her eyes.

"Are *you* okay, Mom? How are you dealing with all of this?"

Jason asked as he stepped back to look at me. "God, I can only imagine the shock it must have been for you to discover all of this."

Leave it to my firstborn to consider my feelings first. "I'm better now. I've had time to think about all of it. I couldn't tell either of you about this when I first found out. I needed time to deal with it and figure everything out."

Following his brother's lead, John said, "Yeah, I can sure understand that. No wonder you went to Paris."

I smiled before saying, "I was pretty angry. Hurt, betrayed, and angry, but over these two months, I've come to see that your father was simply human and humans make mistakes. I've now been able to forgive him."

Both boys nodded in understanding.

"So now what?" John said. "Did she get the money in the account?"

I went on to explain that, no, I hadn't signed the documents yet. Then I took a breath and said, "We did speak on the phone . . . and she wanted to meet us. Before I just signed the money over to her, I thought that might be a good idea."

"Oh! Wow!" John said, as the realization hit him. "She's our *sister,* isn't she? We have a sister."

"You do, although technically she's your half sister, but she very much expressed a desire to meet both of you."

"So when is she coming, Mom?" Jason asked, and I laughed for the first time in the conversation.

"I know you," he said. "You wouldn't deny her the chance to meet us. You're not that kind of person."

I glanced over and saw the tears in my mother's eyes.

"She's coming tomorrow," I said with a smile.

"I'm really sorry that you had to go through this," Jason said. "I know it couldn't have been easy. But I'm glad you told us, and just so you know . . . it doesn't make me love Dad any less. He was always a good father to us . . . and like you said, he made a mistake."

My eyes were now stinging with tears. Andrew and I may not have had the perfect marriage, but we had certainly done something right in raising our sons. We had two boys who had grown to be men we could both be proud of. Men who understood, at a fairly young age, that humans had frailties, but that didn't diminish the fact they were still good people.

John confirmed this by saying, "I agree with Jason. I know this couldn't have been easy for you, but ... I *always* did want a younger sister."

I smiled as I brushed away my tears, because I was certain that was a definite expression of excitement I saw on his face.

✤ 43 ✤

Worth had offered to drive with me to the airport to pick up Fiona, but I felt perhaps it might be best to meet her for the first time alone. Although he extended the invitation, he agreed and said Fiona and I would probably need that hour on the drive back to talk. Jason and John also felt that I should go alone to get her.

Driving along Archer Road, I thought about the conversation with the boys the previous day. I really was fortunate. It had gone way better than I'd hoped for. I'm not sure if it was because they were boys and that might cancel out any jealousy factor, but they had accepted the situation just as my mother and Worth had predicted.

Worth. I felt a smile cross my face. I'd figured I was on a roll after telling them about Fiona, so before the afternoon was over I plunged in and told them about Worth. That he was more than a friend, that we had fallen in love in Paris—that we were a couple. I'm not sure what I expected their reaction to this news to be, but again, it was more than I'd hoped for. Both of my sons seemed genuine in their happiness for me. When they found out he was staying at the Faraway, they insisted I invite him over so they could meet him. We'd spent the previous evening together, and when I'd glanced at Worth talking to my boys and laughing away, it seemed so natural. Before the evening was over, both of my sons made a point to let me know that they approved.

By the time I turned into the short-term parking area at the airport, I was feeling mighty good. I had hit some major bumps during this past year, but I had weathered the storm and come through the other side a much different person. A person who had learned and grown. Somebody who was in her element and felt that all was right in her world.

I walked into the small airport, saw I still had about fifteen minutes before Fiona's flight would arrive, and got myself a cup of coffee. I stood sipping the liquid, my eyes glued to the doors where arriving passengers would enter, and found that, like John, I felt excited about meeting Fiona. Any nervousness I previously had was gone. I felt confident that having her come to stay with us was a good thing.

And then . . . I glanced up as the doors opened, and one of the first people through was a tall, slim young woman with long dark hair and a face that closely resembled Jason's. I'm not sure how she recognized me, but I saw her walk in my direction, and that was when I saw it. Despite being slim, she had a bump that protruded from her stomach. My gaze flew from her midsection back up to her face as I heard her say, "Marin?"

I nodded as a million thoughts raced through my head. My God, she was *pregnant?* This young woman was carrying Andrew's *grandchild?* Why hadn't she said anything to me? Where the hell were we going from here?

She looked like she was about to hug me, but I'm sure the expression on my face halted her.

"I know," I heard her say. "I'm sorry. I guess I should have told you, but . . . I was afraid you'd say I couldn't come, and I only found out for sure a few weeks ago."

I nodded. *Okay, Marin, get it together,* I thought. The first thing I needed to do was move us away from the people exiting the aircraft. I took her arm and steered her off to the side.

That was when I noticed the look of fear on her face and saw the tears in her eyes. "It's okay," I said, not believing a word I was saying. I put my arms around her and felt how thin she was. "Welcome to Florida. It's okay." I took a deep breath as I took her arm, attempting to reassure her as much as myself. "First things first. Let's go get your luggage."

We got her two bags and headed to my car, both of us remaining silent. She slipped into the passenger seat, while I put the luggage in the trunk and got into the driver's seat. I saw that the digital clock on the dash read 1:05.

"You're probably hungry," I said, paying the parking attendant and heading out of the airport. "How about we stop for lunch before heading to Cedar Key?"

"That would be great," she said and then remained quiet until I pulled into Cracker Barrel on Archer Road.

Since it was Christmas Eve afternoon, the place was fairly quiet, and I asked for a table in the back that might give us a bit of privacy.

Once our order was given, a BLT and cup of soup for her and a salad for me that I knew I wasn't going to be able to swallow, I said, "So? Are you married?" I knew so little about her that the thought had crossed my mind in the car that perhaps she wasn't a pregnant, single young woman after all.

But she quickly dashed this idea and shook her head. "No. No, I'm not. I know what you must be thinking."

She did? I wasn't even sure what I was thinking. I looked at her, waiting for an explanation.

"Like mother, like daughter."

"Oh," I said and then blurted, "Is the father of the child married?"

"No. At least I didn't follow in my mother's footsteps by being with a married man."

I nodded as the waitress placed two glasses of ice water in front of us.

"But Greg is ten years older than me," she said, causing my head to snap up as I waited for more information. "He's a professor at BU. Teaches English lit."

Okay. So he was twenty-nine, not married, and had a good education and career.

"How does he feel about the baby?" I asked.

"He doesn't know," Fiona said, like it was the most natural thing in the world not to tell the father of your baby that you were pregnant.

"Oh." I took a sip of water. "Why not?"

She let out a sigh while pushing a strand of hair behind her ear. "Well . . . we've been together a little over a year. I met him a year ago August." She paused to also sip water.

Okay. So she had already turned eighteen but hadn't begun her freshman year of college yet, so she couldn't have met him there. "How did you meet?" I asked.

"My roommate, Katy. Greg is her older brother. He had been teaching out west but took a temporary position at BU last July. She introduced us and we began dating a month later, and by Christmas . . . we'd fallen in love."

I was failing to see the problem. "So did you not get along? Did he not treat you well?"

The waitress placed our food on the table, and Fiona waited before replying. "Oh, no, we got along really well. He was very good to me, but . . . I also knew he had no desire to get married. He never lied about that. He wants to pursue his doctorate and just isn't ready to make a lifetime commitment. That was why we were careful and used protection . . . which obviously didn't work."

I took another sip of water as Fiona took a bite of her sandwich. "So are you trying to protect him by not telling him about the baby? Does he know where you are?"

She shook her head and wiped her mouth with the napkin. "No, I'm not trying to protect him. I just feel that under the circumstances, he doesn't need to know. What would be the sense? Then it would be like my father." She paused and looked at me. "I don't understand why my mother even bothered to tell him. She never allowed us to visit. We had no communication. We didn't even know each other. So why did she even feel the need to tell him if she didn't want us to have contact?"

"Maybe you're wrong," I told her. "Maybe it was Andrew who pulled back and relinquished any contact."

She reached into her handbag and slipped a black-and-white photograph across the table. "Is this my father?" she asked.

I looked down to see an attractive, tall, slim woman with thick dark hair wearing slacks and a cotton blouse standing next to a little girl who appeared to be around six and strongly resembled Fiona. On the other side . . . was Andrew, laughing into the camera, with his arm around the child's shoulder. I felt an ache in the pit of my stomach. They looked like a typical American family out for a day of fun.

"Yes," I whispered, unable to take my eyes from the photo. "Yes, that's Andrew."

"I thought so. That day when we met him, I always thought he was my father, but my mother said no. She introduced him as a *friend* of hers. That was all she'd ever tell me about that day. We went to a park and out for lunch. Even years later when I questioned her, she'd only say he was a friend. Never that he was my father. Sometimes I believed her and sometimes I didn't. But I never saw him again."

I saw the hurt on Fiona's face as I tried to regain my composure. I also wondered how Andrew had managed to arrange the only meeting he'd ever had with his daughter, but realized it had to have been during one of his trips to teach a seminar or workshop.

"So do you see?" she said. "Do you see why I felt compelled to at least come here to meet you and my brothers and maybe learn as much as I can about him?"

I nodded. "I do. But I still don't understand why you wouldn't at least tell the father of your child that you're pregnant. Don't you think he at least has a right to know?"

She shook her head. "No. I refuse to do what my mother did. To tell a man he has a child, knowing full well that he's unable to accept that child—either because he's married or . . . because it would interfere with his own life plans. When I found out I was pregnant, I broke up with Greg. It wasn't easy, but I told him I had a lot going on in my own life with my mother's death, finding out about my father, dropping out of college. He tried to change my mind, but he finally agreed that we wouldn't see each other anymore. Katy is my best friend, and she does know the real reason I broke up with him—but she agreed that it's probably for the best."

I wasn't so sure about that, but of course, it wasn't any of my business. I stabbed a piece of tomato in my salad and made an effort to eat it, while Fiona spooned soup into her mouth.

After a few minutes, I said, "So what's your plan?"

"Plan?" she said, like she'd never heard the word.

"Do you plan to keep the baby? Give it up for adoption? Get a job? Stay living with your roommate?" I felt a twinge of annoyance that she was so young, probably had no direction whatsoever, and yet she was now responsible for another human being.

"Oh," she said, wiping her mouth with the napkin again. "Yes, I'll definitely be keeping the baby. There's no way I could give away my own child. I'm not quite sure yet how I'll accomplish it, but I'm hoping to return to college in the fall. I'm due for the baby in May. So I plan to look for a good day-care program that will allow me to take my classes. I finished my first year as a nursing student and I plan to return. There's no way that I could support myself and a child without a good education and a well-paying job. So I feel going back to college isn't an option. It's mandatory. I inherited my mother's town house, and it's paid for, so that helps. Plus, I have Katy living with me and paying rent. She's a sophomore at BU, and staying with me in Marblehead is an easy commute for her. So for right now, it works."

I felt ashamed. This young woman seemed to have it together. At least she had her priorities, and they were sensible ones. I realized that although she looked young, she was quite mature for a nineteen-year-old who was on her own.

I nodded. "Okay," I said. "Finish your lunch so you can go and meet your brothers."

The huge smile that covered her face touched my heart.

❦ 44 ❦

If my sons noticed the bump in Fiona's midsection when we walked in the door, they made no mention of it, but I saw the quizzical expression on my mother's face. I watched as both Jason and John pulled Fiona into a warm embrace, introducing themselves and then leading her to the sofa, where they sat on either side of her.

My mother extended her hand. "I'm Dora, Marin's mother. Welcome to Cedar Key."

"Thank you," Fiona said. "And thank you so much for allowing me to stay in your home. That was very kind of you."

"Would anybody like coffee or tea?" my mother asked.

Jason and John wanted coffee, and I heard Fiona say, "Would you have any herbal tea?"

"I do," my mother said, heading to the kitchen.

"I'll help," I said, following her.

"So how did it go?" she asked once we had some privacy. "Is that bump in her tummy what I think it is? Or is she just carrying a little extra weight in one spot?"

"She's pregnant. I could hardly believe my eyes when I saw her. She's pregnant . . . with Andrew's grandchild. She's not married, hasn't even told the father, for reasons I'll explain later, but . . . she does seem pretty mature for nineteen, so—I don't know what to say or think."

My mother nodded as she prepared the coffeemaker. "Well, I can understand your surprise. But she probably figured if she told you beforehand you'd have second thoughts about her coming here."

"That's pretty much what she said. God, just when I thought we were finished with crises, now not only does Andrew's daughter show up, but she shows up pregnant." I heard my mother laugh and turned around. "What?"

"Oh, Marin. You should know better than that. Life is filled with one crisis after the other. It's all the good things in between that keep us going. Remember what I always used to tell you—life is great, if you don't weaken. And you won't. You'll get through this."

"True," I said, slicing the loaf of banana bread my mother had baked that morning. "And besides, she's only here short term."

"Hmm," was all my mother said.

By the time Bella returned from downtown later in the afternoon, the boys and Fiona were surrounded with photo albums, each of my sons sharing anecdotes about growing up with Andrew, about what he was like, and I could tell by the look on Fiona's face that she was enthralled, laughing, asking questions, and soaking up every bit of information.

After I introduced Bella, we joined my mother on the patio for a glass of wine and let the kids continue getting to know one another.

"She seems very nice," Bella said, settling onto one of the lounges.

Since Fiona hadn't stood up, I realized Bella had no way of knowing her condition. "She's pregnant," I said.

She shot me a surprised look, eyebrows arched. "Oh? Really?"

"Yeah, really." I went on to explain to her and my mother what I knew.

"Sounds like she plans to raise her child alone with no input from the father," Bella said. "That sure won't be easy."

"No, it won't," my mother agreed. "It also sounds like she's a bit resentful toward her mother for denying her the opportunity to know her father. Yet she's going to be doing the same thing."

I nodded. "Yeah, but I guess she justifies it by not letting him know at all. Unlike Bianca. I couldn't believe it when I saw that photo of the three of them together, and she didn't even tell her daughter that the man was her father."

"It's very sad," my mother said. "I have a feeling Fiona didn't get much guidance from her mother growing up. I'm glad you invited her to come here, Marin. From the sound of the laughter inside, I think she's a hit with the boys."

And she was. When we went back into the house, the first words out of John's mouth were, "Hey, I'm going to be an uncle."

Jason laughed. "Yeah, not only do we get a sister; we're going to have a niece or nephew in May."

No judging. No harsh words. My boys had not only accepted Fiona's news but displayed excitement about it. I smiled. Again I thought, *Andrew and I must have done something right.*

My mother and I were up early Christmas morning to prepare for a house full of people. Rather than a sit-down dinner later in the day, we had opted to have a buffet-style meal, but that still involved a fair amount of work and preparation.

We had just finished our first cup of coffee when Bella appeared in the kitchen.

"Why didn't you wake me up?" she asked, rubbing her eyes and stretching.

"Oh, don't worry," I told her. "You'll be able to pitch in and help, but grab a cup of coffee first, and there's some muffins on the counter to go with it. Then we'll put you to work."

Bella laughed as she filled a mug. "Fiona still sleeping?"

I nodded. "Yeah, I'm sure she's exhausted after yesterday."

"Has she seen an obstetrician yet?" my mother asked as she began peeling potatoes for potato salad.

"Oh, I don't know. I didn't think to even ask her. I guess I was more concerned about what she was planning to do long term concerning the baby."

"Well, from what you said, she has a good plan as far as going back to college in the fall and completing her education, but except for that girlfriend—her roommate—she doesn't have any support in Boston."

"No, she doesn't," was all I said.

Shortly before nine, Fiona walked into the kitchen carrying Toulouse. She had showered, was dressed, and looked more rested than she had the day before.

"Is this your cat, Dora? He's just gorgeous."

"No, Toulouse is mine," I said. "I brought him back from Paris with me. And, yeah, he's quite a handsome boy, isn't he?" I stroked the top of his head. "You like cats?"

"Oh, I do. And dogs, too, but my mom would never let me have a pet. She said with her working full-time it was just too much work."

I recalled the dogs and cats my boys had grown up with and felt a twinge of sadness for Fiona.

"Did she always work full-time?" my mother asked, now cubing the potatoes into a saucepan.

Fiona nodded and continued to cuddle Toulouse, who was soaking up the extra attention. "Yeah. Until I got older, I went to after-school programs for a couple hours until she was done teaching her classes."

Again, I thought back to when my boys were young—how they always returned home to find me there, waiting for them with a snack.

"So," she said, putting Toulouse on the floor and going to the sink to wash her hands. "What can I do to help?"

"How about some coffee or tea and a muffin before we put you to work," I told her.

"Thanks. Tea would be great," she said, taking a muffin and joining Bella at the table. "You have very nice sons. I always wanted a sibling, and now I have two brothers."

I glanced at her breaking off pieces of muffin and popping them into her mouth. "Thank you. I wanted to ask you . . . have you seen a doctor yet? You know, for the baby."

"Yeah, I did. Once. He confirmed the pregnancy with a blood test. He also gave me a prescription for vitamins. Oh," she said, jumping up and heading into the other room. "Be right back."

She returned a few moments later with a large bottle. "Can't forget to take these. May I have a glass of water?"

It made me feel good that she seemed concerned for the baby's welfare. "Do you like juice? We have orange, fresh squeezed."

"That would be great. Thanks."

"I hope you won't feel overwhelmed later today," my mother said. "We're going to have a pretty full house. You've already met Jason and John, but my niece Sydney and her friend Noah will be coming for dinner, and also Marin's friend Worth."

Fiona took a sip of the juice I handed to her and waved a hand in the air. "Oh, no. Not at all. I love being with people. Especially at a holiday gathering. It was always so quiet at my house. You know, just my mother and me."

I felt a sliver of guilt when I recalled that I'd seriously considered not having her come until after the holidays.

"We're glad you can be with us this year," I said. And I meant it.

By two o'clock all of the food had been prepared and was waiting in covered dishes and bowls on the counter and a long table the boys set up in the kitchen. Worth arrived first, bringing squash casserole and a yummy-looking apple pie, followed by Sydney and Noah carrying the turkey they had cooked along with more bowls and platters.

Jason and John began pouring wine and soda into glasses as I made the introductions. I had managed to send off a quick call to both Worth and Sydney the evening before, alerting them to Fiona's pregnancy so they'd have fair warning.

I noticed that Fiona was wearing a long dark green skirt with a blousy top that managed to camouflage her tummy more than the jeans and top of the day before had.

"It's so nice to meet you," Sydney said, giving Fiona a hug. "I hope you'll enjoy your stay here."

"Yes," Noah said, extending his hand. "It's good that you could join us for Christmas."

Worth also extended his hand before saying, "Welcome to Cedar Key."

A few minutes later, Worth placed a wineglass in my hand and steered me outside to the patio while everybody was talking and visiting.

"Merry Christmas," he said, placing a kiss on my lips. "So how's it going?"

I shrugged before taking a sip. "Okay, I think. She seems very nice. I was just so surprised about her being pregnant."

"I can imagine, but you said she seems to have her head on straight as far as what she plans to do."

"Right. She does. But God, it's sure not going to be easy for her. Pretty much on her own."

Worth nodded. "No, it won't. Did she say how long she's staying?"

"Not a word."

He glanced inside the house. "Well, she certainly seems to be enjoying herself. I'm glad it went so well with Jason and John."

I followed his glance to see Fiona standing between my boys, talking to Bella and Sydney, throwing her head back and laughing, and felt a smile cross my face. "They really have hit it off well. I'm proud of my sons for accepting her as they have. I think I did the right thing having her come here to meet them and spend the holidays with us."

I felt his arm around my shoulders as we headed back inside and heard him say, "I *know* you did the right thing."

❧ 45 ❧

By Tuesday morning, my mother's house had resumed the pre-Christmas quietness. Bella and the boys had left to return home over the weekend, and as I sat in the kitchen sipping my first cup of coffee, I recalled how well the visit had gone.

It had been wonderful to spend some quality time with Bella. We'd managed to slip away on Friday to walk around downtown together and have lunch while the boys continued their visit with Fiona. Friday evening I was able to spend time alone with the boys on the patio while Bella and Fiona went for a walk around the neighborhood with the dogs.

The boys were sincere in their fondness for their newly found half sister. Phone numbers and email addresses had been exchanged with a promise to keep in touch. It made me feel good that both of my sons displayed concern toward me, questioning if I was really okay with everything that had transpired. I assured them I was.

All of it had gone well—very well—and I was relieved. The only thing nagging at me was the fact that Fiona had not made any mention of when she might be returning to Boston. And today I was moving into my new home.

I looked up as she entered the kitchen. "Good morning," she said before heading to turn on the kettle for her tea.

"Sleep well?"

"I did. And you?"

I nodded. "Yes, and a good thing, too, because it'll be busy today moving into my new place. The movers are due at the house around noon."

"You must be so excited. I bet it's really nice."

With Christmas and the company, I hadn't even had a chance to take Fiona over to show her where I was moving.

"I am a bit excited. A new venture, and yes, I think the house will be ideal for me. You can go over with me later."

"Oh, I'd love to see it. Yes, you have a lot to look forward to with the house and then opening the needlepoint shop."

I almost said, *With a baby on the way, you also have a lot ahead,* but I refrained from saying anything.

She poured steaming water into her mug and joined me at the table. "Worth seems like a very nice man."

"He is."

"I like him. Is he different from my father?"

"I'm not sure I know what you mean."

She took a sip of tea before answering. "Well, from what I learned from Jason and John, Andrew was a good dad to them, but ... it seemed like he could also be reserved. Maybe not all that outgoing. Worth is just so friendly. He made me feel really welcome here, just like you and the boys have."

I smiled. "Yeah, I think Worth is quite a bit different than Andrew in that respect."

"Did you love him?" she blurted, and then said, "Oh, I'm sorry. I have no right to ask you that."

"It's okay. Yes, I did love him, but sometimes, over the years, things change. People change. Yet we keep going on."

She nodded, like she understood. "I don't think my mother ever loved him."

I was surprised by her honesty. "Why do you think that?"

She shrugged. "I think my mother was a very self-contained person. Oh, I'm sure she was attracted to my father, but . . . I just don't think she really loved him. I think if she had, she would have allowed us to have a relationship, but she denied both of us."

I couldn't help but wonder what would have happened in my own marriage if Andrew had sprung a daughter on me years ago, when he was still alive, when our boys were still young.

"Would you have liked that? Maybe coming to visit your father a couple times a year or having him go up to visit you? Do you think it would have changed anything in your life?"

Fiona thought about this for a few minutes and then said, "I'm not sure, but I'll never know, will I?"

By six o'clock the bulk of moving in had been completed. Without the help of Chloe, Grace, Sydney, Monica, Suellen, and Fiona, that never would have happened.

I finished arranging glasses in my cabinet and glanced over to watch Fiona emptying the last box of kitchen linens and filling the closet. I had enjoyed having her with us all day. In addition to being very helpful, she had been pleasant to have around. I could tell that my friends also enjoyed her company.

"Time to eat," Chloe announced, walking in with large boxes of pizza.

"Perfect timing," Grace said, coming from the bedroom area. "I just finished unpacking the box of towels for the bathroom."

"You guys are so great," I said, uncorking a bottle of Beaujolais. "Thank you all so much."

Sydney, Monica, and Suellen came into the kitchen. "The bed in the guest room is all done up," Suellen said and eyed the pizza. "Oh! Food! I'm starved."

I laughed and joined them at the table. "Would you like soda, Fiona?"

"I'll get myself some ice water," she said, causing me to acknowledge that since she'd arrived she had not expected to be waited on.

We all dug into the pizza, creating sounds of pleasure as we ate.

"So how long do you plan to be on Cedar Key?" Suellen asked between mouthfuls.

Fiona had been with me a week, and there had been no word as to when she might be leaving. I silently thanked Suellen for broaching the subject.

But when I glanced across the table, I could tell Fiona felt uncomfortable.

"Oh, well . . . um . . . I'm not sure," she said, throwing me a glance.

"Right." I took a sip of wine. "As you know, Fiona's pregnant, so she's not in college at the moment, and the restaurant let her go a few weeks ago, so . . . she really has no commitments to return home immediately."

I could have sworn that was a look of gratitude she shot me.

"Well, that's really great. So you might even still be here when Marin opens the needlepoint shop, and of course that will call for another party," Chloe said, causing all of us to laugh.

"Are you a knitter?" Monica asked. "Because we meet at the yarn shop on Thursday evenings, and you might want to join us."

"Oh, really?" I could tell by the expression on her face that she was pleased with the invitation. "I do knit."

I was surprised to learn this. "Oh, I had no idea."

Fiona nodded. "Yeah, there was an older woman who lived next door to us. She taught me when I was around ten. My mother didn't knit at all, so I was lucky I was able to learn so young. I do have my knitting with me, but we've been so busy I haven't touched it yet."

"That's great," I said, reaching for a second slice of pizza. "Well, you'll definitely have to come with my mother and me on Thursday evening."

"What are you making?" Suellen asked.

Fiona paused before answering. "A baby sweater."

Monica nodded. "I knitted a lot when I was pregnant. Good thing too—ending up with triplets."

All of us laughed except Fiona, whose face had paled. "You have *triplets?*"

"I do," Monica said. "Two boys and a girl. They'll turn four in February."

"Oh, my goodness! How on earth did you handle three babies at once? I'm not sure I'll even be able to handle one."

I reached across the table and patted Fiona's hand. "Of course you will."

"I did it with a lot of help. Believe me, if not for most of the town pitching in to help, I wouldn't have gotten through it. My family and friends were great."

Monica abruptly stopped talking, as if realizing that Fiona was returning to the Boston area and would be alone while raising her baby. And as if realizing the same thing, Fiona also remained silent.

To break the uneasiness, Grace said, "But I don't think you have to worry about triplets. Or even twins. You're due in May? Gosh, you're not that big at all. You should have seen Monica at four months along."

We got off the subject of babies and moved on to other topics.

By the time we finished up the pizza, Fiona seemed more herself.

I got up to begin loading the dishwasher and said, "You guys need to scoot on home. It's New Year's Eve, for goodness' sake. I'm ashamed I kept you here so long."

"Yeah, right," Chloe said. "Like I had any big plans tonight."

Suellen laughed. "Same here."

Sydney brought glasses to the dishwasher. "Noah and I are just going to have a quiet evening with a bottle of champagne at midnight."

"And Adam and I will probably be asleep by ten," Monica said, causing us to laugh.

"Lucas has a nice bottle of French champagne for us, but I can't promise I'll last till midnight either." Grace began wiping down the table.

"Well, most of you have men waiting for you," I said, pushing the button on the dishwasher. "And I'm not throwing you out, but . . ."

"And what about you?" Chloe questioned. "Where's Worth tonight? It's your first New Year's Eve together."

It was, but he had been so understanding about my move and having my friends help me.

"He knew we were having a moving-in party, and . . . well . . . he's over at the Faraway. We'll see each other tomorrow. It's fine."

"No, it's not," I heard Fiona say, and all of us stared at her. "Could one of you drive me back to Dora's house, please? I can stay there tonight, and Marin . . . you need to get on the phone and call Worth. It's only eight. Tell him to come over and spend New Year's Eve with you."

Before I could protest, the six of them grabbed their belongings, gave me hugs and kisses, and wished me a Happy New Year, and they were gone.

I was left standing in the middle of my kitchen floor, a huge smile on my face, as I reached for my cell phone.

∼ 46 ∼

I awoke the next morning to sunlight streaming through the curtains and Worth beside me. *Girlfriends are the best,* I thought. They know precisely what we need, and since Worth and I had hardly seen each other in a week, being able to spend New Year's Eve with him had been very special. But I also thought of Fiona because it had been her idea to return to my mother's house and allow Worth and me to have some privacy.

During the week that I'd come to know Fiona, I had discovered that I liked her. This wasn't all that surprising, because I had known from our brief telephone conversations that she seemed like a nice person. What had surprised me, upon meeting her, was that I felt a connection to her. This was silly, because we weren't related by blood—as she and Andrew were. But there was something about her that drew me closer. Something that made me want to know her better. I sighed as I felt Worth stir beside me. I realized that I'd probably never have that chance, because before too long she'd return to the Boston area, have the baby, and get on with her life, and although she'd stay in touch with Jason and John, I might not ever hear from her again. Just before I felt Worth drape his arm across my body and whisper, "Happy New Year," I experienced a sense of emptiness.

*   *   *

"Those pancakes and grits were delicious," Worth said, wiping his mouth with a napkin.

"I'm glad you enjoyed them." I got up from my stool to grab the coffeepot and refill our cups.

I felt his arm slide around my waist as he placed a kiss on my cheek.

"That was pretty considerate of Fiona to suggest you call me last night."

"It was," I agreed before returning to my stool.

"You seem quiet this morning. Everything okay?"

I shot him a smile. "I'm beginning to think you might know me a little too well."

"And that's a bad thing?" he asked, causing me to laugh.

"I guess I'm just feeling unsettled—about Fiona. I thought maybe when I mentioned the money that Andrew had provided for her she would tell me she'd be heading back to Boston soon. I told her yesterday morning that I'd be signing those documents, that I felt the money was rightfully hers and I was sure between having the baby and going to college that she'd put it to good use."

"And what did she say?"

"Thank you."

"That was it?"

I nodded. "Yeah, that was it. No mention about when she planned to leave."

"Hmm," was all I heard Worth say.

"What do you mean by that?"

"Did it ever cross your mind, Marin, that maybe she doesn't *want* to leave?"

"You think she might want to stay here? With me? Why would she want to do that?"

"Because she's alone. Because she has no family in the Boston area. From what I've seen over the past week, Fiona likes it here and she likes you. I think she feels happy and secure. Your own family and friends have accepted her and have made her feel welcome."

Now it was my turn to say, "Hmm," as I pondered what Worth had just said.

"How would you feel about that?" he asked.

"About having her stay here permanently? I don't know. I never expected this might be a possibility when I invited her to come for a visit. I do like her. She's a nice person, easy to be with, and she's certainly a wonderful houseguest."

"I think you need to give this some serious consideration, and then . . . you need to have a talk with Fiona. Put it out there. Tell her if you feel comfortable allowing her to stay here on a full-time basis, and if you do, you both will need to agree on the arrangements."

I nodded. Worth was right. "I think I might enjoy having her here with me, but even more important, I hate the thought of her returning home with nobody to give her support. If she weren't pregnant, I wouldn't be as concerned. But . . . having a baby alone is not easy, and that's another thing—I'm not sure that I agree with her about not even letting the father know that she's pregnant. I understand her reasoning, but . . . I'm just not sure it's the right thing to do."

"Then you have to be honest with her. Tell her how you feel and explain why you feel that way. Don't forget, Marin, she doesn't have a mother to walk her through this, to give her some guidance."

Worth was right again. Not only did Fiona not have a mother— she also had no father in her life.

The following week Fiona and I were in my kitchen baking cookies for the opening of my needlepoint shop the next day. I still hadn't broached the subject with her about any plans to leave, but after more thought, I hoped she would choose to stay.

"So do you think you'll have a lot of people at the grand opening?" I heard her ask.

I continued to spoon chocolate chip cookie dough onto the Teflon sheet and nodded. "I'm sure all the women that you met last Thursday evening will be there and a lot of locals. We'll probably also have a fair amount of tourists dropping in."

Fiona continued pressing a round cookie cutter into dough she had spread out on the table. "They're a really nice bunch, aren't they? All the women at the knitting group."

I laughed. "For the most part, yes. As you noticed, Miss Raylene can be a bit condescending."

"Yeah, but I liked her. She's feisty. She wasn't the least bit shy asking about my pregnancy and then going on about being an *unwed mother* in her day." Fiona laughed and shook her head. "I suppose women in her age-group find it difficult to accept how much society has changed and become more accepting."

This girl was definitely mature in her thinking. "You're going to make an excellent nurse," I said. "You have great insight."

"I hope that insight helps me as a new mom too."

I slid the cookie sheet into the oven, wiped my hands on a towel, and said, "Time for a break. How about a cup of tea?"

"Sounds good. Let me just get these on the cookie sheet and in the oven with yours."

I set the timer on the oven, turned on the kettle, and placed a few of the peanut butter cookies we'd made earlier in the morning on a plate. "It's so nice outside. Let's have our break on the patio."

Fiona and I enjoyed the warm January air as we sipped our tea.

"It's so pretty out here," she said. "So the house is called Safe Harbor? I like that. I like the comforting sound of it. That a house can represent security and family."

My gaze was caught by movement in the air near the shore, and I felt a chill go through me. Dragonflies. The dragonflies were back, hovering near the water.

"Didn't you have that sense of security and family growing up in your house?" I asked.

Fiona nibbled on a bite of cookie. "Being an only child was always tough. Nobody to play with, share secrets with, build a history with. But not having a father around made it even tougher, I think. My mother always worked, and when she was home, she was wrapped up in her own life. Oh, don't get me wrong—she was a good mother. And I did all the kid things, ballet lessons, piano lessons, gymnastics, summer camp. But my mother didn't have a job; she had a career. So a lot of her time at home was spent grad-ing papers, doing research, that sort of thing. Sometimes we did things together, but not often. She was a good mom, but we just didn't have a close mother-daughter relationship."

A twinge of sadness went through me. It sounded like while Fiona had had a good childhood, she also had had a lonely childhood.

"How do you think she would have reacted to your pregnancy?" I asked. "Do you think she would have been supportive or angry?"

Fiona let out a chuckle. "I don't think she would have been angry, based on her own situation. She probably would have been supportive, but I don't think she would have been too excited at the prospect of becoming a grandmother. I really don't think she was that fond of children, to be honest, and I used to sometimes wonder why she kept me. It would have been much easier to give me up for adoption, especially since she didn't include my father in my life."

I blew air through my lips as I continued to watch the dragonflies. This young woman seemed to have an exceptional understanding of reality. Not only did she seem to understand, but she didn't seem to place blame on her mother for any shortcomings.

"Fiona," I said. "I wanted to discuss something with you. About your return to Boston."

Her head shot up as she stared at me. "Have I overstayed my welcome?"

I heard the concern in her words. "No, no. Not at all. It's just that . . . well . . . you've been here two weeks. I've enjoyed having you. Very much. But . . . we need to figure out what, exactly, you're going to do. It's probably time to be seen by the doctor again, plans have to be put in place for the delivery, and frankly, I don't like the thought of you returning home and only having your roommate to depend on."

She remained silent, her eyes not leaving my face.

"And so . . . I was wondering . . . if maybe you'd like to stay here. Permanently. Have the baby and maybe even attend the university in Gainesville to complete your degree. You'd be able to have a lot of support here—people to help you—but this would have to be your decision, and of course, we'd have to agree on certain things."

I looked up to see tears in her eyes. Tears that she wasn't even bothering to brush away.

"Do you mean that? Do you really mean you'd be willing to let me stay here? With you?" The tears were now falling down her face, and she swiped them with her hand. "When I first met you at the airport, I knew I liked you. A lot. I immediately knew why my father chose to stay with you. Why he didn't break up his family for my mother and me. And since I've been here, I felt like I *did* belong, and that was because of you. But I didn't . . . allow myself to think it was possible that I could stay."

I was humbled by what this girl had just said to me.

She swiped at her tears again. "I would love to stay here. I've always wanted a family, and you've made me feel like I was part of yours."

I nodded and felt a lump in my throat. "Okay," I said. "Okay. Well, there's a few things we need to discuss. Things that we both have to agree on to make this work."

Fiona stared at me, an expectant look on her face.

"I know it's none of my business, but . . . I do think you should at least let the father know that you're pregnant and where you're at. Beyond that, it's up to you what you choose to do concerning him. But I feel he has a right to know. You'll have to get established with an obstetrician in Gainesville, and you'll have to get your transcript transferred to UF and put in an application to hopefully begin classes in the fall."

"That's all?" she said as she jumped up to pull me into a tight embrace.

I laughed and said, "Yes, that's all." I felt her arms around me and her cheek next to mine, and for the first time in my life I had a feeling what it must be like to have a daughter.

❦ 47 ❧

By mid-February, life seemed to be on a more even keel. Fiona had moved in with me, we had visited an obstetrician in Gainesville whom she liked, she had already had her transcript transferred to the university and applied for the fall semester, and I wasn't sure if the happiness she radiated was due to pregnancy or to the fact that she truly did feel part of a family.

"Hey," Berkley said. "I love those new hand-painted canvases you got in yesterday. I'm thinking of doing one of the cat ones. You have one that's an amazing likeness to my Sigmund, but then of course Brit will feel left out."

I looked up from the silk threads I'd been placing in the correct drawers and laughed. "Oh, I could order you one that would resemble Brit. Dogs are pretty popular with needlepoint."

"That would be great, but I'll definitely purchase that cat one today. So how's everything going?"

I was almost scared to say it. "Actually, very well. Fiona is due into Gainesville at twelve-thirty, and Worth has gone to pick her up for me at the airport."

"Oh, that's right. She flew up to Boston last week to get things settled up there and talk to the father, huh? How'd that go?"

I nodded. "Yeah, her doctor said she can't fly after seven months, so she decided to go now, and I think it went pretty well. I'll get more details when she gets back, but she did call Greg, they've been together discussing everything, and from the sounds of it, he was pretty excited about the baby."

"Oh, that's great. I'm happy for her. She seems like such a nice kid."

I smiled. "Not so much a kid anymore. She turns twenty in April and will be having her own child the next month."

Berkley nodded. "True. When's her due date?"

"May ninth, but the doctor said she could be early. The baby's a pretty good size."

"Well, at least she knows it's not triplets like Monica. Do you know if it's a boy or girl yet?"

"She doesn't want to know. Said it would be more fun to be surprised, so we've been knitting baby items in green, white, or yellow."

"You seem to be enjoying this, Marin. Your new role as impending grandmother."

"Oh, I'm not the grandmother." Was I?

"Of course you are. Fiona is your husband's daughter. You might not be a blood relative, but . . . you're still going to be a grandmother."

I smiled. I certainly had not considered this, but I rather liked the idea.

I removed the cat canvas from the clips where it had been hanging. "Is this the one you want?"

"Yeah, that's the one. Now I have to choose my threads," she said, walking to the cabinet containing all the various cotton and silk threads.

After I rang up her purchase and she left, I stood looking around the shop and felt a sense of contentment. Despite the delays and disappointments, the needlepoint shop had finally become a reality, and during the past month, I'd been doing quite well with business. I gave some thought to what Berkley had said about me becoming a grandmother and smiled. Although Fiona had not referred to me with this title, Berkley was right. If Andrew were still alive and had contact with his daughter, her child would be *our* grandchild.

Later that evening I sat at the table over dinner listening to Worth and Fiona discussing various news events and felt grateful for the paths my life had taken over the past year. Not only had Worth come into my life sharing his love, but now I also had Fiona, and soon her baby would be joining us. I liked how Worth and Fiona got along. It was obvious that they liked each other, and I couldn't help but wonder if possibly Fiona looked up to him as one might a father figure.

"Okay," I heard her say. "Enough chitchat. I'm sure you both want to know what happened with Greg."

Worth had told me after they arrived back from the airport that Fiona wanted to wait till we were all together for dinner before she shared any information.

"From what you've told me so far, it seems like it went pretty well?"

"I think it did." She fingered the linen napkin beside her dish. "He said he loves me and didn't want me to break up with him, but . . . he felt if I didn't love him in return, our relationship had no hope." She looked up at both of us across the table. "I do love Greg. Very much. He's quite excited about the baby," she said, and I saw a smile cross her face. "And you were right, Marin. Telling him was the right thing to do." She let out a sigh. "But we both agree we have to be practical. In other words, it would be foolish to rush into getting married right now. I need to complete my education, and that will take three years. Greg also wants to work on his doctorate. So . . . we've decided to make a commitment to each other; Greg will be a part of our child's life and will be involved. He plans to fly down here in a few weeks. He'd like to meet you both. He also wants to be here as soon as the baby is born and . . . he's in the process of applying for a teaching position at UF."

Life was most definitely on a more even keel. "Oh, Fiona, that's wonderful. It sounds like you both made some very wise decisions. In the years to come, I don't think either one of you will be sorry for completing your education. And of course, we look forward to meeting Greg."

Worth nodded. "He sounds like an intelligent man. And I give my approval," he said, which caused Fiona to giggle.

I got up to lean over and give her a hug. "I want you to know that I support you one hundred percent, and . . . your father would also approve of your plans."

The following Thursday evening, the knitting group was gathered at Yarning Together.

"So can you believe it?" Raylene said. "There really *is* going to be a movie filmed here on the island. I knew that Carl and I were right."

Corabeth shook her head and laughed. "Yes, Raylene, but technically it's *not* a movie. It's a documentary about sea life in Cedar Key. I tend to doubt that you'll be getting a part, so I'd say your actress days are over before they begin."

Laughter erupted in the shop as Raylene tossed her head and sniffed. "Oh, don't be too sure of that. I might be able to convince them that they need a local with lots of information."

"Right. But I wouldn't be running out to purchase a gown for the Academy Awards," Flora said, causing all of us to laugh again.

"It's the university that's doing the documentary, isn't it?" my mother questioned.

Chloe nodded. "Yeah. I believe it's the journalism department in conjunction with the science department."

"Well, it's still a good thing," Sydney said. "It'll be informational and promote some interest in the island."

I looked around at the women, all knitting away on the Compassion Shawl, and smiled. My gaze fell on Fiona, and I felt my smile broaden. This shawl seemed even more significant now. My mother had been right. Because I had allowed myself to forgive Andrew and in doing so had accepted Fiona, my life had taken off in a whole new direction, and I realized that compassion had been a vital part of making that happen.

"Hey, everybody," I said, standing up. "Time for our pastry break. I brought the dessert tonight, and it's Friendship Bread."

"Oh, I love that," Berkley said. "There's so many variations of it, and I like the fact you can create it to be whatever you want."

My mother helped to slice it as I filled coffee cups.

"This is delicious," Corabeth announced. "Now, what on earth is that special taste?"

I laughed. "It's key lime. I added the juice of key limes to the batter, and it does give it a unique flavor."

"Oh, it certainly does," Monica agreed. "I love it."

After we were seated with everyone enjoying the bread and coffee, Monica said, "Fiona, I meant to tell you, I'm not sure what you have for the baby, but I have three of everything. I'd love for you to use anything you might need. I have cradles, cribs, swings, car seats—you name it, I have it."

Fiona laughed. "You sound like a baby store. Thank you. I might take you up on your offer for a few items."

"Which reminds me," I said. "I was hoping the two of us could go shopping next month after your doctor appointment. I wanted to buy some things for the baby."

Fiona's face lit up. "Oh, that would be great. Since you're going to be the grandmother, I have a feeling this child might be a little bit spoiled."

I felt my heart turn over. Had she really said that? That *I* would be the grandmother? "Really? You're going to consider me the baby's grandmother?"

The look on her face told me there was no doubt whatsoever. "Well, of course you are. Gosh, I thought you knew that. Unless . . . you'd rather not be."

"Are you crazy?" I burst out laughing. "I'm thrilled. I couldn't be any happier," I said and heard clapping fill the room.

"Congratulations," Chloe said. "You beat me. I'm still waiting."

"Your life will never be the same. Becoming a grandmother brings so much pleasure and joy," Sydney told us.

"So what would you like to be called?" Fiona asked. "Because, of course, Dora will be the great-grandmother, and she's called Gran."

I looked over to see a huge smile covering my mother's face.

"You can call me *Nana,*" I said and heard more clapping and laughter fill the room.

48

It was one of those wonderful spring days in March, when parts of the north were still getting snow dumped on them but Florida was enjoying sunshine, mild temperatures, and blooming trees and flowers. I walked into Toys R Us with Fiona beside me. We'd just come from her doctor appointment, and everything was on schedule. She was now looking very pregnant. The bump that I'd first noticed at Gainesville Airport had grown to a mound. She was in good health, had gained a proper amount of weight, and seemed to be quite happy being pregnant.

"Okay," I said. "Now the fun begins. Baby shopping has got to be one of the most fun things to do."

Fiona laughed as her gaze strayed to an adorable teddy bear mobile for the crib.

"Do you have any particular theme in mind for the baby?" I asked.

"Animals. Dogs, cats, bunnies. That sort of thing."

"Then I think this mobile would be perfect." I wound up the music box attached to it and heard the strains of Brahms's Lullaby.

"I love it," Fiona said as I placed it in my cart.

"Now, I know you're borrowing the cradle, swing, and car seat, but I want to buy the crib and carriage," I said, leading the way.

"Oh, Marin, no. You don't have to do that."

"I know I don't," I said, giving her arm a squeeze. "I want to. Hey, it's a grandmother's prerogative, right?"

She laughed and nodded. "It certainly is."

I couldn't remember the last time I'd enjoyed shopping so much. Fiona and I simply had a good time—together. We wandered the aisles, looking at various items, seriously considering some and laughing at others. We debated over different brands, trying to decide which would be the safest for the baby. I'd hold up a stuffed animal, waiting for Fiona's reaction, and smile as she cocked her head from side to side and then give an emphatic nod or shake of her head. By the time the cart was overflowing, I knew one thing for certain. My joy hadn't come only from shopping for baby items—the joy that I felt was because for the first time in my life, I knew what it was like to have a daughter. No, she wasn't a daughter that I had birthed, but that didn't matter. The older I got, the more I realized that family didn't have to be about birth. It could be something that we created, on our own—because of *love*.

Four hours later we were back on Cedar Key after a very successful shopping spree. In addition to the crib and carriage, I had purchased infant nightgowns, receiving blankets, tee shirts, little stretch outfits, bottles—Fiona had made the choice to bottle-feed—and assorted other items. The trunk and backseat were loaded.

"Do you mind if we stop at my mother's house first? I know she's anxious to hear about the doctor appointment and our shopping."

"Definitely. Besides, I have to pee again."

I laughed and headed to Andrews Circle.

My mother and Oliver greeted us as we walked in.

"Bathroom," Fiona explained, rushing past.

My mother laughed. "I take it everything went well?"

"It did," I said, following her to the kitchen.

"How about some cranberry bread with coffee?"

"Sounds good, but herbal tea for Fiona."

"I really love coffee," we heard her say as she walked into the kitchen. "So I'll be glad to go back to it after the baby."

"And the doctor is pleased with your progress?" my mother asked as she turned on the kettle.

Fiona nodded. "Yes, everything is going well, but I'm afraid your daughter went a little crazy shopping. You should see everything she bought today. The car is filled to capacity."

My mother laughed. "And I'm sure she had a great time doing it."

"I did. My goodness, we haven't had a baby in this family in twenty-two years, since John was born."

My mother put a plate of sliced cranberry bread on the table. "Have you thought of any names yet?"

Fiona reached for a slice. "I've thought of a few but nothing definite."

For some reason she'd been avoiding discussing names.

"Was the shop busy today?" I asked.

My mother shook her head. "Nothing that Chloe and I couldn't handle. You had a few needlepoint sales, and Chloe took care of them. Raylene dropped by, and she's convinced the film crew for the documentary is going to ask her to be interviewed."

I got up to get the kettle and laughed. "She just won't give it up, will she? I think she missed her calling as a Hollywood actress."

I placed the mug of tea in front of Fiona.

"Thanks. Well, you do have to admire her determination."

"True," my mother said. "Is Worth at the house?"

"He is. Told us he's preparing spaghetti and meatballs for our dinner."

Fiona smiled. "I told Marin that man is definitely a keeper."

Seems I'd heard those words before. "I agree with that," I said.

After the dinner cleanup, Fiona said she was going to relax in her room. It had been a long day for her with the doctor, shopping, and travel to and from Gainesville.

I kissed her cheek before she headed into her bedroom. "Remember, if you need anything, even during the night, get me."

She nodded and smiled. "Will do."

"How about a glass of wine outside?" Worth said.

"Sounds great." I headed to the patio, waiting for him to join me.

We had mutually agreed the month before that Worth would give up his cottage at the Faraway to move in with me during the week. It had actually been Fiona who encouraged this. She insisted that if she weren't with me, it probably would have already happened. She was right. And it was working out very well. I smiled as Suzette came over and curled up at my feet. Even Worth's dog had fit right in, getting along very well with Toulouse. And Toulouse, being the laid-back kitten he was, got along as well with Suzette as he did with Oliver. On Saturday afternoons, Worth and I headed to Ocala to spend some alone time at his home, and I think Fiona also liked having some time to herself while we were away.

"Here you go," Worth said, passing me a wineglass. "I picked up a nice Santa Cristina Sangiovese when I was in Gainesville last week."

I took a sip. "Excellent," I said. "Thanks."

He reached over for my hand. "Tired?"

"A bit. But happy."

He gave my hand a squeeze. "Good."

"You were right, you know."

"What do you mean?"

"You had told me months ago that everything would work out. And it has."

"Things usually have a way of doing that."

"I really liked Greg too. I'm glad he came here last month so we could meet him."

He was a very nice fellow, tall, good-looking, and obviously quite in love with Fiona. The way he looked at her said a lot, but he also displayed a caring concern toward her, and before he left to fly back to Boston, unbeknownst to Fiona, he'd taken me aside to tell me he loved Andrew's daughter and welcomed the baby and he planned to support Fiona and his child, both financially and emotionally. I don't think a parent could ask more than that for her daughter. He also made me promise to call him the moment Fiona went into labor because he planned to grab the next flight to Gainesville.

"I liked him a lot too," Worth said. "And I'm glad he was able to spend a few days here. It gave them both some time to discuss their plans in depth. I think their decision to go slow is a good one."

I nodded. "Yeah, but I do hope he's able to get a position teaching down here. That would enable him to be more a part of the baby's life."

"He seemed fairly confident that would happen. Apparently, he knows a couple of the professors in the English department, who are going to put in a good word for him."

"It also worked out well that Katy wants to keep renting Fiona's town house. It will give her some extra income, and I don't think she's ready to sell it yet."

"Well, it's really the only home she's ever known. She moved there with her mother when she was five."

"For a girl who had no family to speak of, family really means a lot to her."

"I'm sure that's why it meant so much when you asked her to stay here with you."

Worth brought my hand to his lips, placing a kiss on top.

"You're the one who hinted at that, and I'm not sure I ever thanked you. So thank you. You know . . . I've come to realize that family doesn't have to be defined by *blood relations*."

"Absolutely not."

I nodded. "Family can be a group of persons forming a household—just people, sharing mutual interests, good times and mostly . . . love."

"That's right."

I took a sip of wine and smiled before squeezing Worth's hand. "Then Fiona and I have found a new family. Right here at Safe Harbor. In this house."

49

The first of May arrived on Cedar Key with sunshine and low humidity, and before the day was over the town would have one more resident.

I woke shortly before six-thirty and found Worth already in the kitchen preparing the coffeemaker.

"Good morning," I said, going to give him a hug and kiss.

"Good morning. Sleep well?"

"Always," I said, bending down to scoop Toulouse into my arms. "And how's my little boy today?" I received a musical trill in answer.

I went to the counter and began spooning Iams cat food into his bowl and glanced out the window. That's when I saw them. Down by the water, in the bright sunlight, a swarm of dragonflies hovering in the air. They were back. I remembered when I'd seen them the first time I'd come to look at the property and recalled what Berkley had told me about them. That they symbolized renewal, positive force, and the power of life. They also represented change and the sense of self that comes with maturity. I let out a sigh as I placed Toulouse's bowl on the floor.

"Let's have our coffee on the patio," I said, heading outside.

Worth followed me out and sat beside me at the table.

I nodded toward the water. "The dragonflies are back."

"I noticed."

I took a sip of coffee. "You know, yesterday I was thinking back to where I was a year ago. Andrew had been gone not quite two months. I still hadn't accepted the fact that I was a widow. I had no idea where my life was going." I continued to stare at the dragonflies swirling and dipping as their translucent wings caught the sunlight. "I hadn't met you yet and I didn't know a thing about Fiona. And now . . . I don't know what I'd do without either of you in my life."

Worth leaned over and placed a kiss on my forehead. "I don't think you're going to have to find out. I love you, Marin, and I'll always love you."

Later that morning Worth left to go downtown to the bookshop. He said that Lucas had called the day before to let him know a book he'd ordered had come in.

Fiona had slept in later than usual and emerged from her room just after Worth had left.

"Good morning," I said, bending over to fill the dishwasher. "Sleep okay?"

"Not really," I heard her say and spun around to see a strange expression on her face.

"What's wrong? Are you okay?"

"I started to have a backache about four this morning. I've been awake since then."

"Oh, God, Fiona. Why didn't you wake me up?"

"I don't think it's anything to be concerned about," she said, waving a hand in the air as she went to pour herself some juice.

She had no sooner said this than a gush of water hit the floor and Fiona gripped the counter.

"Oh, my God! I think my water just broke."

"I think you're right." I ran to grab her arm. "Okay. Come on. Sit here while I get some towels. Maybe I should call Worth first, though," I said, halfway to the linen closet. "No, towels first." I grabbed an armful, racing back to the kitchen, feeling completely disorganized.

I threw the towels on the floor, attempting to soak up the liquid as I shot questions at Fiona. "Any blood? Have the cramps increased? Still only in your back? Oh, I have to call Worth. He's on standby to drive us to the hospital. Your bag. Your bag is packed and ready, right?" I looked up to see Fiona doubled over with laughter.

"What?" I said, my concern increasing. "Are you okay?"

She held a hand in the air. "I'm fine, but I don't think you're doing so well. Calm down, Marin. Really, I'm fine. Ouch," she now said, bending forward, and I knew it wasn't from laughter this time.

"Right. Okay, I'm going to call Worth. You just sit tight." As if the poor kid was going anywhere. God, I felt like a character in a sit-com.

He answered on the second ring.

"I think Fiona is in labor. Her water just broke. She's been having back pain since four. I think this is it. We need to get to the hospital, Worth. Like *now*." I knew I was babbling, but I couldn't help it.

Was that a chuckle I heard come across the line? Damn him. Men had no idea how serious this could be. I mean, God, Fiona could deliver her baby right here on the kitchen floor if we didn't move fast.

"Marin," I heard him say. "You need to calm down. Hold on a sec. Josie is right here in the coffee café. Let me relay the info to her and see what she says."

Josie? Josie Sullivan? Oh, thank God! She was an RN.

A few moments later Worth said, "Okay, Marin. I'll be right along. Now, calm down. We'll be at the hospital within an hour."

I had just finished helping Fiona change into dry clothes when Worth walked in, followed by Josie. I wanted to rush over and kiss the girl, but I was assisting Fiona to the sofa.

"Oh, Josie, thank you so much for coming over. Will she be okay? Do we even have time to get to the hospital?"

Josie shot me a smile as she knelt down in front of Fiona. "First babies usually take a while. I don't think this one will be born on Cedar Key." She proceeded to ask Fiona a few questions, nodding and placing her hand on Fiona's abdomen.

Standing up, she said, "You're definitely in labor, but you've got time to get to the hospital. Is there anything I can do to help?"

"Are you sure?" I questioned. "Do you think maybe we should call an ambulance to take her?"

Josie laughed as she patted me on the shoulder. "No, there's no need for that. Take her in the car, drive safely, and I guarantee you won't be delivering a baby on the way."

"Okay," I said, beginning to feel a semblance of calm returning. "If you could call my mother at the yarn shop and let her know we're on our way to the hospital, I'd really appreciate it. Ask her if she could come over later today to let Suzette out, and tell her I'll call her as soon as I can."

"Will do," Josie said. "Now, go. I'll lock up here."

I raced outside to see that Worth had already assisted Fiona into the backseat of my car and placed her bag in the trunk. I jumped in beside Fiona, and Worth pulled out onto the road and headed to Gainesville.

During the drive, Fiona began to have some pretty good contractions. She gripped my hand as perspiration began to dot her forehead and upper lip.

"Doing okay?" I asked.

She nodded. "Yeah, but, Marin . . . will you come into the delivery room with me?"

We had never discussed this, so she caught me by surprise.

"Are you sure? Are you sure you want me in there with you?"

"I do. Very much. Please."

"Of course," I reassured her. "Of course I will."

Worth was pulling into the emergency room entrance when another strong contraction caused Fiona to bend forward, gripping my hand tighter.

"Okay," I said. "We're here. Hold on a little bit longer."

Worth pulled the car to the side, jumped out, ran inside, and returned with a nurse pushing a wheelchair.

I got out of the backseat, allowing Fiona to scoot to the edge, then holding her arm and guiding her into the wheelchair.

"Hi," the nurse said, "I'm Susan. First baby?"

Fiona nodded as I increased my pace to keep up.

"Are you registered to deliver here?" she asked.

"Yes, Fiona Caldwell."

The information was given to the woman in the cubicle we now found ourselves in. While Fiona produced an insurance card, information was entered into the computer, and Fiona experienced a couple more pretty good contractions, Worth went to park the car and returned.

Just when I was convinced that maybe Fiona hadn't given birth on Cedar Key but she most definitely would probably do so in this hospital admitting room, I heard the nurse say, "Okay, off we go. I'm from labor and delivery, so I'll take you up there."

Finally, I thought.

"Will you be with her for the delivery?" the nurse asked, looking at me.

Before I could answer, Fiona said, "Yes, she will. She's my stepmom."

"All righty, then," Miss Cheery Nurse said, like this was just another ordinary occurrence in her shift. "And you are?" she asked, looking at Worth.

"He's my significant other," I said.

We were just about at the bank of elevators now, and I prayed we made the delivery room.

"Okay, that's fine," Miss Cheery Nurse said. "You're probably not going into the labor and delivery room also, but we have a nice lounge that you can wait in, so follow us."

The elevator doors had just closed when Fiona had her strongest contraction yet. Her hand shot out for mine, and she squeezed. Tight.

The doors were opening as the nurse said, "Breathe, honey. In and out. Work with the contraction."

"Caldwell," she called out as we passed the nurses' station and waved her arm to the right. "There's the waiting lounge."

I felt Worth take me by the shoulders, place a kiss on my lips, and say, "You'll both be fine. Now, go become a grandmother."

I raced to catch up with Fiona and the nurse.

"Okay," she said as I followed them into a nicely decorated room. It resembled a lavish hotel room more than a hospital room. "We're going to do an exam first to see where we're at and get you hooked up to the monitor. Then we'll take it from there. There's a call out to your doctor."

I looked around the room and let out a huge sigh. My stress level had decreased dramatically. We were now in a controlled environment. We had proper medical personnel, should anything go wrong. We were safe.

"Everything seems to be going along great. You're in active labor and about five centimeters dilated," the nurse informed us after the exam, grabbing a clipboard from the maple bureau against the wall. She pulled a sliding stool up to Fiona's bed, reached over to squeeze her arm, and said, "You doing okay? Need anything for discomfort?"

Fiona shook her head. "No, I'm okay so far."

The nurse looked at the papers attached to the clipboard. "Okay, well, the doctor ordered some pain med if you need it, and they'll do an epidural right before the delivery. What time did your water break?"

"Around ten?" Fiona looked at me.

"Yes, I'd say it was a little after ten." I glanced at my watch, surprised to see that it was already going on one-thirty.

After the nurse asked the routine questions, I said, "Will she deliver in here?"

Susan smiled and nodded. "Yes, the bottom half of the bed breaks away and becomes a delivery table. Any other questions?"

"I'm very dry. Can I have some water?" Fiona asked.

"I'll get you some ice chips," the nurse said, leaving the room.

"You're doing great," I said, pushing strands of hair off Fiona's forehead.

Another contraction gripped her, and I knew they were now coming closer together and lasting longer.

"Still okay?" the nurse asked, walking in with a paper cup and spoon and passing them to Fiona.

"They're getting stronger," she said before spooning ice into her mouth.

"That's a good thing." The nurse nodded. "That's what we want."

I saw her glance at the monitor as Fiona clasped the bed rail with one hand while reaching out for me with the other.

About ten minutes later, her obstetrician entered the room.

"Hey, Fiona," he said, perfectly at ease and friendly. "So you decided to have a May Day baby, huh?"

She laughed. "I guess so." And a minute later she doubled over in pain again.

"Okay," he said, waiting for the contraction to subside. "Let's have a look and see how you're progressing."

I stood at the head of Fiona's bed and let out a deep breath.

A few minutes later, he said, "Things are moving along pretty fast now. You're almost at seven centimeters. The baby's in position, so the contractions are going to get even stronger and they're going to last longer. I need you to start using your breathing techniques and focus. Mom," he said, looking at me. "She'll be going into transition soon, so your job is to use a cool cloth on her forehead, rub her back, anything that will help her to relax."

I nodded and let out another deep breath and looked over to see the nurse had placed a basin of water on the table beside me with a washcloth.

Within fifteen minutes I knew it wouldn't be much longer. Fiona was struggling to maintain her composure, but fifteen minutes later she began to moan, moving from side to side. Sweat poured down the sides of her face, and I passed the washcloth over her forehead, down her face to her neck.

"I can't," I heard her say. "I can't *do* this."

I turned her face so she had direct eye contact with me. "Yes, you *can,*" I said with more force than I felt.

"The baby's coming too fast for an epidural," I now heard the doctor say. "Fiona, the baby's head has crowned, and I need you to push."

She shook her head from side to side, reminding me of a five-year-old having a tantrum. "I *can't.* I want to go home."

I took her face in my hands, forcing her to look at me. "I *know* you can do this. Fiona, listen to me. You have to focus and push. Your baby is almost here."

She let out a guttural sound, and I heard the doctor say, "Good, Fiona. Very good. Bear down. Give me another push."

I felt her entire body tense with the effort and a minute later heard the doctor say, "You have a daughter. It's a girl. Well done, Fiona."

I looked to the foot of the bed and witnessed the miracle of life as Fiona said, "A girl? Really? Is she okay?"

It was then that I realized we were both laughing and crying, clasping each other's hands.

"See for yourself," the doctor said, holding up the most beautiful newborn I'd ever seen. "Give us a minute to get her cleaned up and you can hold her."

Fiona looked up at me with pure love in her eyes. "Thank you," she said, still weeping. "Thank you so much for being here, Marin. I don't know what I would have done without you."

Hearing those words caused me to start sobbing with profound love for Andrew's daughter and gratitude that I was able to be a part of this momentous occasion.

The nurse placed the swaddled baby into Fiona's arms, and I looked down at Andrew's granddaughter. *My* granddaughter. The look on Fiona's face radiated pure joy, all the pain of the previous hours forgotten as she looked into the face of her daughter.

Fiona gently stroked the baby's forehead. "She has a name," she said softly. "I'm naming her Andrea, after my father, and her middle name will be Marin, after you."

In that moment I didn't think that anger or hurt or betrayal had ever existed—because all I felt was an intense and powerful love surrounding me.

❧ 50 ❧

We had Fiona and Andrea back home at Safe Harbor by early the next afternoon. I was sure I wasn't going to be able to sleep a wink the night before, after such an emotional experience, but after one glass of wine to celebrate the birth of my grand-daughter, I nodded off in bed against Worth's shoulder, and the next thing I knew it was six in the morning.

When I had gone out to the lounge to let Worth know Fiona had a daughter and everything was fine, that was when I first thought of Greg.

"Oh, my God," I'd told Worth. "I was supposed to call him right away. I was supposed to call him as soon as she went into labor."

Worth had pulled me into his arms and laughed. "I called him when I went to park the car, Marin. I knew you were a little frantic."

And Greg would be arriving within the hour to meet his daugh-ter for the first time.

I had just finished preparing crab salad for sandwiches later, along with clam chowder, which simmered in a pot on the stove, when the phone rang.

I answered to hear my mother. "How's everybody doing? I take it Fiona and the baby got home from the hospital okay?"

"They did. They're both resting, and Greg should be here shortly. Are you coming over to see your great-granddaughter?"

"I don't want to intrude," she said. "Do you think it would be okay? I really would love to see her."

"Don't be silly. Of course it's okay. Fiona would be disappointed if you didn't come."

"I'll be there in about an hour," she said, and I was certain a smile covered her face.

My mother had visited with Fiona and the baby and we were sitting on the patio with Worth when Greg arrived.

Fiona was resting on the sofa, surrounded by pillows, Andrea sleeping away in the cradle beside her. He went directly to Fiona, placing a kiss on her lips, and passed her one of the largest bouquets I'd ever seen.

"Oh, my gosh, Greg," she exclaimed. "Did you leave any flowers in the florist shop?"

He laughed. "Hey, it isn't every day that a guy has a daughter. And you did a super job," he said.

"She did, didn't she?" I agreed. "She delivered that baby within three hours of arriving at the hospital. I'm very proud of her. And did you ever see such a beautiful baby?"

He was leaning over the cradle as he held Fiona's hand. "She's gorgeous," he whispered.

Fiona swiveled on the sofa to get up and reached in to take the baby in her arms before sitting back down. "Andrea," she said. "I want you to meet your father."

I saw the tears in Greg's eyes and the look of rapture on his face, and I realized that those words had never been spoken to Fiona.

I turned around to rejoin Worth and my mother on the patio, allowing the happy couple some private time.

Worth was removing a bottle of champagne from the ice bucket. "I do believe a celebration is in order," he said, popping the cork.

I smiled and accepted the flute after he passed one to my mother. Raising his in the air, he said, "Here's to baby Andrea. May she have a long and happy life. And here's to Andrea's grand-mother and great-grandmother."

"To Andrea," my mother and I said, touching glasses.

"Very nice," she said after taking a sip.

She sat back in the chair and let out a sigh. "It's moments like these that make life so special, isn't it?"

I nodded. "It is."

The three of us sat there for a few moments lost in our own thoughts, and then I heard my mother say, "Annalou would be very happy, you know."

I looked over and saw a smile on her face. "I know I didn't want you to purchase this house, and you know the reason, but I was wrong. Because something tragic had occurred here, I didn't think this would be a good place for you to live. But it wasn't up to me to decide that . . . so I'm glad that you listened to your own heart, Marin. I know that you have brought a lot of love into this house over these past months. And now—a baby has been brought here. A baby that is so wanted and surrounded by so much love." She nodded her head slowly. "Yes, I know without a doubt that An-nalou would be very happy about that, and that makes me happy."

"Me too," I said, reaching over to squeeze my mother's hand.

We finished our glass of champagne and my mother got up to leave.

"I'm just going to pop in to say good-bye," she said, kissing my cheek. "But I'll be back tomorrow to see that beautiful baby."

I laughed. "You'd better be."

Worth pulled me into an embrace as he kissed my forehead. "Another glass of champagne?"

"Yes," I said, glancing down toward the shore.

He refilled our flutes and touched the rim of mine. "Here's to the most beautiful grandmother I know."

I smiled. "That has a nice sound to it, *grandmother*." I took his hand. "Walk with me down to the water."

We stood there, holding hands, sipping our champagne, watch-ing the water ripple where mullet were jumping. I thought of Julian Cole. I thought of Annalou Carter, and I thought of Andrew.

I leaned over to kiss Worth's cheek. "You know," I said. "If not for Andrew, I never would have received the gift of Fiona and Andrea."

"You're right," he said, sliding an arm around my shoulder.

"And if not for Andrew . . . I never would have received the gift of *you*.

"Thank you, Andrew," I whispered, and my gaze was caught by dragonflies once again hovering over the water, causing me to smile.

AUTHOR'S NOTE

The Maine coon cat in my story is based on my very own Maine coon kitten, Toulouse. He's the third one we've owned, and while I love all cats (and dogs!), I have a special place in my heart for this breed. Our Toulouse was born in October of 2012 and came from the breeder Lisa Red at Icoons Cattery in Youngstown, Florida. I had fun writing the fictional Toulouse into my story, and I hope my readers will also enjoy this delightful ball of fur. If you'd like to follow the real-life antics of Toulouse, along with photos, he has his own fan page at Facebook: Toulouse The Maine Coon Cat On Cedar Key.

A lot of my fans raved about the Cedar Key Friendship Bread that was served at my knitting retreat, and I've mentioned it in this book. For the retreat, it was made by local islander Dottie Haldeman. Everybody wanted to know the special ingredient; it was fresh juice from key limes! A basic Amish bread recipe from the Internet can be used, but if you squeeze in some real key lime juice . . . that's what will give you that extra-special taste.

Cedar Key Fudge is also mentioned in this book when somebody brings it to the knitting group to go with coffee. We really do now have homemade Cedar Key Fudge available on the island, and I can vouch for the fact that it's delicious! And it's not at all sweet, because it's made with cream. Thank you to Roberta and Bruce Wilson, owners of Ada Blue's, on SR 24, for making this great fudge. It has quickly become an island favorite!

In this book Miss Dora designs a shawl for her daughter, Marin, and has called it the Cedar Key Compassion Shawl. Dora is pleased that Marin has learned to forgive, despite the difficulty of doing so. Once again, I called upon my friend and personal assistant, Alice Jordan, to design the shawl for my story. I wanted something fairly simple for my readers to make, but a finished project that would be both pretty and practical. If you made the Cedar Key Scarf in *Postcards from Cedar Key,* then you'll recognize the pattern of waves that Alice designed. Along the edges, she incorporated some yarn overs for a lacy effect because I feel in order to show compassion and forgiveness, one must be open. I chose the shade of orange (but you can make it in any color you choose) because orange is known to be the color of forgiveness. Both Alice and I hope you'll enjoy making the shawl, and we'd love for you to e-mail me photos of your finished project at dulongterri@gmail.com.

Cedar Key Compassion Shawl

DESIGNED BY ALICE JORDAN

Supplies

4 skeins Cascade Ultra Pima; color: Paprika #3771
Size 10 needles

Cast on 100 stitches.

Knit 6 rows.

Row 1: K4, K2tog, *YO, K2tog, repeat from * to last 4 sts, YO, K4

Row 2: K6, P to last 6 sts, K6

Row 3: K4, K2tog, YO, K to last 6 sts, YO, K2tog, K4

Row 4: K6, P to last 6 sts, K6

Rows 5–20: Repeat rows 3 and 4 (8 more times).

Row 21: K4, K2tog, YO, K to last 6 sts, YO, K2tog, K4

Row 22: K across

Rows 23–24: Repeat rows 21–22.

Pattern Rows (rows 25–31)

Row 1: K4, K2tog, YO, *P3, K3, P3, K3, P4, K3, P3 repeat from * 3 times, YO, K2tog, K4

Row 2: K6, *P3, K1, P1, K1, P4, K1, P1, K1, P3, K1, P1, K1, P3 repeat from * 3 times, K6

Row 3: K4, K2tog, YO, *K4, P1, K5, P1, K6, P1, K4 repeat from * 3 times, YO, K2tog, K4

Row 4: K6, *P4, K1, P1, K1, P4, K1, P1, K1, P4, K1, P1, K1, P1 repeat from * 3 times, K6

Row 5: K4, K2tog, YO, *P1, K1, P1, K4, P1, K1, P1, K4, P1, K1, P1, K5 repeat from * 3 times, YO, K2tog, K4

Row 6: K6, *P5, K2, P5, K2, P5, K2, P1 repeat from * 3 times, K6

Row 7: K4, K2tog, YO, K to last 6 sts, YO, K2tog, K4

Row 32: K across

Row 33: K4, K2tog, YO, K to last 6 sts, YO, K2tog, K4

Rows 34–35: Repeat rows 32–33.

Row 36: K6, P to last 6 sts, K6

Row 37: K4, K2tog, YO, K to last 6 sts, YO, K2tog, K4

Row 38: K6, P to last 6 sts, K6

Rows 39–54: Repeat rows 37–38 (8 times).

Row 55: Repeat row 21.

Rows 56–58: Repeat rows 22–24.

Repeat pattern rows 1–7 and then rows 32–58 (6 more times).

On last repeat, end with row 54.

Next row (RS) K4, K2tog, *YO, K2tog, repeat across to last 4 sts, YO, K4

Knit 6 rows.

Bind off.

Glossary

Odd rows: Right side (RS)

Even rows: Wrong side (WS)

YO (yarn over): Bring yarn forward between the two needles. K (knit) the next stitch, taking the yarn over the right needle. If the next YO is to be a P (purl), again bring the yarn forward between the needles over the right needle and then back around to the front to P the next st (stitch).